D1239758

ABOVE EVIL

A SCIENCE PREDICTION NOVEL

BY

STEPHEN PHINNEY

Disclaimer. *This is purely a work of fiction. The events and actions of all of the characters portrayed in this story are fictional. They do not represent, nor are patterned after, any individuals the author has known or heard of. The use of the names of specific individuals, institutions, businesses, cultural groups, and places is merely to provide a context for an imaginary series of events taking place 2 decades in the future. Experimental results stated or implied by the author may seem plausible to some readers but are not the actual results of scientific research.*

Acknowledgement. Lyrics to Grateful Dead songs copyright Ice Nine Publishing Company. Used with permission.

ISBN-13: 978-0-9834907-2-2

Cover design by Brian Zimmerman

To Huong, Lauren, and Eric

ACKNOWLEDGEMENTS

A scientist attempting to write science fiction is performing an unnatural act. If I have succeeded at all in this attempt, it was only through the thoughtful guidance of many individuals. Gerald Maffeo, James Nach, and Shelley Schlender assisted greatly early on in the project. My co-author on other projects, Dr. Jeff Volek, offered encouraging words at a key juncture, as did Doug Bibus. Matthew Hanf, my unofficial editor, taught me much, much more than I ever got from college literature. And across its 4-year gestation, my internist-wife adopted the dual roles of nurse and obstetrician. Without her steadfast support, this project would never have been born.

OTHER WORKS BY STEVE PHINNEY:

The New Atkins for a New You

Eric Westman, Stephen Phinney, and Jeff Volek
Simon & Schuster, NY. 2010.

The Art and Science of Low Carbohydrate Living

Jeff Volek and Stephen Phinney
Beyond Obesity LLC, Miami, FL. 2011
Available at https://www.createspace.com/3608659

TIMELINE

PROLOGUE

Drifting	December 1, 2034
Rods from God	December 2, 2034

BODY

China Cat	Summer 2028
The Milkman	Summer 2028
Me and My Uncle	Summer 2028
Milk Wars	Winter-Spring 2029
The Newdle Touch	June 2029
Shakedown Street	June 2029
Hyperbarics	June 2029
Jamaica Rum Works	June 2029
The Flood	February 3, 2030
In the Wake of the Flood	February 3, 2030
Grateful – Dead	February 2030
Going Up	Winter-Spring 2030
Birth of the NC	Summer 2030
Hell in a Bucket	August 2030
Close to Heaven	August 2030
Out of Dodge	October 2030
The Northern Route	November 2030
The Maui Connection	November 2030
Uno Uno	February 2031
Uno Dos	February 2031
Uno Tres	February 22, 2031
(Prologue)	*(December 1 & 2, 2034)*
Jamaica	December 21, 2034
Waitsfield	December 26, 2034

EPILOGUE

Angel	January 2036

BEIJING
22 July 2010

In a 73-page report released today, Human Rights Watch detailed the actions of Chinese Security Forces in their crackdown on Tibetan Protestors in 2008. Based on eyewitness accounts, the report documents beatings and troops firing into protestors in the largest anti-government protest that has occurred in Tibet in 50 years. The protests started in Lhasa and spread to other towns and cities in this 'autonomous' region claimed by China in the 1950's. The Chinese Government claims their actions against the protestors were legal and downplays accounts of rights abuses.

A Conspiracy With a Silver Lining
by William D. Cohan
NY Times
March 2011

In March 2010, *(Andrew)* Maguire released his e-mails publicly, in part because he felt the (*Commodity Futures Trading Commission's*) enforcement arm was not taking swift enough action. He was also unhappy over not being invited to a commission hearing on position limits scheduled for March 25. Then came the cloak and dagger element: the day after the hearing, Maguire was involved in a bizarre car accident in London. As he was at a gas station, a car came out of a side street and barreled into his car and two others. London police, using helicopters and chase cars, eventually nabbed the hit-and-run driver. Reports that the perpetrator was given a "slap on the wrist" inflamed the online crowds that had become captivated by Maguire's odd story.

International Network News
3 February 2030

All contact with the cities Christchurch in New Zealand and Hobart in Tasmania has been lost. Early indications are that both have been obliterated by a massive tsunami coming from the south. There has not been any earthquake activity of adequate intensity in that region to generate a tsunami. However there is a report that highly unusual seismic activity on the surface in Antarctica occurred a few hours ago, but its relationship to the tsunami remains unknown. Authorities have posted an international tsunami alert for the South Pacific region, especially for south-facing coasts. The speed, size, and eventual range of this wave are unknown, so remain connected to INN for further updates as more information becomes available.

Ted Kaczynski
The Unabomber Manifesto

Freedom means having power: not the power to control other people but the power to control the circumstances of one's own life.

CHAPTER ONE

DRIFTING

December 1, 2034

Michael Anderson was 6 miles up, sailing east-north-east at 68 miles per hour just above the brown tinged clouds, and his lunch was ready right on time. He opened the flap, removed the cup from his food dispenser, and raised it to his lips. He paused. This was his original fruit smoothie; the one he'd constructed from four fruit flavors – pineapple, raspberry, banana, and melon.

This is what makes us different from the groundlings, he thought. Up here, we make our food from yesterday's poop.

Mike's thoughts drifted back to days 6 years ago when his Mars Mission team first realized that they could recycle yesterday's human waste to make today's food. It was almost inconceivable back then. Now he held it in his hand, did so three times a day, and rarely gave it a second thought.

He took a sip, savoring the taste and aroma of fresh, sweet fruit, followed by the thick creamy texture sliding across his tongue. He took his time emptying the cup, making the pint of unctuous liquid last. No need to rush. He raised his left hand and used his index finger to touch the virtual cup icon projected out in front of him on his three-dimensional, heads-up display[1]. Up popped his menu on the left, and on the right were the nutrient contents of each option. At his current weight of 162 pounds, Hal, his auto-pilot, was giving him 775 calories in each meal including 37 grams of protein and 67 grams of fat. He smiled at the paradox – his food was so satisfying because of its fat and protein content, and at the same time the unique properties of this diet were protecting his health.

Mike shifted his gaze back to the cup. There was maybe a teaspoon of it left, beaded up on the bottom like a drop of dew on a tropical leaf. Nothing adhered to the helical carbon liner of the cup. It was the ultimate non-stick surface. He raised the cup and slid that last bit of the smoothie onto his tongue and swallowed.

"See you tomorrow," he said to himself with a chuckle.

Mike placed the cup back in the dispenser, raised his finger to the control plane of his heads-up display, and set the dispenser cycle to 'clean'. The way he got his food up here really wasn't all that different from how it had happened down there on the ground for millions of years. People ate, and people pooped. Animals ate, and animals pooped. All that shit got returned to the soil or water and then re-entered the food chain. Animal and human manure had been used as fertilizer since agriculture was invented. The difference was that down there, most 'civilized' people did their best to ignore their shit. Up here, it was a cornerstone of Mike's existence. Along with sunlight and water, his body waste was a precious resource that supplied almost all of his daily needs.

Water, Mike thought. Ah, yes. The next thing on my 'to do' list.

•   •   •

Two hours later he was performing with the Grateful Dead in 3D virtual reality, rocking Winterland with 'Sugar Magnolia', New Years Eve in San Francisco, 1970. *"Jumps like a Willys in four-wheel drive..."* Mike looked over the neck of his bass guitar at Jerry, who smiled back at him, the notes from Garcia's Gibson SG dancing high above Mike's bass groove. The crowd in front of him was twirling, some to the beat and some to another beat only they could hear. It was all here except the stale smell of skunkweed – that would be way too 'real-world'. The last thing Mike wanted to breathe was smoke.

Raising his fingertip into the control plane out in front of him on his heads-up display, Mike split the image to check altitude and Doppler imaging. His rig was down to an altitude of two miles with another thousand feet to descend to get below snow level and into the heaviest stream of raindrops. He was relieved to see that the current level of turbulence looked about as bad as it was going to get. Mike tipped the split closed and gave himself back to the Dead. Hal could handle the job for the next half hour – plenty of time for the band to improvise a transition into the quiet despair of 'Morning Dew".

Of all the hassles that came with being a drifter, Mike had a particular distaste for turbulence. It wasn't fear – he knew his disc and tether would hold up just fine. His rig was good to at least turbulence factor-8 and the Doppler showed there was nothing here worse than T-4. It was just the lack of being in control, bouncing around inside his gondola at the whim of weather. He knew his anxiety in turbulence was irrational. But when Mike was 4, his father had died trying to pilot his small plane around a thunderstorm. He'd heard the police tell his mom what happened – that his dad's plane had been torn apart before it finally crashed. For years after that, there were nightmares.

Playing with the Dead on VR helped – at least the motion of the gondola slung beneath his disc-shaped balloon fit the scene. Besides, catching a load of fresh rainwater 2 miles up sure beat going all the way down to sea level and having to suck up a bunch of salt water. And letting his rig go dry when there was sunlight available to process water into hydrogen was not an option.

Twenty-five minutes later, Garcia was crooning *"Can't walk you out in the morning dew my darling"* when Mike felt the high pitch vibration of the mini-pump filling the water storage bladder under the gondola as the rainwater began streaming down off the disc. He could also feel the faint jerking of the tethers adjusting above the gondola as Hal inflated the second layer of the balloon array to compensate his rig's lift for the increased load of rainwater and prepare to hoist them back up out of the clouds and into the sun.

Mike had been drifting – living the life of a high-tech nomad – for almost 4 years. None of this was new. In each seven day cycle he'd get a 'drink' of 300 liters of rain or surface water and use the power from his solar electric array to process it down to hydrogen. It took 3 cycles to produce 100 kilograms (aka 'keys'), and then he had to find a buyer through the Newdle Consortium – hopefully at a reasonable place to do some ground time. And if that didn't work out, he could always use his Jellybelly glider[2] to drop it, 10 keys at a time, down to sites where the NC determined there were groundlings in need of an energy fix.

This time up, he had another cycle to go after this one. This would fill his hydrogen stores to 100 kg. In these 2 weeks or so, he planned to complete another circumnavigation. Hopefully that would bring him back close to where he was now, over the mid-Pacific. If he couldn't manage to put down at an up-wind spot like Maui, then Santa Barbara, or even Puerto Vallarta, wouldn't be too bad. He could negotiate a shuttle home from any of these places in exchange for 100 keys or less, depending on the spot price of hydrogen through the NC.

Mike normally didn't stay this far north after the fall equinox. The days were longer and thus provided more sunlight for processing water in the southern hemisphere. But this year he wanted to get back home to Vermont for Christmas. It was a big deal for his mother even if she didn't state it openly. The last time they'd talked, she reminded him he hadn't been home on Christmas day since he began drifting. Shuttles coming up from south of the equator cost more, and the spot price for keys was higher north of the line this time of year, so staying north of the line was a win-win for Mike, given where he wanted to be in 3 weeks.

Besides, being from Vermont, he wasn't worried about the cold. That meant he could drift higher, bleed less power off his solar panels for heat, and get more processing done despite the shorter days in the Northern Hemisphere. The math was pretty simple. He also didn't have to worry about the consortium giving him any grief about sub-optimum hydrogen production. His status in the NC was pretty secure. After all, he'd been there at its creation.

•   •   •

By the time the Dead were finishing their 4-hour Winterland set, Mike felt the ride go smooth and gondola rotate and sway as Hal positioned it to the south side under the disc. Mike handed the bass guitar back to Phil Lesh with a grateful nod, cancelled the VR video, and punched up his tech status. He was pleased to see that the trip down through the cold front had netted him a full load of fresh water. Hal had brought them back up into the clear at an altitude of almost 7 miles, well above the cold front below. The disc was canted at 38° to the southwest, and at that angle the afternoon sun was cranking out enough watts off his solar array to make 0.8 keys an hour. Too bad he'd only get 4 more hours of sun today. Then he'd have to zip up, power down, and ride the jet stream east through the night.

Mike instinctively enjoyed the freedom that came with sailing his rig, a cocoon-like gondola slung beneath the disc-shaped balloon, in the air currents high above the ground. Although they called this drifting, in reality this was more akin to sailing a ship, adjusting altitude to selectively ride air currents that would take him where he wanted to go. To do this, he had to overcome the randomness of the atmosphere with a combination of data, probability, and a bit of luck. Trusting a bit of his fate to chance didn't bother him anymore because he'd learned that no amount of planning could completely eliminate the unexpected. Mike realized that his quality of life had improved when he accepted the unexpected. Looking back, he could see that it was often the unplanned events in his life that propelled him to where he was now – not the events he'd planned or anticipated.

He raised his finger tip into the VR display to open the NAF icon, the animated Newdle Atmospheric Flow chart that allowed him to see both current and predicted future airflow around him in three dimensions. He ran his options off his current coordinates. He wanted to stay as far south as he could without losing the opportunity to cross over Hawaii next time round and he didn't want to have to go up and 'park' 10 miles up to wait for better currents to ride. This time of year, north of the line, it was too cold to process water or grow bugs effectively above an altitude of 7 miles, so parking above the weather with all 3 layers of his balloon deployed and running a big heating bill was literally burning up money. Hydrogen was just too valuable to waste like that, and being a hydrogen consumer rather than a net producer felt too much like being a groundling.

The NAF software offered him two course options. If Mike stayed above an altitude of 6 miles, he would ride the upper jet stream out across central California to dawn over Kansas. However, if he descended to 5 miles, he could catch the top of the cold front he'd just climbed up out of. That would take him on a bit more southerly route, crossing well above the brown soup over LA and getting him to dawn 12 minutes earlier over central Texas. Instinct told him to take the southern route, but he could wait an hour or two before committing to it. The longer he stayed up here in the sunlight above the clouds, the more hydrogen he could make.

Once Mike made the choice, Hal could watch the NAF data stream to manage their altitude. Altitude didn't matter too much when drifting at night as long as Hal didn't get them into any turbulence stronger than T2. At dawn, however, they'd have to get back up into the clear above 6 miles to get the best yield out of the solar array on top of the disc, otherwise processing would suffer, and there were also bugs to grow, so he'd have something to eat. Choices … choices…

Mike thought back to the first drifters – sports balloonists like Steve Fossett[3] who had ridden over oceans and then eventually circumnavigated the Earth at the bottom of his big floppy gas bag. How things had changed in 40 years. Back then, they froze their butts up here. Now Mike had the solar-flex fabric that gave him 30 kilowatts of electric power off the top of his 10-meter disc. Most importantly, back then they didn't have NAF to help them accurately navigate through the chaos of the atmosphere.

Of all of the great things that Barry and Ivan had done for drifters, NAF was the quintessential key to the freedom that Mike now enjoyed. With NAF, he could get to almost any place on the globe in just 2 circuits although even the boys from Silicon Valley hadn't completely conquered chaos. Nonetheless, Mike's likelihood of getting somewhere specific on the globe within 20 days was good to a probability of 0.9. Then again, 9 out of 10 ain't bad odds when you rarely needed to be anywhere specific in the real world. That's why they call it drifting.

Now that he was back up in smooth air, Mike opened the access flap of his smoothie machine and took out the insulated cup. He had to think for a second to remember what he'd told Hal yesterday to make for today's final meal. Oh yeah, broccoli cheese soup. He took a sip and savored the thick, warm concoction. He thought of the thousands of other drifters drinking similar meals around the globe. For Mike though, the satisfaction was perhaps a bit more than for most. He and his friends from the Mars Project had invented both the bacteria (which everybody called 'bugs') and the machinery that made this miracle of today's food from yesterday's poop possible.

While the sun was still up, Mike lowered the opaque inner curtain on the southwest side of his gondola, exposing the faintly tinted, transparent outer fabric. His VR exterior status panel showed everything in the green, so he knew that no one, powered or drifting, was nearby, but he wanted to enjoy the real-world view. He flipped up his VR display visor, put on the old sun glasses he used for surfing, and looked out over the north Pacific from his perch seven miles up. Not much to see down below given the weather – just the bright, puffy, brown-tinged clouds that had filled his processing tank an hour ago. But off to the south the clouds were more broken, and through the brown layer, he could just catch the blue of the ocean surface. There, higher up, Mike wasn't surprised to see 2 white ribbons arching up from the horizon to end at the dark blue edge of the atmosphere at the top of his view – steam trails left by afternoon shuttles, probably coming up from vacation destinations in the South Pacific and heading for the US mainland.

Mike, like many drifters, enjoyed doing ground time in Polynesia or Samoa this time of year. Both archipelagos had enough high ground that they'd survived the tsunami and were pretty well recovered. If it wasn't too crowded, he could drop his sea anchor into a leeward bay or lagoon and leave the disc deployed, processing at low efficiency under the brown layer. Every little bit helped, so while Mike was off-catheter and eating fresh fish in spicy ginger sauce or Thai curry under palm trees on the beach, Hal could be managing his rig out in the lagoon, processing water to make a few extra keys of hydrogen to help pay the rent.

He wondered if he knew anybody aboard those shuttles going back to the US today. Probably not; it was too expensive crossing the line. Most of his drifting friends wouldn't waste good hydrogen going somewhere now when they could drift a lot closer within the next few cycles. Those 2 shuttles were probably loaded with big-carbon-footprint groundlings heading home after some beach time in the relatively clean air of the South Pacific.

Still, duty called. Mike dropped the sunglasses back into their pouch on the wall, flipped his VR visor back down, and punched up a series of frames: rig status, all green with processing rate holding at 0.8 keys per hour; gondola temp was 17°C; ambient O_2 inside the gondola at 63%, CO_2 at 0.3%; variance of real path from desired was within 2%; external envelope was clear of drifters to 3 miles; and powered aircraft clear out to 60 miles. He thought for a moment about how dramatically the use of this space up here at an altitude of 6-7 miles had changed over the last 5 years. Up until the tsunami, they were still flying carbon-fueled aircraft around the globe at this altitude. That would have made things messy for drifters, having all those big fast-movers slicing through prime drifting space. Now the few shuttles just went up and down through drifting space, spending most of their time at altitudes above 100 miles. The only remaining fast movers in drifting space were a few old national defense units, and because the Consortium had become a force to be reckoned with, they made a point of keeping well away from NC rigs. Then there were the 'Burgs' [4], but they spent most of their time drifting, too.

Just to be sure, Mike ran a check on this transponder. "You're being neurotic", he chided himself. Maintaining radar transponder function was near the very top of Hal's priority checklist, and the hardware had triple backup. Still, it was every drifter's nightmare to be taken down, whether on purpose or by mistake, because of a non-functioning transponder. That was cardinal rule #2 of Consortium membership: be absolutely sure that everybody knows exactly where you are (but never who you are) whenever you are up.

Having covered the basics, Mike moved his index finger up and scanned the incoming data stream from the last 4 hours. There were a bunch of orders from drifters and others wanting to buy his food-producing bugs, a reminder of the Consortium Council meeting at noon GMT tomorrow, and two video postings. One of the vids was from Klink at Ham U and the other from his mother in Townshend.

Still nothing from Senator Nyce, however. "Damn," Mike thought. "What's his problem?"

Mike took the easy ones first. The bug requests he separated into three groups: NC members, NC applicants, and 'others'. Consortium members and applicants were easily identified by the characteristic web addresses available through Newdle only to drifters. As for the 'others', Mike didn't really care where they called home.

Mike's fee structure was simple: members got the lowest price; applicants paid a bit more; and 'others' were charged a lot more. Sure, there were some among the 'others' who wanted the bugs for personal use, but mixed in with them were the industry stooges interested in trying to reverse engineer his bugs for unlicensed retail production on the ground. Mike had attempted to figure out how to separate sincere individuals among these groundlings from industry shills, but it was impossible. The guy with an address in Idaho Falls, Taos, or Bangor was just as likely to be a front for a big company as he was a homesteader trying to live clean off the grid. Therefore, if they weren't drifters, they'd have to pay big.

Mike sent the bug orders off to Tina at the Rum Works to be filled. Next he plugged 'noon GMT' into his two track projections to get an idea where he'd be when he needed to hook up to the consortium conference tomorrow. Given the 6 hour difference between Merry Old England and US central time, that would put the meeting at just about dawn Mike's time. He decided to take the southern route option, so he could be powered up and processing before the start as this meeting would take his full attention for at least a few hours.

Mike used his index finger to activate his tracking program, set the goal for central Texas, and commanded Hal to use NAF to decide when they should drop down to catch the more southerly flow of the cold front below. Immediately, Mike felt the mini-pump beneath the pod activate as it pulled hydrogen out of disc two to take them down. Clearly Hal's little nano-chip brain had been waiting impatiently for this decision and now was eager to get them down into the more southerly flow. Well, Mike thought, unlike Kubrick's version of HAL, at least his 'Hal' didn't talk back.

Along with his passion for the Dead, Mike was also a big fan of Kubrick. With the development of modern VR software and the ability to insert oneself in three dimensions into any previously recorded event or movie, both artists had experienced resurgent popularity with large groups of 'participants' around the globe. In the 4 years he'd been up, he must have played in "2001, A Space Odyssey" at least 20 times. Despite its age, it was one of Mike's favorites. This 66-year old classic dealt with a relatively simple storyline about human versus machine while the thinly veiled back-story addressed humanity's uncertainty about its origins. Despite its age, it still spoke to Mike about the passion for self knowledge and the resilience of the individual.

Particularly now, 33 years after the supposed time of Clark's and Kubrick's fantasy, the Earth's remaining inhabitants were struggling to balance the benefits of technology against its tendency to amplify humanity's negative effects on the planet. Just as in "2001", the real technology of today had tremendous potential to help the planet or harm it. Humanity's challenge was to figure out how to use their machines for good rather than evil.

Evil. Klink. That was an easy transition to make. Mike hesitated, trying to wipe away his memory of that sinister smile. Resigned, he moved his finger tip up to the video icon and activated the selection identified by Klink's face above his Hamiltonian University address. Klink's head and torso appeared and began to speak:

> *"Hi, Dr. Anderson. I hope you are staying well up there in the big, blue sky. Are you sure you've got the radiation issue solved? I noticed your three new patents, so I guess you haven't lost your touch. I just want to remind you that my offer of a faculty slot here at Ham U still stands, but I can't keep it open forever. So-*

cial conditions here have improved a lot in the last 12 months. If you accept the position, you could do it either physically on-site or virtual. This job is perfect for a guy like you. You have a lot to offer our program here. Both our students and faculty stand to benefit. And as you know from our prior work together, our close relationships with industry can get you a lot more income from your patents than you could possibly get as an independent drifter. Let me know what you need from us to bring you on board. And if you happen by St. Louis, why not drop in?"

Klink chortled for a second at his own joke, and then continued:

"If you are still up to it, we could even resume our friendly tennis competition. But I've got to warn you, I've developed a killer backhand. Hope to hear from you soon."

Sending Professor Steven Klink a polite, but firm, 'no' by text wasn't that hard to do, but then again, it was. It brought back a flood of memories of his time working for Klink and the Mars Project at Hamiltonian University. Along with the good ones, there were also a lot of infuriating memories from these seven years of having to deal with Klink. Eventually, they'd reached the breaking point. Soon after that came the tsunami, and then the technological leap to drifting. The irony of it was that Mike's work in the Mars Project lab there at Ham U – some called it brilliant – became a key piece of the technology that made safe and sustainable drifting feasible. Not too shabby when a nerd in the lab could help 10,000 people ascend into the heavens (well, almost).

Mike reflected for a moment on Klink's reference to tennis. Klink just couldn't help himself. He'd always had that self-congratulatory, sarcastic streak. As a junior faculty, Mike used to soundly beat his department chair in tennis (not to mention skiing and Frisbee football). Back then, Mike had been a bit too self-absorbed to realize the harm that his prowess in sports was doing to his academic career. Klink hated being beaten at anything by anybody. Now that he was drifting, it would take Mike months on the ground before he could build himself back up to his prior level of fitness. Klink knew the toll that drifting took on muscle strength, and he just couldn't resist the chance to goad Mike about it. Klink just didn't seem able to comprehend that no matter how much power he wielded in the academic-industrial complex, there was no way Mike would ever opt for a job that forced him to deal with such pettiness. He shook his head as if to rid himself of Klink.

Next on his list, Mike thought about trying to reach Senator Nyce directly, rather than approaching him through his staff. For the last month, the senator's staff at the Foreign Relations Committee had kept Mike at arm's length by repeatedly promising a video link or a call-back from the Senator tomorrow. The Consortium needed the Senator's support for an international treaty to guarantee the safety of drifters, but some in the Senate felt that the Consortium had pre-empted national rights to maintain borders and security. In their view, the thousands of drifters floating overhead, landing where ever, and exchanging things with groundlings using their funny, little Jellybelly balloons broke every Customs and Immigration law on the books. While this was partially true, the NC arose when the US government (along with most governments around the world) was in near collapse. Now that some national governments were re-covering, they were struggling to catch up with how much the world order had changed in the last 4 years.

As best Mike's contacts could tell, Senator Nyce might be won over to the Consortium's view, but as Committee Chair, he was obviously playing his cards carefully. Now it had come down to the wire. Mike had really wanted to talk with the Senator before tomorrow's Con-sortium conference, but clearly that wasn't in the cards. At this late hour on the east coast, it just wasn't worth rubbing a Washington big-wig the wrong way with an after-hours call, especially to a num-ber the senator thought was unlisted. No, he decided. He'd just keep working through normal channels. After all, how many truly interested constituents could a Vermont senator have?

That led Mike's thoughts to his mother. Mike touched the virtual clock icon and pulled the cursor from his current location to Town-shend, Vermont. The clock read 9:30 pm local. He touched the video icon from Stephanie, and her image popped up to say that she had "important news, so call back soon". He touched the call-back icon, waited a few seconds, and there she was in real time, her long, light brown hair pulled up on top of her head and held there by what looked like a pair of chopsticks stuck through it. That had to be Tina's idea.

"Hi Mikie," she said with a smile. "How are you?"

"Good. You?"

"Fine. Where are you?"

"Mom, you know I can't tell you that," Mike said, holding out both palms in exasperation. "Let's just say that I'm over the Pacific somewhere off the California coast, and I should be over Texas tomorrow morning. What's up?"

"That's okay, Mikie. I wasn't asking for your GPS coordinates. The reason I called is I thought you'd like to know that we got the probate papers on your uncle. It's all settled, honey."

"You sure? Nobody snooping around the Rum Works asking questions? Did anything show up in the local press?"

"Nope. It was all very quiet. We did it through a judge in Brattleboro, and there aren't many reporters in Brattleboro these days. And I've got our accountants working on the financial side of the settlement. They should have that done for us in a few days."

"Good work, Mom. That's going to make a lot of things less difficult." He paused. "Does... does Tammy know about the trust fund yet?"

Stephanie nodded once to acknowledge her son's ambivalence, and then shook her head.

"No" she replied. "We'll finalize the papers once the financials on the estate are completed. Then I'll have copies delivered to her in Chicago. In the mean time, I've just kept sending her the monthly $10,000 'grandmother check' like we've done all along... And she still keeps cashing them."

"Do we know, uh, in general terms, how big the trust is going to be?" Mike stammered.

"It looks like it will be somewhere north of three million, Mikie."

"Thanks, Mom. So, what do you think? Will this thaw some of the ice on that end?"

"I hope so, Mikie. As much as I love talking to Angela, what I really want to do is put my arms around my granddaughter and hug her."

"Yeah, I know the feeling" Mike agreed.

"So, hey," he said, changing the subject. "I'm going to go for another loop and should be back to Hawaii in... well, pretty soon. I'll drop my rig there and grab a shuttle into Beantown. I want to try the new hyperbaric mag-lev up through White River. I'll give you a call next week when the schedule is firm. Can you come down to Brattleboro to pick me up?"

"Sure thing, Mikie. Just let me know when. I'd come on as little as an hour's notice if that keeps you safe, but twelve hours warning would be nice".

"By the way", Stephanie continued, "Tina is teaching me to make Chinese stir fry using our green-house veggies. Would you like to try some while you are here? And we will move Ping Jr. out of your room. He can sleep with his mom and dad while you're here"

"Okay, Mom. I've got to go. I love you. Bye"

"Love you too. Bye."

This was good, he thought. She'd been running the Rum Works[5] pretty much by herself for almost 4 years. At least now she'll get some credit for what she was doing. And maybe... just maybe... Tammy will let her come to Chicago for a visit.

Mike's last call of the night was to a yellow 'A' icon that occupied a permanent location on his display. It was 8:38 pm in Chicago.

The blonde head that appeared had striking blue eyes, much like Mike's. Angela had an old-fashioned paper book in front of her. "Doing homework, Honey?"

"Hi Mike. Yeah. Chemistry."

"How do you like It? Does it make any sense to you?"

"Yes, but I learn more from the web tutorials than from this dorky book. Mom got me a new VR set, so I can see the stuff in 3-D. So where are you, Mike?"

"I'm about 10 kilometers up over the Pacific, and I've come about 4000 kilometers since I talked with you 2 days ago."

"Did you stop in Maui again this trip?" She asked.

"Not this time, Angel, but I'm hoping to set down there in the next week or two."

"I really want to visit your place in Hana, Mike. I loved the pictures you sent me a couple of weeks ago."

"Yeah, and I'd love to have you come out there sometime, Honey, but there's more surfing there than tennis. That would be a break in your training, so I doubt Tammy would let you waste your time there. By the way, how'd tennis go this weekend?"

"Fine. I played in a tournament over at the University Club. I did pretty well yesterday, but today I was better. I took first place in the under-18 singles bracket. Mom said she's going to take me to Boston or San Francisco next summer to find some stiffer competition."

"Congratulations, Angel. I'm proud of you. If you let me know when, I'll try to come see you play."

"Sure, Dad. But this next time we should work it out in advance so mom's bodyguards don't try to break you in half. I didn't even know it was you until mom started to laugh when they frog-marched you out of the arena."

"Tammy is such a merry soul, isn't she? Yeah, in retrospect I should have let her know I was in Chicago when I came to see you play last summer."

"So, anyway Mike, I have to get back to work. Mom still makes me go to bed at 9:30 'cause I practice every morning at 6."

"Okay, Angel. I love you. See you soon."

"Bye, Mike. Love you too." The blonde head disappeared.

As he habitually did after most of his conversations with Angela, Mike touched the Guns 'N Roses icon right next to Angela's 'A" and heard the bell-like opening riff from Slash's Les Paul guitar leading into "Sweet Child Of Mine". Mike didn't attempt to join the band on-stage. He just sat on the stage staring into the 3D video, and once the vocals started, he turned down the volume and let it play.

This was the price he paid for his conversations with his daughter – guilt and recrimination. Well, that plus Tammy's persistent demands for inordinate child support while at the same time denying him any visitation rights. At least, he thought, that hatchet might get buried when the trust fund papers are delivered.

"She's such a great kid," he thought. "Maybe I should have married Tammy and moved to Chicago back when she wanted me to." But Mike had plowed through this field of rocks a thousand times. When the tennis coach at MIT first suggested that they play mixed doubles together, Tammy had rejected the matchup with condescending laughter. She was 22 and doing her MBA; blonde, beautiful, headstrong and rich. Mike was just 16 and a country boy from nowhere. Eventually the coach prevailed, and Tammy was pleasantly surprised to find that she wasn't constantly dodging Mike's racket or getting hit in the back with his thundering return shot. By the end of that first season, they became a force to reckon with on the court. Off the court, however, they'd lived in totally different worlds: he in the lab and she among the Martha's Vineyard weekend elite. Nonetheless, they played together for all of her 3 years at MIT, culminating with their winning the Regional Open Tournament at Longwood in May of 2019, the same month that Mike completed his undergrad coursework at MIT.

To celebrate, Tammy took Mike to bed. During the three years they'd played together, Mike had morphed from the skinny kid with zits into a tall, muscular, blue-eyed man-boy with dark brown hair, a wicked serve, and a growing notoriety at MIT. In her eyes, he must have appeared ripe.

Barely a month later she'd informed him she was pregnant, insisting that they marry and move back to her family compound in Skokie, north of Chicago.

Mike knew that would never have worked. If they'd tried, Angela surely would have suffered more in the bitterness of their daily lives together than in the vacuum of their lives apart. No, Tammy and her family had provided well for Angela – perhaps too well – but the kid seemed to have her head on straight. Over time their internet-based relationship had evolved into something more like big brother and kid sister than father and daughter.

And then, of course, there were the events of the last 4 years. After the tsunami that literally rocked the world, humanity could have slipped back into the dark ages, or worse. The dinosaurs actually hadn't been killed by that asteroid 55 million years ago. It had just been the triggering event that destabilized their already tenuous relationship with the planet after which they'd been unable to adapt before they slid into extinction.

Mike killed the Guns 'N Roses track. He lay back in silence and stared at the top of his gondola. Was he justified in thinking that he was helping a bit in guiding humanity away from its pre-tsunami failures and towards a more sustainable future? He wouldn't be doing this if he'd been stuck in Tammy's hometown of Skokie helping man a perimeter defense against the less fortunate mobs from downtown Chicago to the south. Perhaps the path he'd chosen, however emotionally painful in its own right, had allowed him to do more for his daughter's future (not to mention the other seven billion souls on Earth) than anyone realized at the time.

Mike took off his headset, rearranged a few things in the gondola, and did an hour of yoga. Then he adjusted the flow rates and infusion temperature of his catheters and settled into his sleeping pad. Like Angela, he too would be up early.

CHAPTER 2

RODS FROM GOD
December 2, 2034

Mike slept well knowing he had Hal standing guard. While he knew that Hal was just a bundle of nanocircuits with imbedded software, over the years his autopilot's soothing voice and can-do attitude generated the kind of confidence one usually reserves for a trusted friend. But that was common among drifters, and one more piece of the puzzle that made the improbable reality of a drifter's life tolerable.

One of Hal's tasks in keeping Mike secure was tracking all objects in his proximity, or any object that could rapidly penetrate Mike's safety envelope, a virtual sphere extending out to 6 miles in all directions.

Another of Hal's tasks was keeping Mike's rig totally anonymous. When they were up, they had to look and act like every other of the thousands of rigs in drifting space. If no one knows which of the thousands of drifting rigs you are in, you can't be targeted by someone wishing you ill. That way, an attack on any one drifter became an attack on all drifters, and the NC was a formidable opponent. To maintain this anonymity, among other things, all communications in and out of the rig that could possibly identify Mike had to be embedded as random bits in a terabyte flow of data through Hal's circuits.

The only exception to the total anonymity of individual drifters was a closely guarded program at NC Central. This program used an encrypted unique ID to track all drifters: members, applicants, and the occasional idiot who tried unregistered drifting. The latter were closely watched, as no one knew who or what was in these rigs. In contrast, both members and applicants for NC membership were all screened before going up, and if an unregistered rig came within 6 miles of another rig, most drifters' security systems activated countermeasures. For NC members, however, approach within 1 mile was tolerated before action was taken to maintain minimum separation. All of this was automatically done by Hal and the other NC autopilots without disturbing their occupants.

Another of Hal's functions was to stay in touch with NC Central to monitor the behavior of other rigs in his region. Most people would assume that all rigs in the same region would move through the air together as a group. But that ignores the 'chaos factor'. Within any one piece of the atmosphere, there are minor currents and eddies that work to vary the positions of any two adjacent objects relative to each other. Thus over days of travel, rigs that started out close together tend to separate. And if they don't, that's either a rare anomaly or a sign of intent – that one rig is purposefully adjusting altitude to capture flow differences to remain in proximity to another rig.

And that had Hal worried. Eight days ago, NC Central had alerted him to a rig that had left Maui an hour after Mike, 5 days before that. Over those initial 5 days, its relative position to Mike had varied from 10 to 30 miles behind – never coming closer but also never farther away. At those distances, using pixel accumulation technology via high resolution cameras, one rig could effectively maintain visual contact with another. And in the last 8 days, as Hal watched, this pattern continued despite the NAF prediction that they would become separated. In the same period, every other rig near them when they'd lifted out from Maui was now at least 150 miles away.

Now, earlier this evening, the automated program at NC Central had identified 5 other rigs that had lifted off from the California coast ahead of them as Hal and Mike came over on this circuit. These 5 rigs were separated out ahead of them and seemed to be holding fixed positions relative to each other. Other than this fact, nothing made these 5 rigs stand out. It was just that NC Central's surveillance program identified their behavior as a group to be non-random.

Because the 5 rigs out in front of Mike represented a potential threat, the automated surveillance program at NC Central flagged these observations for human attention, and as it involved Mike Anderson, the issue got rapidly kicked upstairs to someone who immediately called Dave Erickson, the administrative chief of the Newdle Consortium. It was one a.m. in California, and as Dave and the security team conferred, the picture they pieced together wasn't pretty. All six rigs in question were registered as Consortium members, all of whom had been 'up' for more than a year. None of the rig owners seemed to have prior affiliations with one another. But all six had been on the ground for at least 2 weeks before coming up this last time, and some had been down for 4-6 weeks. In short, their combined behavior was highly anomalous. It looked very much like they had all been in position waiting for Mike to leave Maui 13 days ago.

Next, they ran a check on the recent behavior of these six drifters. While the content of every drifter's communications through the Consortium's hookup were completely private, the Consortium did have the legal right and ability to look at their individual patterns of use. This gave the Consortium the ability to generate a functional fingerprint of each drifter, based on generic aspects of what they did (video, text, gaming) and when they did it. But within this pattern, there was also a small amount of variance – a second order derivative. No one behaved precisely the same every day. And here Dave and the security team found their red flag. Over the last 1-2 months, each of the 5 drifters up ahead of Mike had exhibited precisely fixed patterns – too precisely fixed patterns. It was like their communication behavior was generated by a recorded loop being played over and over. This was compelling evidence that the 5 pickets were hijacked rigs being run on auto-pilot.

At this point, without being asked, the security director on duty set up a 3D plot of all seven rigs, including Mike. Over the last hour, the tracking rig behind Mike had adjusted altitude to move up to within 6 miles, and all 5 of those out front had popped up above 45 thousand feet altitude and rising. This effectively took them up above the jet-stream, stopping them high above Mike as his rig approached. Clearly they were forming a picket line 30 miles wide under which he'd necessarily pass.

Although it was obvious what was happening, so far no one had done anything illegal, so there was nothing that Consortium Security could officially do to stop them. But they decided it was now time to alert Mike. In his gondola, Hal activated a soft chime, which increased in intensity every 5 seconds until Mike awoke. As Mike sat up and rubbed his face, Hal said, "We have a security alert, Mike. Please put on your headset for a video link with Dave Erickson".

"What's the threat level, Hal?" Mike asked groggily.

Programmed to avoid eliciting anxiety, Hal responded: "Not urgent, but we need to talk with Dave now."

Mike adjusted his headset and extended the video boom. Dave and another familiar face appeared, but Mike couldn't attach a name to the second face. "Seems like we always talk at odd hours, Dave," Mike grumbled.

"Good morning, sleepy head." Dave grinned but then turned serious. "You've got a potentially dangerous situation building. Some rigs up ahead of you seem to have formed a high picket line, and you've also got a tracking rig that's been shadowing you since Maui. That one is 6 miles behind you."

"When did we pick up the tracker?" Mike asked.

"NC Central tagged the potential tracker 5 days ago, and your autopilot has been watching it since then. But there wasn't a credible threat until we identified the pickets up ahead of you half an hour ago. Let's have Julian give you a quick briefing…"

Ah. Yes. Now Mike remembered. Julian Aldous was one of the Consortium's security chiefs, by his accent either British or Canadian.

"Okay, Mike. First we've got maybe 30 minutes before something might happen. You are moving at 85 kilometers per hour and the pickets are 45 kilometers ahead of you and close to stationary."

"There are five of them," Julian explained, "all above 15 km altitude and climbing, and they are spread out across your path covering a span of 50 km. There's no way you can avoid them unless you go to ground, but that would expose you by letting the tracker over-fly you. And that's not a good idea, eh?

That 'eh' erased any doubt about Julian's nationality – clearly Canadian.

"And if you go up to parking altitude", Julian continued, "it could become an extended waiting game. We think that the pickets are unoccupied rigs running on autopilot, and with less weight to carry, they'll have an altitude advantage over you that will put you at risk if they can get even a few thousand meters above you. We haven't been able to tease a direction stream out of their data flow, so we don't think that they are being actively guided. If they were, we could shut them down by taking their communications off-line. Their autopilots are probably acting on a pre-planned scenario that is slaved to their position relative to the tracker. We think that the tracker rig is occupied and his actions dictate how the others respond."

"Do we know who the tracker is?" Mike asked.

"The rig is registered to a 31 year old engineer from southern France named Fabien Bissonette," Dave replied. "He joined the Consortium 19 months ago. According to our records, you and he have no history of interaction. His record in the NC is spotless, but it appears he's not done really well generating income since he's been up. He did a few contracts for some European defense industries, but that's not been a lucrative area since the flood. Bottom line, he may be a paid mercenary."

"Do you think he knows that we're on to him?" Mike asked.

"Probably not yet, but he's gotta know that the pickets will stand out like a sore thumb shortly. He probably hopes they can take you out while he remains anonymous. And we want him to keep thinking that's true as long as possible, Mike. Now here's what we think will happen. When you pass under the pickets, one or more of them is going to drop kinetic weapons on you. You've heard of 'rods from God', right?"

"Yeah, but weren't they supposed to be launched from low Earth orbit satellites? All of them are toast since the Iridium cascade." Mike responded.

"True," Julian agreed. "But a depleted uranium or tungsten rod with tiny winglets and guidance fins will be falling at over twice the speed of sound at your altitude if dropped from 8 km above you. At that speed, it can easily penetrate helical carbon fabric. It will go right through your rig. No flash or big bang, just a silent blow that will instantly destroy your balloon."

"So we think you have only two options" Dave continued. "First, you can jump with your emergency chute right now, wait and open it low, and hope that your tracker doesn't follow you down and use a kinetic weapon on you when you land. If you're going to jump, you need to do it now."

"I'm not abandoning my rig", Mike said emphatically. "And I'm not abandoning Hal!" He added lamely.

"Okay, option number two is we try to thread you between the pickets, and if they make a move on you, we dodge and try to divert one of their rods into Bissonette's rig."

"Can you do that?"

"Rods don't have propulsion or on-board guidance". Julian explained. "Instead, they track on a laser designator from a third location – in your case from your tracker. Ten minutes ago, we recruited 26 drifters within 80 km of your position, and now we have them rising slowly to get above your tracker. None of them are within 6 miles of your tracker or his pickets, so we don't think he'll notice. On our signal, they'll dot your tracker with a variety of infrared lasers. Hopefully at least one of those lasers will be similar to the one Bissonette's using, making him a target for his own weapons. What you have to do is pull him in and down, so he's drawn into the kinetic weapon's cone of effect. We're working on an estimate of how wide that is, and we should have it for you shortly. Meanwhile, we want you to ease your altitude down another 3000 feet, making it look like a routine auto-pilot navigation adjustment. That will slow you down a bit and bring him in closer and above you which will please him because it makes his job of targeting you seem easier. Your autopilot already has this move uploaded, so initiate it now, please."

Mike raised his finger into the control plane and touched the blink-ing 'alternate route' icon. He could feel the gondola starting a slow descent as Hal pumped hydrogen down from the disc.

"So what are my chances of getting through this unhurt?" Mike asked.

"Maybe he'll figure out that we've drawn him into danger, and he'll let you through," Julian said. "But I wouldn't count on that. And in the event that they drop any weapons, things are going to happen super fast, Mike, so our counter-measures need to be done instanta-neously by your autopilot off of our algorithm."

"So I just sit back, relax, and enjoy the flight?" Mike put his hands behind his head and leaned backwards on his sleeping pad.

"No," Julian said. "You have to be prepared to take a couple of actions, depending on how things play out. First, get your emergency chute and oxygen on. Because if your rig is hit by one of those kinetic suck-ers, you are going down, and you'll need to get out of there in a hurry."

Mike swallowed hard. "And if the rig takes a hit, what's the chance I'm not instantly hamburger?"

"The top of your balloon has a surface area of 80 square meters, Mike. Standing up, you have a surface area of less than 1 square meter. So your chances of surviving a hit are better than 98%, as long as you can get out of the rig and activate your parachute. But the best scenario is you don't get hit. And to do that, on weapons release, your autopilot will swing your gondola under your balloon all the way over to the side closest to your tracker and do an emergency pump-down. That will cause your rig to slide away from and down. By the time the first weapon descends to your altitude, you'll be 2,000 meters down and 3,000 meters closer to your tracker's vertical coordinates. We'll keep you dropping like a rock until you are in the clear, or you reach an altitude of 2000 meters above the surface. You ever tried one of these before, Mike?

"Nope" Mike replied. "I've heard of drifters doing them for a thrill, but I've never been tempted. However I remember Brian telling me he'd designed these rigs to withstand a programmed free-fall in case there was a sudden failure in the gondola oxygen supply. I recall he said something about pulling the tethers in tight once the balloon was deflated to prevent them from tangling. Is my autopilot programmed to do that?"

"Actually, we've got Brian working on that right now, Mike," Dave replied.

"Oh, where is he?"

"He's over the Indian Ocean," Dave replied. "I had someone talking to him as soon as the pickets showed up, and he's updating your descent algorithm for this particular situation. But we need to make some decisions, Mike. Are you okay with playing innocent for as long as possible, doing the emergency pump down on weapons release, and jumping if your rig takes a hit?"

"Yes, Dave." Mike raised his hands over his head in a gesture of surrender. "I'm with you...'cause I don't seem to have a lot of other options. What's next?"

"We wait and watch really close," Julian replied. "And we'll update your autopilot with Brian's evasion algorithm as this dance plays out."

"Has anybody in a rig been taken out by kinetic weapons in the past?" Mike asked. "I seem to remember something about some kind of weapons being used over Russia a couple years back."

"Yeah," Dave replied. "There were those two Chechen guys funded by that Saudi prince who dropped a cluster of them on the Russian Ministry of Defense in Moscow shortly after we got Russian approval to overfly their territory. That set us back a bit but also helped clear the skies of non-NC rigs after we re-negotiated exclusive over flight permission with the Russians and Chinese for NG members only. And we also found out what a Russian surface-to-air missile can do to a rig."

"As for rigs being taken out by a kinetic weapon, we don't know of any for sure" Dave continued. "But there have been 12 unexplained rig disappearances in the last 3 years, and who knows how they went down? The beauty of using a dropped rod is that there's no smoke trail or huge bang like you get from a missile, so it's the ideal tool for a stealth take-down."

"Sorry, but that beauty is lost on me," Mike snapped, ending their conversation for a minute.

At that point, Julian gave them access to the 3D image showing the positions of all 7 balloons. Mike's was slowly descending which took him away from the closest picket but closer to the next in line. Under each picket, Julian now displayed an inverted cone to indicate the probable effective circumference of its falling weapons. Their goal was to move Mike out to the edge of the cone while luring Mike's tracker into the same cone that Mike was in. Then they'd activate multiple lasers from nearby NC rigs to divert a falling rod into the unsuspecting tracker before he could initiate effective evasion.

At this point, Mike was about 5 minutes away from entering the first cone, and the tracker, being higher up where the cone was narrower, was maybe 3 minutes behind Mike on his fateful track into the death zone. They had to hope that the picket would hold off on the weapon drop until Mike was dead center in the cone to increase the probability of a kill.

A second 3D image in a box in a corner of Mike's field of vision showed an expanded picture that included the 7 primary balloons in the dance plus the additional NC drifters farther out who were rising into position to designate the tracker. At this point, there were 17 NC rigs within range, and another 9 were about to get look-down access over the tracker. It reminded Mike of the old on-line computer games he played as a child in which teams of players co-operated in battle scenes to try and kill off other teams in the same game. However in this instance, he'd be on the receiving end of a lethal object going more than twice the speed of sound. He felt a shiver down his spine. His thoughts drifted to Angela, Stephanie…

"Weapons launch, weapons launch" Hal's voice penetrated Mike's brain. "Activating pump-down. Mike! Detach your catheters! Stand up NOW! Hold on tight!"

On Mike's display, the diameter of the cones under the pickets suddenly doubled. Julian's estimate of the weapon's outward angle had been too conservative. Mike was now well inside the cone, and the edge of this revised cone just intersected Mike's tracker. Mike's gondola lurched as Hal abruptly adjusted the balloon tethers to swing him over under the west side of the balloon. The combination of the pump-down plus canting the balloon turned his disc into an air-foil that slid Mike rapidly to the west as he descended. This pulled him under his tracker which increased Julian's chance of diverting a rod from the picket into the tracker. This, however, put Mike at risk if the tracker also carried any rods and dropped them onto him.

The force of his balloon's maneuver threw Mike against the side of his rapidly falling gondola where he clung to the top of his food dispenser, trying to remain as upright as possible. The speed of his fall accelerated as more hydrogen was pumped out of his balloon, and the falling gondola began to gyrate. Brian had never designed it to fly like this.

Mike broke into a cold sweat. Turbulence! He hated turbulence. He tried to concentrate on his display and was able to see three bright dots coming towards him from the picket, but before he could see whether they were going anywhere near the tracker, his gondola began to spin, throwing him down and pinning him against the side. He tried to get up, but the spinning and buffeting were too great. In the chaos, he was unable to focus on his display.

"I'm spinning. I'm down. Can't get up," Mike shouted. "Stop the pump-down!"

"Over-ride. Over-ride" Mike heard through his headset. In his terror, he didn't know if the over-ride command came from man or machine. As he plunged, the turbulence began to throw him about the cabin. He curled into a ball to protect himself. He was helpless – his worst nightmare. There was nothing he could do. Getting to the access flap and jumping clear was out of the question. He thought of his father as his plane was torn apart in that thunderstorm 30 years ago.

Mike heard someone screaming and only slowly realized it was himself. Then in his headset he heard another scream; but unlike his scream of abject fear, this was that primal victory-sound that one human makes when killing another. The contrast registered in Mike's brain, but its meaning did not. He was out of control. He couldn't get out. He was going to die.

He wanted the end to come quickly, but his fall in the wildly gyrating gondola seemed to last forever. Then the screaming abruptly stopped. Mike couldn't scream because he couldn't breathe. He was suddenly pressed so hard against the floor of the gondola that he couldn't fill his lungs. There was unbearable pressure in his ears. His head was about to explode. He couldn't hear, see, or breathe. As Mike wondered if this was what death felt like, he blacked out.

•   •   •

"Hey Amigo."

The voice registered in Mike's brain. Friendly. Familiar. His brain struggled with recognition. Only one person called him Amigo. It was Brian. Mike lay sprawled face down across the floor of his gondola. His head was pounding, heart racing, mouth bone dry. He opened his eyes and struggled to focus. The few loose objects that had been in the cabin were scattered about in front of his face.

"Hey Amigo. That was one hell of a hot drop! I'm glad you're still with us."

Mike rolled over on his back and adjusted his headset, slowly managing to focus on the image: Dave, Julian, and now Brian was with them in the composite image. "What happened?" He croaked.

"First things first, Mike," Brian said gently. "Plug your catheters back in, sit up, and get a drink of water. You've been out for a couple of minutes. And please, none of your lame lyrics from the Grateful Dead."

"Where's the bastard that tried to kill me? Am I in the clear?" Mike slid over to the food dispenser, sat up, selected water, and removed the cup. The cool water revived him a bit and swallowing helped ease the pain in his ears.

"We think you're safe for now," Julian replied. "Fabien Bissonette, or whoever it was, is a bug-splat on the canyon floor below you, along with the tatters of his rig. His balloon took two rods, and one of them went on through his gondola as well. It went down like a rock and no one got clear before impact. The five picket rigs all self-destructed when the tracker went down. Obviously they didn't want to leave any traceable evidence behind. But they obviously didn't think we'd take down Bissonette. So once we have a bit more information, we'll send a 'Burg' in to recover his wrecked rig and see if we can figure out who was behind this."

Mike raised a shaky finger and brought up his rig status. He was a bit over a mile above the Black River in southern Colorado which put him only a couple of thousand feet above the rocky plateau on either side of the canyon. His rig status was nominal – everything seemed in good working order. "Who drove my rig during the fall? I tried to stop it when it spun out of control and someone over-rode my command. I was scared shitless." Mike paused, smiled weakly, and then added: "But then, with these catheters in, I guess

I'm always shitless." The others chuckled, as much because they were pleased that Mike was able to try a joke after his near miss with death, as in response to his lousy humor.

"I came online a few minutes before the rods were dropped on you, Mike," Brian said. "I was still working on the descent parameters for your rig when we had to initiate your emergency pump-down, so we kind of played it by ear. I was the one who over-rode your stop order, and I was driving your rig until all six rods were clear of you."

"Six?" Mike exclaimed. "I only saw three."

"The same picket dropped another three, right after you executed your slide-away descent. The first three missed because you slid outside their maneuvering envelop. Two rods from that second group took out Bissonette above you. The last one in the second group lost guidance when Bissonette got taken out, extinguishing his laser." It missed you by 200 feet. By then you were less than a mile above the ground, so I dumped all your water, most of your hydrogen, and did an emergency re-deploy of all three layers of your balloon. It had to feel like landing on a big sponge going 200 miles per hour. You and your rig pulled at least eight g's. I finally stopped your descent 1000 feet above the plateau. I'm sorry I was so rough on you, but I didn't want to see you hit those rocks down there."

"Thanks, Brian. I owe you big-time," Mike said, gratefully. He tried to stand up, but his legs were shaking so much that he sat back down. He took another swig of water, looked at Dave and asked, "Who do you think was behind this?"

"Whoever it was, they had lots of resources, and it was meticulously planned," Dave replied. "They had at least six rigs; five of them we know had been hijacked for at least 2 weeks without anyone complaining. And frankly, the Consortium didn't see this coming. That took a lot of advance planning. They had to find rig owners who could be taken out without being missed for weeks. It's possible that they had an insider with access to Consortium records. We'll check that out, but I doubt it. More likely, they had a lot of people at popular spots where NC members do their ground time, cruising for likely candidates. It's sad how much information a pretty girl can extract from a horny geek who's been up all alone for months at a time. Whatever happened, it's going to be a grisly tale, and that kind of work doesn't come cheap."

"We also have initial analysis on the six rods dropped by the picket," Julian added. "Given their rate of acceleration and terminal velocity, they had a density signature characteristic of depleted uranium. You don't just buy these things on eBay. They were probably modified anti-tank sabots, and the only sources of these are from Russian, British, French, Chinese, and US military arsenals. Some Russian and US arms depots were compromised during the post-tsunami unrest. The Chechens got theirs from Russia. But getting them and modifying them with infrared seekers is no small feat. That would have taken a well-financed, technically-advanced, and highly secure infrastructure."

"We'll know more in the next few days, Mike," Dave continued, "but this was a hundred million dollar hit. Congratulations, my friend. You've made it to the big time. Someone down there really doesn't like you, and I'm not talking about your ex-girlfriend here."

•   •   •

As Mike lay exhausted and sleepless, he asked himself how things had come so far. This was the second time they'd tried to kill him. Why? He was just a science nerd who'd figured out how to use bacteria to make food out of shit and sunlight.   Well, at least that was where it had started. Over time, he realized his work had become a small but critical piece in a larger process. While the Consortium members just wanted the freedom to live as drifters, an unintended consequence was that they were fundamentally influencing how all humans either lived or hoped to live. Giving people control over the circumstances of their own lives – the essence of drifting – meant taking power away from those who'd previously held it. So who was it? Big agri-business upset by his milk-machines, the power monopoly losing market share because of NC hydrogen, or did it go back further than that?   He wondered: did it start when he was 14 and created that first ethanol bug? Or maybe it was when he met Lhamo…

CHAPTER 3

CHINA CAT
Summer 2028

Their first meeting was a disaster.

Mike had been working with the Life Support Project of the US-China Mars Mission for more than five years. In that time, he'd made a couple of big steps forward in getting a single strain of sunlight-powered bacteria, which everybody referred to as his 'bugs', to crank out a complex mix of nutrients. Photosynthesis had been the source of energy at the bottom of the food chain for a billion years. Eight thousand years of agriculture had honed its products to a fine point. You could now grow tons of soybeans, corn, or rice on a single acre, but Mike and his team were now on the verge of doing it all without seeds, leaves, or dirt; and his 'crop' would grow and be ready for harvest in just 24 hours.

At this point the Mars Nutrition Group was grappling with the problem of how to separate the bacteria and their leftover waste from the good stuff – the food components that Mike's team had programmed the 'bugs' to make. This turned out to be a frustrating hurdle for the engineers on the separation team. The two teams had held a number of meetings to deal with it, but so far to no avail.

Some jerk on the other team wisecracked that they should program the bacteria to make yogurt protein, and then have the Mars astronauts eat the whole slimy mix. "Plain yogurt tastes like shit anyway, so they won't even notice".

Someone else suggested that they squeeze out the water and make a bar out of it. "Call it a 'Mars bar' – maybe they'll think it's candy". That got a few chuckles out of the team.

Finally, Brian Solis, the Life-Support Project leader, got out of his seat at the back of the room, tried unsuccessfully to scowl with his habitually jovial face and offered: "There's a Chinese woman at Cal Tech who's doing some interesting work on continuous chromatography. She's gotten it really small, like the size of my fist. Let's get her out here to tell us about it. If it's promising, there shouldn't be a problem getting her help because everyone agrees that we need more Chinese members in the technical group anyway."

Mike knew a bit about Chinese girls from LA. There had been a quite a few of them in his undergraduate class at MIT. Stuck up, perfect princesses who did exactly what they were told, supported by rich families who tended to be the worst high-end consumers. These were not the kind of folks who gave up their suburban mansions and big gas hybrids for efficient housing and light weight hydrogen scooters. A person who made her mark by leaving a huge carbon footprint was not likely to fit into the spirit of a team designing a way for humans to make all their food and oxygen from sunlight while recycling their urine, feces, and expired carbon dioxide over and over again.

•   •   •

What turned up 2 weeks later was not quite what he'd expected. Tall and skinny – check! Long, straight black hair and high cheek bones – check! But the simple, almost austere clothing and no hint of makeup didn't fit his 'China doll from LA-LA-land' stereotype. As soon as she opened her mouth, it was obvious she hadn't grown up in LA. Her English was so challenged that Mike had to use his headset translator to understand her. Even then, he had a hard time following her presentation about her separation technology. Something about complementary molecular surfaces, laser-etched nanoparticles, switched electrical charge properties, and attraction/release cycles. This was supposed to simultaneously pull 10 different nutrients out of his bacterial soup? After getting both his bachelors and PhD degrees from MIT in less than 7 years, he figured anyone talking over his head was blowing smoke.

Mike listened politely, but he wasn't buying it. He'd be happy to trade all this magic pie-in-the-sky for a little bit of real pie on his plate. All he needed was something small and dependable to pull the protein out of his bacterial soup. Then another to pull out either sugar or starch, one more to pull out the fat, and presto! You'd have a rudimentary if boring energy mix. Forget this magic nanoparticle surface crap.

When she had finished her presentation, he asked: "Why not just one nutrient at a time, like protein, fat, and carbohydrate, so we might have something ready to fly in less than 10 years?"

She calmly met his gaze and answered that her multiple component extractor was development ready; they could have it ready for beta-testing in 6 months; and then she quietly said something that came out of his translator as: "And you'll need at least 40 different nutrients in your mix, not just protein, carbohydrate and fat, or your Mars astronauts will die of malnutrition before they get a quarter of the way there".

This was too much. He'd worked miracles to get his little green bugs to make food components from sunlight and shit, and here was some skinny Chinese FOB engineer telling his team how to do their job. He stood up and said: "That's OK, Honey, I'm all over it" and walked out.

That afternoon, Brian left a vid-clip in his in-box, saying:

> "I've hired her on the project, Mike, so whatever your problem is with her, get over it. And by the way, our Chinese Co-director checked up on her, and they love her in Beijing. 'Got her PhD there, and they were pissed as hell when she went to Cal Tech. We need her here, Mike, so don't drive her away. Okay?"

Mike dealt with this problem by using his time-tested technique for dealing with women: he buried himself in his work. Maybe she

wouldn't come. What had Brian said? She'd be here in 2 months?
In the mean time, he'd given her the nickname 'China Cat' from
the Dead song: *"Crazy cat peeking thru a lace bandana...Like a one-eyed
Cheshire, like a diamond-eye jack"*

Now he had bugs that made all of the vitamins, and he was starting
to think about using his bugs to produce flavors. By the time that
Lhamo (that was her name – strange – didn't sound Chinese) got
there, he was thinking that the opportunity to pull 40 nutrients out
of his soup was sounding pretty good.

• • •

The second time they met, things went a bit better. A bit, not a lot.

A week after she made the move from California, Brian took Mike
over to the engineering center to meet with Lhamo and her team
leader. Maybe it was his imagination, but her English seemed better, and he had an easier time following her as she walked them
through the functional details of her 10-compound extractor.

When she had finished, she turned to Mike and asked: "What are the
precise surface characteristics of the nutrients you want to isolate?"

Always the good student, Mike had done his homework. He liked
this job, and the last thing he wanted to do was piss off his boss.
While he appeared to be your standard issue, easy going Hispanic
from Texas, Brian (no one called him Dr. Solis) had his PhD in bio-
medical engineering from UT Southwestern. Nobody bluffed him,
so Mike had read Lhamo's publications on transforming surface
continuous chromatography, and when he discovered that she had
5 US patent applications filed on the process, he'd read those too.
He'd come prepared and maybe a bit impressed. Sure Mike had 5
issued patents and 8 pending applications, but his were just about
bugs. Hers were for hardware. And those five were just the US ones.
Who knew how many she had pending in China.

Mike leaned forward towards her computer microphone and spoke
a keyword sequence to open a shared file off the University Cloud.

Her screen lit up with a list of 41 nutrients, each with the necessary molecular structure data from which the surface characteristics could be determined. Lhamo briefly scanned the length and details of the list, turned back to face the forward leaning Mike, and just said "okay".

•   •   •

Their third meeting came the next day, when China Cat showed up unannounced in Mike's lab. Mike heard a conversation that his head-set identified as Mandarin outside as Tina Chin, Mike's Chinese graduate student, directed her to his office door. Mike first caught sight of her as she navigated her way through the lab benches, incubators, and instruments. Lhamo was wearing a denim jacket, loose denim jeans, and a stern look pasted on her high-cheek-boned face. She looked like a cowgirl on her way to a gunfight. All she needed was a 10-gallon hat and a six-shooter.

Mike kept his face neutral. "Hi, what's up?"

"I wonder about your list."

Mike pointed her to an empty chair and then leaned back, stretching his legs under his desk. "What about it? Too long?"

"No. I have just three questions."

"Go ahead. Shoot." He tried not to smile at his own lousy pun on his gunfighter fantasy.

"First, you have only the alpha-form of vitamin E. Why not one of the other kind, too?"

As far as he knew, vitamin E was vitamin E. Mike bit his tongue for a second. "And your other 2 questions…"

"Why do you include biotin? No one runs out of it in less than two years."

Mike raised his eyebrows in a gesture for question number three.

"Why nothing for flavor? Your mix will taste like paste."

Mike held Lhamo's gaze for another second and then replied: "number three first: our minimum mission parameter is that the nutrients are fed through a stomach tube – no one is going to taste it." She held his gaze. "Two: two months ago, you told me that people needed 40 nutrients to stay alive, but I figured I should add biotin, even if that makes a total of 41. It is a known vitamin." Her gaze didn't waver. "One: I have no clue if two kinds of vitamin E are better than one. I'll have somebody look it up".

Holding his gaze, she said: "I have read your patents, Dr. Anderson. You have a rare gift for working with bacteria. It is a shame that you have not found time to develop a similar ability to work with people".

She stood up and started toward the door.

"You are right", he replied hurriedly. "That's probably because I'm still young and foolish. But I learn quickly. Let me buy you lunch, and you can teach me all about vitamin E."

She turned to look at him inquisitively for a second, and then nodded slightly.

During the 7 minute walk across the campus to the faculty club, each used their headsets to scan the menu and order lunch. Otherwise they walked in silence. Mike used the time to monitor progress on Tina's thesis project. Lhamo was doing something on her display too, but Mike couldn't tell what.

When they arrived in the dining room, their table was ready and the food delivered a minute after they sat down. Mike had a veggie burger, fries, and a salad. Lhamo had tofu in a spicy red pepper sauce over rice. After a few bites, he asked her: "how's the food over here in the US? Is it a big change for you?"

"Not bad," she replied. "They did this Sichuan sauce a little better at Cal Tech, but nothing ever matches the food we grew up with at home, right?"

Mike nodded as he swallowed a bite and asked: "Where's home for you? I heard you speaking Mandarin with Tina, but 'Lhamo' doesn't sound like a Chinese name to me."

"Lhasa," Lhamo replied. I'm originally from Tibet"

Kiss goodbye to my 'China Cat' nickname, he thought. "Isn't it unusual for a Tibetan to go to the University of Beijing?" he asked.

"Yes. Mostly the Han Chinese come to Tibet. My people usually don't get to go to China."

"So, how did you do it?"

"I don't know. The Dali Lhama was always curious about science and engineering, so we were taught well in school. I work hard, and I am good with machines. The Han people may be arrogant, but they are not fools. They have always been good at importing the talent they need. How do you think they built that wall? And you, Dr. Anderson, how did you get such an important job while you are still so young and foolish?"

What was it about this woman and eye contact? He met her gaze and saw a suggestion of laughter rather than sarcasm in her dark eyes, but the mouth was still all gunfighter.

He shrugged. "Like you, I left my home in the mountains to go down to the big city. I grew up in a little town in Vermont. My uncle had a microscope, so I'd go find bacteria in a swamp, on trees, even on the snow, and study them. My uncle kind of tutored me. We found one that very efficiently made alcohol out of wood, and he helped me write a patent for it. Actually, the patent was on an engineered version of that 'bug' – we inserted a modified Hayflick gene[6] into it, so they only live for a month or two before they go senescent and die. That way we could sort of rent our bacteria for people to use without giving away the original one that grows forever. We keep the original one that lives forever locked up in a vault in Vermont."

As Mike spoke, Lhamo listened to him with quiet intensity. It felt as if she was listening not just to what he said but simultaneously understanding why he was saying it. It wasn't anything clinical, like being analyzed by a shrink. Still, it made him a bit uneasy. He was used to people trying to understand what he was saying, but this woman seemed to want to divine his inner feelings and motivation. In addition, she seemed oblivious to interpersonal barriers and thus able to apply more of her energy to the interaction.

He paused in his story, and she nodded to indicate her continued interest. "My uncle now runs our business in Vermont." Mike continued, "using my bug to make biofuel ethanol from waste wood, and we also sell the bugs to others who do the same. I was 14 when we filed that patent, and that helped get me into MIT at 16. They liked my fascination with bugs there. I figured out how to change them – to make them want to do things for me. My bugs and I get along pretty well together; maybe, as you pointed out, better than I get along with people. So I filed a few more patents, made the old men at the Institute happy, and they gave me a PhD. End of story. So, now you need to teach me about vitamin E."

"No, Dr. Anderson. I am just an engineer. But to get a molecule to like my surface, I study it. I get to know it. I found that there are many forms of vitamin E, and they do different things. Not everyone likes the one called 'alpha'. But you have people in your group who can figure that out. What I want to talk about with you is flavor."

"What about flavor?" This woman might be fascinating, but she was as unpredictable as hell! Busting me over biotin, quizzing me on vitamin E, and now she wants me to have good taste? Geez!

Lhamo paused a second, did that eye contact thing again, and then said: "I'm new to this project, and I recognize that you have all worked hard on it for years. I know the Mars astronauts will have catheters for waste collection, but I do not think that feeding through a stomach tube is a good idea. Most people will not miss it if they don't – how do you say politely – pee and poop? But going without the taste of food for 2 years will be very hard for them. There is virtue in the appreciation of one's food"

Mike paused, trying to understand what Lhamo meant by that, but shrugged and continued. "So you want us to make our paste taste good? How many of the 40 necessary nutrients do you want to give up, so we can add taste to our paste?" Mike struggled to keep his expression neutral and his voice free of sarcasm. Two months ago, he would have reacted to her comment by terminating the conversation, maybe by addressing her as 'honey'. He wondered what was making him hold back.

Again she held him with her steady gaze, maybe a bit of fun at the corners of the eyes, but still the quiet intensity. She replied: "Our weight limit for the complete nutrient extractor to fly in the Mars Mission crew capsule is five kilograms. Right now, each prototype ten-compound sub-unit weighs 1.2 kilograms, so we can get our 40 molecules from an instrument having a total weight of 4.8 kilograms.

Mike nodded and waited. She had told him all of this yesterday. There had to be more coming, and he was beginning to think it might be worth the wait.

"But in six more months" she continued, "with the excellent engineering team we have here, I think we can get each subunit down to 800 grams. That means we could get 60 molecules extracted from 6 subunits together that still weigh a total of 4.8 kilograms. You could have your biotin, two types of vitamin E, and still have 18 molecules left to add taste. Maybe you could train your bugs to make this Sichuan pepper sauce," Lhamo said, pointing to her plate.

The centers of her eyes were still serious, but there was obviously mirth in the corners. Still, he sensed she wasn't joking. Mike felt that she was tempting him, wanting to see if he'd join her in this fantasy. He remembered their first meeting two months ago, when all he had wanted was a way to get three pure compounds out of his bug soup, and she'd jacked him up by a factor of more than ten.

So what was another 50% improvement in her instrument's performance-to-weight ratio to this woman? Maybe she could do it, extracting 60 individual nutrients from his bug soup with an instrument weighing less than 5 kg. Had she hacked his lab computer? Did she know that he was already working on simple fruit flavors – apple, banana, strawberry, pineapple, and maybe melon – each fruit flavor composed of a mix of four or five simple molecules. He could almost taste a fruit smoothie made with those 18 added molecules coming out of her 4.8 kg extraction device.

Lhamo took the last bite of her tofu in Sichuan sauce. When she looked up at him, Mike's gaze was steady. "In a month, I can give you bugs that make five fruit flavors, each composed of four or five molecules. In six months, I think I can make meat and vegetable flavors, green tea, cocoa, and maybe coffee."

She smiled. It was Mike's first Lhamo smile.

"Okay" she said.

CHAPTER 4

THE MILKMAN
Summer 2028

After his lunch with Lhamo, Mike went back to his lab, spending the rest of the afternoon immersed in creating the bugs that could give taste to paste. The fruit flavors were relatively easy. If a banana plant or a melon vine could make the combination of chemicals that together constitute a characteristic flavor, a bug could be equipped to do the same thing. It was just a matter of sorting through his virtual library for the chemicals, finding the enzymes in a plant that produce each of the chemicals, inserting the gene for that enzyme into the bug, and voila! Taste for the paste. Oh, yes...and make sure that none of those chemicals did something bad to the bugs. Pissing off a bug with the wrong chemical could stunt its growth, make it die, or worse, induce it to make a toxin. Bacterial poisons are common in nature, like the toxin that causes botulism – not a disease you'd want to have crop up and be dealing with half way to Mars.

Meat flavor was another story. Most humans prefer not to eat chicken sashimi. They'd rather eat most types of meat cooked, and that's a different flavor from what the animal creates in raw meat. You can't find chicken cells that make the cooked flavors characteristic of chicken soup or fried chicken. That would take more work – maybe all 6 months. Mike would have to screen a list of thousands of compounds to find combinations that could mimic cooked meat flavors. In addition, because drying changes some chemicals, green tea would also pose more of a problem than fresh fruit or vegetables, but it was going to be less of a problem than cooked meat.

Coffee and cocoa, on the other hand, would be an absolute pain in the ass to solve. Coffee beans and cocoa pods are processed at high temperature to get their roasted flavors, but bugs don't naturally make high temperature flavors, not even those bacteria that evolved to live around undersea volcanic vents. This was going to be tough. Maybe he'd over-reached a bit when he'd promised coffee.

Before he knew it, his visual display began flashing the 10 minute warning for his 6 p.m. tennis game with Klink. Oops! Professor Steven Klink was one of the few really good tennis players at Ham U. He was in his early forties, brash, and Chair of the Molecular Biology Department. What else? Oh, yes; even more than losing, he hated waiting for anybody, especially Mike, who usually beat him at tennis. Showing up late for tennis with Klink was not an option.

Technically, Klink was Mike's boss. The US-China Mars Mission Life Support Project was part of Hamiltonian University in St. Louis, thanks to an ear-mark inserted into legislation by some dead white senator named Bundy. Thus, when Mike was recruited to join the Mars team, he had to be assigned to an academic department within the university. Since he worked with bacteria, it was logical that Mike would have his "academic home" in Molecular Biology. However, Mike's salary, research support, and laboratory were all provided through the Mars Project budget, so his appointment in Klink's department was supposed to be a mere technicality.

Except, that is, when it came to patents – those pieces of paper that make department chairs and old fart university administrators dream of money. Mike was writing patents to cover all of his newly created bugs, and Klink insisted that all of Mike's patents had to be filed through his department. That was uncomfortable, but Mike did not see it as a major problem.

None of those issues got solved in the 12 minutes it took Mike to sprint to his hydrogen-powered scooter, park at the tennis bubble, get through the airlock, slip into his tank top, shorts and shoes, and come out of the tunnel by court three. There was Klink, hands on his hips - probably thinking 'billable minutes'. He reminded Mike of his ex-partner Tammy, the rich heiress and now a corporate lawyer who billed her clients just as much for waiting as for actual service performed.

"Sorry, Professor". At 27, Mike was not about to call his department chair by his first name.

"It's okay, Mike. I just talked to Tina in your lab, and she said that you left there at sub-light speed about 10 minutes ago. So I figured you were either running toward me or away from me. Either way, I'd find out the result soon enough. And, by the way, good job with Tina. I'm always glad to see it when a graduate student works late. Now let's get going. We only have the court for an hour. I'll serve."

Fifty-five minutes later, Mike had won their first match in straight sets 6-3 and 6-3; now they were at 2-2 into another set when the 7 p.m. players showed up.

I guess we'll call this one a draw. Too bad. I was just getting warmed up," said Klink, wiping the sweat from his brow.

"So next time, let's get the court for two hours and play five sets" said Mike.

"Can't, Mike. The only courts available for two hours are outside, and I'm not about to play out there in that unfiltered air. So, same time next week?"

"Okay," Mike said, turning for the exit doorway.

"And Mike, make sure to keep up with the patent applications on all those bugs you're creating." Klink had turned to face him in the doorway. "You know, nailing down the intellectual property on them is the key to translating your brilliant work into the real world marketplace. And I mean it, you're doing great stuff!"

Klink patted Mike condescendingly on the shoulder and went off towards his car – a big gas-powered Lexus. Mike found his scooter, slid under the canopy, powered it up, and headed home. On the way, he used his heads-up display to order takeout from a Chinese restaurant. He decided to spread his carbon foot-print just a bit and ordered Sichuan beef rather than the tofu. He'd make it up to the green-house gas gods later.

•   •   •

After having a beer with his dinner, Mike checked his message vids and was disappointed to find nothing from Angela. She was only eight, but she usually sent him a smile and a "Hi Daddy". Unless Tammy had diverted her again with those damn kid games on VR or had worked her to exhaustion on the tennis court. Between the spicy food, the beer, and thinking about his failed relationship with Angela's mother, Mike's gut ached. He wished he had a glass of milk to cool it off. But milk and beef in the same day? That would take some serious penance before the greenhouse gas gods. Instead, he just went to bed early.

Four hours later, Mike awoke and sat bolt upright. What was it? The room was dark and quiet. He felt okay. In fact, he felt good. That was it – the taste of milk. He'd dreamed that he had been drinking a tall glass of cold milk. The dream was so real, even his gut felt good. And there was no guilt. Why? What WAS it? Ah, yes! In the dream, the milk had come from Lhamo's extractor – her new 60-compound extractor. Could you make milk out of just 60 compounds? Yes, but the fat – there was something about the fat that puzzled him…

While pondering that thought, Mike sank back into sleep, his brain freed from the inhibitions of consciousness.

At five a.m. Mike awoke again. Something about the fat, he thought. Huh? What fat? Milk fat; it's in globules. What's it called – an emulsion. Could his bugs be trained to emulsify fat? Can I get cream from bugs? Yes! All I'd need is the cell machinery from a cow's udder – and no roasting required.

So that was it – a dream about making fresh milk using his bugs and Lhamo's extractor. A tall glass of cold milk. Mike burst into laughter. Now that was one hell of a strange wet dream. How was he going to explain this to Lhamo? Nope. Don't even try it, kid.

Mike sat up and put his feet on the floor. I've got to think this through – cheap milk without greenhouse gasses – zero carbon emissions. All we'd need are the chemicals found in human waste, sunlight, and a bunch of Lhamo's magic surfaces, including one that could capture the emulsified butterfat globules and carry them out of his bug soup and into a glass.

Mike stopped. Vermont is one of the last strongholds of dairy production, he thought. They still love Ben and Jerry back home. My neighbors will kill me if I do this.

"Shit! I've gotta talk this through with Uncle Mike."

CHAPTER 5

ME AND MY UNCLE
Summer 2028

"Hey, kid. How's life inside the evil academic-industrial complex?" Only half of his uncle's face was visible. Clearly the video boom on his headset was not extended, but his right eye was darting back and forth, trying to follow something he was doing with two hands.

"What're you working on, Uncle Mike?"

"It's the truck I told you I was building. The patents finally ran out on the combined turbine-generator I developed 20 years ago back at RPI, so now I'm free to use it like it was intended. I just got the carbon-fiber body, and I'm trying to bolt on the power train. This damn thing was built to specs, but I can't quite get this bolt aligned. Give me a second here."

Mike's video feed went blank for a minute, and then his uncle appeared, wiping his hands on a grimy red rag.

"So, how's the Rum Works doing?" Mike asked. "You know it's illegal to drink the stuff my bugs are making for you."

"Everything in moderation, I always say. Actually, partner, we're doing pretty well. Here in town we've increased our cutting rights up to 5200 acres, and we've now got 68 franchises from other independent producers that purchase and use your bug. Our ethanol production here in town is up to three million gallons per year, and over 100 million gallons total at all of our franchises. We're beginning to rock the fuel business up here in the North Country. Folks are starting to notice. If your patent continues to hold up, and nobody figures out how to reverse-engineer your bug to defeat the Hayflick gene you inserted, this alcohol gig might make you rich some day."

"That's great, Uncle Mike. But look. Whatever my share is, just keep putting it back into the business. The less that goes into my bank account, the less Tammy will think she can claim for child support."

"Okay, kid." His uncle shot Mike an angry scowl. "I can keep doing that for now, but there's only so much capital this little business can absorb. Before long, you're going to need another strategy to keep looking poor to hold your ex-girlfriend's lawyers at bay. And besides, to keep our partnership equal, I have to match your investments, so your endless spat with Tammy is making me poor, too."

Mike knew his uncle's anger was all show. He bought maybe two outfits of work clothes each year, owned his Vermont farm outright, never took a vacation, and bummed most of his meals off Mike's mom. He was the original skin-flint.

"How about upgrading our timber harvesting system?" Mike asked, trying to steer the conversation away from his personal problems. "Is this truck you're building something that might replace the skidders? They really tear up the forest floor."

"Funny you should ask, Wonderboy. Great minds think alike," Uncle Mike replied, his face lighting up. "While my truck will be light and very agile, it won't have anything like the power or weight needed to haul whole trees out of the forest. But I've been looking at this new helical carbon technology. Have you been paying any attention to this stuff?"

"You mean that Superman fiber they claim is a hundred times stronger than steel?"

"Two hundred fifty times stronger," his uncle chided. "Yeah, it's pure carbon fiber made from tar that naturally forms itself into a helix – kind of like an unfolded, continuous Buckyball[7]. And the funny thing is, the stuff looks for all the world like diamond – white and lustrous. A strand the size of kite string can hold a couple of tons. So, look, they're starting to make fabric from this stuff that weighs almost nothing and yet it can stop a bullet. You can weave a balloon from this stuff, and it'll hold hydrogen forever."

"Great. So you can make kids' balloons that can't be popped and never deflate. That'll wreck the party balloon market pretty damn quick buy your kid one balloon, and it'll last a lifetime" Mike said, cynically. "But what does that do for us in the woodlot?"

"Okay, Kid, listen up. If we make a balloon out of this fabric and fill it with a million liters of hydrogen, we can lift almost 2 tons. Then we put it on a 10 km loop of super-string made from the same stuff. That way, anywhere within 6 miles of the Rum Works, we could cut a cord or two of waste-wood, hoist it up beneath the balloon and pull it down to the factory without ever touching the ground. That gets rid of the skidders and all the fuel they use. And no more ruts in the mud or rocks stuck in the bark to kill our chippers. What do you think?"

"Get a grip, Uncle Mike. It costs me close to 200 bucks for 1000 liters of hydrogen whenever I fill up my scooter, and half the time I try, there isn't any hydrogen to buy. That's $200,000 to fill your balloon to get enough wood into your chipper to make $2000 worth of alcohol. How does that work?"

"*Think…this…through…with…me..,!*" Uncle Mike sang.

Crap, Mike thought. When Uncle Mike starts singing Grateful Dead lines, I'm toast. What's the next line…? *Let…me…know…your…mind.* With his unruly red hair and thick beard, Uncle Mike looked the part of a strawberry-flavored Jerry Garcia. They should have named that song "Uncle Mike's Band". Mike stayed silent and waited.

"You with me, Wonderboy?"

"Yeah, I was trying to figure out where you were going with those lyrics. Something to do with 'walls built of cannonballs', maybe?"

"Relax, Kid. I told you this before. You're supposed to just listen to the Dead – not take them literally. So here's how it works. We send the balloon on a superstring tether up the hill almost empty, we load it up with a bunch of trees, fill it with just enough hydrogen to carry the load, pull it and the load back down to the chipper, pump the hydrogen back into its attached storage tank, and send it back up the hill almost empty. The hydrogen is either in the balloon or in the tank, which stays with the balloon – all we do is just pump it in and out. So that $200,000 of hydrogen will last us about forever."

"This Superman carbon fabric doesn't leak," Uncle Mike continued. "Even the local NRA guys can't rain on our parade, 'cause it will stop anything up to 50-caliber, maybe even a cannonball. Unless they get a loose nuke, there's no way anybody puts a hole in our pretty balloon. Once we use that initial hydrogen 200 times, we break even. And I think we can cycle it back and forth from the woodlot 20 times per day, so we've pretty much paid for that hydrogen by the end of the second week. After that, it's all profit. Capiche?"

"Okay, okay! What's our little 'Hindenburg' going to cost? And are you going to paint 'Jamaica Rum Works' on it like those blimps at the football games?"

"Sorry, Wonderboy. No advertising on this one. The surface is like diamond, so nothing sticks to it. Not paint, not grease, not water. It stays perfectly clean. There's a startup in Alberta called Diamond Fabrics that's hurting for a sale. This stuff can only be made from fossil tar, and they've got lots of it up there. I think I can get them to make us a trial balloon for less than $100,000, so our total for balloon plus hydrogen to get up and running is about $300K. You in?"

"Okay, I'm in."

"That was easy."

"Uh, Uncle Mike?"

"Uh oh, here it comes. I knew you were calling about something other than wanting to hear about my balloon fantasy. But thanks for letting me get that in. What's up?"

"How much do you like cows?"

"For food, cows are great. For sex, sheep are better. Come on, kid. Help me here. What's the question?"

Mike had a flashback to being an eight year old kid trying to see what his uncle saw through the microscope. What his uncle saw tended to be much different than what normal humans saw looking at the same thing. What others saw in black and white, Uncle Mike saw in Technicolor. Now, sometimes, their roles got reversed. This was never easy.

"Uncle Mike, I'm working with someone who can pluck selected molecules out of the goop my food-producing bacteria make. In addition to meeting our Mars Mission objectives, I think we can use a similar system to make milk from sunlight and waste-stream nutrients. Where it gets messy is, I think we can do this a lot cheaper than real milk from real cows."

"Wow!" Mike could see instant recognition of his problem cross his uncle's face. "This is heavy, Wonderboy. I trust your fake milk is pretty close to cow's milk straight from the teet. Like having the same nutrients, and it'll taste okay?"

"No different."

"What's the cost difference?"

"Initially I'm guessing that ours' will cost maybe half as much to produce, and that might come down more as our volume goes up," Mike replied.

"You going to use the same senescence gene we put in your alcohol bug, so folks can't just buy it once and walk away?"

"Actually, I've come up with a better one. That'll make it even harder for someone to do the reverse engineering to get back to bugs that live and reproduce forever. But in this case there's another reason to do this besides making the customer keep coming back for more."

"And that might be...? Uncle Mike asked with raised eyebrows.

"Most bacteria can make toxins that would harm people if they slipped through the extractor", Mike continued. "I know how to turn off toxin production in my engineered bugs, but given enough time some of them will eventually mutate back to become toxin producers. That's not a concern for the Rum Works bug as long as you don't drink the alcohol. But you don't want to run a culture of these food-producing bugs for too long before you toss it out and started with a fresh batch."

"Okay, I get that. So where are you taking me? What's the carbon footprint of your ersatz milk?"

"It's not ersatz milk, Uncle Mike – it'll be real milk in every chemical and taste analysis. Except ours is made by bacteria plus a machine, rather than by cows. Our bacteria live on sunlight and human waste, and actually take up CO_2 from the atmosphere. So no methane emissions, no acres of forage crops pumped up with fertilizer, no more erosion caused by over-grazed pastures, and no carcass disposal issues when production drops."

Uncle Mike thought for a moment. He remembered when this 'kid' declared that he had found a bacterium on some moss from the north side of a tree that turned wood into ethanol at 56% efficiency. He was 14; he had ear-to-ear pimples; and every girl within a hundred mile radius treated him like small-pox. Now that little moss bug provided the core technology for the Jamaica Rum Works, making them over two million dollars in profit last year. It had also brought a spark of life back to their little backwater Vermont town, so when his nephew got a bone in his teeth, he knew enough to give him some space to maneuver.

"So", his uncle continued, "you're telling me you can make real milk in a sun-powered machine, sell it cheaper than milk from factory dairies, and you do it all with a carbon footprint the size of a mosquito. Not too shabby. But let me guess – you're worried about putting dairy farmers out of business. Right?"

"Right", Mike replied. "This might be great for kids, but I'd hate to destroy the livelihoods of thousands of farmers."

"Listen, Mike", his uncle paused.

"I'm listening." It was rare that Uncle Mike called him 'Mike' rather than 'Kid' or 'Wonderboy'. But when he did, Mike knew they were both going to act like grownups for a little while.

"Cows and jet planes are history, Mike. When you factor in the cost of cleaning up the mess that both make on the planet, we can't afford either one. So your milk machine is a big deal, and your timing is good. If you can make it work, it's good for kids, good for the planet, and you'll get stinking rich doing it. Go for it. You've got all the intellectual property sewed up on this, right?"

"I'm writing the patents on the bugs, but because I'm technically on the faculty here at Ham U, they own the IP, not me. So no, I won't get that much money back from them, but it will help the University a lot. I think I get something like 20% of the profit on the first $500,000, and then 10% of the next million, so I'd max out on this at $200,000 per year. It's pretty much like my contract with MIT for the patents I filed there."

"How about this person who does the separation step after the bacteria are done? How does that work? Does he use high pressure filtration through membranes? Does he have this covered with IP as well?"

"It's a 'she', Uncle Mike. And she uses continuous chromatography, no high pressure, no high temperature. It's a remarkable device. She did the initial work on it in China, and she has US patents filed from there. I don't know if she has other patents in China."

Uncle Mike snorted. "A patent filed in China is about as useful as cotton candy in a downpour. I'd suggest that you talk with her about the IP on her device because your bugs – no matter how cool they might be – are worthless without her widget. If somebody else buys up her IP, you're completed blocked. No milk with your cookies. Nada!"

"You're right, I kind of assumed that Ham U would have licensed her US patents, but I haven't talked with anyone about that. But her instrument is vital to the Mars mission, so they must have nailed it down. I'll talk with her and see what gives."

"Yeah, you definitely need to do that. Sorting out this crap in that academic piranha tank you live in is where most of the perspiration comes from after the inspiration. It's why I'll never work for either a university or a big company. The academic-industrial complex sucks."

"I think I've heard you tell me that more than once."

Michael Barber gave his nephew a sharp look. "It's true. And here's one more tip for you, Mike. Remember when we wrote your alcohol bug patent back in '14? You wanted to put everything into the patent to prove to them how smart you were. I told you to tell them just enough to prove 'novelty' and hold the rest back? Remember that?"

"Yeah." Mike recalled how they'd butted heads on that. "You told me to write it so that it had a back-door, if I ever wanted to do a work-around on my own IP later. I remember."

"You still doing that?"

"Pretty much. But is that so important when these aren't actually my patents? They belong to Ham U. It's not really honest if I leave a hole in their patent on purpose."

Uncle Mike scowled again and the strawberry-colored face behind his red beard grew even redder. "You're so much like your mom. I love my sister dearly, but honestly, you two drive me friggin' crazy. The terms 'innocent' and 'idealist' fit you two like a pair of silk gloves."

"And by the way", Uncle Mike continued. "Care to guess who taught me this 'back door' trick."

"Who?" Mike asked.

"Your father, Mike. When I was doing graduate work at RPI, sometimes he'd pick me up on Friday afternoon in Troy, flying home from New York to Brattleboro for the week-end. My research on mini-turbine generators was creating a lot of potential intellectual property, and the tech-transfer folks down there weren't keeping up with me. So over those few years your dad taught me patent law. He was one of the best."

Mike sat there looking at his uncle's image suspended in front of him – ruddy skin under red hair and beard, with those intense blue eyes looking back at him. When his father's plane went down in turbulence, Mike was four, and Uncle Mike was still working on his PhD in engineering at RPI. Mike felt a slight shiver of fear. Uncle Mike had never mentioned that he could have been aboard the plane that day as well. Shortly thereafter, his uncle had his infamous spat with his professor, abandoned his nearly completed dissertation, and walked away from academia for good. He'd come back to Vermont, took over the family property in Jamaica, and never left.

From the moment of his return home, the uncle and the boy were inseparable. Since there wasn't much work to be found in Jamaica, Uncle Mike had the time to help care for his nephew while the grieving Stephanie held down her job as school nurse in Townshend. But Uncle Mike was never idle. First he fixed up houses, then ran a firewood business off the Jamaica farm, and eventually along came Mike's alcohol bug. At every junction in life, it seemed that Uncle Mike had taken Robert Frost's less traveled path, and yet he always seemed to come out ahead. So when those eyes got that intense, Mike knew to pay attention. Something important was happening.

"I don't think you ever told me that about my father," Mike said solemnly. "Okay... I'm listening."

"Good, because your dad would have told you this too. Not everybody out there has your Eagle Scout mentality, Mike – not in business and certainly not in academia. So you've got to watch your back and always be thinking a couple of moves ahead. This milk thing you're doing is fundamentally different from what you did with your alcohol bug."

"What WE did", Mike corrected.

"Shut up and listen, Wonderboy. Your alcohol bug was truly innovative, but nobody saw it as an immediate threat. Other than the Jamaicans down in the Caribbean hassling us because our little Vermont town has the same name as their island, nobody pushed back when we started the Rum Works. It allowed us to make waste wood into fuel for homes and cars without smoke, and we return the fermenter sludge back onto the forest floor, so nothing is lost. People here in town like it because it's both a paycheck and a sustainable business, as do folks near our franchises. But each franchise by itself is small potatoes, so there aren't any big waves, big egos, or big salaries. E.F. Shumaker[8] would have liked it. It's a good, sustainable business model. But your milk thing is fundamentally different, and you are right to be worried about it."

"Why," Mike asked. "Our milk machine will recycle human waste and get its power from sunlight, so it's sustainable, too."

"Right. But here's the difference," Uncle Mike continued. "There was a guy down at Harvard a few decades ago who divided innovation into two classes, 'incremental' and 'disruptive'. Incremental innovations enhance existing business structures, and that's what the Rum Works franchises have done. People can add from 10% to 85% ethanol to gas and drive pretty much the same cars."

Mike nodded, and his uncle continued. "But disruptive innovations destroy existing business. This Harvard guy used computers from the last century as an example: in the 1960's they filled a room, by the 1990's they fit in your briefcase, and now we wear them like jewelry." Uncle Mike said, pointing to his headset. "Each time the device got smaller and cheaper, the previously dominant companies missed the boat and were wiped out. Startups grew up to take their places in the market until they grew too big and clunky, and then they got wiped out by the next wave of disruptive innovation."

"So here's the punch-line, Mike. This milk machine of yours is the poster-child for disruptive innovation. Yeah, the farmers are going to stop doing the dairy cow thing. That's already a given. But when the cows are gone, they'll still have their land. They can grow something else. The folks who are really going to be hurt by your milk machine are the magnates of agribusiness – the guys in suits with big egos and big salaries who sell the chemicals, feed additives, antibiotics, and that hormone they shoot the cows up with. Those are the guys who are going to seriously not like you because you will destroy their existing market without creating another one for them to move into."

"Who's this guy at Harvard? I want to read his stuff."

"Christensen. His best book was called 'The Innovator's Dilemma'[9] He tried to help big companies learn to deal with innovation, but elephants can't dance on pinheads. It was all about size. Shumaker had it right, 'Small is Beautiful'."

Mike remembered when his uncle made him read Shumaker's book at age 14. He'd had huge plans to sell the ethanol bug and be as rich as Bill Gates, but Uncle Mike wouldn't let the big guys in the door. Now the Rum Works was supplying 68 other towns under franchise making their own bio-fuel, and he and his uncle still controlled the whole operation. He was right back then, and he was probably right again. "So what should I do?" Mike asked.

Uncle Mike stared up for a few moments. Maybe he was watching a hawk circling outside his office window. Then he looked back at Mike and asked: "If Plan A is working this through Ham U, do you have a Plan B?"

"Uh...no".

"You need one, Mike. Have you thought about doing it through the Rum Works? As I mentioned, we've got some working capital."

"I can't do that if I'm working for Ham U."

"And if they screw you on this thing, will you still be working there? When word of this new milk thing gets out, your enemies will try anything to shut it down, including coming at you through Ham U."

Mike shook his head. "But I really like the Mars project. This is where the rubber meets the road in my field, Uncle Mike. We're pushing out the human envelope by going there."

Uncle Mike scowled again. "Seems to me that's an awful long way to go to play in some red sand. There're much better beaches closer to home, and ours down here provide water and surf at no extra charge. No really, Mike, this milk thing of yours is potentially huge. Stick with it, but be careful. Make sure that all of your IP has a back door. And let me know if we can do anything to help secure this Chinese woman's patents."

"She's not Chinese, she's Tibetan. And Uncle Mike. Thanks! Give mom a hug for me."

"You'll need to come here and do that yourself, Wonderboy. The only things I hug are maple trees."

CHAPTER 6

MILK WARS
Winter-Spring 2029

Seven months after he had the dream of milk from a machine, the first drops of white liquid started dripping into a flask in the lab. Six of them stood around and watched the white drops accumulate. Mike and Brian, Lhamo and her boss, Tina and another graduate student looked at one another and smiled. But then the smiles started to fade.

Brian asked the obvious question. "Who's going to taste it?"

Everyone but Lhamo unconsciously took a half step back. She looked around, shrugged, picked up the collection flask, and poured an ounce into her empty tea mug. No one moved. She raised her mug to her lips, and took a sip. She paused and then scanned the assembled group. "It tastes like fresh grass and flowers!" she exclaimed.

Mike smiled. Success! He'd patterned the chemical profile of his milk after that of unpasteurized milk from Vermont cows eating June pasture grass – the best tasting milk in the world. Well, maybe equaled by some milk produced in the Alps and Ireland. In all of these locations, fresh grass and flowers came through in flavors imparted to the milk.

They had done this by working lots of extra hours, so their primary task of providing food for the Mars Mission was still on schedule. They already had fruit smoothies and chicken soup coming out of

Lhamo's extractors. And now with the added ability to make milk and cream, their range of flavors was increased to include creamed soups and milk shakes. Mike almost had the chocolate flavor nailed down, so cocoa and chocolate would soon be added to the list, and if he could solve the coffee problem, they'd have lattes and mocha, too.

While Mike was pleased by his and Lhamo's success on the Mars Project, his delight at seeing – and then tasting – fresh milk from her machine was infinitely greater. It had taken him a while to understand why he felt this way. Feeding five people on a space mission for two years using human waste and sunlight was a remarkable feat, but it was Lhamo who pointed out that in the end, all of this effort only fed five people.

By contrast, the milk machine could help to feed millions, with many of them being kids whose families could not afford the increasingly expensive version of milk made by cows. Then there were the added benefits of making inexpensive milk without all of the methane, carbon-dioxide, and ground-water pollution that came with milk production on factory farms. From the perspective of personal satisfaction, the milk machine won hands down.

However, no one was planning to send kids to Mars any time soon, and the Mars astronauts could complete their mission without chocolate ice cream or milk in their coffee, so they had kept the two projects organizationally separate. This meant that Lhamo and Mike scheduled regular Saturday morning meetings to plan the milk project and deal with the practical development of the Earth-bound milk machine.

To their pleasant surprise, Brian Solis joined them from the start, bringing to bear his valuable project management skills. They even drafted a business plan for a start-up company within the Ham U business incubator to build the milk machines and lease them to schools. Locating their milk machines at schools was a natural choice. After all, that was where the kids were, and it offered the least appearance of competing with the dairy industry's distribution through grocery stores.

While there was a lot of commonality between the Mars Mission machines and the Milk machines – like extractor surfaces and the bugs
that produced the components – there were a lot of differences as
well. One was simply the size of the device. One fed five people everything they needed, but the other had to make enough milk for as
many as a 500 kids per machine per day. This meant that they had
lots to do on Saturdays. Particularly for Lhamo, the scaling-up process, the waste collection system, and mounting the incubator panels in the sun on the roof, all took a lot of extra engineering effort.

Furthering Mike's sense of surprise, as the string of Saturday meetings progressed from winter into spring, was that the size of the group
kept getting bigger. One by one, other members of the Mars Project
team, and then faculty and students from other Ham U departments,
showed up and offered to lend a hand. By word of mouth, the buzz
on campus was that 'The Martians' were doing something with their
little green bugs that might actually help ordinary Earthlings.

It turned out there was a fair bit of thinly veiled envy on campus
directed at 'The Martians' because of their fancy new facilities and
guaranteed research funding. Frankly, even some members of the
Mars team were a bit embarrassed by the resources being spent on
their project while there were so many other worthwhile problems
sorely in need of attention here on Earth.

When word of the Milk Machine project leaked out, it began to
change the image of the Mars Project. Brian liked this change, but
not wanting to be accused of losing focus, the official word on the
Milk Machine was silence. Nonetheless, Mike and Lhamo began to
get a lot of unofficial attention on the web. This made Mike uneasy.
Keeping Brian happy was the key to getting the milk machine out
the door and feeding good nutrients to kids, but the politics here
were delicate. Mike knew from past experience, being young and
foolish, that politics was not his long suit.

Then came the Saturday meeting in late June when Lhamo, Mike,
and 33 others sat in the conference room for 15 minutes waiting
for Brian to show up. Mike kept checking his headset display to see
if there was something from Brian. This was unusual. Brian was a

poster-boy for punctuality. After 20 minutes, they knew that something was wrong, and this was confirmed a few minutes later when Brian walked in the door. He looked really unhappy, like there had been a death in his family or something. He motioned for Mike to come over to him as he remained in the doorway and then turned and walked back out into the corridor with Mike following him.

Outside, Brian turned and said: "I just got summoned to a meeting with the University Chancellor and the VP who oversees the Mars Mission. They're shutting this group down. They told me that they've sold exclusive rights to your milk patents, and this project is in violation of that license agreement."

"They can't do that without my okay!" Mike shot back. There was a second or two pause as Mike thought about this, and then he asked lamely "Can they?"

"That's what I've just been trying to get a handle on, Mike. The short answer is, yes they can. You get a share of the royalty on each of them, but you gave the university complete control when you signed on as faculty in Klink's department. He maintains tighter control over patents than NASA does."

"But our draft agreement for the start-up has all of the royalties coming through Ham U. We ran it by the university lawyers when we chartered the startup. They'll get their cut the same either way. Nobody's had a problem with that for the last few months. Why now?"

"I don't know, Mike," Brian replied. "All I know is that the university VP who's legally my boss told me they can't license the patents for your bugs back to us for the School Milk Project, and he ordered me to shut it down."

"What the hell are they thinking? This is good business for the university, it helps kids, and it's great PR for the Mars Project." Even as he said this, however, Mike realized that this was what his uncle had warned him might happen.

Brian sighed. "The chancellor said they have a better arrangement lined up. He wouldn't tell me what that is. He did reassure me that we can still license the milk bugs back to the Mars mission. Look Mike, you've got to stop thinking of these bacteria as your personal bugs. Based upon your contract with Ham U, they are the University's property, so they are legally in the clear to do this."

"So what if I go to the press and get on the blogs? Have they thought about how much they have at stake in terms of bad PR?"

Brian looked Mike square in the face, dead serious, and said; "Please think carefully about that before you do it, Mike. Believe me, you don't want to take them on without having some serious legal talent behind you. They can and will hurt you if you piss them off. And personally, Mike, you are a key player in the Mars Mission, and I don't want to lose you."

"But what's their better deal? Maybe we can negotiate up the royalty from the School Milk Project without screwing the kids."

"I don't know, Mike. We'll probably find out in due time. But for now, let's send these folks home," Brian said, nodding towards the conference room.

"You do it, Brian," Mike retorted. "Handling bullshit like this is way above my pay-grade."

As soon as he'd said it, a part of Mike felt bad for Brian. Over the last few months, Mike had affectionately but privately given Brian the nick-name 'Señor Dude' because although he was the boss, his easy-going, Hispanic personality made him so easy to work with.

However at this point, Mike was seriously angry. He turned and stalked down the corridor, kicked the door as it cycled through its automated opening sequence, and stormed out into the mid-morning St. Louis haze.

Mike's head was spinning with a combination of rage at the university, but also anger at himself for failing to nail down rock solid access to the IP before he'd shown his hand. But then, in the same breath, he silently thanked his uncle for warning him about maintaining his back-doors. Uncle Mike was right again. Like, what did that son-of-a-bunch-of-hippies have anyway, a crystal ball or something?

Mike also felt bad for Lhamo. He had a lot of financial security from his stake in the Rum Works, but she was probably living hand-to-mouth and maybe even sending money back home to Tibet. Given the clandestine deal done by Ham U, there was no telling what if anything they'd get back from these patents. Losing even the modest royalties from the milk project might be a big financial hit for her.

As Mike sat on a concrete wall outside, trying to get control of his anger, the milk project volunteers began filing out. Some looked his way and shook their heads. Others stoically avoided his gaze. The last two out were Brian and Lhamo. Brian walked over to where Mike was sitting. Lhamo hung back.

"I'm really sorry this happened, Mike. Honestly, I didn't see it coming." he said.

"No, Brian. It's my fault," Mike said with slumped shoulders. I should have nailed down clear access to the IP before we wasted everyone's time. And it obviously wasn't smart for me to assume that the University would be altruistic."

"Hang in there, Mike. We still have the Mars Mission, and I'll find out what I can about this screw-up. Maybe we can work something out."

"Thanks, Brian. But please, don't stick your neck out. Maybe they'll come to their senses."

"Hope so. See you Monday," Brian said over his shoulder as he walked away.

Mike turned to look at Lhamo. Her expression was relaxed, almost happy. His surprise must have shown because she raised a hand to check his question. "I know you really want this project to succeed. So do I. Perhaps we can still keep it alive."

"Come on, Lhamo, we're busted!" Mike exclaimed with complete exasperation. "We can't make milk without your extractors or my bugs – excuse me, I mean the University's extractors and bugs!"

"Twice you have asked me about the patents on my machines, and I avoided your questions, yes?"

"Yeah, you did. I thought you were being overly protective, but I didn't want to be pushy."

"Well, maybe it is time we talked about my machines and your bugs," Lhamo replied.

"You mean the University's…" Mike retorted, but she raised her hand again.

"No, I don't," she replied. "The Chinese government has US patents on enough of my technology that they can exclude others from, what is the word, 'infringing'? But no one has patents on my surface technology. That is a trade secret, like what they put in Coca Cola, yes?"

Mike looked in amazement at Lhamo's relaxed face and smiling eyes. "You have a back door?" he asked, almost in a whisper.

"I trust you, Dr. Anderson," she said, sitting down beside him, "so I will answer. Yes, because the milk machines can be big and heavy, not small like the Mars Mission extractors I can use the same surfaces but make them work another way that is not covered by the existing patents." She turned to face him. "But now you must tell me: do your bug patents have a back door? Can you make new ones that do the same thing?"

Mike knew that he had to answer her question. Lhamo had just entrusted him with information that could get her fired and maybe even deported back to China. If the University found out that she had purposefully maintained a workaround for her extractor patents that they had licensed from the Chinese, they would fire her in a heartbeat; and without a job, her visa would be revoked. She had taken a big risk telling him this. He might have had his headset on and recorded the conversation.

Mike removed his headset and rotated it, so she could see that it was turned off. Silently, she did the same.

"Yes," he replied. "All of my bug patents have back doors." Mike paused and held her gaze.

She nodded solemnly but said nothing, so Mike continued. "When I was 14 and filed my first patent on the alcohol bug, my uncle taught me how to do this, and why. Seven months ago, I watched you eat tofu in hot sauce when we had lunch. So I tried it for dinner, and went to bed with heartburn – you know, pain here," he said, pointing to his chest. She nodded but raised an eyebrow as if to ask, 'so'?

"So," he continued, "that night I awoke from a dream that I'd just had a glass of cold milk from your extractor, my heartburn was gone, and by the next morning I had it figured out. Whenever I get a crazy idea like that, I always talk it through with my uncle. His first response when I explained my idea was to warn me to keep my backdoors open. He called my idea a 'disruptive innovation', and he predicted this crap would happen" Mike said, pointing at the building they'd just left.

Lhamo rewarded him with a mischievous smile. "I would like to meet this uncle of yours. Now I understand how you can be so good, Dr. Anderson – foolish boy has wise uncle."

Mike felt his face start to flush. He was tempted to retort, but her placidly mirthful gaze checked him in mid-thought. He took a breath, let it out slowly, allowed his face to relax, and then asked: "So who taught you to build back doors and hold back trade secrets? Do they teach that at Beijing U?"

"In Beijing, they taught us to trust the State and give them everything, but I am not Han Chinese. I see the world through different eyes. My brother and uncle in Lhasa taught me to give them only as much as they expect."

"I would like to meet this brother and this uncle of yours," Mike said, and they both laughed.

"Come Dr. Anderson. Let us eat an early lunch. We have much to discuss. Maybe you can have the tofu in Sichuan sauce and get another good idea."

CHAPTER 7

THE NEWDLE TOUCH
Late June 2029

Mike sat on the edge of his bed, bare feet on the floor, elbows on his knees and head in his hands. The day had been a rollercoaster. First there was the cancelled meeting and getting back-stabbed by the university, then discovering their mutual attention to backdoor strategies, and finally a highly productive afternoon with Lhamo charting a potential course forward to revive the School Milk Project outside the university.

It actually seemed feasible, but the obvious stumbling block was money. Not only did they need a new 'home' for the milk project off campus, but clearly they were going to need the help of a high-power law firm to build a new IP estate and to fend off the inevitable attack from Klink, Ham U, and whoever had bought up their old IP as soon as their new workaround patent applications published. All of that took a lot of money up front – more than either of them had.

Most of the rest of it turned out to be not that difficult. Lhamo's brother in Lhasa could front for her as inventor of record for the milk extractor patents. Uncle Mike could do the same for the modified milk bugs. After all, Uncle Mike already had a bunch of patents, starting with his mini-turbine generator combinations to power hybrid automobiles, and he was also co-inventor on Mike's original alcohol bug filing. They could also use the Rum Works as the project's new business home.

As for money, the situation also wasn't totally bleak. Although Mike rarely revealed his equity value in the Rum Works to anyone, he'd made an exception for Lhamo. He trusted her, and that felt very strange after his decade of sparring with Tammy, the spoiled rich girl who'd tried to snare Mike into a marriage he wasn't ready for. Well, Mike thought, in Lhamo's case it was just business.

Lhamo seemed appreciative that he was offering to put his own money into the project, but pointed out that their legal costs would far outweigh the development costs for the bugs and extractors. What that meant was that even if Mike leveraged all of his Rum Works equity to come up with about 5 million dollars for the development costs, they'd still need something like another 25 million dollars for their legal umbrella. This was a high stakes game, and without top-notch legal cover, they'd be flying straight into disaster. Clearly this required more capital than Mike alone or in combination with his uncle could free up right now.

As alternatives, they had talked about grant applications, venture capital funds, and angel investors. However, the latter two always wanted to get back at least 10 times their original investment, sooner rather than later. And most grants required revealing what you wanted to do before the request was even considered, which was a stone-cold non-starter. Clearly they couldn't give the University a year's notice that Mike and Lhamo were planning to undermine what the University thought were solid patents.

In the end, they agreed that they would somehow find a way to revive the School Milk Project, and that finding discrete funding was the key to moving it forward. They also knew that their hopes for resuscitating the project could not be revealed to anyone at Ham U, NASA, or anywhere else with the exceptions of Uncle Mike and Lhamo's brother, Dorje. They had parted with a hand-shake that became a hug, followed by slightly embarrassed smiles.

His clock said it was 10:10 p.m. Mike killed the light, swung his feet up under the covers, and was fluffing his pillow when his headset twittered. His gate-keeper protocol should have directed almost all traffic to his avatar. Only his mother, uncle, and Angela had the over-ride option. "Damn," he thought, "has Tammy pushed Angela so hard on the tennis court that she's ready to run away at age 9?"

He put on the headset and queried the caller ID. There was no picture, no address, and the caller's return number came up all zeros! Clearly this caller didn't want to be identified, and knew how to do that. That took a lot of talent. He could reject the call, but there was no way to block the caller, who officially didn't exist. Therefore, the only way to find out who it was and send them packing was to take the call. Mike opened the line.

"Mike, you don't know me, but we need to talk," the male voice said firmly. There was no video signal, so Mike still had no clue who was calling.

"You know where I live and what time it is here. And frankly, I'm not in a good mood. If you want to talk, call back Monday during working hours."

Mike was moving his finger up to touch the 'end call' icon on his display when the voice said: "I know you've had a bad day, and we want to make it better."

"Who are you?"

"I don't think I should tell you that over an open line," the voice replied.

"Tell me about my day," Mike countered.

"You were trying to do something good, and you got screwed by some bureaucrats at Ham U who are owned by big business."

"How do you know that? Do you work here at Ham U?"

"No, we're a long way away from St. Louis. Look Mike, I like what you are trying to do, and I work for a group that might be able to help you keep it going," the voice replied.

"How could you help?"

"Mike, I need you to trust me. We need to do this in person."

"I'm not in a really trusting mood. Frankly, I don't like the fact that you bypassed my avatar and defeated caller ID. If you want face time, just come here and meet me in my office on Monday."

"I could do that, but you really would rather come visit us. And this has to be discrete. Frankly, we don't want to be seen on campus there."

"Who is 'we'?" Mike asked.

"Like I said, I can't tell you that on a voice line, but we have been very interested in your carbon-neutral milk project for some time."

"Great. I just love being stalked. Tell me how and why."

"Okay. Let me tell you that we are very interested in the environ-ment, and we tend to know a lot about what's happening in the world," the voice said, coyly.

This was beginning to feel to Mike like a game of 'Twenty Questions', and not really going anywhere. "Government agency? He asked.

"No."

"Business?"

"Yes."

Bingo! Mike thought. It's either an interested third party, or it's someone from big agribusiness like Santo Dominus trying to trick me into revealing my work-around.

Then Mike made a flash connection. He and Lhamo had been get-ting a lot of attention on the web, and Newdle knew everything that was happening on the web, didn't they? Not just volume but change in volume. They were famous for tracking informational derivatives which told them which direction things were going.

Mike had not Newdled himself or the School Milk Project today, but maybe news of its shut-down had already gone viral. Newdle still appeared to be a positive force in the world. They did solar on their office roofs. Their workers got the most efficient company cars. They had invested a lot in jumpstarting the hydrogen economy when the oil companies wouldn't touch it.

"Mike? You still there?"

"Thinking. Give me a moment."

"Okay."

It's worth a shot, Mike thought.

"Not mentioning any names," Mike said to the voice on the other end of the line, "I wonder if you know about me because you have a finger on the pulse of the web?"

"Maybe. And if that was us, could we meet?"

Mike was into old movies almost as much as he was the Grateful Dead. Besides Kubrick, one of his all-time favorites was Clancy's 'Hunt for Red October',. He remembered the Soviet submarine captain saying:

> *"Give me a ping, Vasily."*
> *"A ping, Captain?"*
> *"Yes, one ping only, Vasily. "*

"You need to convince me," Mike replied. "Give me a ping."

"A ping? As in 'one ping only, Vasily?'"

"Oh. You like that movie, too? Yes, something I'd recognize only you could do. Like, rock the web for me."

There was a pause on the other end. It sounded like the caller had put him on mute for a moment, and then the reply: "Okay, I think we can do that for you. Give me a 3-word phrase."

"Jamaica Rum Works," Mike replied without thinking.

"That's your uncle's place in Vermont, right?"

Oops, Mike thought, feeling a slight chill, but I can't back out now. "Right", he replied.

"You online? The voice asked.

"Yes."

"Open this attached data stream," came the instruction.

A virtual icon popped up; Mike touched it with his fingertip; and there in front of him was the famous search frequency cascade displayed in Newdle's main office lobby. As he watched, 'Jamaica Rum Works' worked its way up to the top line of the cascade, stayed there for about a minute, and then slowly fell back below various images of women with and without swim suits and movie star gossip.

"Okay." Mike said. "What's next?"

"Catch the seven a.m. high speed to Boise tomorrow morning."

"Boise? Idaho? What's in Boise?"

"We are; well, pretty close anyway. You will be picked up outside the station, and we'll have the afternoon to meet. Then you can either take the night train back to St. Louis or stay overnight with us and go back on Monday. Tell them you are taking a mental health holiday to go fishing."

"Okay. I'll be on the morning train, and I'll come back tomorrow night."

"Good. The ticket's in your name. Just scan your ID to get aboard."

"Who's meeting me? Wait. Let me guess. You can't tell me that."

"Right. We'll find you. But make it easy for us. Wear your green Jamaica Rum Works baseball cap when you come out of the station."

"Okay."

"Thanks Mike. Good talking to you. See you soon. Bye."

The line went blank. Mike flicked the 'calls received' icon. Nothing there! The call never happened.

With the light back out, lying in bed, Mike processed the call and the caller. Friendly, clandestine, and confident. It was either someone who was really, really clever with code, or it was Newdle, and the situation fit their company motto: 'be not evil'. But why all the secrecy? Maybe his uncle was right again. Maybe there were big players out there determined to kill the project and delay his carbon-neutral, no methane milk machine as long as possible.

That was Mike's last thought of the night. No dreams, no heartburn, and no more earthshaking good ideas. The next thing he knew, it was 5:30 a.m., and his alarm was insisting that he rejoin the conscious world.

Thirty minutes later, he was on his scooter en route to the STL high speed rail link. Almost as an afterthought, he swerved into the left turn lane, cut across traffic, and pulled into the drive-thru of a coffee-shop that was just opening. As he rotated to reach into his back pocket for his wallet, he saw two other scooters make the same turn, but neither pulled into the drive-thru behind him. The building on his left prevented him from seeing where they went.

His latte in his scooter's cup-holder, he drove slowly through the parking lot and turned right, going back up the street the way he'd come. Four blocks later, he took a right, accelerated, took another right, and zipped through four stop signs on the empty Sunday morning side-street. Looking back, he saw nothing suspicious. Maybe I'm getting paranoid, he thought.

At 6:30 he was in the enclosure with a few other sleepy folks, sipping his soy latte. None of them appeared to be paying him any attention, but he had his video monitor take mug-shots of everyone on the platform. He sent Lhamo a brief vid-clip telling her that he'd decided to spend a day in the country and be back tomorrow. He thought about talking to Uncle Mike but realized that he didn't know anything yet, and maybe it wasn't a good idea to be talking over voice circuits right now. If the Newdle guys worried about that, maybe he should too.

•   •   •

The train ride was quick and smooth. At up to 400 kph with just 3 stops, they did the 1500 kilometer trip in a bit under 5 hours. Once into Wyoming, Mike took off his headset and watched the mountain scenery dappled with spring green race by in the morning light. At a quarter to eleven, he stepped off the train into the Boise station. No one paid any attention to him, but just to be sure he had his video monitor check everyone who got off the train and confirmed that none had boarded with him in STL. Then he stowed his headset in its pouch, put on his green JRW cap, and walked out to the street.

There was light traffic consisting of scooters and some hybrids. Half a block to his left, a new ultra-light hydrogen-electric sedan eased away from the curb and came silently to a stop next to him. With a faint hiss, the right side of the sedan rotated up, revealing 3 empty seats. The fourth was occupied by a trim, crew-cut man who Mike estimated was in his mid-40's.

"Hi Mike. Hop in,"

Mike dropped his pack into the back, eased into the empty front seat, the door hissed closed, and the car silently pulled out and up the street. The man extended his hand and said; "Dave Erickson. I'm VP of Sustainable Innovation at Newdle. Thanks for coming."

"Hi Dave". They shook hands. "'Sustainable Innovation'?" Mike asked. "Have you ever read some old stuff by Christiansen at Harvard?

"Have I read Christensen? I got my MBA working with him at Harvard, and I taught his course there for 5 years after he retired. My job at Newdle exists because of him. How do you know about him? His best known stuff was written before you were born."

"My uncle introduced me to his writings."

"The Rum Works uncle? Sounds like he does a lot more than cut wood," Dave said with a chuckle.

"Where are we headed?" Mike asked.

"There's a hunting lodge up in the hills outside of town," Dave replied. "The rest of the group is up there. We came up on Friday, and then your little event popped up on our screen during a strategy session yesterday. Sorry for the short notice."

"Who are the others?"

"Barry, Ivan, and one or two more may sit in. One of those is Anton Brinkman, our head of competitive intelligence and maybe someone from the IP group."

"*THE* Barry and Ivan?" Mike had to ask.

"Yup. They like your milk project a lot, and they think they will like you. In case you are wondering, in the local vernacular, they tend to like folks who have a lot of cattle but wear small hats."

It took Mike a second to figure out that this was the flip side of the dismissive phrase 'all hat, no cattle'.

"And what about all this clandestine stuff?" Mike asked. "I thought you guys don't do evil."

"If forced to choose among good, evil, and innocent, we try to avoid the last two. Even the good guys in business have to watch out. Give the other guy half a chance, and he'll take everything you've got."

"Okay, you're not the first person to tell me I'm naive," Mike admitted, "but I learn pretty quickly. What's the agenda?"

"First off, I need to find out what you want for lunch. Where do you hang out on the food chain?"

"I grew up in rural Vermont, so I'll eat almost anything. But I try to keep my footprint small when there's a choice."

"Well, the rest of us are having elk tenderloin with raspberry port sauce, salad, and roasted spuds. Everything is local and sustainable except for the port. That work for you?"

"Wow! Sure."

Dave flipped his headset down, entered, and sent a short message. "Good. In this sweet little car, we're about 20 minutes from the lodge. After lunch we want to explore options for getting your school milk project back on track. And we also need to discuss how to hold your antagonists at bay."

"Who are they?" Mike asked.

"We'll talk about that in the group. That's Anton's area of expertise." Dave replied.

Just then Mike's headset twittered with a priority call. His headset was still in its pouch in his pack behind him. "Sorry," Mike apologized as he slid it on. "At least I know it's not you this time," he said with a smile.

The icon was Uncle Mike's. "Hi Uncle Mike. Happy Sunday", he said, breezily.

"I know it's Sunday, Wonderboy. That's precisely why I'm calling. What did you do to us?"

"What do you mean? Mike asked, realizing belatedly that he probably knew what his uncle meant.

"Mike. It's Sunday afternoon here. It's supposed to be a day of rest, which I need because I'm old, I've been working hard, and I'm tired. But all day the frigging com lines have been clogged with reporters asking what we make and why we are the hot new thing. And mixed in with them are people who've already figured out what we do and want to sign up for a franchise. This is crazy. You did something, right?"

Mike glanced over at Dave, who was watching him with a curious grin. "Well," he told his uncle, "I didn't do anything on purpose... well, not intentionally, anyway."

"What did you do, Wonderboy?"

"Seriously, Uncle Mike. I can't talk about it just now. I'm still trying to figure out what's going on myself. Can I call you back when I know more, maybe tomorrow afternoon?"

"Good luck getting through. We are totally jammed. But yes, whenever you think you could let me know why you sent these press harpies after me, I'm all ears."

"Sorry, Uncle Mike. But can you get some new business out of it?"

"Sure, but one town at a time, not 500! I was just talking to a town in the Mojave Desert, for Christ's sake! There ain't enough vegetation within a hundred miles of them to run an ethanol operation. This is totally frigging crazy. Bye, Wonderboy."

Mike looked back at Dave and said, "I guess I should have picked a different 3-word phrase".

"It kind of rattled his cage, didn't it? I thought that might happen, but it was late, I was hassling you, and I figured those were the first 3 words into your head. But no major harm was done. Your uncle gets some free attention for his business; I got you to come out here, and my bosses will be happy you did."

Dave waved towards the front. "Here's where we start up towards the lodge. We've got 43,000 acres, most of it forest and upland meadow, a few hundred are farmed for potatoes, and we've got a geothermal greenhouse for year-around vegetables. Most of the land is left as habitat for elk, moose, mule deer, and bear. We've got some wolves, but there aren't enough of them yet, so we manage the herds to hold them down at the carrying capacity of the property, and we get to eat the rest. Our lunch is part of the 'rest'."

For the last 10 minutes, the scenery was particularly beautiful as the car followed its programmed track up to the lodge. The buildings were virtually invisible up against the hillside until they were almost there. Mike liked what he saw. These humans chose to blend in rather than stick out. He wondered if they'd consider setting up a Rum Works ethanol operation here. "No", he could almost hear Uncle Mike's voice telling him, "don't press your luck, Wonderboy." He took off his headset and put the green JRW cap back on.

CHAPTER 8

SHAKEDOWN STREET
Late June 2029

Mike had debated if he should even show up. Within an hour of his return from Boise, he'd gotten a call from Klink's secretary, Anna. He liked Anna, so although Klink was now number one on his shit list, Mike had taken her call. Her voice was neutral, but her expression was sad, almost apologetic. Klink needed to see Mike in person right away, either today at 3:00 p.m. or tomorrow morning at 9:00. Mike hadn't slept that well on the train ride back from Idaho, and he figured he'd need to be well rested and in top form to handle Klink, so he'd opted for tomorrow at 9:00, which was now.

Mike sat in Klink's outer office working on a file on his display. He'd declined Anna's offer of coffee, assuming that the meeting would be short. Besides, he'd rather not have anything in his hand available to throw at Klink.

At 9:09, Klink opened his office door. Mike started to get up, grumbling to himself that Klink's insistence on punctuality was a one-way street. In that instant, Tina walked out as Klink held the door open for her, the smile on her face morphing into a look of surprise when she saw Mike.

"Good morning, Dr. Anderson," Tina mumbled as she avoided his gaze and hustled out of the office.

Klink smiled and said, "Come on in, Mike."

Mike tried to process what was happening. He'd come expecting an open confrontation with Klink. Then, here was his graduate student, who had bypassed him to meet with his boss, her smile rapidly replaced by embarrassment. What was Klink up to, standing there smiling like a cobra eyeing a squirrel? Nothing good, Mike was sure. But the squirrel who finds himself in a cobra's den necessarily does the dance, and if said squirrel feigns eye-contact but watches the snake's neck muscles, he just might survive until lunch rather than become lunch. Mike got up and walked past Klink into his office.

"Have a seat, Mike."

Mike remained standing. What's up with Tina?" He asked.

"I had some good news for her, Mike. And I've got good news for you, too. Please have a seat."

Reluctantly, Mike sat. Klink walked around and sat at his desk. It was the old-fashioned type made of brightly polished wood. There was one neat pile of paper on the desk plus a flat-screen. Klink didn't use a headset. Mike had only been in Klink's office a few times, but it was always exactly the same. Mike wondered how he got anything done when nothing on the desk ever got moved.

Klink interrupted Mike's thoughts. "I know you've got a lot of questions after last Saturday, Mike, so let me fill you in on what's going on."

Mike nodded, sitting upright on the front edge of the chair.

"Like I've told you before, what you're doing with your bugs is brilliant, and a lot of people are getting interested in your work. This is where I can be a big help to you, Mike. I know how to leverage your work to get you the kind of benefits you deserve."

"Do I get any say in what's done with my bugs?" Mike asked.

"Sure, Mike. That's why I invited you here for this talk. But give me some credit for having done this stuff for 20 years. This is why

I'm department Chairman. I know how the system works." Klink paused. Mike remained quiet, keeping his face neutral.

"So here's the story," Klink continued. "If you insist on using your bugs for straight licensing deals, all you can get from Ham U are your capped royalties, and that's held to a maximum of $200,000 per year. But there are strategies that can net you a lot more from them if you know the ropes. Your bugs can yield much more value in other ways. For instance, if someone really wants them, they might be willing to compensate you indirectly at a much higher level."

"How does that work?" Mike asked.

"Let me put it to you directly, Mike. There are people who like your work enough that they are ready to endow a Professorship for you. They'll give the University $25 million up front, and you'll get 5% interest on that each year. That's $1.25 million for salary and research support, year after year. And effective immediately, your appointment at the University leap-frogs from assistant professor to full professor with tenure. That's a huge honor and a damn good deal for somebody 5 years out of graduate school. You're what, 28, 29?" Klink asked with a knowing grin.

Mike could feel his heart start to pound. Yeah, some day he'd love to make full professor and have an endowed chair. But this was wrong, and at an instinctive level it really pissed him off. He couldn't believe that Klink was so dense to think he couldn't see through this. There had to be more.

What's up with Tina," Mike asked again. "Why did you have my graduate student in here without me?"

"Take it easy, Mike. It's not just you I'm trying to help here. When we get this Chair for you, you'll need to move your lab over here into my department's space. After all, we can't have an endowed chair dangling from a congressional cobweb like the Mars Project. Just a few votes switched in Congress and your supporting infrastructure disappears just like that. Your endowed Chair needs a stable home in my department. What with all these administrative changes, I just wanted to reassure Tina that her position and stipend are secure. Oh, and I've also arranged an assistantship for her husband in electrical engineering. You know, what's his name, Ping, came over here with her from China in hopes of getting a position in the Engineering graduate program, but that didn't work out for him. Now it's a done deal. Without my help, he might lose his visa and be deported."

Mike looked at Klink. The face was smiling, but the eyes were blank. No, on their surface Klink's eyes looked blank, but behind them Mike could see the viper eyes, lidless horizontal slits that knew they had their squirrel.

Mike thought of his uncle's epic break from his professor at RPI. The story was it had been a two-way shouting match, and it had ended his uncle's chances for an academic career. That wasn't the way Mike wanted his to end. What was the phrase that Lhamo had taught him last night? "The person who makes you angry controls you". Well, he certainly had reason to be mad as hell. Trying to extort him through Tina was the final insult. Mike, however, was determined that Klink wasn't going to have the satisfaction of seeing him lose it. The only down-side to what he was about to do was that Ping wouldn't get his assistantship, but maybe he could fix that by having the Rum Works or the Milk Project fund the kid.

Mike stood, leaned across the prefect desk, and reached out his right hand. Klink took his hand with a grin. As he held Klink's eager hand, Mike said, "Thanks, Professor Klink." The grin broadened into a smile. "But I'm happy where I am. No thanks."

Klink stiffened and jerked his hand back. "What!" he shouted. "Only an idiot would turn me down. How far do you think you'll get without my help?"

"You can have my bugs, Professor Klink," Mike said evenly, "but you can't have me."

Mike turned and strode to the door. As he opened it, he could feel the viper eyes on his back, and he could feel his hand begin to shake.

Just a few more steps past Anna's puzzled face in the outer office, and now his whole body began to shake. Out in the corridor, he sprinted to the men's room, pulled the door closed behind him, and shouted "You bastard, you slimy BASTARD!" to the empty room.

Mike stood leaning forward with both hands on the edge of the basin. After a minute, his breathing slowed, and the shaking subsided. He splashed some water on his face, dried it, and went to the door. Opening it a crack, he checked the corridor back towards Klink's office to be sure it was clear. Just then, a stall door behind him squeaked open, and a young man stuck his head out – probably an undergraduate. Mike gave him a quizzical smile, pushed the door open, and marched proudly down the hall.

One hundred feet away, Klink sat at his desk, pondering his next step in this dance. He liked Mike, which for Klink meant that he liked what Mike could do for him. He'd had to deal with this type of willful stupidity before. This kid was one of those young stars who burned with such brilliance and passion that they blinded themselves to the big picture. Mike just couldn't see that the world wasn't ready for cheap milk from a machine, so even when someone like Steven Klink went out of his way to negotiate a safe, secure, and lucrative refuge for him, Mike was incapable of appreciating it. Here he could have an endowed chair, work on his bugs to his heart's content for the next decade, and then he and his Oriental honey could get rich from their milk machine when the world was ready for it.

Klink sighed. Much as he'd like to help Mike, the real world was not going to wait. He'd given it his best shot. Lining up a position for that Chinese kid in Engineering had taken a lot of extra time and effort, and should have sealed the deal. But if this brilliant hick from the backwoods refused to appreciate his efforts, he'd have to wash his hands of him.

Klink activated his computer, dictated a short message, and sent it.

●　　●　　●

Senator Donald Nyce put down the draft bill he was reading when Suzy Adams knocked on his door and swept into the room. She had a red 'eyes only' folder in her left hand and a worried expression on her face. This bothered him because he much preferred her face when she was excited.

His office manager had an athletic build and long, auburn hair. She reminded him of his former paramour when he was starting his law career in Vermont. Although Suzy dressed conservatively here in Washington, he knew that she was firm but supple. Like his former auburn-haired lover, her passion for tennis kept her very fit, which helped her cope with their long days here in the Senate office building, and sometimes with the evenings that followed.

"Don. We need to talk about this," she said tersely, handing him the folder.

Inside was a single page fax printout, a form of communication that could be shredded, leaving no electronic trace. It was a message from Bob Tharp at Santo Dominus.

> *Don*
> *That Anderson hick from your state blew us off. We can't let them launch this fake milk project with Newdle. If you don't have a prompt and effective way to reel him in, we'll be forced to initiate action against him, his uncle, or (as you so delicately call her) his oriental honey. This is of highest importance to us. Your continuing assistance in accomplishing our goals is why we have faithfully supported you through the last two election cycles.*
> *Bob*

Nyce looked up at Suzy. "What does he think I can do – wave a magic wand and make him quit? This guy and his uncle make money out of trash and live like monks. Not only are they revered locally because of all the jobs and their payments to landowners, they have more than 30 franchises in Vermont stretching from Bennington to St. Johnsbury which means they've got a strong political base. The uncle's so weird he scares people, but frankly my dear, if that Anderson kid decided to run against me next year, I'd have to take him seriously. Remember Bernie Sanders? I couldn't touch him until he retired in '18. He was another one of those righteous, squeaky-clean do-gooders."

Suzy smiled outwardly at her boss. She hated constantly having to show him how to do his job. "Come on, Don. You could solve this little issue in your sleep. These guys have to be vulnerable somewhere. My intern found out that they're cutting wood on National Forest land. Why not tell them to back down, or we'll cut off their access to government wood?"

"I'll give you an 'A' for effort on that one sweetie," Nyce said with a smirk. "You're from Missouri. Not a lot of National Forests out there, so you're forgiven this time." Nyce patted her fondly on her hip. "But now listen to Papa. Normally, a permit to log National Forest land is nothing more than a government sanction to rape Mother Nature. Most loggers cut off all of the good stuff, tear up the land, and hopefully it starts to grow back 50 years later."

"What these two hippies are doing is just the opposite. They cut away the shitty timber that no one else wants, make it into high-value ethanol, leave the forest as pristine as the Garden of Eden, and go laughing all the way to the bank. If we tried to shut them out of National Forest land, those ass-holes at the Sierra Club would nail us to a redwood cross."

Suzy smiled appreciatively at Nyce. There was a reason why he'd survived almost 2 terms in the senate. "How about his bastard child in Chicago. The court records prove that he's a dead-beat dad. Maybe there's a way we can leverage that to shut down this fake milk thing."

"I agree there's some potential dirt to be turned there; but if you do, you'll almost certainly find yourself square in the middle of a minefield. The slightest wrong move, and you'll be missing one of those beautiful legs. Our Montpelier office has been all over this kid since they started expanding franchises across Vermont 5 years ago. Once they started using those gas-bags to pluck up trees, their star has been rising fast. Here's what our people in the home office told me."

"First, the guy refuses to pay child support unless the mom proves paternity and gives him visitation rights. It's been 9 years, and neither side has budged. But get this, meanwhile the Anderson kid's mother has been voluntarily paying child support every month since the blonde girl was born. Those checks have all been cashed, so they are sweet as spring-water."

"Second, that love-child's mom is from old Chicago money. They control a major piece of the pharmaceutical industry. For her, this is a battle about pride rather than money. If you think you can score points by helping her get more money, she'll just laugh in your face."

Again, Suzy smiled appreciatively. "You are so amazing, Don. You have so many fingers on the arteries and veins of your constituency. But they have to have some weakness – something we can exploit to turn them. We just have to figure out what it is? And frankly, it would make my job easier if you'd let me run the Montpelier office. That would, among other things. save you the task of telling me all the details of this hick's Chicago dysfunctional connections."

"Suzy. Darling. Relax. You've been with us for, what, ten months?" Senator Nyce smiled kindly and continued. "I've been building my Vermont base since the early 1990's. When you have my Washington office fully under your thumb, then I promise you I'll hand over the Montpelier office as well. As for the Jamaica hicks, they have no obvious vulnerabilities at this point. If we find one, you'll be the first to know. In the mean time, how about dinner at Morton's?"

"I've got tennis tonight at seven, Don," Suzy said apologetically, "and in the mean time we've got to respond to Bob Tharp at Santo Dominus. We can't just ignore his request or tell him we're completely stumped."

"Yeah, you're right," Nyce said with an understanding nod. "Before you leave for your tennis, draft out a note saying that I was concerned he wouldn't go for the money in the first place, and that we'll keep trying to come up with something that will pull the plug on their project. Make it sound earnest. When you get the wording right, I'll sign it, you can fax it, and then we shred both copies as usual."

"Okay, Don." She turned to go.

"Oh, and Suzy." She turned back, her auburn hair sweeping across her shoulders. He gave her a warm smile. "I've got to stay here for a few hours to try and punch a few loop-holes into this foreign aid bill, anyway. By 9 p.m. I'm going to be really hungry, so how about you meet me at Morton's after your tennis. Remember I'm one of the most eligible bachelors in this town, so think twice before you consider turning me down, sweetie."

"Sure, Don." She conjured up a warm smile. "I should be pretty hungry by then, too."

CHAPTER 9

HYPERBARICS
Late June 2029

"Uncle Mike? You there? I can't see you on my headset."

"Yeah, Kid. I'm here, but I'm under my truck. Can't extend the camera boom or it'll break off."

"Is this the same truck you've been working on for the last year?" His nephew asked. " Come on. Slide out from under, and turn your camera on. I'd like to see it."

On his headset, Mike watched the camera boom extend out past his uncle's red nose, refine its image to show his whole face, and then swing around as Uncle Mike directed the camera towards the truck. What he saw looked like a rectangular plastic hot tub with a large wheel at each corner and a pod-like cab at the front.

"What do you think?" Uncle Mike asked with a triumphant gesture. "It weighs 800 pounds, seats four, and carries 1500 lbs of cargo. The turbine and generator together weigh 55 lbs, each wheel/motor/suspension assembly weighs 70, and the battery pack weighs a bit over 100. On the road it goes 80 miles per hour, and it runs on 100% joy-juice out of the Rum Works still. I call it my 'goat-mobile'."

"I think you should loan it to me, so I can run over some people out here," Mike said, acidly.

Why? What's up? You don't look real happy," his uncle said, cocking his head and scanning Mike's face.

"I'm massively pissed. They shut down my School Milk Project."

"Who did – the University? Don't tell me I didn't warn you about those bastards!" Uncle Mike stabbed an index finger in Mike's direction. "You did what I told you to protect against this crap, right?"

"Look, I don't want to talk about it right now. What I need to do is come back there to mom's place in Townshend. We could talk about this on Saturday. You free then?"

"Sure, but isn't this why we use these fancy video things. Why fart a lot of carbon into the atmosphere just so I can see you live?"

"Trust me. We want to do this in person."

"Fine with me, Wonderboy. Maybe then you can explain why we've got all these guys in suits sniffing around the Rum Works."

"Absolutely", Mike replied. "That's part of what we need to talk about."

"Can I tell my sweet sister that her long absent son's gonna show his face here, or do we keep her in the dark?"

"Sure. I was going to call mom to let her know, but you can break the news. Tell her if she can get some local Bambi steak, I've got a great recipe for a sauce to go with it."

"You cooking now? This Chinese girl give you a cookbook for your birthday?"

"She's Tibetan; and no, I got this recipe from Newdle."

"Yeah, I know. Nobody uses cookbooks anymore. But you'd better watch out. Remember what your last girlfriend did to your wallet." Uncle Mike scowled at Mike for a moment and then changed the subject. "Hey, any chance you have a few more minutes now? Something's come up that I want to run by you.

"Sure. No problem."

"You know that startup in Alberta, Diamond Fabrics, where I get the timber harvesting balloons made? Well, I filed a patent on the balloon, tether and pump combination almost a year ago, and once it published, I licensed it back to them gratis, so we're pals. Most of our franchises have switched over to using their balloons, so this was already getting to be a major part of their work before you unleashed this perfect storm on us last Saturday night. Now they're going to have to expand if they want to keep up with demand. The bottom line is they need working capital, and I'd like to put some more money into them."

"Do we already have a stake in them? Did you tell me, and I forgot?"

"Yeah, I think I mentioned it as an opportunity back when we bought our first balloon a year ago. Remember you told me to keep plowing our profits back into the business? Seeing how well the balloons were working for us and our franchises, I've made two small investments totaling a couple of million dollars to help them. First so they could get better equipment to fabricate the things and second to buy options on a lot of tar sands up in Alberta to guarantee their access to raw material. Currently, that's the only source of carbon that can be used to grow the helical fibers. And once it's made, the diamond fabric is so strong that it takes really high tech tools to work with it."

"Anyway,' Uncle Mike continued, "we already own about 25% of them. Now one of their other angel investors is looking to cash out, and he'll sell to me. I want to take us up to around 50% of their stock, and that would get us a seat or two on the Diamond Fabrics Board. Can you imagine me on some company's board of directors?" Uncle Mike asked with a quizzical look. "I don't even own a suit. But I digress. Where was I? Oh yeah, that will take most of our current cash reserve – about eight million – but our cash flow is good and about to get better. Right now it looks like we'll double our number of franchises this year. It's a bit of a gamble, but we know there's more business coming, both for us at the Rum Works and for them, so it's a no-brainer, really."

"We've got eight million in the bank? Wow! I guess I've lost track of how good business has been this last year. Okay... so who's their competition?" Mike asked.

"Lots of people are experimenting with the fabric, but we are the first to make industrial balloons. Most of what the other guys are doing is ordinary stuff like body armor and ultra light camping tents. And so far, the only source of helical carbon is tar, and because it's considered a waste stream, we were able to tie up lots of it with a ridiculously small investment."

"Okay, it sounds like a win/win, Uncle Mike. You've got my vote."

"Good," his uncle said with a grin. "Now let me tell you why I really want to do this and why I want to be on their Board."

"It's a good fit with the Rum Works. I get it."

"That's part of it, Wonderboy, but only a small part. What I really want to do is get them started making hyperbaric structures."

"What? You mean the high pressure chambers they use on divers with the bends?"

"Nope. I'm talking about bridges that are stronger than steel ones, weigh almost nothing, and never fall down; houses that can stand up to a hurricane, but then be deflated and transported in the back of my goat-mobile. The world is at a turning point. Concrete and steel just became archaic. Truly modern structures will be held up by helical carbon fabric tubes filled with high pressure hydrogen.

Mike held up both hands in a mock surrender. "Whoa! I'm just a dumb Double Brass Rat from MIT[10]. Help me catch up here."

"I'll show you my plans when you come out here, but think about this. This fabric is one tenth the weight of steel, but 25-times stronger. That's a strength-to-weight advantage of 250 compared to steel. So you weave a fabric tube and pump in hydrogen to, say, ten atmospheres. A car tire is only inflated to two atmospheres, so ten atmospheres makes it very hard. But hydrogen is the lightest gas, weighing about one fifteenth as much as air, so with ten atmospheres of H_2 gas inside this ultra-thin, ultra-strong tube, the whole object is lighter than air and floats up like a balloon."

"You never saw the dome house that your grandparents built before your mom and I were born. The frame was steel pipe covered with plywood. It leaked in the rain, and when it snowed, it swayed and creaked under the load. As kids, we were always afraid it would collapse on us. With this new fabric, you could weave a geodesic dome out of these tubes, cover it with two layers of the same fabric, and you've got an indestructible dome house that never leaks or creaks and would have to be anchored by a ring around its base filled with water so that it doesn't float up and away."

Uncle Mike was getting really animated, pacing back and forth in his workshop. Mike had seen him this way before. His uncle had gone through a 6-month manic phase when they'd discovered the alcohol bug, wrote their patent, and founded the Rum Works. Mike had been 14 that winter, and everyone in Jamaica and Townshend seemed to step back, awaiting the obligate depression phase that they expected would follow.

"He's doing it again," Mike had heard people whisper with knowing nods. But they were wrong. Since that year when he and Uncle Mike discovered the ethanol bug, his uncle had had his 'ups', but even his worst 'downs' were more like what most folks considered 'being normal'. And best of all, this had occurred without his uncle having to take lithium or accepting the chemical shackles of anti-psychotic drugs.

Mike loved this man that others considered 'crazy'. Not only was he Mike's surrogate father, he was also Mike's muse – his connection to his own creativity. Even when his uncle went on a tear, like now, and Mike felt like he was riding backseat in a Top-Gun fighter jet, he knew it would end up okay. Starting with his ethanol bug, in his 15 years of flying back-seat to his uncle, both of them had walked away from every 'landing' after Uncle Mike's manic periods.

"These tubes are so strong that 10 atmospheres is nothing," Uncle Mike continued. "Potentially they can hold up to 1000 atmospheres if we get the fabrication right. At that pressure, hydrogen is a virtual liquid at room temperature, which makes storing it to power fuel cells in cars, scooters, and small devices safer and lighter. And that's not all. If you fill your tube to only 100 atmospheres, you've got a rigid beam that's stronger than steel and about as heavy as styrofoam. This is a whole new class of structural materials we call 'hyperbarics'. Think of bridges that can hold a tank, weigh almost nothing, and never rust." Uncle Mike's face was flushed and covered with a big grin.

"Yes," retorted Mike, "and if that tank's engine backfires or its track throws a spark, you've got yourself another Hindenburg."

"Good try, Kid, but that was a century ago. Our friends at Diamond Fabrics have made a lot of progress in their fabrication techniques. One of the three partners up there is a former textiles guy from Taiwan who cashed out and left before the mainland Chinese took over. He's got them spinning fabric tubes out of continuous fibers with no seams, kind of like women's pantyhose, on computer-guided looms. So as long as the connectors and valves are good, these structures are really safe. Although it's made of carbon, the molecular composition of diamond fabric is similar to graphite. It doesn't burn. The only way to set one on fire would be a thermite grenade or a long pulse from a very high energy laser. For larger structures, we compartmentalize them so that one hole releases only a small fraction of the total hydrogen. I've written a patent for that part, too."

"So how many filings are you working on?" Mike asked.

"Well, right now it's a suite of 18 patents covering tubes, valves, and connectors; with application claims for houses, bridges, mag-lev rails, balloons… Think of a long string of patents kind of like a picket fence."

"Wow. This is serious. You think this is the next big thing?"

Uncle Mike put his hands on his hips, almost defiantly. "Not think, Kid. Know!"

"Okay. Know." Mike conceded. "So you're talking about taking this stuff from its current niche into mainstream commerce. Right?"

"Right. This is the real deal, Wonderboy. If we keep this thing on track, it will be really big."

"How big is really big?"

"Like in five years, you could use your share to buy all of Ham U outright, fire the bastards who screwed you, and get your original milk bug patents back."

"Hold that thought", Uncle Mike. "We'll see you Saturday morning."

"We?" His uncle asked with a puzzled look.

"Yeah," Mike responded. "Lhamo wants to come with me to meet you and mom."

"You can bring her along if you like, Wonderboy, but I'm not dressing up for her. No way."

"It's okay, Uncle Mike. She's pretty cool around geeks like us."

•   •   •

Luckily Mike and Lhamo slept for most of the train ride, waking only to change trains in Hartford. But starting from the moment they were picked up in Brattleboro, they were deluged under his uncle's passion to replace steel with diamond fabric hyperbarics. There was so much in there that just had to come out – kind of like draining an intellectual abscess. So rather than make him hold all this back, Mike and Lhamo let Uncle Mike's passion run its course. There would be time later in the day to tell him about Newdle and the School Milk Project.

Mike had a pretty good idea how his uncle's mind worked. An idea would take root and grow subconsciously deep in his brain for weeks or months, functioning almost like a parasite that sapped some of his energy. During this phase he would appear totally absorbed, even a bit withdrawn. When the idea matured, however, what came out was remarkably complete and complex.

This hyperbarics concept had probably begun when his uncle had stood outside the Rum Works watching his shiny, white balloon come and go from the woods to the factory on its almost invisible tether. Something about it fascinated him, but he wasn't quite sure why. Once he'd made the leap in his mind from a big, soft cigar filled with hydrogen at 14 pounds per square inch to high pressure tubular structures, all the rest had probably come on like a land-slide…and Mike had to admit to himself, what his uncle wanted to do was perfectly credible. In fact, it was very exciting.

Throughout the morning, Lhamo watched and listened intently. Mike could tell that she was processing what Uncle Mike was saying, but she said little. He also noticed that Uncle Mike seemed a bit uneasy with her there, avoiding her gaze and talking more to Mike than to her.

Mike's biggest issue had been his uncle's insistence on using hydro-gen to fill the high pressure tubes in his structures. It made obvious sense in a low pressure balloon designed to lift something, but why use a flammable gas to fill the high pressure tubes? When his uncle slowed down enough to explain it, however, the answer turned out to be rather simple. Volume for volume, helium weighs twice as much as hydrogen, and helium is also much more expensive. Ditto for all of the other noble gasses. Nitrogen is cheap and non-flam-mable but weighs 14 times as much as hydrogen. Given its weight at 100 atmospheres in a carbon fiber tube, you might as well use a wooden two-by-four. Ditto for oxygen. No, because of the strength and impenetrability of the fabric, hydrogen was the ideal filler to form light-weight structures, and over time you could make as much hydrogen as you wanted wherever you had water and sunlight.

As noon approached, Mike began thinking about food, but his uncle opened up one more virtual file to show them. The title was "RV in the Sky." The first diagram that popped up on their displays was a large balloon in the shape of a flattened cigar. In the back there were two ducted fan engines incorporated one each into stubby horizontal tail fins. Otherwise the object was completely smooth. The second page was a cutaway diagram of the interior showing a crew cabin, a cargo area, fuel bladders, the primary lift bladders filling most of the center, and smaller buoyancy trim chambers in the nose and tail. The cutaway also showed the lacework of hyperbaric tubes that gave his uncle's dirigible a unique combination of strength and aerodynamics.

The next page had specifications for carrying capacity, altitude limits, and range at various speeds of flight. On top of the balloon was an optional 30 KW solar array linked to an electrolysis unit to make oxygen and hydrogen from water. The next page listed life support systems, and Mike was surprised to see his bugs and Lhamo's extractors listed, along with other components from the Mars Mission technology.

Uncle Mike let the two of them look through the file for a minute. "This is where all the stuff the two of you are developing for the Mars Mission finds a down-to-Earth application," he said. "Your combination of bugs and extractors is much more valuable here than that stupid idea of sending humans to Mars to do a job better accomplished by robots. By the way," he said darting a quick glance at Lhamo, "your extractor technology is absolutely elegant – at least twenty years ahead of its time." For this, she rewarded him with a shy smile.

Returning his attention to the file, Uncle Mike said: "Rather than one unit going to Mars and then being hung up for eternity in the Smithsonian, this is a much more practical application. It's a carbon-age mobile habitat that can efficiently carry people and cargo long distances. One of these things could feed you, keep you warm, and let you tour the world. You harvest water from the clouds and then use sunlight to make oxygen to breathe, which allows you to fly at whatever altitude you want. The higher you go, the more we increase the percent oxygen in the crew space. That way, you don't need a pressurized cabin, even up past altitudes of 30,000 feet. This ultra-light structure far exceeds the performance envelope of those heavy old dirigibles with metal frames. And the hydrogen that you get as a byproduct of hydrolyzing water can power a fuel cell for electricity when there's no sun or used in the turbine engines to extend your range.

"How big is this thing?" Mike asked, squinting at the numbers. "And how can it lift a 30 KW solar array. Isn't that pretty heavy."

"Good call, Mike. You put your finger right on my sore spot. The dirigible is big enough lift the solar array okay, but you put that heavy thing up there on top where the sunlight is, and in simulations, the whole thing flips over upside down. Even if we put all the other heavy stuff like crew and the fuel bladders as low as possible, we can't solve the center of gravity problem. The best current solar panels are way too heavy."

"But you can build it with a smaller solar array, one that doesn't affect its stability," Lhamo volunteered. "You actually only need 2500 Watts to make oxygen for up to five people, supply enough energy to power our life support system, and make a small amount of hydrogen for the fuel cell to use at night. For the turbines, you can fly it just on ethanol, yes?

"Yep," Uncle Mike replied, grinning at Lhamo. Mike was relieved to see that his uncle was getting a bit more comfortable with Lhamo. "Even without the extra hydrogen for the turbines, I think it will have a range of over 2000 kilometers carrying a normal fuel load. And once I get my seat on the Board at Diamond Fabrics, I'll try to convince them to build one as a prototype. The other thing I want them to do is experiment with doping the fabric with metals when the fibers are formed. The molecular structure of each fiber is a helix, so it forms long fibers that act like carbon nanotubes, right?"

Both Mike and Lhamo nodded in unison.

"So those nanotubes could be doped with conducting metals like silver, aluminum, and copper; or with semi-conductors like germanium or gallium. It's possible that if we got the right mix of conducting and semi-conducting fibers, you'd get an ultra-light, flexible solar panel.

"Have you tried that yet?" Mike asked.

"No," Uncle Mike admitted. "The whole focus up in Alberta has been on manufacturing the fabric. To do this conducting/semi-conducting stuff, we'd need a separate team led by an experienced materials chemist. There are some good people out there we could hire, but that takes a budget, and we're a few months away from being able to make that kind of commitment."

Lhamo fixed Uncle Mike with her gaze. "I do not think you need worry about a few months. You are so far ahead of everybody with this technology, it will be years before they catch up."

Mike took a deep breath, and let it out slowly. His head was swimming. He and Lhamo had come to Vermont to tell his uncle about Newdle's commitment to back the alternative School Milk Project. But what Uncle Mike had just laid before them trumped their hand in spades. This could be the end of the steel age and the dawn of the carbon age – a fundamental shift in how humans lived and functioned in the world. Kind of like transistors leading to computers and the information age – only bigger.

Mike turned to look at his uncle, whose face was relaxed now, bearing just a slight smile. He'd gotten it all out, shared it with someone who could comprehend. No. Actually Mike realized that now there were two people he was comfortable sharing his ideas with. Uncle Mike was smiling at Lhamo.

"How about we see if Stephanie has anything for lunch?" Mike suggested.

CHAPTER 10

JAMAICA RUM WORKS
Late June 2029

Lunch at Stephanie's was a large salad made with Chinese noodles and venison sausage, along with rice and tea. Afterwards, the four of them climbed into Uncle Mike's goat-mobile to check out the Rum Works up the road in Jamaica. Mike hadn't been there since they installed the balloon harvesting system almost a year ago, and Uncle Mike wanted to show him how much it had changed their operations.

As they approached the tiny town, Mike noticed two changes right away. First, there was a large, white dome on the other side of Route 30 from the Rum Works buildings. It looked like a huge, white mushroom cap resting next to the river. "That's our new Diamond Fabric greenhouse?" he asked.

"Yup," his uncle answered. "We put it up in December and harvested our first radish in January. Now we have tomatoes, beans, and cucumbers coming out in marketable quantities. We use waste heat from the ethanol fermenter to keep it warm, and we also pump in some of the waste CO_2 that your bugs make to promote plant growth. We're still figuring out the best rotation of crops to grow year around, but it already provides fresh vegetables for everyone associated with the Rum Works, and then some."

The second thing that Mike noticed was that the factory was in full operation on Saturday afternoon. In the cutting yard, the balloon had just dumped a multi-ton load of whole trees. Using hydraulic scissors, saws, and winches, the 4 person crew were cutting everything into 6 foot sections and loading them onto the recessed conveyor that went to the chipper. Mike was struck by how clean the yard was. It had previously been a mess of muddy ruts, bark and branches left by the big logging trucks that brought in the timber. Now it looked like a big skating rink.

Within 10 minutes of the load being dumped, the crew had everything bigger than a twig cleared away and were sweeping up the last bits with a tractor-mounted broom. Then the crew took off helmets and gloves, had a drink of water, and relaxed until the next load arrived. Uncle Mike commented that they did this 4 times per hour for a six hour shift.

"Why are they were working on a Saturday?" Mike asked. "Up until now, we've always been a 5 day per week operation."

"Most of our employees are former dairy farmers." Uncle Mike explained. "They were used to milking their herds twice-a-day, 7 days per week. So now that they only work 5 days per week, covering the occasional weekend shift was not a big issue."

"Since installing the balloon, we've doubled our ethanol output here in Jamaica," Uncle Mike beamed, waving his hand towards the mountainside above them. "Although the balloon has an operational radius of only 10 km, it has paradoxically increased our access to wood. Because it can silently pluck up trees off of any terrain without damaging the forest floor, almost all of the landowners within the balloon's radius have now signed up for the harvest. Previously many were unwilling to have noisy, smoke-belching skidders tearing up their woodlots. This increased our access to wood so much that we now run the harvest operation 12 hours per day, 7 days per week."

"Right now, we are pretty close to our full capacity of 6 million gallons of ethanol per year," Uncle Mike said, turning his attention to Lhamo. "That's enough to heat a home and power a car for 7,000 families. We employ 96 people full time, most of them from right here in the Jamaica area. And next month we'll open our second fermenter along with another greenhouse in Townshend up north on Grafton Road. That will give us a potential capacity of 12 million gallons per year. A lot of these people still own their land here in town because of our Rum Works. They either sell us their timber, at a fair price I might add, work for us, or both. This puts a lot of money back into the community. And best of all, the forest is a lot better off due to our new management practices. Come on. Let's go up to the current harvest area in the National Forest so you can see for yourself."

They rode up the forest track in Uncle Mike's turbo-electric truck, the carbon fiber body barely swaying as the 4 electric motors each drove its own independently suspended wheel. Now Mike understood why his uncle called it the goat-mobile. It was just as agile navigating over roots and rocks as on the highway. The alcohol powered mini-turbine spun the generator with only a faint whine. It was a far cry from the big and noisy diesel trucks Mike had grown up with. The lightweight vehicle barely disturbed the leaves on the track as they climbed the hillside.

Mike began to see individual standing dead trees mixed in with the bright, green summer forest. His uncle explained that the Rum Works' forester had selected the trees that they wanted to harvest and killed them by girding the previous fall, so now they were completely dry and therefore a lot lighter. This simple trick alone increased the efficiency of the balloon harvesting process by more than 30%.

Coming around the hillside, Mike caught a glimpse of the balloon up ahead with 2 large trees suspended beneath it. The truck pulled up next to a couple of scooters. They stopped and got out. Below them to the left, the forest was dense, with lots of brush and fallen logs, but up to the right, it was more open with larger trees spaced at intervals and a few tall straight young trees reaching up towards the canopy in between.

Noticing Mike's curious expression, his uncle explained. "The balloon has fundamentally changed our harvesting practices. Back when we used the big diesel skidders to drag out logs, they had tended to stay down in the valleys where the going was easier, harvesting less from the hillsides and ridges. That tended to wreck the watershed along the streams."

"Now we leave the watershed areas completely undisturbed, reducing erosion and improving habitat for the forest wildlife. In spite of this, we can still harvest trees from three-fourths of the forest surface. And because in any one year we select less than 10% of the standing wood within the harvest area, the nine-out-of-ten trees left standing get bigger and stronger. This is a dramatic change in the management of land that has either been clear-cut for pasture or repeatedly shorn of its best timber trees for the last 3 centuries."

"In 50 years," Uncle Mike said, pointing to a mixed stand of maple, ash, oak, birch, hemlock and white pine, "these trees will be two to three feet in diameter and 50 feet up to the canopy. And some of this young growth in between will have reached the canopy to challenge them, straight and knot-free for 50 feet." He smiled at Lhamo. "Who knows? If we give them room to grow and stop dumping acid rain on them, maybe we can help some of our native sugar maples survive in Vermont after all".

As they walked up the hill to where the harvesting crew was working, they passed through an area that looked like the site of a recent mud fight. Grey muck was plastered on the foliage and forest floor. It smelled a bit like fresh bread.

"The balloon just dumped its load of fermenter-sludge here," Uncle Mike looked at Lhamo and pointed to some of the muck. "The wood we harvest has a mineral content of about 2%. You know, the stuff that makes ashes when wood is burned. When Mike's bugs turn the wood into alcohol, this nutrient-rich solid stuff settles out in the tank."

Lhamo nodded her understanding. "A 5-ton load of logs leaves about 200 lbs of solids behind after we've digested out the cellulose and lignin," Uncle Mike continued. "We mix the sludge with 100 gallons of water and sprayed back on the forest from the balloon. We used to struggle with getting the fermenter sludge back to the forest, so we didn't deplete the soil of minerals. Now we just send it back up in a dispenser hung under the balloon and spray it onto previously harvested plots. We even add a bit of calcium carbonate to counteract the effect of acid rain. That helps the maples survive."

Up ahead, two people in hard hats were at work on a dead tree. One had a fuel-cell powered saw, and the other had a long pole. The one with the pole was just guiding a hook dangling from the balloon into a harness attached high in the tree. With the hook engaged, the line was taken up by the balloon. They saw it dip slightly as the line came tight.

"They're adding volume to the balloon now," Uncle Mike said. "They calculate each tree's weight to within a few percent based on diameter, height, and species. So when they cut it, the tree doesn't fall, and the balloon stays airborne."

The worker with the saw stepped up to the base of the tree, positioned the blade at the base of the trunk, and in a few seconds severed the tree from its roots. The tree rose silently into the sky.

"Now that solves an old question," Mike said to Lhamo with a smile. "Trees will no longer fall in the forest, so we don't need to decide if they make sound if no one is there."

Lhamo looked at Mike and just shook her head. Uncle Mike chuckled. Now Mike realized why the cutting yard was so clean. Because the harvested trees never fell to the ground, they never got dragged in the mud. It made the whole operation that much cleaner.

With its full load – in this case 5 trees – the balloon silently departed back towards the Rum Works. The harvest crew took off their hard hats, and the one with the long pole let down a cascade of red hair. Uncle Mike walked over to them.

"Cindy, Bob, this is my nephew, Wonderboy, the one who discovered the magic bacteria that got the Rum Works started. And this is his friend, Lhamo, one of the true brains behind the Mars Project. Cindy and Bob here are our most efficient harvest crew, which I can't fathom because they are husband and wife. As you saw as we walked up here, they can get the balloon loaded in less than 6 minutes."

The couple walked over to Mike and shook his hand. On their faces, Mike saw confidence and something more – maybe gratitude or appreciation.

Cindy gave Mike a lasting hug and whispered in his ear. "Thanks, Mike. Our son Bobby is a chem-major at UVM up in Burlington because of the Rum Works. And don't let your uncle get to you – all that growling is his cover for being all brains and no teeth".

"Cindy, let go of Wonderboy. You're old enough to be his mother. And give him a heft of your tether pole."

Cindy smiled at Stephanie and Lhamo, and Bob gave Mike a firm handshake. Cindy returned with a 40-foot long rigid pole about two inches in diameter. By the look of it, it should have weighed about 80 pounds, but when Mike reached out and took it from Cindy, it felt like a feather.

"It's our first hyperbaric tool," Uncle Mike said proudly. "It's helical carbon fabric inflated with hydrogen to 45 atmospheres. It weighs two pounds. What do you think?"

Mike swung the pole among the branches above him. He slid its hook over a dead branch and gave a small tug. The branch snapped off and tumbled to the forest floor. He tapped the pole against the upper trunk of a maple tree, hearing and feeling the firm "thunk" of solid against solid. The pole felt like it was made of metal, but at the same time it was almost weightless. He handed it to Lhamo who hefted it appreciatively.

"And at the end of the day, Cindy pumps out the hydrogen, folds it up, and carries it home in her backpack," Uncle Mike said.

"Sorry, Mr. Barber," Bob said. "Gotta get ready for the next load." Cindy took back the pole, waved goodbye with a smile, put a collar on the hook, and lifted the hyperbaric pole up among the branches of the next dead tree.

As they headed back down towards the truck, Uncle Mike and Lhamo walked ahead. Lhamo was listening intently as Uncle Mike used his hands to describe something intricate in the air in front of them.

Stephanie took Mike's hand and held him back a bit. "Thanks, Mikie. I know the two of you have something you're bursting to tell us. You've both been saints letting my brother get this hyperbaric stuff out. He's been on the verge of exploding for months. It started with one of his quiet phases, and then he locked himself in his house for 5 weeks and just wrote pages and pages of text. I had to bring his food up there or he'd have starved. But today he seems a lot better now that he's had a chance to tell you all about it. And I'm amazed how comfortable he seems with Lhamo. She's a remarkable woman, Mikie. Look at how she's drawing him out of his shell. Forgive me for saying this about my brother, but she's a world-class dork-whisperer."

Mike nodded but then glanced at his mother with a slightly embarrassed grin.

"Also," she continued quickly, putting her arm around her son as they walked downhill, "I just want to tell you how proud I am to be your Mom. You've made a difference for the people here. I grew up with them. I know."

Mike smiled inwardly as he and Stephanie walked arm in arm towards the truck. Coming home was good. Coming home with Lhamo was better. Maybe they should do it more often.

•   •   •

Later, the two Mikes were sitting on Stephanie's porch sipping iced tea. The two women were out taking a tour of Stephanie's vegetable garden.

"So tell me, what did those bastards at Ham U do to make you come all this way for face time?" Uncle Mike asked.

"I heard rumors that you were screwing up the Rum Works, so I came back to check on you," Mike deadpanned.

"Don't be a smart-ass, Mike. It's your milk project, right?"

"Sorry. Yeah." his nephew replied. "So here's the story. Up until a week ago, we had a team of volunteers, some from the Mars Project and some from other labs collaborating on a project to use our bugs and extractors to make milk for schools. It was in the process of being set up as a non-profit corporation within the University's small business incubator. All of the players stood to benefit. The University would get reasonable royalties on the patents, and the Mars Project was getting huge positive PR. And then, out of the blue, the University shut down our project, claiming that they'd get better royalties on the patents from another source."

Uncle Mike held his hands out palms up, as if to say, 'so?'

"Three days later," Mike continued, "this last Tuesday, my department Chair, a weasel named Klink, calls me into his office. Out of the blue he offers me an endowed chair worth $1.2 million per year and promotion to Full Professor rank at Ham U, independent of the Mars Project. He said the endowment came from an anonymous donor who was impressed by my research. It was an obvious attempt to buy me off. I couldn't have lived with myself if I did that. So I shook his hand, smiled at him, said 'no thanks', and walked out."

"You walked out on an endowed chair?" His uncle's face burst into a huge grin. "No shit! I'd have loved to have seen that. Maybe there's hope for you yet, Wonderboy! But what happens now?"

"It's obvious that the money came from the Santo Dominus Corporation, the company Ham U licensed my milk bug patents to, and they were trying to buy my complicity with twenty-five million dollars of endowment. Meanwhile they'll sit on the patents and continue to sell billions worth of feed additives and growth enhancers to the dairy industry."

"I know that part. What do you plan to do about it, Mike?"

"Well, I'm going to keep working for the Mars Project. But what's important is what you are going to do about it, Uncle Mike."

"And that would be...?"

"I think you should file patents on an alternative milk bug, and partner with some smart people in Tibet who can make extractors just as good as the ones we have in the Mars Project."

"So you really want me to front for you on a workaround for the milk machine?"

"Why not?" Mike asked. "You suggested that path months ago when we first discussed the milk machine idea."

"For starters, as I mentioned on Wednesday, we've just committed most of our spare cash at the Rum Works to our joint venture with Diamond Fabrics in Alberta. There's not a lot of working capital available for anything else just now, particularly not for something this big."

"Yeah, I realize that now. But really, that's okay. Let me tell you the rest of the story." Uncle Mike gestured with his fingertips to indicate 'bring it'.

"A week ago today, right after we got shutdown by Ham U, Lhamo told me in confidence that her brother in Lhasa, a chemical engineer, is the exclusive manufacturer of her extractor surfaces. And get this: they never patented that part of the device. How they make the disc surfaces fit the molecules to be extracted is a tightly guarded trade secret that neither the Mars Project nor the Chinese have access to."

"Why am I not surprised? In case you haven't noticed, Mike, your lady friend is not only a brilliant engineer, she's also got one hell of a lot of street smarts," his uncle interjected.

"So," Mike continued, "the two of us began to think that we might build an alternative milk machine. But money is a problem because we want the business of providing carbon-neutral milk to schools to be a break-even enterprise, like a charity, so there is no big, quick score there for the typical investor."

Uncle Mike nodded. "Not to mention your legal defense costs against a giant like Santo Dominus."

"And," Mike continued, "Lhamo and I had that conversation off line, outdoors with headsets off, so nobody could have been eavesdropping. But late that evening, my phone rang, and it was someone who knew what the University had done, really wanted me to come visit him to talk about it, but wouldn't give me a name over an open line. That's when we played a short version of 20 questions, and to verify his identity, he made the Rum Works become the most popular search in the world for a minute or two."

"Newdle?"

"Yeah," Mike nodded. "His name is Dave Erickson, and his title there is VP of Sustainable Innovation. You'll like this guy. He got his MBA from Harvard, worked with Christensen, and he stayed on to teach Christensen's course for a few years after the old man retired. Anyway, I took the morning train to Boise and spent Sunday afternoon talking with them."

"Boise? Them?"

"Newdle has a huge ranch north of Boise. I think it belongs to Ivan, kind of like his American dacha, but they use it as a company retreat. The meeting involved just 4 of them: Barry, Ivan, Dave, and a CIA-type named Anton who's their VP of Competitive Intelligence. They knew a lot about the Mars Project, lot about me, and a lot about you and the Rum Works. They want to meet you."

"Why me? I'm small and they're big. And in case you haven't noticed, I have a rather high antibody titer to big business."

"That's the really interesting part that I didn't understand until I talked with them," Mike replied. "Barry and Ivan have handed over the reins for most day-to-day operations at Newdle to a younger management team. But they've hired this guy Dave Erickson as an empowered free agent to shake up the business, and they've given him a fair bit of their time and money to do it. He's their in-house silo-buster. It's his job to question their established practices, and also to bring in new ideas that enhance Newdle's overall goals, like free access to information, clean energy and sustainable food. That's why they're interested in you, Uncle Mike. I think they've cracked Christensen's conundrum so that 'big' can learn from 'small'."

"I'd like you to talk with them" Mike continued. "They've made a commitment to sponsor the School Milk Project through their foundation. Even before I got there, they'd done the due diligence and decided that a Rum Works subsidiary would be a good home for the milk business. As they pointed out, you are a credible originator for the workaround IP. And you already supply bugs and equipment to your network of ethanol franchises, so the business models are similar, once the milk machines are set up at schools. Of course, some might suspect that Lhamo and I are working behind the scenes, but since there will be no salaries, profit, or equity coming directly to either of us, nothing can be proved. We just need to keep all of our communication absolutely private."

Uncle Mike looked down at his boots for a moment, and then back at Mike. "You trust these guys?"

"Anton is seriously scary. You wouldn't believe how much information he has at his fingertips," Mike said, holding his fingers up like he was working his heads-up display. "But yes, I trust them."

"Have you asked yourself why Newdle is all that interested in your milk project?"

"Think about it, Uncle Mike. These guys have been running a green company for 30 years. They have become the world's dominant trader in hydrogen because no one else dared to buck the oil companies and do it. They've recognized that factory farms are a major problem for the environment, and they see the milk machine as an important step in the right direction. They don't want Santo Dominus to buy it and bury it. And remember, their motto is 'be not evil'."

"Are they are going to set up secure communications for us? If we do this thing, it needs to be kept very tight."

"It's remarkably simple. We'll get new headsets from them that have massive bandwidth capability. Then they redirect a fraction of their routine search volume through it – we become a walking part of their pipeline, so to speak. Imbedded in that terabyte flow will be our few megabytes of communication, pulled out by an encrypted filter on either end. Anyone trying to listen in will drown in a digital river if they try to drink in all that volume."

"So when do I get to meet them?"

"They are going to be in New York next week. After that, they thought they might drop by the Rum Works for a chat, see the balloon harvester and the fermenters, trying to stay as anonymous as possible – kind of like a couple of prospective investors."

"And you want me to play nice and do what they tell me."

"No, Uncle Mike," his nephew said sternly. "I want you to listen to what they say, and then decide if you can do it along with all the other stuff on your plate. Lhamo and I can't be paid for this or connected to it in any way, but you will be well compensated for making it happen. And you should hire any staff you need to advance the project."

"Fine. I'm probably going to say 'yes' because I know you want this, Mike, even though the last thing I need right now is more work or more money. Just make sure you keep your distance and watch your back. Because if this works, it's going to be very disruptive, and those guys at Santo Dominus will seriously not like you even more now than before."

CHAPTER 11

THE FLOOD
3 Feb 2030

Vermont wasn't supposed to look like this in early February.

There was no snow on the ground. In sun-exposed places, bits of green grass defied the Winter Gods. Even the squirrels seemed uncomfortable in their thick winter coats.

The two Mikes sat in their shirt-sleeves on the south porch of Stephanie's Townshend house as the afternoon sun floated just over the hilltop to the south. They were poring over a paper printout of their school milk project business plan. The Newdle Foundation was funding the first 100 units, and now they had to decide where to put them.

They had two demonstration units already up and functioning, one here in Townshend and the other up the road in Jamaica. Mike wanted to spread the rest of them around, like two per state, so no one felt left out. Uncle Mike favored clustering them in one non dairy state – both for ease of servicing and also to lessen the political blowback from the dairy lobby. Mike had about given up defending his position when suddenly Stephanie yelled from inside.

"Mike, Mikie! You've gotta see this!"

A second later she ran out onto the porch, holding the door open. "What? You're not connected?! Get in here! NOW!" She disappeared back inside.

Both Mikes sat frozen for a moment. Stephanie never lost her cool. Then her son jumped up and sprinted into the house, her brother not far behind.

Stephanie stood transfixed looking at an old, flat screen on the wall. The image was of a coastline seen from an aircraft.

The logo at the bottom identified it as "International Network News: live feed".

What had once been a small coastal city was devastated for a couple of miles inland. The camera zoomed in on a ship, a freighter or maybe a large ferry, lying on its side in a jumble of smashed trees and rubble at least half a mile in from the shore. The voiceover was saying that this was Christchurch, New Zealand, taken from a New Zealand military aircraft.

"What happened?" Mike asked. "Did they have an earthquake and tsunami?"

"Hush!" his mother hissed. "No one knows yet."

The voiceover changed from female to male. "The USGS Earthquake Information Center in Golden, Colorado reports no earthquake activity near New Zealand, but they report unusual surface activity in Antarctica, possibly in the area of the Ross Ice Shelf, about three hours ago. Because there was no seismic activity characteristic of a tsunami generating earthquake, no warning was issued."

The picture abruptly shifted to another feed. This showed another coastal city with similar devastation. The crawler under the picture identified it as Hobart, Tasmania. It reminded Mike of the pictures of the Japanese tsunami he'd seen when he was eleven years old. The voiceover reported that a massive wave coming from the south had swept over the low-lying areas of the city half an hour before. Again, all but the largest structures were completely gone, and vast piles of rubble, boats, cars, roofs and trees were thrown up into tangled piles far inland. In the harbor, rafts of floating debris surged back and forth as individual large waves marched in from the south at 2 minute intervals.

'Shit," breathed Uncle Mike. "Two south facing cities a thousand miles apart. This is no localized event. I'll bet a big chunk of the Antarctic icecap must have let go. This is the mother of all tsunamis, and it's going to scrub the Pacific basin from guzzle to zatch, all the way up to the Bering Strait. This could kill millions. I hope they've gotten a warning out."

As if on cue, the picture shifted to a podium bearing a US Government seal. An agitated man in a uniform walked up. The caption identified him as Commander Eric Sims, US Coast Guard. "There has been a major event in Antarctica that has generated a massive tsunami heading north into the Pacific Ocean. Coastal cities in New Zealand and the southern tip of Australia have been devastated. We do not know the speed of this wave, but a tsunami warning has been issued for all coastal regions on the Pacific Ocean as far north as Hawaii. Residents of low lying areas are advised to seek higher ground, especially on south facing coasts."

Mike looked at his uncle. "How fast do tsunamis travel?"

"Depends on how deep the water is. Most of the Pacific is deep, so it can move really fast."

"But this doesn't make any sense," said Mike, thinking out loud. "Ice shelves are already floating in the water. If they break free, they don't raise the sea level, and they don't make waves. They just float away and become icebergs, and ice coming off the land moves like, you know, a glacier, one chunk at a time."

"Well, Kid, this one's obviously different. Didn't they say that the USGS picked up seismic activity on the surface in Antarctica? The only explanation is that something very big and high up came suddenly downhill. What do you think might happen if a block of ice a mile thick and the size of Pennsylvania came skating down off the high Antarctic plateau and into the south end of the Pacific? For something that big sliding down from 2 miles up on the plateau, once the edges break free, friction would be inconsequential. [11] That means it's gonna accelerate like it's falling straight down. Remember, "32 feet per second per second" from high school physics? So when the bulk of this hummer got to sea level, we're talking a forward velocity into the Pacific at something like the speed of sound. This was no glacial event. This is the ice avalanche from hell!"

Mike tore his eyes away from the screen. "I've gotta get connected! I've gotta talk to Lhamo". He sprinted up the stairs and grabbed his Newdle headset off the dresser, switching it on as he adjusted the earpiece. It took a couple of seconds to boot up, and immediately he had 3 icons flashing red. He ignored the "news alert", skipped past "Mars Program – urgent", and opened his "Vids – urgent" array. There were two messages, one from St. Louis, one from Chicago, but nothing from out of country.

Mike extended the camera boom and hit record. "Lhamo. There's been a disaster in the Southern Pacific, and a massive tsunami is heading north. No one knows how far it will go. If you are still in Lhasa, sit tight. But if you are back in China and near the coast, please get to high ground. Call me when you get this. Bye." He hit send. The system responded with "message sent", followed almost instantly by an audio warning: "All links to Asia are busy. Message will be re-sent in 30 seconds".

Mike ran downstairs and rejoined Stephanie and Uncle Mike in front of the flat screen. The image was back to Hobart where one shot zoomed in on two bodies and a large teddy bear floating with the trash in Hobart harbor. Stephanie was staring transfixed at the picture, her head held in her hands, and tears flowing down her cheeks. Uncle Mike looked grim.

The INN feed switched to an apparently untouched harbor. The caption identified it as Sydney, Australia. As the camera panned to the right, the iconic harbor bridge and the opera house behind it came into view. The picture was probably coming from a helicopter because the camera angle was pretty low. When the camera zoomed in on the bridge, it was jammed with traffic. In the harbor, there was a glut of boats and ships of all sizes heading out under the bridge and past the opera house. Adjacent to the opera house, a large cruise ship was docked, but the thick smoke coming from its exhaust stacks suggested it was about to get underway. Clearly the word had gotten out and people were trying to clear the coast and harbor areas. The voiceover was explaining that an expert had told INN that tsunamis traveled at an average of 350 miles per hour and that it was 600 miles from Hobart to Sydney, so the wave was not expected for another hour.

Mike directed his attention to his headset display, selected 'search', and asked verbally, "distance from Ross Ice Shelf to Christchurch?" Almost instantly, the voice said, "2114 miles or 3932 kilometers". Then he asked: "Speed of travel, tsunami in deep water, miles per hour?" The answer came: "variable, but may be up 500 miles per hour in deep water".

He turned to his uncle. "How long ago did they say that seismic event was?"

"About 3 hrs ago."

"Well, it's 2100 miles from Ross to Christchurch, so this sucker is doing more like 700 miles per hour, not 350. So it might take less than an hour for it to get from Hobart's latitude to Sydney's. They'd better watch out there."

"Like I said, Wonderboy – 'speed of sound'." Uncle Mike said flatly.

By this time, the helicopter supplying the INN feed had crossed over the bridge and was east of the city, nearing the Pacific coast. Its camera was focused on the cruise ship, which was attempting to pull out of its slip without any tugs to help. There was a stream of boats coming out under the bridge as they sought to get out to deep water, and this made it impossible for the cruise ship to safely maneuver out into the channel. Farther out, 3 large warships, less inhibited by the small boats, were moving east up the channel at high speed.

The helicopter camera swung around to the south. On the left was the Pacific Ocean, looking completely normal. On the right of the screen was Sidney international airport. The camera zoomed in on the airport, showing the two runways extending out into the bay to the south. Both taxiways along the runways were lined with planes waiting to take off. There had to be 20 planes on each taxiway. Clearly a lot of folks were wanting to get off the ground in a hurry. Mike did a quick calculation: if they took off at standard 60 second intervals, this was going to take 20 minutes or so.

The camera pulled back, showing the terminal area. There were still at least a dozen more planes either at the gates or in maintenance areas. Probably not enough crews to get everything airborne on short notice, Mike thought.

At that moment, the camera swung to the left out over the Pacific. An excited voice, perhaps the camera operator could be heard shouting: "There it is!"

As the camera zoomed out, a long dark ridge less than a meter high could be seen racing towards the coast, looking more like a shockwave than any ocean wave Mike had ever seen. Within a minute, it had traveled most of the way from the horizon to the shore. Then the most amazing transformation occurred; it looked like it was shifting from fast forward to slow motion. As it slowed, it rose up from the sea like a cliff. More and more water began to build behind its face as it slowed.

There was no voiceover. Whoever had the microphone at INN was, like the rest of the connected world, transfixed in horror. The camera swung to the airport, showing most of the planes still in line for takeoff, then up to the harbor mouth where the warships were just nosing out into the Pacific. The cruise ship, now out in the channel, was hemmed in among hundreds of smaller boats. The camera swung back to the headland south of the airport. To the left stood a small hill covered with oil tanks and a refinery, then a low isthmus connecting it to the mainland on the right. Closer in was the small bay behind the isthmus. Across that bay was the airport.

The wave was huge. Because there was so much water amassing behind it, it didn't break; it just plowed forward as it came up the beach. Like a foaming bulldozer it came in over the isthmus, flowing up and around the hill, tearing away many of the tanks and refinery equipment in its path. At the center of the low isthmus, the wave came across into the bay intact. Now at two-thirds its original height, it drove foaming across the bay towards the airport.

Alerted to the danger, the remaining aircraft were scurrying to get in the air. Safe spacing between takeoffs was obviously being ignored, and there were two or three planes at a time using each runway. In the two minutes it took the wave to cross the bay, only half the remaining planes on the taxiways made it into the air. The 10-15 meter high wave drove up the five meters or so onto the runway, and as millions of horrified eyes watched, smashed into the big jets stuck in line at the south end of the runways. The camera zoomed in on one last lucky aircraft that was lifting off seemingly out of the wave itself, moments ahead of destruction. Behind it, the next jet in line was overtaken by the wave, flipped up on its nose and then crumbled, spewing baggage and bodies into the foam. Carrying this collected carnage, the wave smashed its way through the terminal buildings and parked jets before proceeding inland towards the south side of Sidney.

But then the camera swung abruptly north, taking in the mouth of Sidney harbor. At the bottom right of the screen, the headland south of the harbor mouth was facing the advancing wave. This headland looked like it could stop the wave, but at the expense of the elegant beach-front homes that covered it. And because it opened towards the northeast, the mouth of the harbor looked like it too would be spared the brunt of the wave advancing from the south.

And there, just clearing the harbor were the 3 Royal Australian Navy ships, almost into deep water. The wave rose up from the depths less than a kilometer in front of them. Unfortunately, the ships were heading east out the channel, whereas the tsunami was advancing cross-wise towards them from the south. They had neither sea-room nor time to maneuver. It hit them, along with the other fleeing boats, almost broadside. Against a 30-meter high cliff of water, they were no match. Broaching sideways, every boat at the harbor mouth was rolled over and swept back into the cove to the north.

One of the navy ships could be seen upended and tumbling in the foaming face of the advancing wave, its bow torn completely off.

For another few seconds, the camera followed the wave up the cove towards the northern coastal suburbs of Sidney. Then it swung back to the west to follow a smaller wave up the main channel into the harbor to the west. The cruise ship, opera house, and then the bridge came into view. The wave in the channel was less than a third the height of the primary wave, but the surge of water behind it was creating a massive current, converting the channel into a raging torrent flowing to the west towards the opera house and the bridge.

The camera focused on the cruise ship. The crew had it lined up in the channel, and seeing the approaching peril, they had increased power, driving a large white plume of prop wash behind it. This caused some of the smaller boats in the channel to spin out of control behind it. Having made it out past the opera house, the advancing cruise ship driving forward under full power met the wave head on, drove its 20 meter high bow up into the 10 meter wall of water, and there it came to an abrupt stop.

For an agonizing 15 seconds, small boats and debris spun past the big ship as it used its massive engines to hold its position against the flow. Whether it was the smaller ferryboat thrown up against its bow, or something else fouling a propeller under its stern, the huge ship slowly began to slew to the right, threatening to get crossways in the channel. To avoid driving its bow into the opera house, the crew cut power, maybe even reversed engines, and while struggling to realign itself in the channel, the ship drove backwards into the bridge at midspan. Part of the stern slid under the 49 meter high span, and then the superstructure struck the bridge. The roadway suspended under the arch of the bridge swung backwards and then held. As the wave forced its bow around, the ship became stuck broadside between the flow and the bridge, heeling over onto its side. Lifeboats, passengers, crew, and deckchairs cascaded into the torrent racing under the bridge. Then, as if in slow motion, the arch gave way and the bridge collapsed onto the ship beneath it, causing it to completely capsize.

At the same time, at the bottom of the screen, the drama of wave-versus-opera house was playing out. The initial wall of the wave had hit the landmark with a good three meters of water flowing in over the rail and striking the iconic structure. Perhaps because it was built on pilings over the water, it seemed like much of the power of the wave was flowing beneath the structure. It appeared to be swimming in the wave for a full minute as the overturned cruise ship drifted helplessly backwards behind it into the inner harbor. There was no voiceover. No words could describe the power and the horror being played out on the INN feed from Sidney. Then the screen went blank. The feed was lost.

The screen stayed blank for a few more seconds. Then, with another shift in the picture, the voiceover identified the location as Valparaiso, Chile. Here the picture came from a fixed camera, and the damage did not seem to extend as far inland, but everything near the water, maybe lower than 15 meters elevation, was completely wiped away. At this point, it seemed the tsunami was trading height for width, but clearly it was headed inexorably north.

Stephanie sat sobbing. Uncle Mike stood, his face a mask. Mike put his arm around his mother. She accepted the arm but didn't move. Uncle Mike turned his back to the screen, walked to the window, and looked outside. There were tufts of green in the early February lawn – in Vermont.

"This is because of those idiots in Washington," Uncle Mike said bitterly, more to himself than anyone else. "All these years of warnings, and they couldn't do jack shit!"

At that moment, Mike's head-up display flashed "New Vid – Urgent". Instinctively he cued the real-time connection. It was Brian Solis in St. Louis. "Mike, tell me you're not surfing on Maui".

"I'm safe, Brian. I'm in Townshend, Vermont. Not a lot of exposed coastline here."

"Where's Lhamo?" Brian asked.

"She left for Lhasa 2 weeks ago. She went there for the Chinese New Year. We last talked on the 29ᵗʰ. She was debating whether to fly back via Beijing or Shanghai. You know the Asian mandate – price trumps everything else. I just sent her a heads-up, but received no delivery confirmation. I don't know if she's still in Lhasa or down in the Chinese coastal lowlands".

"I've got 'eyes only' information from NSA. A huge piece of Antarctic ice avalanched down off the eastern plateau. That's what unleashed this tsunami."

"Yeah, I know. My uncle figured that out from watching INN close to an hour ago."

"It must run in the family, Mike."

"Give it a rest, Brian". I grow bugs. I don't read the future."

"Prove it by me…Look Mike, seriously, I'm getting a lot of pressure to keep you on board with the Mars project. There are a lot of important people who like you, but your stand on this milk machine thing is a big headache. Can we talk about this?"

"No, Brian. Look at what's happening out there. Do you really think there will be a Mars Project come tomorrow?"

At that moment, another "New Vid – Urgent" icon popped up on Mike's display.

"Sorry, Brian. Got to go."

Mike hit 'accept', and Lhamo appeared on his display, looking like she'd just awakened. Beautiful.

"Where are you?" Mike asked.

"Lhasa," she replied. "At my family's house. Why?"

"Because the world has changed. Stay there. Please."

CHAPTER 12

IN THE WAKE OF THE FLOOD
3 February 2030 – the Year of the Dog

The Lunar New Year of 2030, welcoming in the Year of the Dog, was the worst day the world had experienced since Noah's flood.

Celestial clockwork dictates that once every 28 days, the moon and sun are aligned together on the same side of the Earth. When this occurs, their gravitational effects are combined. Not just the cause of ocean tides, even ice and rock move slightly to the rhythm of the sun and moon. Whether by chance or design, the ancient astronomers during the Han Dynasty decided to reset their yearly calendar on the one day in the year that the Antarctic pole of the Earth was most closely angled towards the sun and the moon.

While there is no proof that this alignment of the South Pole to the combined gravitational pull of the sun and moon triggered this cataclysmic event, the Antarctic avalanche of 2030 did indeed happen on the Chinese New Year. Once unleashed at the far end of the Earth, it then sent its tsunami messenger racing north to touch the land of those ancient astronomers.

Whatever set it off, it was horribly compelling. A fascination with the enormity of the disaster riveted the world's attention – at least for those survivors who still had power and remained connected. Hourly and then daily, casualty estimates and details of the physical destruction were updated.

As the action of the wave was reconstructed, its origin was an avalanche-front 240 miles wide that delivered 30 thousand cubic miles of ice into the Pacific in four minutes. The resultant wave advanced northward at a relatively constant speed of 710 miles per hour in water over 3000 feet deep, slowing down only in shallower water. As it progressed north, its energy decreased somewhat as it spread over a wider front and encountered more obstructions. So the 80-100 foot wave that smashed into south-facing coasts in the southern Pacific decreased to an average of 60 feet in Hawaii and 30 feet in Japan. For the most part, only south facing coasts were seriously affected.

As any surfer knows, however, the shape of the ocean floor, especially bays and coves, can amplify a wave. Thus a city at the head of a south facing bay experienced a bigger wave than a straight coast or point of land, making such cities particularly prone to massive surges of seawater. And because a bay or river mouth opening to the south typically offers protection from the prevailing weather patterns in the Pacific, it was precisely in these geographic locations that humans built harbors and ports. As a result, large numbers of moored watercraft, from pleasure boats to massive tankers, containerships, and warships, were lifted off their moorings and deposited up on dry land – some largely intact and others hideously broken apart. This, along with the destruction of docks, warehouses, and port equipment resulted in an immediate and long-lasting interruption of transportation and commerce.

A horrific example of this effect was seen in Ciudad de Panama. This city on the Pacific end of the Panama Canal looks south out over the Gulf of Panama, which amplified the wave. Besides wiping out much of this low-lying city, the tsunami drove a 50 foot wall of water over the first lock in the canal three miles inland, completely obliterating it. The next lock, located another two miles inland received a 30 foot surge. At this second lock, the diminished wave was just big enough to drive a giant cruise ship just to its west back through both sets of gates. There it turned in the swirling water and came to rest on its side across both the east-bound and west-bound lock structures as the wave receded. Looking like a huge beached whale in aerial photographs, it was obvious to even the casual observer that no ship was going to pass through the Panama Canal any time soon.

Another effect of the wave that made it unique in history was its effect on ships at sea. The wave appeared to be very small in deep water. Its front was estimated to be less than a foot high in water more than 3000 feet deep. However because it was traveling at near the speed of sound, when it hit a floating object, it delivered an impact like a hammer. Older and less flexible craft tended to rupture seams and sink outright. More modern ships were better able to absorb the blow and remain afloat, but the impact of the passing wave damaged bearings and shifted the delicate alignment of propulsion systems. If ships that suffered this type of damage continued to operate their engines, they self-destructed in a matter of a few hours, but there was no way a crew at sea could repair this damage. That would take months to repair in a first class shipyard. Thus most of the merchant fleet in the Pacific that avoided being destroyed in port was sunk or disabled at sea. With very few tug boats surviving to assist them, those ships that remained afloat but powerless at sea had to be abandoned and most eventually ran aground.

The world's greatest fascination and horror was reserved for the loss of life in coastal areas. New Zealand and Australia were struck without warning. For those inhabiting South Pacific island groups such as Fiji, Samoa, and Polynesia, there was some warning but often no place to go. Those with boats often made for deep water, only to be disabled or sunk. Curiously, traditional sailing outrigger canoes seemed to fare the best – their aboriginal pilots instinctively seeking refuge north of their islands. However, many who survived by this means sailed back to find their low-lying island homes wiped completely clean. Even those islands with high ground often had most of their infrastructure clustered along their southern coasts, and thus were functionally devastated.

•   •   •

For the US population, the wave's arrival in Hawaii was the first taste of its strength against the US homeland. On the southern tip of the Big Island, rugged and sparsely populated, news cameras were perched high up on the coast highway at the top of the volcanic bluffs. With seven hours of warning, almost everyone had cleared the beaches and low areas.

Multiple live feeds captured the fast-moving dark line racing up from the south, followed by the sudden rise of the wave as it thundered up against the steep coast. As most of the cameras swiveled north up the coast to follow the wave front, a few focused in on the backwash coming off the land, carrying back the remains of boats, houses and trees that had been too close to the water. Farther to the north, the more populated towns of Kona and Hilo were angled out of the wave's path, suffering little damage and leaving the island's infrastructure pretty much intact.

The next island in the chain, Maui, was less lucky. Shaped like a dumbbell, Maui is anchored by the 10,000 foot volcano Haleakala to the east and the 5800 foot Pu'u Kukui to the west. In between lies the fertile lowland cane fields stretching from Kehei in the south up to Kahului in the north. At its center, this thin veil of soil between giant volcanoes rises only 80 feet above sea level. South of Maui, there is nothing but the deep blue Pacific for thousands of miles – nothing to break up the power of the wave. They knew it would probably be a big one, but no one was prepared for the power of the wave that came ashore at 4:13 p.m.

The tsunami sirens had been wailing intermittently for hours. Police and firefighters had cleared the south side beach resorts and residential areas for a mile back from the beach and 100 feet up from Waimea to Lahaina. The roads had initially been jammed with cars and trucks hastily loaded with people and possessions moving inland to higher ground. Now the roads were almost empty. Maui knew and respected waves...except this wave was different. Humanity hadn't seen a wave like this for thousands of years

Their first visual warning came from the tiny islet of Molokini just to the south. One minute its rocky crescent was visible to those looking down from the slopes of Haleakala; the next minute its position was marked only by a foamy streak in the sea down the back of the massive wave that rose up like a proverbial monster from the deep. Female hump-back whales instinctively called to their calves and sounded as deep as they could dive. Northward up the sound the wave marched, channeled by the underwater shoulders of Haleakala to the east and the small island of Lana'i to the west.

No one got an exact measurement of its height when the wave came ashore on South Maui, but photographs put its height between 80 and 100 feet. At opposite ends of this 10-mile long, south facing crescent, the two beach-front towns of Ma'alea and Kihei simply disappeared. In the middle, a quarter mile inland and directly in the path of the wave, stood Maui's base-load electric generator. Although Maui got more than half of its power from wind and solar, these three big flex-fuel turbines served the function of keeping Maui's grid up. That is, until the 100 foot wave swept over its 80 foot tall exhaust stacks. Then, as its base load generator disappeared, Maui's electrical grid went down.

It is nine miles from Kihei to Kahului on the north side of the island. The wave surged across this distance in just 11 horrifying minutes. Those foolish souls who had parked their cars a mile or so inland from Kihei in the cane fields, thinking that the wave would break before getting to them, had less than a minute to recognize their fatal error. Then they became part of the foaming monster, along with palm trees and sugar harvesters, sweeping inexorably north to engulf the city of Kahului and the island's international airport. Before sinking back into the ill-named Pacific Ocean, the wave filled Kahului's north-facing harbor with cars, mud, broken airplanes, and thousands of bodies.

For those survivors watching from higher ground, their international airport, major city, and base load power supply vanished before their eyes in an event of biblical proportions. And the world knew as well because live feeds went out on multiple channels. Before the eyes of the world, on this island alone, an estimated 25,000 people died. Being north of the equator offered no refuge. For those poor souls left alive on Maui, simple things like water and food suddenly became the only things that mattered.

The wave, stopping for no one, swept northward. On the island of Oahu, Honolulu and Waikiki were devastated by a 50 foot tall wave that disabled or destroyed all shipping left in Pearl Harbor. On the US mainland, San Diego took a glancing blow – a surge rather than a wave disrupted, but did not destroy, the harbor. Many boats of less than 100 tons displacement got lifted and moved up on shore.

Larger craft, like cruisers and aircraft carriers, got banged about but most remained afloat, and much of the port's infrastructure remained intact.

In contrast, for south-facing seafronts, fate was dealing dark cards from the bottom of the deck.   Long Beach, California, a major military harbor and container ship destination, experienced a 40-50 foot surge.   The Queen Mary, a 1930s relic used as a floating hotel, was wrested free of its moorings and propelled half a mile up the concrete aqueduct euphemistically called the Los Angeles River. Riding the surge like a titanic surfboard, along its path, bridges, houses and skateboarders who did not even know they lived near a river were smashed into oblivion. Thousands of acres of warehouses and homes were swept north and then back out to sea as the wave crested as far as two miles inland before receding.

A bit to the north, Santa Monica suffered a similar fate. Thousands died. Los Angeles Airport, a few miles south and just a mile inland, was saved by its position 150 feet up on a bluff.

One uniform effect of the tsunami as it marched north up the west coast of North America was its complete destruction of undersea cables where they rose up onto the continental shelf. The underwater currents generated by the wave, often called 'under-tow', were intense and highly destructive. These currents also wrought havoc with the cooling water pipes used by seaside power plants. Even if the plant itself was located high enough to avoid direct damage, loss of its access to cooling water effectively shut it down.

Going north from there, other than idiots who watched from the beach or the Pacific Coast Highway, little major damage occurred for three hours. San Francisco, Seattle, and Vancouver, big harbors with small entrances angled away from the diminished wave, experienced small surges.   North America was again lulled into thinking that the wave had dissipated.

Small clues from low lying but south facing towns on the British Columbia coast were missed. Silent surges came in, sweeping away boats, people, houses and cars, and then were gone. Alaska's hillside capital, Juneau, whose only links to the world were by sea and air, was mostly spared. Situated deep in the glacial valleys of the inland waterway, there was just a silent surge that rose 20 feet high. However, in the process it washed away most boats and inundated the low-lying Juneau airport, leaving the city largely intact but cut off from the world. Skagway, however, 40 miles up a south-facing deep-water fjord, was scrubbed off the shore by a 50-foot, ice-ladened wall of water. One moment it was there, and a minute later, Skagway was gone.

Then came Anchorage. Alaska's biggest city lay at the top of a huge, south-facing arch formed by the Alaskan panhandle on the right and the Aleutian Islands on the left. This geological position functioned as a lens to focus the diminished but still inexorable power of the wave coming up Cook Inlet. Twenty minutes after Skagway vanished, the wetlands between Anchorage and Wasilla started draining out to the southwest. Two minutes later, a 90-foot tall wave rose from the Pacific and swept away everything that was important on the south coast of Alaska. Anchorage, Seward, and Valdez ceased to exist as functioning ports and cities. Alaskan oil stored in shoreline tanks and aboard tankers was instantly claimed by the wave. The oil still in the ground had no outlet as pipelines suddenly had no terminus, and the few remaining intact tankers had no docks to tie up to.

•   •   •

As devastating as the destruction in Hawaii and the continental US was, as destabilizing as the loss of its Alaskan oil reserves was, the United States got off lightly compared to Asia's Pacific coast. After the destruction of Maui and the south side of Oahu, Japan had only three hours warning to clear its south-facing harbors and coastal cities, but there weren't enough cars, roads, trains, and busses. About half the people in exposed lowlands made it to safety. The other half died. The Japanese ports of Yokohama, Nagoya, Kobe, and Osaka suffered destruction greater than if they had been hit by nuclear weapons. Worst of all, the fertile coastal farmlands were inundated with salt water, poisoning the land against growing rice for years to come.

The worst blow struck by the Antarctic avalanche tsunami was saved for the shores of its most distant target – the Yellow Sea. Like the Gulf of Alaska, the Yellow Sea sits at the apex of a funnel formed by Taiwan to the South and Japan and Korea to the north. Into this funnel rose the wave from the deep Pacific, building in height and force as the funnel narrowed to the north. Shanghai, on the southern lip, had a 50-foot surge, destroying a third of this low-lying city. Inchon to the north, the major port for Korean commerce, was powerless against a 70 foot wall of water. At the north apex of this funnel lay the Chinese city of Tianjin, the port city for the inland capitol of Beijing. Here the surge rose up over 100 feet high – greater than any blow struck to cities north of the Equator. And because so much water was pushed up into the funnel, the surge coursed for miles inland.

In China alone, it was estimated that 50 million people died immediately. Across the Pacific basin, the estimate of total fatalities was 85 million. Perhaps worse, however, was the destruction of the infrastructure of commerce. Every undersea cable in the Pacific basin became so much coiled junk on the sea floor. Ports serving half of the world's commerce lay in ruins, and a major fraction of the world's commercial shipping was sunk or disabled. In just a few hours, the livelihoods of more than a third of the world's population disappeared.

In the inland city of Beijing, itself untouched by the wave, the Communist People's Party leadership promptly and accurately assessed the far-reaching implications of the disaster. The People's Army and the People's Militia were mobilized, military rule was declared across the entire country, and food rationing was imposed under military supervision. Recognizing that the stability of the State was uncertain, the Central Committee made a perfectly rational decision to pull back their forces to focus on maintaining order in the heavily populated eastern half of the country.

Out to the west in Tibet, to the amazement of the indigenous population, whole units of the Chinese People's Army suddenly packed up and departed to the east in trains, trucks and buses. And as the army left, so did many thousands of police, government bureaucrats, and ethnic Han immigrants who feared for their safety now that the army was leaving. Such was the power of this wave that it was felt at more than 11,000 feet elevation and over a thousand miles inland. After 75 years of stoic, mostly non-violent resistance, Lhasa and the Tibetan people were, at least temporarily, free of Han Chinese rule.

CHAPTER 13

GRATEFUL-DEAD
February 2030

On the seventh day after the tsunami, the power grid in New York and New England went down, but before the lights went out, everyone in the region already knew too much to believe that this disaster was in any way temporary.

The failure of the electric grid occurred despite guarantees by national leaders that it was dependable and secure. It began in Mexico and southern California with just seventeen disabled coastal power plants. Nine of these could have been promptly repaired, but the necessary parts had been in manufacturers' warehouses in coastal China or Japan. California grid operators attempted to compensate for their local deficit by purchasing additional power from other southwestern suppliers. After a few days, this added burden drew down the onsite fuel reserves at these generators, forcing the Southwest to pull more power from the mid-west, and so the burden shifted progressively to the east. Across the United States, deliveries of everything from fuel to spare parts were stressed and then began to fall behind. As with the California generators, reliance on 'just-in-time delivery' from parts manufacturers half a world away became the fatal flaw. Finally, a localized but intense blizzard from Pennsylvania to Virginia shut down regional rail deliveries of coal for three days. This was the proverbial last straw that broke the camel's back. Starting with the Mid-Atlantic States, the whole system collapsed.

Some states and cities detached themselves from the grid and tried to operate independently, but the loss of the national grid drove a knife into the heart of commercial transportation. Abruptly, pipelines no longer pumped oil or natural gas. Trains no longer delivered coal. By making their best effort to stay online, some operators overloaded their generators, damaging parts that could no longer be replaced from inventories half a world away. Before the tsunami, these parts could have been in hand within 48 hours. Now they might as well have been in a warehouse on Mars.

For fifty years, 'just-in-time-delivery' had been the paradigm of the efficiently run marketplace. Now it became the Achilles heel of an infrastructure that allowed two-thirds of humanity to live an urban lifestyle. The US electric grid fell like a perfect line of dominos from east to west, and with it went commerce, jobs, heat, and light.

In most US cities and towns, from Miami to Seattle, by the seventh day, food had long since disappeared from grocery store shelves due to hoarding. Then the loss of the electric grid effectively shut off movement of food from warehouses into the cities. When it did, the civil unrest began. In some places, it was contained by law enforcement. But in most places, by the tenth day, 'peace officers' were rarely seen. The National Guard, exhausted by 30 years of overseas deployments, had little to offer when their 50 respective governors called. The US Army did its best to use the Posse Comitatus Act of 1878 to sit on the sidelines. Most local military commanders understood the simple metric that they had less than one month's essential supplies on any given base, and that did not bode well in mid-winter for a base that housed 10-20 thousand armed men and about twice as many dependents.

In St. Louis, for example, the breakdown in public order was swift and seemingly irreversible. The city's general demographic had the economically disadvantaged living to the east and the wealthy west of downtown. The Ham U campus was about in the middle, so when looting broke out in the east, the campus was quickly caught up in the violence. Brian Solis, who lived with his parents in a house just northwest of the campus, was forced to flee to the west as looting spread into his neighborhood. They ended up camping on the Creve Coeur golf course next to their car in February with little food and only his father's shotgun to protect them.

Small towns, particularly those in financially challenged regions, tended to do better. Most small town cops tend to live in their jurisdiction and know everyone in town – who the opportunists are and who can be relied upon in a pinch. Also, folks long accustomed to food insecurity tended to squirrel away some flour, lard, canned tuna, and corned beef to have enough in the pantry to sustain them for a month or two.

Therefore, when the inevitable caravans departed the troubled cities to seek food in the countryside, they were met with armed road blocks rather than open arms. The outlying towns knew they had a chance to make it by themselves, but there was little hope if they had to carry lots city folks on their backs as well. Finding themselves cold, cut-off, and hungry, many major population centers erupted into violence and self-destruction. It was ugly, and some of these images got out before the power went down.

In Townshend, they were grateful for their distance from these troubles – a hundred miles north of Hartford and over 150 miles from Boston and Montreal, with lots of towns in between to stop marauders. Their nearest metropolitan area was Albany/Troy in up-state New York, and that was 90 miles away with Bennington in between. Thus, Mike was less concerned with trouble coming from a distance than he was with the simple issue of how their two small towns would make it through the rest of the winter with enough food and heat for the local population. As he tallied up their 'assets', it became apparent that the two Rum Works with the pair of greenhouses they'd added in the previous year, plus the two prototype milk machines, would be key factors in their survival. That is, if they could be kept operational.

As was typical of Uncle Mike, he instinctively understood that the survival of their towns was a given. His attention had already leap-frogged ahead to what a post-tsunami world would look like and how it might be served by Rum Works and Diamond Fabrics technologies. As a means to that end, he saw his nearly flight ready hyperbaric dirigible, which he'd wickedly christened the 'Alberta-burg', as a key asset. Without gas at gas stations and unchecked civil disorder in the population centers, flying over it all in a highly efficient dirigible looked increasingly attractive.

One of his immediate goals was to get access to the Mars Mission technology – the bugs, smoothie machine, life-support hardware, and the catheters – for use in the Alberta-burg. His previous bids to license them from NASA had been rebuffed as inconsequential. But in the first days after the tsunami, while the government was still operating, he renewed his offer with the promise to pay the first 2 years of licensing fees upfront. Not only was his offer accepted, but with uncharacteristic speed, the deal was completed in 3 days.

When the grid went down on February 10th, making Townshend and Jamaica just two more cold, dark spots on the map, Uncle Mike was confident that he had the pieces in hand to maintain and grow his businesses in the post-tsunami world. With that done, he then turned his attention to how they might create and maintain local power grids in proximity to the two Rum Works facilities in Jamaica and Townshend. He had previously installed alcohol fired turbine generators at both sites to provide backup power. These were adequate to power both Rum Works operations, but to maintain even a small local grid plus run the Rum Works, they'd need a lot more capacity.

As he tallied what was available locally, he realized that they weren't too far from making it work. There were a fair number of homes in both towns with rooftop solar panels and also a number of wind turbines that had been tied to the grid. This included the 150 KW turbine on the hill north of his house that he'd bought on a whim the previous summer and installed on a 65-foot steel column. With the grid down, it was currently sitting idle, but his experience with it over the last 6 months suggested that it would provide meaningful power about two-thirds of the time.

With these resources in mind, Uncle Mike considered the practicalities of setting up local grids. The base load power would have to come from the Rum Works' alcohol fired turbines because they could run in the dark and on cloudy or windless days. That meant that they'd have to be opportunistic in operating the Rum Works machinery, drawing power for the winches, chippers, and pumps when sun or wind provided extra capacity above base load requirements. Of course, everyone on the two mini-grids would need to draw the absolute minimum of power and avoid peak load times whenever possible, but he was convinced it could be done. After all, more than half of the folks who'd be connected together in these local grids were Rum Works stakeholders, which meant they were family.

On that afternoon, the seventh day after the tsunami, Uncle Mike left the Townshend Rum Works facility on Grafton Road north of Stephanie's house and drove his goat-mobile south to the high school at the junction of Route 30. He'd gotten a message earlier in the day that the milk machine at the school had stopped producing any milk that morning. Mr. Lambert, the biology teacher who was tasked with monitoring and maintaining the prototype, had checked out the digester and extractor that were mounted inside the building. Both were functioning well, so he figured that there was a blockage in the circulation of the bacterial soup through the translucent tubes up on the roof. However, Mr. Lambert had no experience working on the roof installation, and he didn't want to touch it without supervision from Mike or Uncle Mike. Uncle Mike figured he still had enough daylight left to get up on the roof and check out the problem. Perhaps it was just a minor kink in a tube that he could clear, allowing the installation to be back in operation at dawn the next morning.

There was no one at the school, which was cold and dark. He got a ladder from the maintenance shed and set it against the east facing roof where the tubing array had been installed. With the final glow of the late afternoon light fading in the southwest, he climbed up on the roof and made a cursory inspection of the entry/exit lines down to the inside installation. Everything looked fine there, so he followed the tubing bundles up to the arrays that covered 50 sq. meters of the roof surface. Here he found the blockage – one of the main feeder lines was kinked. It looked like the translucent tubing had somehow become tangled around one of the mounting clamps that held it firmly in place on the roof.

Easy enough to fix, Uncle Mike thought. He reached down and lifted the tubing to untwist it, and only then did he see the flat plate with two thin cables that had been concealed under the tubing array. As he wondered what this strange object was doing up here, a red light flashed on the flat object and its fuel cell-powered capacitor discharged 750,000 Volts up through his arms. The force of the electric shock contracted his muscles and threw Uncle Mike's body back onto the roof where it lay still in the growing darkness.

An hour later, back up the street at Stephanie's house, she and Mike waited from Uncle Mike to arrive for dinner. Her ham and potato casserole, hot out of the flex-fuel oven, sat cooling on the table. With the grid down, their headsets didn't work, so they'd started using old hand-held FM frequency radios. Their repeated attempts to reach Uncle Mike by radio got no response. It was not like Uncle Mike to be late for a free meal, so after waiting half an hour, Mike took his scooter up to the Townshend Rum Works. Uncle Mike's truck wasn't there, so he headed back down Grafton Road towards Highway 30, planning to check Uncle Mike's house up in Jamaica.

As he slowed to turn west on Highway 30, Mike just caught the shadow of the goat-mobile in the dark parking lot of the school on his left. He wondered why it was there and what had kept his uncle from dinner. Swinging left into the parking lot, he stopped and called his uncle's name. No response.

Mike parked his scooter and checked the truck. The keys were there, and it was unlocked. Another call to his uncle went unanswered. Taking the fuel cell-powered headlamp off his scooter, he began to explore the school grounds, first coming upon the ladder, and then his uncle's body on the roof.

My God, he's dead! What happened? Mike's mind struggled to comprehend. He's too young for a heart attack, he thought. There was no sign of injury, except his uncle's hands seemed discolored in the light of the LED headlamp. A closer look suggested they were burned.

And then, under the tubing, Mike perceived a hint of red. It was there, and then it was gone. He shut off the scooter's headlamp and waited a few seconds, and there it was again – a tiny red flash under the tubing. Whatever it was, it shouldn't be there. Someone had been tampering with the installation, and his uncle was dead. Mike suddenly felt vulnerable up on the school roof in the darkness. He knelt next to his uncle's body and put his fingers to his neck. It was pulseless and cold. Whatever had killed him, it had happened some time ago.

Mike turned his light back on and examined the tubing that covered the flashing red light. On close examination, he could see a flat, black object underneath with two thin wires extending to what looked like a metal clamp that blocked the tubing. The red light flashed on the flat black object. He killed his light. He had no idea what this device was, but he shuddered. It was something sinister, and it had probably killed his uncle. If it had been an explosive, there would be a hole in the roof. If it released poison gas, why the burns on Uncle Mike's hands. Mike's best guess was that it was electrical, which meant, don't touch it. That deduction saved Mike's life, for by that time the fuel cell had already recharged the capacitor.

Mike retreated off the school roof and drove his scooter the half mile to the home of Sergeant Thomas of the Vermont State Patrol. The Sergeant was the closest thing Townshend had to a town policeman. The trooper's wife let him in and then called her husband in from out back where he was splitting firewood.

"How can I help you, Mike?" Thomas removed his gloves and shook Mike's hand. "You okay? You don't look so good."

"I'm okay," Mike lied, seeing the three children huddled close to the woodstove. He lowered his voice. "Can we talk outside?"

"My uncle's been murdered," Mike blurted out when the door was closed.

Thomas' jaw dropped. "Oh shit, Mike! Where? How?"

"On the roof of the high school. He was checking out a problem with the milk machine. Someone attached some kind of electrical device to a clamp on a tube, which disabled the milk machine. It looks like it electrocuted him. There are burns on his hands and arms."

"Are you sure that device is not part of the machine's normal equipment?" Thomas asked.

"Absolutely sure." Mike replied. "Besides, the grid's down. There's no live power in the system anyway."

"Wait here, Mike. Let me get my pistol, and let's go have a look."

Three minutes later, they were on the roof next to Uncle Mike's body. Sergeant Thomas examined the body carefully but found no wounds other than the burns on Uncle Mike's hands and arms. Next he used his Glock pistol, which was made of plastic, to lift the tubing to look at the flat device with the wires leading to the clamp on the tube.

"You're sure this isn't part of the system – some kind of monitor?" He asked Mike.

"Absolutely sure. My friend builds these, and this is definitely not part of the installation."

"Well, first, I'm sorry as hell about your uncle, Mike. But we've got a bunch of problems. From what I see, I'm guessing that somebody came into our town, placed this device up here, and it killed your uncle. But this might just as well have been intended for you. And we don't know for sure if the person who did this is from outside the area. I doubt it was one of our local people, but you never know. You and your uncle are pretty well liked in these parts. Do you know if anybody in town had it in for either of you?"

"I've been away for most of the last 15 years," Mike replied. "I've only been back home for 3 weeks now. And beyond the fact that most people in town probably found Uncle Mike a bit strange, he seemed to be appreciated for bringing the Rum Works to both towns."

"Yeah, that's my impression, too," Sergeant Thomas agreed. "Those that didn't love him still respected him. So we're probably looking for someone from out of the area. I've never seen anything like this thing here, but I'm guessing it's our best connection to your uncle's killer.

"But here's my problem, Mike," Sergeant Thomas continued. "Things are really difficult right now, what with the breakdown in the food supply, the power going off, and riots in the cities. The State Patrol is really concerned about maintaining public order here in the North Country if the power doesn't come back on. What I don't want in the meantime is a witch hunt for your uncle's killer among our neighbors. Yes, everybody knew he was a bit strange, disappearing into his house sometimes for weeks at a time. But your uncle was really well liked in these parts, even revered as a local force of Nature. If word gets out right now that he was murdered, it could push some people perched on the edge over into a bad place. Can we keep this quiet for a while? Let's just say he's fallen into one of his famous 'blue funk' phases."

"Okay, I guess so..." Mike replied. "We'll have to deal with this officially as soon things settle down. But I agree with you. Besides, right now, the last thing I want to do is give my uncle's killer the satisfaction of knowing he succeeded. And my mom and I need some time to figure out how to keep the two Rum Works operating through this energy crisis without Uncle Mike at the helm."

"Good. Look Mike, you know I'm really, really sorry about your uncle. He did a lot for Vermont, and he never caused us a lick of trouble. But we need to get his body down off here. Let's take him back to your mother's house until we figure out what to do next."

•   •   •

The next morning, Sergeant Thomas, Mike, and Pete, the Rum Works' electrician, were crouching on the roof of the Townshend high school, looking at the flat device hidden under the tubing.

"Well I'll be damned!" Pete exclaimed. "I think this is like an electrical claymore mine – kind of like a taser on steroids. 'Heard rumors about these things recently at a trade show, but never expected one to show up here. It uses a small container of hydrogen to power a fuel cell that charges a very large capacitor. If you touch it, it discharges a massive voltage that is designed to kill."

"Can you disable it?" Sergeant Thomas asked.

"Yes, I think so. It's got very high voltage but not a lot of amps, and once discharged, it takes a while to recharge. So all I need is to short it out with these jump-start cables, and then attach those two wires together to keep it from recharging the capacitor. You guys stand back!" There was a flash and a popping noise, and then Pete was holding the device up like one would a poisonous snake.

Half an hour later, they were up on the roof of the elementary school up the road in Jamaica, looking at an identical device. It was just a hunch that made them check the other milk machine. Luckily no one had found it before they did. In a minute Pete had it harmlessly stashed in another evidence bag provided by Sergeant Thomas. They put it in the trunk of his cruiser along with the first one.

"I wonder why someone decided to place two of these damn things?" the sergeant asked. "For sure, once one of them claimed a victim, nobody would touch the second one. It's almost like a statement to us, emphasizing that they have free access to these places in our towns."

"And both were placed on the milk machines," Mike continued his thought. "Uncle Mike repeatedly warned me that some people would stop at nothing to scuttle this technology."

"So what you're saying is that they were aimed at you and your technology, no matter who they killed. You have anybody in mind, Mike?"

"Nobody I can name, but I know people who can track this back towards its probable source. Well, 'could' if the power were on. And I wonder about the timing of this. This has probably been in the works well before the tsunami, like maybe someone followed me when I came back home 3 weeks ago. So these being placed the day the power grid went down was purely incidental. But now, we won't be able to make any more milk machines anyway; at least not until we get the power backup and restore commerce across the Pacific to Tibet. If that was their goal, maybe whoever did this will back off for a while."

"I'm sorry about your uncle, Mike." Pete said. "If I'd found one of these in daylight, I might have figured it out. But that's over, and we can't change it. Is there anything I can do for you now?"

"Yes." Mike relied. "You can help us bury my uncle in his woodlot this afternoon. We found his will last night, and that was his request."

"And Pete," Sergeant Thomas continued, "I'd appreciate it if you can keep this death very quiet until things settle down, and we figure out who's behind it."

• • •

That afternoon, after Sergeant Thomas and Pete had left, Mike sat in Stephanie's kitchen as she made them some tea. Mike stared at Uncle Mike's favorite chair – its emptiness a metaphor for the void in his existence now that his uncle was gone. Mike remembered that 'Bird Song', (a eulogy for Janis Joplin) was one of his Uncle's favorite Dead tunes. The line: "*Sleep in the stars, don't you cry, dry your eyes on the wind*" came into his mind and remained there almost every waking moment for weeks.

• • •

Two days later, Sergeant Thomas was called down to Bennington, where a small group of Vermont National Guard troops, police, and local citizens were attempting to defend the town from a large caravan of marauders who had come up Highway 7 out of the cities of Albany and Troy in upstate New York. Known subsequently among Vermonters as the 'Trojan War', the three day battle fought west of the Bennington Airport was ultimately successful in holding off the marauders, but at the price of 12 defenders killed – one of whom was Sergeant Thomas.

When they brought Sergeant Thomas' body back to Townshend, it was in a pickup truck, not his cruiser. Mike wondered what happened to the two lethal capacitors.

The village rallied around Sergeant Thomas' widow and her three children. But after the funeral, Stephanie asked Mike. "Wasn't he our only official link to my brother's death?   What do we do now?"

"Let's wait and see how things play out," was the best answer Mike could give her. Besides, he thought, there's no government bigger than a town working right now. We just need to get through the winter. If we make it, we can worry about legal issues come spring.

CHAPTER 14

GOING UP
February to July 2030

The six months after they buried Uncle Mike among the maples above his Jamaica farmhouse felt like swimming in a whirlpool. Stephanie and Mike worked nonstop to adjust to the effects of a complete meltdown in international and national trade and services. For the first month it was touch and go keeping the Rum Works operating despite shortages in supplies, the loss of the electric grid, and even shortages in food. Gas and diesel fuel had completely disappeared by the end of that first terrible week, shutting down those hydrocarbon consumers who hadn't converted to ethanol.

As a result of their efforts, the Jamaica Rum Works managed to keep chugging along, and by spring they even managed to increase output a bit. At the same time, fuel prices went through the roof, increasing their revenue. Because much of the Jamaica and Townshend area population was involved with the Rum Works as employees or woodlot owners, Mike and Stephanie continued Uncle Mike's policy of local discount pricing. They also used a significant fraction of their ethanol output running their generators to support their local power grids. As a result, they didn't make out as well as they could have if they'd taken full advantage of the market.

Partially because of this, but mostly because they were typical Vermont towns with a rich history of community and self-reliance; Jamaica and Townshend had less of a struggle than much of the rest of the country. Relatively speaking, they came through the winter without the starvation or social unrest that was all too common elsewhere.

The Trojan War that claimed the life of Sergeant Thomas down in Bennington was the closest that outright conflict came to them.

Just as Uncle Mike had anticipated, they were able to link together their local wind turbines and solar arrays using the ethanol-fired turbines at the Rum Works sites to provide base-load power. At first these mini-grids offered power intermittently, shutting down in the middle of the day, so they could operate the Rum Works, and then again late at night to conserve fuel. However, soon the two towns figured out how to cobble together enough capacity and limit use so that they could keep both local electric grids up continuously.

Similar stories came back to them from other towns that had franchised the Rum Works technology. Many of these towns and villages also pulled together in the face of adversity, conserving and rationing their local fuel source for the common good. Around the Rum Works franchises, people still drove their flex-fuel vehicles, houses had some heat, and the lights started coming back on. Now more than ever, any town within six miles of a tree wanted Mike's bugs and the balloon harvesting system to go with them.

Growing the bugs, and even fabricating the balloons, was not a problem. Mike's bugs were processed in Townshend in an expanded lab adjacent to the new Rum Works. Up in Alberta, they had plenty of power from the tar sands where Diamond Fabrics made the balloons, but the collapse of most interstate and international transportation presented their biggest bottleneck. Once grown, Mike's wood-eating bacteria were concentrated and freeze-dried, so a month's supply of bugs for a typical Rum Works operation only weighed ten pounds. The basic balloon harvesting system was also relatively light weight – a hundred pounds or so without the hydrogen, but when nothing drove far or flew, there was no way to get the balloons down from Alberta, or the bugs very far out of Vermont, for that matter.

Here again, ingenuity, cooperation, and Uncle Mike's prescience provided a solution.

The 'Alberta-burg', nearly completed before the tsunami, became a high priority project. A week after Uncle Mike died, it lifted off and flew around in circles on a ten kilometer tether – the world's first hyperbaric dirigible.

Once confident in its controls, they unleashed it from the tether and took it through its paces. With its smooth hyperbaric shape and diamond-fabric skin, it was, in the words of its test pilot, "slick and quick", clocking a top speed of 155 mph. Its payload, besides two pilots, was only 1000 pounds, but its flex-fuel turbines gave it a 1700 mile range when burning ethanol at a more economical cruising speed of 100 mph. If the payload was replaced with extra fuel, its maximum range could be pushed out to 2500 miles. Because it was built before Uncle Mike got access to the Mars Mission life support system, they flew it mostly at altitudes between 10,000 and 15,000 feet; but in a pinch they could go as high as 25,000 feet breathing supplemental oxygen. Even with these limitations, however, this meant that the Alberta-burg could make a fully loaded trip out from Alberta to Townshend and back in 48 hours.

By the time spring rolled into Vermont, Mike was coordinating one to two trips per week from Alberta to Townshend and back. On each trip, the Alberta-burg delivered ten balloon harvesters to franchise sites outbound and the bugs and key instruments needed to grow and monitor them to up to 100 sites on the homebound leg.

Rather than having the dirigible come down at each site, the actual deliveries along the route were made via hyperbaric-winged gliders dropped on a tether from as high as 10,000 feet up without any loss of time (or the risk of getting shot at by desperate people on the ground.

The result was a swath of new franchises from Minnesota to Missouri in the west and from Maine to Pennsylvania on the east end. Thus the Rum Works had again doubled its franchises, and growth was limited only by the rate that he could deliver equipment and supplies to both new and existing sites. Pretty soon, the Alberta-burg would be joined in the sky by a sister ship with the Mars Mission Life

Support system installed; and a larger dirigible, the "Big Brother-burg", was taking shape on the shop floor at Diamond Fabrics.

For Mike, while this was not his idea of 'the good life', it was okay. It was good to have something meaningful to do. He was certainly a lot better off than most people and most businesses worldwide. The Mars Project, for example, had been closed down a week after the tsunami and then terminated when China formally withdrew from the project a month later.

Mike had intermittent contact with some of his co-workers in St Louis. Every one of them had it rough, and some died in the increasingly ethnic based strife. His primary concerns were for Brian Solis and Tina Chin, who as non-whites were at considerable risk as the interracial tensions there devolved into outright warfare.

On February 23rd, once they got their local grid up, Mike had a brief video link with Brian. "Hey, Brian. You okay?"

"Not really, Mike." Brian replied with a shake of his head. "How about you?"

"Locally, we're getting things back together. What's your situation like there?"

"The Ham U campus is in no-man's land, and our house is probably burned. Most of that area went up in a conflagration last week. We don't know for sure, and we can't go back to find out. We're camping on a golf course. There's very little food to be had. Worst of all, it's every man for himself here. We've had marauders coming through the camp, but nobody here comes to the aid of others who are being attacked. My dad and I had to shoot two guys who tried to steal our car. It's really ugly here."

"How far are you from open country?" Mike asked.

"There's farmland maybe 15 miles west of here, but there's no reason for us to go there. There are no crops in the fields, and we'd probably get shot if we tried to find food."

"Listen, Brian. If you have enough fuel in your car to get your family into open country, I think I can get you picked up," Mike replied.

"By what, the Starship Enterprise?" Brian asked with undisguised sarcasm. Mike could see that he was really stressed.

"Look, Brian. Back before the tsunami, my uncle was building a prototype ultra-light dirigible. We've got it flying, and it could pluck you out of there within five to ten days if you want to give that a try?"

"This is the uncle who conspired to break the Ham U patents and build the milk machines?"

Mike could see that Brian was struggling to keep his face calm. "That was before the apocalypse, Brian. This is post-apocalypse, and it's a different world. Please try and let that go. I can have you and your folks picked up and taken to our partner's facility in Edmonton. Conditions up there are a hell of a lot more stable than what you're dealing with in St. Louis, and with your NASA background, you'd be very useful to them. It's a gamble for you and your folks, but please think about it."

"Okay, Amigo. I've thought about it," Brian responded instantly. "Where do we meet your starship?"

As is so often the case, this spur-of-the-moment decision had far-reaching consequences. Lifted off of a country road by the Alberta-burg along with his parents, Brian immediately went to work at the Diamond Fabrics facility in Alberta. There he designed new hyperbarics like the tethered delivery gliders and Big Brother-burg, effectively picking up the development of hyperbarics where Uncle Mike had left off.

On successive trips over St. Louis, other members of the Mars Project team were plucked to safety and put to work either in Alberta or Vermont. These 'Mars refugees' included Tina, Mike's Mandarin-speaking graduate student plus her husband and infant son. The five of them were now living together in Stephanie's Townshend house, which the locals had fondly renamed 'Chinatown'.

The town soon came to love Tina, whose talents were applied to producing bugs for the Rum Works franchises, as well as ramping up production of bugs for the milk machines they knew the world needed. Ping, her husband, quickly found his place in the village as an electrical engineer and ace handyman, helping Pete keep their two local power grids up and functioning 24/7.

Mike had also contacted Tammy in Skokie, offering to have her, Angela, and her family picked up and transported by the Alberta-burg to Edmonton or Townshend. Tammy had been characteristically blunt in declining, saying that she was more confident in their defenses there in Skokie than in some small town or a foreign country. To Mike's relief, as the months played out, she seemed to be correct. The Chicago North Shore communities came together and held their southern line at Evanston and Skokie against waves of marauders coming north from downtown Chicago. At the same time they sent their own marauders west into Illinois and southern Wisconsin, and also east across Lake Michigan by boat, to procure food and fuel.

Throughout those first 6 months after the tsunami, two thoughts were constantly with Mike.

First, he missed his uncle. It wasn't just the loss of Uncle Mike's acerbic irreverence. It was the loss of his vision. Mike thought often of his empty chair and the Dead's Joplin tribute. Uncle Mike always knew where to be before the rest of the world got there. Now Mike constantly felt that he was a step or two behind where his uncle would have been. He felt incomplete. He was doing okay, no question, but with Uncle Mike at his side, he knew he'd have been doing better.

There was also a practical reason to think of Uncle Mike. In the chaos following the tsunami and Uncle Mike's death a week later, Mike and Stephanie had not legally transferred the Rum Works out from under Uncle Mike's name. As co-owners, the two of them together owned 50% of the business; but the other 50% belonged to Uncle Mike as senior partner.

Making this right was no simple task. Among other things, when he died, the world was a total mess (including non-functioning state and local governments). There was no way they could get a legal death certificate before they buried him. Without that, the transfer of his ownership in the Rum Works was a non-starter. Nor had Sergeant Thomas had the opportunity to file an official report of Uncle Mike's death before he himself died, contributing to the legal limbo. Through these many months of coping, Mike and Stephanie just signed the paperwork as necessary for day-to-day operations, and Uncle Mike's share of the company grew right along with theirs.

The second person Mike missed was Lhamo.

Communication links were slowly being re-established, and although by early summer audio and video to Alberta were pretty consistent, connections with Asia were marginal, and those to Tibet even more so. When the links were up, they talked, whatever the hour. When bandwidth allowed for video, occasionally they could see each other.

She was living with her brother, the engineer, and she looked good. She said they had enough food – potatoes, lentils, oats, milk, butter, and occasionally some meat. She was still working on her extractors, finding ways to improve the durability of the surfaces so that they could go a year or more without replacement. But what she really wanted were Mike's bugs for the milk machine. She and her brother had a small shop where he had built the prototype milk machine extractors, and what she needed was a supply of the bugs to make milk for the children in Lhasa. "There's more milk out in the country, but not enough of it gets here to the city", she said. "And besides, I think I've acquired a taste for the grass-and-flowers flavor of the milk your bugs make."

In July, Mike told Lhamo about the Big Brother-burg. Brian had flown it down from Alberta to Vermont, taking it as high as 33,000 feet and making most of the trip above 25,000 feet. This was possible because the Big Brother-burg had a modified Mars Mission life support system installed to maintain comfortable cabin temperature and gas concentrations. As Lhamo had suggested to Uncle Mike a year ago, a two kW solar array mounted on top was enough to keep the life support systems operating. To save weight and power, however, Brian had not opted for installing the smoothie machine because their longest trips typically lasted little more than a day.

With its bigger payload (5000 pounds) and larger fuel capacity, they calculated it had a fully loaded range of 3000 miles and an unloaded range of over 7,000 miles. Unfortunately 7,000 miles could get them from Alberta only as far as Korea, but then they'd need another load of fuel either to continue or just to get back home. Given the continued uncertainties in commerce and social order, there was no way they could count on finding fuel along that route to Lhasa. Clearly the Big Brother-burg was not able to bring them together, but Mike wanted to give Lhamo some hope and let her know he was trying.

The bandwidth for that conversion was particularly good, so he had a clear image of Lhamo on his display. Her expression when he told her this was neither sad nor sympathetic. With her hands on her hips, she regarded him sternly and asked: "If you don't use the motors, with our life-support system installed, you can stay up as long as you want, yes?"

"Well, yes..." he replied.

"So you and Brian can fly east with the prevailing winds rather than flying west against them. If you ride with the winds like a soaring bird, use your motors only part of the time, you can travel much farther on one load of fuel. That way you could loop south of the Middle East, cross northern India, and drop in over the Himalayas to visit me. If you bring me the milk bugs, I'll make sure you get enough fuel to get you back to Canada."

Then her face softened a bit. "And maybe I'll come back with you."

"Lhamo, darling", he replied, "I'd love that. Truly I would. But a trip like that would take at least a month, and there's no guarantee we can find the right winds, so we don't get blown right past you."

"I have carefully thought about this," she replied. "It took Steve Fossett only 2 weeks to drift around the Earth in a balloon, and he didn't have any motors. Do your friends at Newdle still have their weather sensors drifting in the stratosphere? Ask them to help you find the right winds."

Mike was about to answer...but stopped. Then something popped into his thought stream. Big Brother-burg with the Mars Project smoothie machine mounted inside the crew gondola, its panels on top growing bugs in the sunlight, and he and Brian enjoying fresh smoothies while floating high above the Earth. This was his uncle's vision. Because they would be drifting with the wind as much as flying, maybe they could afford to add the extra weight of the smoothie machine. It just might work. It was like the Mars project brought down to Earth – well close to the Earth.

Lhamo watched him for a few seconds. Their eyes met, Mike nodded, and they both smiled. "You are going to put our smoothie machine in it. Yes?" She asked.

"Yes," he replied. "It will probably take Brian a month or two to do this. What's the weather like there in late August?"

"There are the Monsoon's to the south, but Lhasa in August is beautiful. Stay north coming in if you can." Her face grew somber, and she asked: "But how can you pay for this. The airship is very expensive, no?"

"My uncle owns half of the company that built it, Diamond Fabrics, so technically we own half of the airship," Mike replied. "And we need you back here to get the milk machine project back on track, so Newdle will almost certainly help us make the flight out there."

"Do you think it is safe enough?" Lhamo asked. She was obviously reconsidering now that the idea seemed possible.

"I need to talk with my friend at Newdle. There are places we definitely don't want to fly over. So you are absolutely right, we need them to help us chart a course to get there, not just drift anywhere the winds blow. But if we can make enough oxygen and heat, we can fly above 30,000 feet most of the way, and I don't think anybody is going to bother us up there. Yes, darling, I think we can get there without too much danger. But what I don't know about is China. Can we fly south from Lhasa and avoid going over China on our way back? They've been pretty xenophobic since the tsunami."

Lhamo nodded. "You are right to be concerned about China. If I leave with you, I don't want to fly over them. They contacted me here in Lhasa 4 months ago. They know I'm here and want me to come to Beijing to help them reconstruct the Mars Project technology. I told them it was too dangerous to travel, but they insisted that I come there. They have agents here in Lhasa, and they will know if your airship arrives. It is big, yes?"

"It looks like a flat cigar, and yes, it is 80 meters long", Mike replied. "But when we land, because it is has a hyperbaric fabric frame, we just pump out the hydrogen. Then it can be folded up and stored in a space big enough for a small car, like a shed or garage. If we come in at night, there will be nothing to see in the morning. So if your friends at our landing site can keep a secret, the Chinese don't need to know about us. And from this end, I don't think we are going to tell anyone where we are going, and we certainly won't ask anyone's permission."

"Mike, maybe we shouldn't be talking about this on an open channel," Lhamo said.

"We use this standard scrambled signal imbedded in bit noise for our business. It's pretty hard to crack from this end," Mike said, "but I'll ask my friend at Newdle how we can make your end safer despite your lower bandwidth there. Secure communications are essential before and during this trip, and maybe they have something even better."

They said goodbye and closed the video link. Mike sat for a while staring out the window. The harvest balloon came down with a load of trees to the Rum Works yard outside. What was it? A year and a half ago, Uncle Mike had told him about his idea for a newfangled diamond fabric balloon on a tether. Now he was seriously thinking of sailing around the world in one. Crazy. And wonderful. But still crazy.

• • •

Three days later, Mike was sharing the crew cabin in B^3 with Brian. They had gotten tired of calling it Big Brother-burg, so its initials, BBB, quickly got re-christened B^3 – 'B-cubed' in geek-speak. It was early afternoon, and they were heading west over Lake Erie, cruising at 60 mph over the ground against a moderate headwind. Other than a brief trip up over southern Vermont in the Alberta-burg a few months earlier, this was Mike's first real trip in a hyperbaric airship. With the turbine engines in the back, the fan blades enclosed in their ducts in the tailfins, and the ship constructed of hydrogen filled tubes rather than a metal frame, up front in the crew cabin there was just the faintest hum. With their headset displays synched with the airship's system, they could see out in any direction and even look down on the ship from a compound lens mounted on a dorsal antenna.

Mike chuckled. He thought about how fast they'd be going if they were heading downwind rather than upwind – 140 mph over the ground rather than 60 mph. Still, they were traveling in a straight line and going where they wanted to go. If need be, they could run the turbines at full power and get airspeed up to 150 mph, but that wrought havoc with fuel economy. Still, not too shabby; but he realized that Lhamo's instincts were correct. This ship was definitely better suited to going with the wind rather than against it on a long journey.

Mike and Brian had been in almost daily communication since Brian had been plucked out of the social chaos in St Louis 5 months ago. However, this was their first sustained time together since before the tsunami. Brian looked years younger than when they were working together on the Mars project, and it was clear from his words and his body language that he really enjoyed working at Diamond Fabrics. In particular, he seemed very proud of B^3 as he took Mike through the practical aspects of airship operation such as airspeed, angle of drift in a cross wind, altitude control, and maintaining level trim.

All of these were technicalities, however, because they could mostly be performed automatically by the ship's autopilot/guidance system when they were in powered flight. All the pilot needed to do was tell the ship where to go and when to get there, and then the options of how to do that came up on the head-set display. Unless the system displayed the dreaded message, "YOU CAN'T GET THERE FROM HERE", all the pilot had to do was select from high altitude or low, bumpy or smooth, certain or highly likely, and then sit back and enjoy the ride – unless, or until, something changed.

On this trip out of Townshend, they'd already made 21 deliveries of bugs and instruments out of the cargo bay, all pre-programmed and preformed by the automated control system. On 20 of these, the hyperbaric glider Brian had designed had been properly retrieved on it tether. The 21st had snagged a tree a bit too big to be yanked out of the ground and had to be cut free. They'd pick it up on their next trip over that site, and because they carried a number of backup gliders, this was no problem. They still had 43 more drops to make over Michigan, Wisconsin, and Minnesota, but these too would be handled by the automated system. From there they would cross South Dakota, which was now controlled mostly by a confederation headed by the Lakota Nation (who were not interested in making ethanol from Black Hills spruce trees), and then across Wyoming for a ground stop at the Newdle retreat. Their ETA in Idaho was 33.5 hours away.

Then Brian moved to the practical details of life in B^3. "Up to an altitude of 10,000 feet, we can breathe ambient oxygen. Worse case: you might or might not get a headache. Above that, because the crew cabin isn't pressurized, O_2 concentration is adjusted to maintain the O_2 partial pressure found at 5000 feet. This means that our bodies get used to living at an altitude similar to Denver. When we encounter 'weather', it's more comfortable to fly over it than through it. So the more time I spend in this rig, the more I find myself selecting the 'go high' option."

"Because the crew cabin is airtight, we only need to add oxygen at the same rate that we use it; but that also means that we have to control against a build-up of carbon dioxide, which our bodies make, and we exhale into this closed space. For this, we use the same multi-stage compressor we developed for the Mars project to scrub the cabin air to remove the CO_2. Right now we just dump that CO_2, but when we install Lhamo's smoothie machine, we'll use it to help your green bugs grow in the thin air up here."

"In the Alberta-burg," Brian continued, "we use compressed O_2 to enrich its partial pressure in the crew cabin when we fly it high. Each of us uses about 18 grams of O_2 per hour, so between us we'll use less than a kg of oxygen if we stayed up high at 30,000 feet for most of this trip. But for our around the world cruise, guessing that it might take as long as 20-25 days, plus maybe adding another body to our life-support system in Lhasa, that's a lot of oxygen to carry. That's why we installed the Mars Life Support system in B^3."

"I know," Mike replied. "My uncle had this epiphany that we should put a large solar array up on the top of the air-ship, collect water from the clouds, not only to make our own oxygen by hydrolysis, but to make lots of extra hydrogen as well. That way the extra hydrogen from the water could be injected into the fuel stream in the turbines to stretch our range. Unfortunately, his analysis said that many solar panels were too heavy and would flip the airship upside down."

Brian smiled. "He was right. I found his notes in the engineering files at Diamond Fabrics. With the best current panels, it wouldn't work. Although they are 28% efficient, they weigh too much. But that's last month's technology. Have my bosses at Diamond Fabrics told you about our recent doping experiments?"

"I know you've tried adding metal ions to the fabric to make it conduct electricity, and my uncle thought the fabric had potential as a semi-conductor. Is this something different?" Mike asked.

"Yeah, well it turned out different than any of us expected." Brian smiled. "Our first try was to make helical carbon fiber into nanowires that conduct electricity. So we did experiments by adding copper, silver, or aluminum to the bath when we grew out the molecular fibers. The one that seemed to fit best into the helix structure was aluminum, but when we tried to pass an electric current through those fibers, they actually contracted violently. Those HC-Al fibers act almost like muscle fibers. They're weird. So we tried transition metals like germanium and gadolinium. But nope, they didn't conduct.

However when we put one of the test preps made with germanium in sunlight while it was still hooked up to the meter, it pegged the dial – not negative for conducting, but positive for generating! The HC-Ge fibers are awesome converters of solar to electricity – just what your uncle was looking for."

"Wow. That's soooo cool!" Mike smiled, silently thanking Uncle Mike. "When did this happen?"

"Ten days ago", Brian replied with obvious pride. "The problem was getting uniform alignment of each fiber to the plus and minus poles of the bundle. That's necessary in order to get net electricity off of a fabric made from the fibers. The trick turns out to be running the bath that generates the fibers in sunlight, and offering anodes and cathodes to the incipient fibers. That seems to work. They just line themselves up."

"And when did you discover this?" Mike asked.

"Three days ago".

"And what kind of efficiency do you see coming from a fabric array made from these fibers?" Mike asked.

Brian held up an index finger, worked his display, paused, and said: "between 42 and 48%".

Mike took a deep breath. He had to ask. "You look like life is being good to you, Brian. So tell me, Señor Dude. What will this fabric weigh compared to the best silicon crystal panel?"

"Maybe a fifth as much."

"So you have a fabric that's a fifth the weight and, what... 48 divided by 28 is ... up to 70% more efficient than the best current solar panels?"

Brian smiled. "Yes".

"'Did you just change the world, Senor Dude?"

"Yeah, Amigo, I kinda think we did".

CHAPTER 15

BIRTH OF THE NC

Summer 2030

They touched down right on time in the field in front of the Newdle lodge. Once they had the nose tethered, Mike and Brian walked away from B^3, and their football-field sized hyperbaric dirigible started to shrink as its pumps sucked the hydrogen gas down into the two hyper-pressurized bladders, one in the bow and one in the stern. By the time they had climbed the hill to the group of Newdle employees gathered at the front door of the lodge, its total volume was almost down to the size of a pickup truck.

On a balcony above, Ivan and Barry watched the process. Barry sent a five word text to Dave. He turned to Ivan and said: "These guys make cool stuff that actually works. You want to go with them?" Ivan nodded. With that nod, the Newdle Consortium was born.

Inside, Brian and Mike were treated a bit like rock stars, but neither one was particularly moved by the adulation. On Brian's part, he'd seen too many great opportunities disappear into big bureaucracies (or be outright rejected) to be impressed by dancing girls with pompoms, let alone a bunch of geeks. Mike had one of his uncle's favorite admonitions echoing in his ears: "If the NIH or the NSF is supporting your research, you're either well behind the curve, or an excellent liar."

But was that true for Newdle as well? Would Mike and Brian have to lie to get their help?

After a few minutes, Dave came into the central area of the lodge. Mike introduced him to Brian. "I'm told that you designed that airship. It's awesome", Dave exclaimed. "Arriving in a football-field-sized airship and then making it disappear in a matter of minutes kind of got our attention here."

"Yeah, it is pretty cool, but it was a team effort", Brian replied. "It's an upgrade of a smaller design that Diamond Fabrics built for Mike's uncle before I arrived. They plucked me out of the chaos in St Louis with that one 5 months ago when nothing else was flying. But actually, the engines are strictly off the shelf and the guidance system is pretty much straight out of a car like the ones you have parked out front. We just put the pieces together. It's no big deal."

"You're way too modest," Dave countered. "Putting those pieces together as you have is even more revolutionary than what the Rutan brothers[12] did 50 years ago when they flew their Voyager aircraft around the World. Using a hyperbaric frame in a lighter-than-air craft is brilliant. But let's go up and see the big guys. They sent me down to rescue you from this flock of geeks. They want to meet you".

Mike and Brian followed Dave out of the room. They climbed up two flights of stairs, down a corridor, and into a spacious room with floor-to-ceiling windows and a view of the mountains. The center of the room was dominated by a massive table made from a single plank of polished spruce surrounded by leather upholstered chairs. The two Newdle founders in casual clothes arose to meet them. They shook hands, and Brian was introduced.

Barry was the first to speak. "We like your ride. Can we get one or two of them?"

"More importantly," Ivan said, "we love its potential. In a resource-constrained world, it's one of the few new ideas we've seen that makes sense."

"We're told you intend to use it to circumnavigate the globe," Barry interjected, "bring back the Smoothie Machine Princess, and help us get our carbon neutral milk program back on track."

Mike let Brian take the lead. "Yes, we can build two of them for you; and yes, we are considering a circumnavigation with a stop in Lhasa," Brian replied, looking at Barry.

"What will happen if you overfly China?" Ivan asked. "Trust us, you don't want to do that. We know how much of a problem their leadership can be."

"We agree that would not be a good idea. But if we can enlist your help, I don't think we need to," Brian replied. "You still operate the drifting look-down weather sensors you launched after the Iridium cascade wiped-out all the weather satellites?"

Ivan nodded.

Brian continued. "We'd like to use that data stream to predict our drifting path at various altitudes. The data are there, but we need a software patch that predicts where a drifting object at various altitudes will go, rather than what the future weather will be at any one place, which is what you do with it now. We plan to start with a light payload and enough fuel for 5000 miles of powered flight, refuel only once in Lhasa, and complete a 25,000 mile trip. That means we need to go at least 60% of the total distance riding the wind. We'll primarily use the motors to nudge us in and out of desirable flow regions...and to get out of a jam if necessary."

"So you need some new software – no problem. And we'll also give you access to our secure data link through the drifting sensors both for tracking and communications. Anything else?" Ivan asked.

Brian looked at Mike and cocked an eyebrow. Both shook their heads.

"Money?" asked Barry.

"Nope, we're good." Mike replied.

Barry turned to Ivan. "When was the last time someone came in here and didn't ask for money?"

"I can't remember," Ivan replied, and they both laughed. Then Ivan's face turned serious. "We're delighted that you two are willing and able to do this without our financial assistance, but please don't be penny wise and pound foolish. We'd rather that you don't take any extra risks for want of money. Your trip is very important to us, too. So think about it. What can we do to add to your chances of pulling this thing off?"

Mike looked at Brian with eyebrows raised and then back to Ivan. "Our communications links with Lhasa are pretty tenuous. Can you help us make them more robust?"

"That was on our 'to do list' with you guys, so it's good you brought this up. We've been struggling to build up bandwidth in Asia. Placing our data transfer nodes along the coasts is relatively easy, but getting one into inland Asia right now is almost impossible. We'd like to place a ground station in central Asia to help anchor communications with our drifting sensors. Lhasa would be perfect for us, and it would also help them with international bandwidth as well."

"What does it weigh?" Brian asked.

"The whole package comes to less than 10 kg", Dave interjected. "They are disguised to look like a plant in a flower pot. The leaves are organic solar panels, and they also collect rainwater to use to make hydrogen, which runs a fuel-cell for backup power at night and on cloudy days. They work best on high ground with full sun exposure, and maybe a rock wall around, so they don't get knocked over by animals. Other than that, their only requirement is a couple of liters of rainwater every 6 months to recharge the hydrogen generator. Can you find a secure site in Lhasa and someone to check it occasionally?"

"Ten kg we can manage, no sweat. How about setting it up in a monastery?" Mike asked. "I'm guessing the monks there are pretty dependable."

"That'd work," replied Ivan. "But tell me. Are you guys able to carry enough food and our transmitter? You're not going to go hungry because of us?"

"We're still working out the details," Brian replied, "but we think we can mount the Mars Mission liquid food generator..."

"You mean the Princess' smoothie machine?" Barry interjected.

"...the 'smoothie machine' in the airship," Brian continued evenly, "and also a larger solar array on top as well. The smoothie machine can feed up to 5 people as long as we stay up in good sunlight. We'll use the solar array to process rainwater collected from clouds to generate oxygen to breathe, but also to make extra hydrogen that we can use in the turbines to extend our range."

"What's our timeline", Ivan asked? Mike noticed he had said "our timeline" rather than "your timeline". He also wondered why they were referring to Lhamo as 'Princess'.

"Adding the smoothie machine and a larger solar array to the airship is strictly cut and paste," Brian explained. "It's completely independent of the hyperbaric tube structure and well within the mission payload, so we can have that done within a month. How long will it take for your software guys to come up with the global atmospheric flow predictor software?"

Ivan looked at Barry, who held up all 10 fingers, and raised his eyebrows. Ivan nodded, and so did Dave. "If we have the key people in that group drop everything else, maybe a week. Letting the programmers go home to sleep occasionally, more like ten days to two weeks. Give us a month, and we'll have it glitch-free and beta-tested by bringing a couple of our drifters down to your operational altitude to see how well we predict where they actually go."

"Sounds good to us," Mike said with a smile.

It felt like they had done what they came to do, but no one moved. After a pause, Ivan asked. "So after you get back, then what?"

"I'm pretty busy at the Rum Works, and there'll be milk machines and bugs to make and deliver," Mike replied.

"And your airships? Are you going to sell them?" Barry asked.

"We currently use them to service the Rum Works franchises, and we'll use them to service the milk machine sites as well," Brian replied. "And like I said, if you guys want a couple, we can arrange that."

"Why not build a fleet of them and re-establish some international trade?" Ivan asked. No one else is dependably getting cargo into the interior of the continents, and the Pacific basin is like the Wild West for surface ships. There's high value cargo out there begging for a ride."

"We've thought about that," Mike replied. "For starters, we'll be happy if we can get in and out of Lhasa just once without anyone knowing what we are up to. But if we try to do it on a regular basis, I'm guessing there are pirate forces out there that would love to take us down. We're almost a three hundred feet long. That's a big target. And besides, despite being much more economical than any heavier-than-air craft, when we drive our airships back and forth on a scheduled route, they are still net carbon consumers. We'd like to find a way to get away from that."

"What Barry is hinting at is that we are looking for stable platforms around the globe through which we can channel data flow," Ivan admitted. "They don't have to be stationary like the one you are taking to Lhasa, but it would help if they were bigger units than our high altitude drifters. Those communications payloads way up there at 25 km altitude are limited to a couple of kilos, and the weather patterns up there dictate that they eventually end up congregating at either the equator or the poles."

"You mentioned the Iridium cascade," Ivan continued, pointing up towards the heavens. "When that chain-reaction of satellite collisions took down all near-Earth satellites in 2015, it forced us down into undersea fiber-optic cables. And then the tsunami tore the guts out of the cable network serving half the world. So right now, at the international level, we're stuck with the drifters. For us, that's like trying to breathe through a soda straw. We absolutely need to get more bandwidth."

Mike leaned over and asked Brian, "you want to tell them about your gondola idea?"

"What else are you guys flying?" asked Barry.

"Nothing yet," replied Brian. "Mike's been on a roll, and he thinks we can keep it going "

"He's right," Mike admitted. "We were brainstorming on our way out here, but our concept is still pie in the sky. Or perhaps I should say, a pie plate in the sky."

"We're on vacation here for the next..." Ivan glanced up at his display "...17 hours. We've got time. Let's hear it."

"Anybody besides me want a beer?" Barry asked. He responded to the universal nods by keying his display.

Brian took a deep breath and decided to stand up. "There are a lot of unresolved issues, but here's the elevator spiel. We've been experimenting with making the diamond fabric into a conductor, and by chance stumbled onto a process to make it photovoltaic. What we've got in the lab right now is much lighter and also more efficient than the best current silicon or organic solar panels. It's the alpha-version of this product that we are planning to put on our dirigible out there for next month's trip to Lhasa. We think we can get 10-15 kW worth of fabric ready in time, which is plenty to supply us with oxygen, power, and a back-up source of hydrogen on the off-chance we spring a leak."

Brian walked to the end of the long spruce table and made a circular motion with his right hand. "But if we put this fabric on top of a 10-meter diameter disc at 10,000 meters altitude," Brian continued, "we could get 25-30 kilowatts of power. If we make the disc into a flat balloon 3 meters thick and fill it with hydrogen, we get enough lift to carry one human, a smoothie machine, and an electrolysis unit to use most of that power to make hydrogen and oxygen out of water. The life support systems are housed in a two meter diameter gondola hung beneath the disc balloon. The occupant uses the oxygen to breathe and saves the hydrogen. If we stack two more 3-meter thick discs on top of each other, we get enough lift to accumulate and carry enough water to make 100 kg of processed hydrogen. Adding one of your 10 kg data transfer nodes to this rig would not be a big problem as long as its power demand is less than a kilowatt."

Dave nodded, and Brian continued. "This would be a passive platform, kind of like your current high altitude drifters, but with one big difference. Although it won't have a motor for propulsion, if your new software works out – let's call it NAF, for Newdle Atmospheric Flow – the occupant in this rig could chart a pretty predictable course to almost any place on Earth by changing altitude to get in or out of the various jet streams."

As Mike listened to this completely unrehearsed spiel from Brian, he knew he'd found a worthy successor to his uncle. Señor Dude was really good at this.

"All that said, there are three major unresolved issues," Brian continued. "First, most people go crazy if stuck in a small container for weeks at a time. They get 'cabin fever'. For the NASA Mars mission, we estimated that we'd need to screen 3000 candidates to find just five people suitable to go to Mars and back. Second, muscles tend to atrophy when they don't exercise, and the payload for this unit does not include a weight bench or treadmill, so over time the occupant will get skinny and weak. Third, radiation up there at 10,000 meters is many times what it is down here, so it's unlikely people could live up there permanently."

The beer was delivered. Dave handed them around. It was a local Boise pale ale.

Ivan leaned over the table and asked Brian; "why 10,000 meters?"

"Because that's high enough to get above the brown layer and most of the clouds," Brian replied. "You need to be up there to get optimum output from the solar panels. It's also the minimum altitude to stay above most of the weather and turbulence, but it's low enough that you can still ride the jet streams and breathe enriched oxygen in a non-pressurized gondola."

"Some of our programmers don't leave their cubicles for a week except to hit the bathroom and vending machines," Barry volunteered. "So maybe we've already done the behavioral screening for you."

Seriously, Dr. Solis," Ivan continued, "we've got employees who could just as well work up there as down here. And with the 10 kg communication nodes aboard, bandwidth won't be a problem. These folks in your balloons will have the best virtual reality environment in the world. They could do real-time megaplayer games without a millisecond of lag. But how do you handle the fact that normal people need to piss and take an occasional crap?"

"For the Mars Project, we were developing ultra-thin catheters to use in the bladder and colon," Brian responded. "Now that we've got diamond fabric tubes that allow us to work at ultrahigh pressures, we've made excellent progress on the catheters. Everything that comes out through the catheters gets sterilized by hyperbaric pasteurization and then goes directly back into the nutrient mix. There it is used to grow Mike's bugs which produce the food components that come back out through Lhamo's smoothie machine. It's a closed nutrient cycle powered by sunlight. We aren't ready to use the catheters on the Lhasa trip, but we're close. Maybe the next trip after that."

"Who owns the IP on the Mars Project technology – like the smoothie machine and the catheters?" Ivan asked. "Do you guys have clear rights to use them going forward?"

"They are jointly owned by the US government and Hamiltonian University, and both owners have licensing rights," Brian responded. "However Diamond Fabrics has negotiated a ten year non-exclusive option on all of that technology. Plus we were able to pick up some key players from the Mars project when it got shut down."

"Interesting. When did you do that deal on their IP?" Ivan asked.

"A few days after the tsunami", said Brian. "Mike's uncle at the Rum Works did it in his capacity as a Diamond Fabrics board member at a very opportune time. The US Treasury was suddenly looking at a world of hurt, so he got their immediate cooperation and really good terms."

"How is your uncle, by the way?" Barry asked, fixing his gaze square-ly at Mike.

Mike looked away and paused a second before answering. "Unfor-tunately, as I'm guessing you already know, he's dead," Mike said, looking at Dave, who nodded sad acknowledgement, and then back to Barry. "He was murdered right after he figured out that the Mars Project was DOA and closed the deal for its IP. He went out to check on one of our prototype milk machines that was malfunctioning and got fried by an electrical discharge mine someone hid under it. In the post tsunami confusion, we never got a death certificate. We quietly buried him among the sugar maples in his woodlot as his will specified. But on paper, he's still alive. Except for my mom, a few of our employees in Vermont, those present here, and a couple of the Diamond Fabrics guys in Alberta, no one else knows. The word in town is that he became a recluse. Can we keep this quiet until things settle down and we figure how to resolve it?"

Ivan looked at Dave, who nodded slightly, and then looked back at Mike. "We're really sorry about your uncle, Mike. But I hope you understand, we had to get that out on the table. On paper, you and your uncle own half of Diamond Fabrics. In addition, he owns half of the Rum Works, right?" Mike nodded. "What we are planning here today depends upon these two businesses being organizationally viable," Ivan continued. "Who's filling in for your uncle right now?"

"My mother and I together own the other 50% of the Rum Works," Mike replied. "I'm helping on the technical side, but the business is mostly done by my mom, and she's doing a great job so far. At

Diamond Fabrics, I've been added to their Board of Directors to effectively represent my family's interests. And frankly, having Dr. Solis up there now as their Chief Science Officer adds a wealth of engineering and organizational expertise that I lack. So I think both businesses are sound, and that's supported by how well we've done these last 6 months, despite the social and economic turmoil." Mike looked from Barry to Ivan.

"We only met your uncle once, but we really liked him, and we admired how he structured your ethanol business. He will be missed," Ivan replied somberly, and then paused. "That said, however, Anton did our due diligence and came to almost the same conclusion you just stated. We think the interlocking teams you have in both companies are sound and form an excellent platform for further growth. So we're okay with this as it stands," Ivan concluded with a reassuring smile. "As long as you want, from a business perspective, Michael Barber still lives."

Mike let out a big sigh. "Thanks".

"So here's what we want to do," said Ivan after a glance at Barry. "We'll fund the prototype of your disc balloon plus gondola rig. If it works, we want an option to buy a hundred of them. Our people will negotiate price with your people after the prototype flies, and we'll tell ours to leave their claws at home."

"We are interested in two things here." Barry continued. "First, we get back a lot of bandwidth in the mid-latitudes. Second, we like the idea of being able to drop an appreciable amount of hydrogen from the sky into selected markets. Your ethanol gig is great, Mike, but it only works in the woods. We think that the world hydrogen economy will be huge, particularly when the population centers come back, and we want to continue to be a substantial player in it. Your disc-plus-gondola rigs could help solve what we foresee as a major distribution headache. Deal?"

Mike looked at Brian and held his hand up palms out. Brian nodded to Mike and replied, "Deal".

Mike locked eyes with Barry and asked, "why?"

"Because there are jerks out there who will try to control regional hydrogen markets, create shortages, and gouge consumers on the ground when they're desperate for power. Remember that Enron thing from the Bush years? No, you were a bit young then, but we sure do. Day after day we went black in Silicon Valley because those jerks in Texas were allowed to steal from us and get away with it."

"Correct me if I'm wrong," Ivan continued, looking down from having done something on his heads-up display, "but I estimate that just these first 100 drifting rigs could produce 1000 kg of hydrogen per day. That's only a small amount on the global scale, but it's the flexibility of distribution that will make the difference. If we could drop that much hydrogen from your balloons into any regional market at will, we'd have a start on a system to prevent price gouging and market manipulation. It's that simple. "

"I like that." Mike replied, paused, and then asked, "but can I change the subject and ask what's with this 'princess' thing?"

"Look, Mike, we know you two are tight," Ivan replied in a fatherly tone. "But you should know, Lhamo's mother was born in the Dali Lhama's family. There's no royal dynasty in Tibet, but she's the next best thing to a princess. She's a special person there. If you are planning on going there and bringing her back here, you need to know that."

•   •   •

As they stood together outside waiting for B³ to complete its inflation, Brian turned to Mike and asked, "So Amigo, do you ever pinch yourself to see if this is real? Like, a couple of years ago I was just a middle-aged, divorced, Tex-Mex rocket-jock punching my time card every day at NASA. Now you've got me volunteering to climb into a big bag of hydrogen, drink smoothies made from yesterday's shit, and sail into an array of international no-go zones with a funky search engine watching my back. If I wrote a book about this, they'd file it in the science fiction section. This is seriously weird."

Mike put his hand on Brian's shoulder. "Yeah, Señor Dude, it is".

CHAPTER 16

HELL IN A BUCKET
August 2030

On their eighth day out, their luck changed.

Up to that point, everything had worked pretty well, and they were a bit ahead of schedule. No one had bothered them as they slid south of Ireland, over southern England, across France and Italy, down the Mediterranean, across the Sinai, Red Sea, and the Saudi Republic. Now they were out over the Arabian Sea, a hundred miles south of Persia. Their plan was to make landfall on the Indian subcontinent south of Karachi, transit northern India, and cross into Tibet just west of Nepal.

Mike had the con, and Brian was sleeping. They were maintaining zero electronic emissions and drifting 8800 meters up in a cloudless sky with the motors shut down. Their first indication of trouble came from one of the tail cameras which picked up motion and then imaged an approaching high speed aircraft about 80 km astern. Mike immediately turned on the radar transponder and powered up their high resolution Doppler radar. It indicated that the aircraft was approaching at close to 900 km per hour – clearly an old hydrocarbon fighter jet. Mike reached down and shook Brian's shoulder.

Five minutes later, the jet rocked them with a high speed pass up their left side a hundred meters away, crossed in front of them, pulled up into a slow and easy loop/roll combination, and then came back down their right side.

Mike's headset lit up with an incoming transmission that was identified as Farsi. "Unmarked white airship. Identify yourself and turn north to heading 16 degrees and follow me to my base, or you will be destroyed."

Mike responded with a message in Farsi. "We are Canadian Airship B-three. We are on an international relief mission, and we are in international airspace. Please clear our area."

Mike muted his headset and turned to Brian. "This guy doesn't sound real friendly, and he's armed with a 20 mm cannon. If he opens fire, we're not going to fare well."

"Damn straight, Amigo. I think we should act like we are complying, but fly really slow on his 16 degree heading. He'll have to circle us, and he's likely to run low on fuel before we get close to land. Maybe we can figure something else out in the mean time."

Their radar showed the aircraft turning about 25 km behind them in preparation for making another pass. Mike was about to start the turbines. At that moment, Mike's headset indicated a different incoming message. It was Dave from Newdle, who insisted "Give me access to your radar and video images. I think we can get this guy off your back." Mike complied.

Within seconds, a new voice hailed the fighter aircraft. "This is the International News Network. We are monitoring your actions and sending live video to millions of viewers. You and your ground control authority may want to consider this before you take aggressive action against an international relief mission."

Thirty seconds later, now less than five km behind them, the aircraft pulled up abruptly, rolled 180 degrees going over the top, cut power, and disappeared out of visual contact going north the way he had come.

Mike immediately shut down the radar and the transponder, fired up the turbines, swung the nose 30 degrees further south, and hustled B^3 away at her maximum speed of 150 mph. If anyone came back to look for them, he wanted to be somewhere else and hard to find. And before he shut down all electronic emissions, he thanked Dave for his help. "What time is it there in California? Four a.m.?"

"Yeah, it's four in the morning here. But a little electronic birdie told me you guys had company, so I got up to watch. Safe travels, Amigos."

"Thanks, Dave." Brian said. "We're happy you've got our back, buddy. Hasta luego!"

An hour later they cut the motors and recalculated their course. It hadn't changed much except that now they were even more ahead of schedule. This wasn't good news because they wanted to come into Lhasa at about midnight the day after tomorrow, and now it looked like it might be 10 pm instead. They'd have to re-calculate. This was the first time they'd asked the software to get them somewhere slower rather than faster, but the Newdle Atmospheric Flow system seemed to respond just fine, taking them up to 10,500 meters where the winds were lighter.

As the excitement drained away, they analyzed their interaction with the fighter plane. First, how had they been spotted? No one had enough jet fuel for routine hydrocarbon aircraft patrols, but maybe the Persians had a MacCready[13] node aircraft orbiting at 25,000 meters with a lookdown camera to monitor their southern border. Clearly they hadn't been picked up on radar because radio waves just went right through the diamond fabric. It generated zero radar reflections. They could only be seen on radar when their transponder was turned on.

Second, the fighter pilot clearly did not have a clue what they were. Thus the two observation passes. Third, for the time being at least, social pressure seemed to work on the Persians. They wondered who else had seen Dave's live feed and heard about their 'international relief mission'. They both used their headsets to scan what live news feeds they could pick up in the area, and no one was mentioning anything about international relief. Maybe Dave had been able to isolate his live feed to southern Persia, so hopefully Pakistan, India, and China hadn't been alerted.

They were also curious to know how Dave had picked up the inter-action with the fighter so quickly. The radio challenge in Farsi was probably picked up by a Newdle drifter, but clearly Dave had set up scanning software that triggered an almost instantaneous alert. Or maybe he'd picked up the communication that had directed the fighter to go check them out in the first place, so he knew it was coming before they did. Either way, it was clear that Dave was invest-ing a lot of computing muscle to watching their path.

•　　•　　•

A day later, their luck seemed to be holding. Dense clouds with tops above 11,000 meters blanketed the coast of southern Pakistan. Down at 10,100 meters, their white diamond fabric clad airship blended in with the clouds, making visual ID virtually impossible.

Across northern India they drifted, mostly among the Monsoon clouds, motors off and emitting no radiation. Then the air currents shifted without warning. Rather than taking them on the predicted course to the north of New Delhi, strong currents developed that held them south, driving them quickly down the southern side of the Himalayas rather than letting them slide across the northern edge of the mountains into western Tibet.

Time for plan B. Their prototype NAF software was designed to navigate by pure drifting. The option of using the motors intermit-tently was not integrated into this alpha-version of their course plot-ting software. They had to improvise by telling the software they were someplace else, and if being there seemed to predict a better option, they could go to that place using the motors and then see what happened. They'd had to do this twice in the last nine days, first when they were south of Ireland and then again over the Alps. It was looking like mountains and islands were navigation hazards for atmospheric drifters.

The good news was that they still had almost half of their initial fuel load. They'd done surprisingly well so far using the winds, so they still had enough fuel to make a fully powered flight to Lhasa from here if need be, even against moderate winds. But not knowing for sure how much fuel they'd actually get in Lhasa, they didn't want to be spendthrift. Both of them sat there on the crew benches, using their headsets to plot options, figuring time and fuel needs to various points north of the mountains.

Finally Brian said, "Got it!" He traced a path in the air out in front of his headset. "If we stay in this current flow pattern for 12 hrs, it will carry us rapidly down to southern Bhutan. If we drive up over the mountains now, we'll have headwinds all the way into Lhasa. But look at this, if we drift past Bhutan and then turn north, we'll have the wind partially with us on the last leg, and we still won't enter Chinese airspace. It's longer, but it uses less fuel, and the timing works out just about right. What do you think?"

Mike synched his headset view with Brian's NAF file, looked at the numbers, and the 3D map of their projected path for a few seconds and then nodded. "I like it. This will also take us over our probable route when we come back out of Lhasa, so it will be good to have scouted it. The less fuel we need to use on that first leg out of Dodge, the more options we'll have going the rest of the way home."

Eleven hours later, they were easing north across the east end of Bhutan at 11,300 meters under moderate power. They were treated to a spectacular sunset over the Himalayas, the alabaster ice-covered peaks rising above valleys shrouded in purple haze backlit by deep reds and gold. Mike captured some of the camera output, including a zoom shot of the sun sinking behind Lotse and Chomolungma, the Sherpa name for Everest. It was breath-taking footage, and he planned to zip it out to Stephanie and Angel once they were in the clear over the Pacific on the home-bound flight. He found himself silently singing the line from one of the Dead's later songs: *'I may be going to hell in a bucket, baby, but at least I'm enjoying the ride'.*

Below them, the mountains began to slope away as they moved north, and they slid the airship down into the darkness below 6500 meters to capture the best northwest flow, easing off on the power. They sailed at an angle against the breeze rising up from China off to their east, heading for their touchdown point just outside Lhasa. They were both excited but alert. Brian, who had the con, made transient use of their Doppler to check for mountain downdrafts that might plunge them into the peaks below. Ten days out and almost there, they didn't want to mess it up now.

The agreement was that they would use a low power directional radio to signal their arrival when they were 50 km from touchdown. Mike and Brian did not know if Dave had been able to get a visual track on them from the Newdle drifters. If so, they might be expected.

Thirty minutes past midnight, and Mike made the call. "B-cubed calling Lhasa".

There was a pause. Then came the reply "Welcome home, big brother. We will turn a light on for you."

Darkness. They came over the last ridge, a few scattered lights could be seen in the city to the left, and what looked like two signal fires burned on the fortress walls high above it to the northwest. But they were supposed to be met east of the city. Down they came. Altitude read 3800 meters, less than 500 meters above the ground. 3600 meters, and there slightly to the right ahead of them, a rectangle of lights suddenly appeared out of darkness.

They could see about 30 people waving small bright lights around the edge of a soccer field. Pointing the nose of B^3 into the wind, Brian maneuvered the ship to touch down at a slight angle on the field. He released the tethers, and simultaneously initiated the hydrogen pumps to rapidly kill lift. Then he and Mike shared a brief hand-shake, released the electrostatic exit flap, and walked out onto the soccer field, where all but one light had been turned off.

Mike walked towards the man holding the light. The solid turf felt funny under his feet after 10 days in the crew gondola with its soft, moving floor. As they approached each other, Mike recognized him from his picture. It was Lhamo's brother, Dorje.

"Welcome, brother," came his greeting. "You have come like a ghost in your white ship. How may we assist you to make it disappear?"

"Thank you for your excellent reception," Mike replied, shaking his hand. "We were very happy to see your lights. Yes, please help us remove the cargo. In a few minutes, it will be pumped down. After we detach the fuel and hydrogen bladders, you can help us fold up the ship. Do you have a place to store it?"

"It is indeed a remarkable ship. Someday I want to fly in it," Dorje said admiringly. He turned and pointed. "Yes. We have an old truck over there. It is covered and can hold up to 36 cubic meters and 8000 kg. Is that enough?"

"Yes, more than enough. We can roll the hydrogen and fuel bladders off the field and cover them. The rest of the ship only weighs 400 kg and should fit easily in your truck."

Twenty minutes later they were done. When the sun rose in the morning, someone would need to be very curious to find evidence of B³'s presence. The group assembled, and they divided up the cargo – enough bugs to supply 2 milk machines for 1 year each, plus the Newdle transmitter. They began to walk west towards the dark city. Brian and Mike each carried a light pack with personal items and presents.

As they passed an occasional light, Mike tried to assess the group. A few of the men wore traditional Tibetan clothing, but most appeared to be monks with shaved heads, dark orange robes, and sandals. Mike felt a bit chilly in the cold mountain air despite his full flight suit and hood, but the monks looked completely at ease despite wearing much less.

After walking silently for twenty minutes, they came to a car parked by the road, an ancient Toyota Corolla. The monks put the Newdle transmitter in the trunk, bid goodbye to Lhamo's brother, and walked on to the west carrying the milk machine supplies. Mike, Brian, Dorje, and one other man got in the car and drove slowly into town.

"What can I get for you?" Dorje asked as he drove. "Food, Tea? A bath?"

"Yes to all three," Mike replied. "And where is Lhamo? Is she okay?"

"She's fine. She's waiting for you. Dave from Newdle saw you come across the mountains east of Bhutan, so we knew when you would arrive."

"Damn!" thought Mike. "I'm sure glad the Chinese didn't succeed in their hostile take-over attempt of Newdle back when the renminbi was strong."

CHAPTER 17

CLOSE TO HEAVEN
Late August 2030

It was a bit awkward. They'd followed Lhamo's brother up the narrow staircase to the second floor. The fourth man, obviously a guard, remained on the street level. Brian and Mike were dressed in their seamless one-piece flight suits made of light silver-gray diamond fabric with hidden electrostatic zippers. Even with their hoods down and headsets off, they still looked like spacemen.

The stairs led to a large room that opened into a central atrium. They were greeted there by Lhamo, who wore a traditional robe, embroidered wool stockings, and a scarf. Her eyes met Mike's, held them for an extra second while she observed him, and then she nodded slightly. Breaking gaze, she walked over to greet Brian first.

"You look like you have just come back from Mars, Brian, but it is very good to see you. And I thank you for teaching my young and foolish friend how to fly and not hit mountains." She was smiling as she gave Brian a hug. She turned to Mike. "Welcome to Lhasa… and to my home," she said, and gave him a long, tight hug. "Please sit. We will have tea."

After the tea was served (Mike declined the added yak butter), they talked briefly about the airship, her extractors, and the new experimental solar fabric. Lhamo was delighted to hear that most of their food during the flight had come from her machine, and that it was still operating well.

"When I built that prototype before the tsunami, it could run for 30 days before the disc surfaces had to be replaced. Now I have discs that should last a year, so we will upgrade your machine while you are here. That will not take long, so we can do it when you inflate your ship before you leave." Lhamo shifted her gaze from Mike to Brian. "How long will you stay?" she asked.

"We have a communication system from Newdle that they want installed here to anchor their network in central Asia, and we need to find some additional fuel for the airship," Brian replied. "We did very well with fuel outbound. We still have almost 40% of our initial load left. Is there fuel we can buy here, and what kind?"

"We don't have much ethanol here. We have methane from biomass and hydrogen from hydropower." Lhamo's brother replied. "But we have been saving petrol for you, and we can get 1000 liters delivered to the field whenever you are ready. Can you use petrol?"

"Yes, our flex fuel turbines like it just fine," Brian replied. "And we probably only need 500 liters."

"We will save the rest for the next trip," Lhamo stated firmly. "And the bugs you brought for the milk machines are more than enough payment. That will supply the monks with 300 liters of milk per day for a year to give to the children. But when do you need to leave?"

Mike struggled to stay with the conversation. He was tired after the ten days of tension, flying B³. His head ached. "How safe is the airship in that truck out there by the soccer field?"

"It is very safe," Dorje replied, his arms folded across his chest. "The people who met you tonight can be trusted, and the truck is being guarded by the monks."

"Then we are in no rush to leave," Mike said. "I'd like some time on the ground to get used to this altitude, to walking, and I'd like to get to know Lhasa."

"Good. Then you two should go to bed," ordered Lhamo. "It will be dawn soon. I will tell Dave you are here. And while you sleep, we will find some real clothes for you. In those spacesuits, the Han spies will spot you from a kilometer away!"

• • •

Mike lay still in the bed. There was sunlight behind the curtain. He was in a small room with masonry walls, a door, and a window. He sat up. The floor was covered by a fine wool rug, thick and warm under his feet. He went to the window and looked down to the street below. A man in loose white pants and a colorful wool cape was leading a yak up the street, pulling a cart full of vegetables. He was probably going to a market. Mike remembered Brian's comment about pinching himself. This was 2030, but he felt like he had flown a couple hundred years back in time.

There was a bowl of water and a pile of clothes on a table next to the door. Dark pants, white cotton shirt, wool cape. Mike wiped some depilatory cream on his face, splashed it off with some water, and dried off on a small towel. The clothes were loose but comfortable. He took a deep breath and opened the door. His third floor room opened out onto the central atrium. He descended an ornate wooden staircase to the second level, and then he followed his nose to a room at the back where he found Lhamo cooking on a small gas burner.

She turned and said, "you look good".

"So do you," he replied. They embraced. She let him hold her for a second. "I've missed you".

"I have missed you too, Mike. I am happy that you are safely here. At first I was afraid after I asked you to travel around the world to come to me, but now I am not. We are following the Vajrayana[14], which means the diamond path, and you have come to me in a diamond airship wearing diamond clothes. It is as it should be."

"I need to understand that better".

"In time you will," she said. Lhamo put her hands on Mike's shoulders and searched his face as she said, "I was very sorry to learn of your uncle's death. He was burdened with a great power that was hard for him to carry. His life has given us many gifts, and we must work hard to pass them on to others."

'He was killed by people who feared him," Mike retorted.

"No, Mike." Lhamo replied quietly. "He was killed by the power of his message. Our message. Now he lives in us. People with his power do not die. They are reincarnated."

"Perhaps someday I'll understand that, too," Mike replied lamely.

"Perhaps someday you will." Lhamo replied. "But now I will feed you. It is just tea, oat porridge, and yak butter, but it will help make your headache go away."

"How did you know I have a headache?" Mike asked.

"This is Lhasa. We are almost 3500 meters high. I think you used too much oxygen while you were flying here. Last night you and Brian were breathless from climbing one flight of stairs. The next time, reduce your oxygen to 40% when you are at 10,000 meters, not 50%, and you will have no headache when you get here."

"Do you always mix religion, physiology, and nutrition?" Mike asked with a quizzical smile.

"They are one," she replied firmly. "Eat."

•   •   •

Three hours later they were climbing the thousand steps up to the palace above Lhasa, the Potala. They'd left Brian in bed with more altitude sickness than tea and porridge could cure . Step after step, turn after turn. The city lay below them, and in the distance spread the high Tibetan plain backstopped by the Himalayas. It was like Vermont but magnified by a factor of four. When they'd started out,

Mike was carrying the Newdle transmitter, but less than a quarter of the way up, he'd relinquished the burden to Lhamo. His breathing was harsh and urgent; hers was deep and relaxed.

"In two weeks, you would become comfortable here," she said.

"I can't wait," he gasped.

She stopped climbing and turned to him. "But I do not think you should stay that long. Soon the Han spies will discover that you are here. I would like for you to stay a long time, but it is not safe. The Han have sealed our borders to the east. They want to isolate us to make us weak. They will be unhappy that you have found a way to come here without walking from the south for weeks over the mountains."

"But even if we made regular trips, we could not bring you much cargo. Why would they worry about that?"

"My people have always been self reliant. What we need does not weigh much, like your milk machine bugs and this Newdle communications node to connect us to the world," she said, pointing to her pack. "Also, my brother is very impressed with your new solar fabric. It will work well for us here at 3500 meters. We will need more power to make the discs. And when you leave, you can take my extractor discs out for your milk machines in America. The machines you may build there, but the discs are only made here."

"Where do you actually make them?" Mike asked.

Lhamo smiled and pointed up. "In the palace. It is secure. My brother directs the monks, and my uncle watches over him."

"And who is your uncle?" Mike asked.

"You will meet him when you have climbed to the top." She smiled and resumed her climb. Mike followed, slowly, finding his pace in the thin air, working his way upward. He tried not to think of Lhamo's lithe body climbing easily up ahead of him, and it took all of his concentration to keep looking down at the steps in front of him.

Now was not the time to break a leg. He wondered if she might learn to play tennis...

•   •   •

The four of them sat in a room with a view of the mountains. Mike thought of Newdle's Idaho retreat and of his uncle's office at the Rum Works. Somehow he seemed to connect with people who liked mountains.

Lhamo's uncle was a small man with delicate features, quiet demeanor, and intense eyes. He wore local clothing, not the robes of a monk. Their discussion started with the Newdle transmitter. The uncle asked about its function and how it was powered. To Mike's surprise, Lhamo's brother answered these questions and clearly knew a lot about the instrument. Obviously, Dave had been talking with the locals. There were no objections to setting it up in a protected place on the palace grounds.

The next topic was the disc business. Lhamo explained how Mike's bugs produced the nutrients and her discs removed them to make liquid food. Neither part was effective without the other. She explained that Mike's bugs were protected by his patents in the US but also because almost no one in the world knew how to create bacteria to do his bidding the way Mike did.

She paused, looked down, and then said quietly, "I do not trust patents, but I can design good surfaces, and Dorje, here, can make them. For now, we will make them only in Lhasa, and we must find a way to ship them to those who will pay us for them."

"Who will use them?" Lhamo's uncle asked.

"Starting now, and increasingly in the future, anyone who wants milk, butter, or cheese," she replied.

"And how many people will you need to make them?" The uncle asked, looking from Lhamo to Dorje.

"Right now we have eight people in our shop using the equipment we assembled for the US-China Mars project," Dorje answered. "Newdle has ordered 100 machines. To make discs for hundreds of milk machines, we will need as many as 50 people and space for more equipment."

Lhamo's uncle thought for a moment. "There is enough space here in the Palace, and our monks are happy with the work. We will also need more of these machines to make milk for our people. But there is the problem of shipping our discs to the United States for your machines there as long as the Han continue their blockade. How will you deal with this?"

"The airship I came in would be able to make a trip here once each month," Mike replied. "But we must find a secure route that avoids flying over dangerous regions. If we can do this, and if there is more demand for the discs, we could build more airships and visit more frequently."

"Then we will invest in making these discs," said the small man with the intense eyes, which he now directed at Mike.

"And now we will talk about you and our Lhamo," he said. "Do you honor her, and can you provide for her?"

Mike was stunned. He hadn't anticipated anything this direct, but his answer came without hesitation.

"Yes." He replied. "I do, and I can."

"Then if she chooses you, we will accept it." The uncle said firmly.

•   •   •

Mike and Lhamo walked out of the palace in silence. She stopped next to a low wall overlooking the city. "You know that my father disappeared in the 2010 unrest. Then, when I was seventeen, my uncle became my guardian when my mother died. He is the oldest son in her family, so he still feels responsible for me.   I am sorry if he offended you."

"Offended? No. Surprised? Yes." Mike paused and met her gaze. "So, will you choose me?"

"Someday, Michael Anderson, but it is not yet the right time."

"When will it be the right time?" He asked.

"There is too much uncertainty in our world right now," she said seriously. "And besides, you are still too young and foolish," she added with a smile.

•   •   •

Before descending to the city, Lhamo took Mike to another part of the Potala, through a series of corridors to an area in the 1500 room palace off-limits to tourists.   She walked up to an unusually modern door with no handle or visible lock, looked into a retinal scanner, and the door released with a faint 'pop'.   She pushed it open and led Mike into a small, glass room that opened into a larger room with modern lighting and a series of benches and work stations. The benches were occupied by ovens, presses and complex instruments being operated by men with shaved heads wearing goggles, surgical masks, and white suits. One corner at the far end of the work space was enclosed with dark glass, and someone inside was sitting before a large device that was giving off bursts of very bright, colored light.

"The good thing about being a monk and working in here is you don't need to wear a hairnet," Lhamo said, smiling. "That's my brother inside the engraving booth. The discs are pressed out of photo-sensitive nanoparticles over a radial lace of silver threads that come together at the center of the disc. The different colored lasers in the engraving instrument make the various nana-particles take different shapes. Different shapes hold different molecules made by your bacteria. The shaped spaces only hold your food molecules when that part of the disc is electrically charged. But when we re-lease the charge on each silver thread, that part of the disc then releases its molecules. That vacuum oven, over there, coats the disc with a layer of gold only a few atoms thick. That is the newest step we have developed in the last few months. It extends the life of the disc to a year or more."

Mike nodded in appreciation. "This is remarkable. And you developed these techniques yourself?"

"Yes and no," Lhamo replied. "I had a lot of help from my brother. I started working on photo engraved nanoparticular surfaces when I was in Beijing. Back then I tried using a paddlewheel and a solvent wash to release the bound molecules. That was too slow and getting rid of the solvent was a problem. It was at Cal Tech that I had the idea of spinning a disc between two chambers and using a releasable electric charge to let the molecules go on the food collection side of the barrier. But the monks here in Lhasa have been working with woven silver and gold plating for a thousand years. There are thousands of tapestries in this building containing silver and gold threads, so that part of the disc comes from my heritage. And a year ago, one of the monks out there suggested that we use a coating of gold to preserve the disc surfaces and make them last longer."

"And you had this operation hidden here in the palace during the Mars project?"

"Oh, no," Lhamo replied. "Until the tsunami forced the Han army to withdraw, they occupied the Potala and had it preserved like a pagan shrine. After the Dalai Lama had to flee in 1959, most of the monks were forced out, and the Potala has been like an empty vessel waiting to be refilled. That has happened only in the last 6 months. The body of the 14th Dalai Lama has been carried back over the mountains from Dharmsala by thousands of our people and is now at rest here in his stupa, and the 15th Dalai Lama has come back to guide us."

"So where did you make the discs for our first extractors?" Mike asked.

"In the house of my uncle's nephew, my second cousin. He did not marry and became a monk after training as an engineer. He is one of the men here today. There, the one operating the press," she said, pointing. "We only moved back into the Potala after the Han army left."

"Is your uncle the Dalai Lama?" Mike asked.

Lhamo gazed at Mike sternly for a second. "You spent a month preparing and ten days coming here. Just five seconds of research on Newdle could have answered that question."

"We were under zero emissions blackout the whole time, Princess. But please, tell me about your uncle."

"Do not call me that," she countered.

"That's what the boys at Newdle call you." Mike replied defensively. "They were the ones who told me you are related to the Dalai Lama."

In a moment of weakness, Lhamo allowed herself to frown. She had spent her whole life dealing with men like this – many of whom called themselves 'geeks' with perverse pride. Some like her brother and Mike were remarkably good geeks and maybe that extended to the 'boys' at Newdle as well. But in school here in Lhasa, at the University in Beijing, at Cal Tech, and at the Mars project in St Louis, she had spent her whole life coping with geeks, typically male, superficially informed, but fully confident. By definition, a geek lacked both balance and insight. She took a deep breath, and she was centered. Her frown disappeared.

"What did you just do?" Mike asked.

"I forgave you for being young and foolish, Michael Anderson," Lhamo replied. "Now I will tell you about my uncle. He is the nephew of the 14th Dalai Lama, but on his mother's side. There were many children in that family, and my uncle's name is different. In 1959, he was a small boy, so he did not need to flee to India. He trained himself in financial management. How do you say? He became a clerk? He worked with the Han invaders. He helped them make the Potala into a tourist destination. While they made money from what they regarded as a pagan shrine, my uncle worked to preserve it. The 15th Dalai Lama was selected as a child and protected from the Han invaders. Now he lives here in the home my uncle helped to save for him. So my uncle has an important position in the palace, but he is not related to this Dalai Lama."

"Oh," was all Mike could manage.

"When I was born," she continued, "my mother had a dream and named me Lhamo, which means 'goddess'. In her dream, she was told that I am the reincarnation of a powerful person. But I am neither goddess nor princess. I am just a woman. And like all people, I am one with my ancestors, and I am part of the future."

• • •

Mike lay in bed thinking. Brian was okay – able to take some tea. Lhasa was amazing. It was completely new to him, but at times he felt like he had been here before. It was total cognitive dissonance, and yet it felt right. People were selling vegetables from carts pulled by yaks while a state-of-the-art lab turned out transformative technology deep inside a 17th century castle.

The Newdle node was powered up and functioning. He'd had good bandwidth on calls to Stephanie and Angela. He'd told Stephanie about the conversation with Lhamo's uncle, and she'd asked: "How do you feel about that, Mikie? After all of that bitterness between you and Tammy, you've been more than a bit gun-shy around women."

He'd responded, "I guess I'll just wait to see if she chooses me."

"Do you truly want her to choose you, Mikie?"

"Hell, yes, Mom! But Lhamo isn't the kind of person who responds to pressure. I may be a dork sometimes, but that much I know."

Stephanie gave Mike a warm smile. "Absolutely no pressure, Mikie, but find the right time to tell her you want her. And when that time comes, don't second guess youself."

Mike and Brian had discussed the timing of their departure and decided that they would leave tomorrow night. While lying in bed feeling like crap from the altitude, Brian had used the Newdle Atmospheric Flow data to analyze alternate routes from Vermont to Lhasa. Surprisingly he'd found that an insertion into Eurasia over Scandinavia, followed by a route over Russia and Kazakhstan almost always provided a faster and more fuel efficient path to Lhasa.

Then Brian had spoken with Dave, who had contacts in Stockholm, Copenhagen, and Kiev. If they could establish a swath of Rum Works franchises across northern Europe, they would essentially be paving a friendly highway complete with 'gas stations' to Lhasa. Given what they had learned about the B^3's performance characteristics, they estimated that the average trip to Lhasa would require only 25% of their maximum fuel load, which meant they could deliver more cargo without taking on additional fuel from Lhasa. All they needed now was a safe route out of Dodge. That would have to be dealt with tomorrow night.

Mike was on the threshold of sleep when Lhamo slipped into bed beside him. She put her finger on his lips and said: "tomorrow I will leave with you. If we survive, we can be together."

CHAPTER 18

OUT OF DODGE

September 2030

The night was windy which made the launch tricky. They had rolled the old truck to a spot upwind of the field, unfolded the airship, attached the fuel and hydrogen bladders, and began inflating the ship while it was tethered to the truck. They inflated it from back to front to reduce the amount of flapping as the ship took shape. Then they were able to load the cargo and install the upgraded extractors. The whole process took less than half an hour. As soon as they entered the crew cabin and had activated the electrostatic seal, Brian boosted the ambient oxygen to 40%. Within minutes he felt better.

They lifted off just after 11 pm, two hours before moonrise. The wind near the ground was against them as they headed south, but as they rose above the peaks of the mountains, its flow reversed. Now the wind was pushing them southeast, partly the direction they wanted to go, but too much towards China. Brian pointed B³'s nose slightly west of south and used the motors to push then straight south over Bhutan. Once over the Himalayan hump, they eased the ship's nose a bit to the east and continued powered flight, bringing them over central Myanmar at dawn. No one had slept those first hours in the air as they pushed to get south around the lower tip of China. However, the ship performed flawlessly, driving them almost silently through the moonlit clouds above spectacular mountain peaks. Monitoring communication links, there was no indication that anyone knew they were there.

Now they went to work on developing their course options to get across the South China Sea and then back across the Pacific. Their best bet was to cross over central Vietnam, stay well south of China's Hainan Island, and cross northern Luzon into the Pacific. There they hoped to find a strong northerly flow to take them up towards Japan and then to the east across the north Pacific about half way between the Aleutian and Hawaiian Islands. Their biggest risk was that September is typhoon season in the western Pacific. These powerful storms could develop rapidly, and about half of them typically drove onto the Asian mainland rather than following the trade winds north to Japan. This year, the onshore typhoons had been particularly powerful, so, much like the sailing ships of the distant past, they needed to be vigilant to avoid being blown ashore on an unfriendly coast.

The other hazard to avoid was the equator. As a rule, the winds near the equator are weak and variable. Back in the days of wooden ships, sailors hated the equatorial oceans because the doldrums there would often leave them becalmed for weeks. Once they were well away from China, they could use B^3's Doppler array to precisely chart local airflow patterns, and this could give them an advantage in navigating their way through variable air. However they would much rather have strong dependable trade-winds to drive them home, so their best course was to thread their way safely south of China but not too close to the equator. It was a big sky they were sailing through, but political realities and airflow patterns made their homeward navigation a surprisingly delicate process.

By the evening of that first day out of Lhasa they had travelled a bit over 1500 km and were drifting east with the motors off in a favorable wind north of Bangkok. These winds looked like they would carry them across Vietnam near Hue. After that, they might need to power up and motor their way across the South China Sea to get into the northern trades east of the Philippines. If so, they would still have more than half of their fuel, while being well positioned to ride the rest of the way to North America on the North Pacific trade-winds.

With three people in the crew cabin and possibly a week or more of flying ahead of them, they worked out a routine of watches. They had two crew benches, so one was used for sleeping while the other two people sat on the second bench, monitoring and navigating the ship. This was done using their headset displays to operate the wireless controls. However most of the time they had little to do but watch the jungles and villages of Southeast Asia float away beneath them or work on other projects. They drew lots, and Brian got the first sleep break, so Lhamo and Mike sat together and flew B³ through the darkness of their second night in the air.

The next morning they crossed the coast of Vietnam between Hue and Da Nang, drifting out over the South China Sea. As NAF had predicted, here their favorable winds died, and they started to drift slowly north towards China's Hainan Island. Lhamo was asleep and Mike was getting groggy from 2 days with only occasional cat-naps, but Brian was fresh and alert. He powered up the turbines and set them on a course for Luzon in the Philippines. At a groundspeed of 150 kph, he calculated that they would cross into the Pacific air currents east of the Philippines before night fall. There, the NAF chart showed them to be strong and northerly, and if they held up, they could shut down B³'s turbines, breathe a sigh of relief, and ride the wind north towards Japan.

On this day, their best altitude to avoid adverse winds was just three km above the South China Sea. This gave them a pretty good view of the ocean surface below, but being off the coast of China, the air was thick with the brown haze of the coal-fired, post-tsunami Chinese economy. So their visual horizon was only about seven km. They were not really comfortable flying without their radar on, but this altitude, in turn, gave them a degree of security. They were unlikely to be spotted by anyone above or below unless they flew directly over a Chinese patrol boat; and the closer they got to the Philippines, the less likely that became.

Mike was now asleep, with Brian and Lhamo running the ship. They were sharing a fruit smoothie fresh from the extractor, its first output from growing up a new set of bugs after departing Lhasa. It was a refreshing change from the packaged food they'd been eating the last two days. "It's hard to believe that this is actually yesterday's poop," Brian said with a wry smile. "It is truly amazing how far we've come since you joined the Mars project less than 3 years ago."

"It is also amazing how little we knew then where that work would take us," she replied, raising her cup in a toast to their progress.

Late in the afternoon, the haze cleared a bit, and they passed over a number of sail boats fishing in the ocean below them. The guidance system said they were less than 30 km from the coast of Luzon, and in a few minutes the green slopes of the island emerged in front of them. Lhamo took B^3 up to 5 km and ground speed began to increase. Half an hour later, as they approached the east coast of the island, she climbed to an altitude of 10.5 km and shut down the turbines as B^3 slipped into the heart of the jet-stream flowing north. They were flying towards Japan, well off the coast of China, and going 135 kph over the Pacific. As the sun set into the haze off to the west over China, they woke Mike up and celebrated by turning on their transponder, powering up their transmitter, and calling home.

•   •   •

From that point on, the trip went smoothly. No typhoons crossed their path, and no more curious aircraft approached them. Other than flying directly over Iwo To, they came no closer to Japan that 300 km, and the north Pacific was remarkably empty. Empty, except for the winds. Just as the Newdle software predicted when they approached the Japanese coast from the south, the trade-winds veered to the east and grew even greater in force. They often flew at 200 kph in unpowered flight as the winds drove them across the northern Pacific.

In two days, they covered almost 7000 km, and on their fifth day out of Lhasa they were approaching the coast of the state of Washington just north of Seattle. They still had a bit of their original Vermont ethanol and all of the petrol they'd taken aboard in Lhasa. Two months previously, Lhamo had told Mike he should be able to fly around the world in 14 days, and here they were on day 15 of flight, about to cross back into the US.

At this point, they had to decide where to land. Their obvious choices were Alberta or Vermont, but they had a load of extractor discs aboard, and they had to make a final decision where to set up operations to manufacture the milk machines. They had an invita-

tion from Newdle to do this at their new secure campus north of So-
noma in California, but for practical reasons they decided against it.
The big population areas still struggled with social unrest, and any
machine they installed needed to be serviced with deliveries of bugs
and parts. For this, the swath from the Midwest to the Northeast in
the US was clearly their best market. They already made routine
deliveries for their Rum Works franchises along this corridor. The
final decision was that the extractors would be built in Alberta at
Diamond Fabrics, and that's where they headed.

The trip over the Canadian Rockies was quick and bumpy. Most of
it was done by drifting, using the NAF software and their Doppler
radar to find good winds. For the last 50 km coming down off the
mountains into Edmonton, however, there was a backflow that they
had to motor through. They approached the field at Diamond Fabrics at 4 PM on their fifth day out of Lhasa, 15 days of flight, and 19
days total from departing Vermont.

Even on their final approach into Edmonton, they were already
planning the next flight to Lhasa. Brian had continued monitoring the airflow patterns over Scandinavia and Russia, and he was
convinced that they could cut two days off the trip from Vermont
to Lhasa. "If we could set up ethanol operations in Russia or the
Ukraine and on the Philippines where we could pick up extra fuel if
needed, we might make the whole trip routinely in 12 days total by
using a bit more powered flight and less drifting. With two airships
and four crews, we could schedule weekly deliveries to Lhasa. And
we'd be doing it without any use of fossil fuel, just ethanol, and at a
tiny fraction of the cost of flying there in heavier-than-air planes."

"Why four crews," Mike asked. "Can't they work 12 days on and take
four days off? It isn't like this is hard physical labor."

Brian grimaced. "Just one minor problem, Mike. Radiation. Since
we are spending a lot of our time around 10 km altitude when we
fly this thing, we really increase our radiation exposure from cosmic
rays. At that altitude, we accumulate double our average annual
exposure in just one month, reach the threshold of risk in 70 days,
and go into the danger zone after about six months of total time

up in a year. We struggled with that issue for the Mars mission, and never found a good solution. But for our airships, if we start making regular long trips, our crews shouldn't spend more than a quarter of their total time up."

"So we can hire people who work part time on the ground and part time in the air," Lhamo agreed. "But can Diamond Fabrics afford to build another one of these?" Lhamo asked.

"We can't afford not to," Brian replied. "And besides, the Newdle boys are buying two of them, so we'll use the profit to build a third. I've been designing them during this trip. Here, take a look," he said, giving them access to his file with its 3D images. "It's roughly the same diameter and shape but a bit longer. It has a bigger, two compartment crew cabin to accommodate up to two passengers plus 2 crew. I've also enlarged the solar fabric array. We've made about five per cent of our fuel needs from solar this trip, and we just strapped that fabric array on top for this trip almost as an afterthought. If we double the size of the array, it adds to range and economy. These small ridges along the nose and back will make it easier to collect rainwater out of clouds, so we can gather water for hydrolysis to make oxygen and hydrogen using the solar power. It's almost self-sustaining".

Brian was clearly excited by the prospects. "And the best part is that it's almost all made of fabric, either cut and pasted together or woven to precise specs on our looms. The motors, the smoothie machine, the guidance system, the pumps and valves, and all of the other equipment are strictly off the shelf now. That means we can cut the total time from design to test flight to less than a month. The other big step we need to take is having the crew use our upgraded catheters from the Mars mission"

"That would certainly be preferable to peeing and pooping into the recycling chute behind that curtain," Lhamo said gratefully, pointing to the cabin's 'potty corner'.

As Brian and Lhamo continued discussing design details of the 'New-New-Burg', Mike swung   B³'s nose into the wind, touched down with barely a bump, dropped the tethers and cut power. He then released the electrostatic zipper on the exit flap, and they all stepped out into the late afternoon Canadian sunshine. They'd let the Diamond Fabrics crew handle the cargo, pump-down, and storage. It was time for a big Canadian steak and at least one beer.

All three of them knew that they had accomplished something remarkable with this circumnavigation, but they also wondered where it would lead them next.

CHAPTER 19

THE NORTHERN ROUTE
November 2030

They were three days out of Vermont, and the flashes off the waves in the Baltic from the morning sun were bright despite the haze. They had made 12 drops of bugs and balloons behind them into Sweden and had 23 more up ahead into southern Russia and northern Ukraine. The routine of being up in B³ had become familiar, but Brian and Mike knew this trip was different. Yes, they were exploring a new, more efficient, and hopefully safer route into Lhasa from the north. And for this trip they were both using bladder and colon catheters connected directly into the waste recycling system. But there was another, more fundamental, difference between this trip and their last one.

Mike had conceived of their first trip into Lhasa as a one-off fling. It had been driven both by a sense of adventure and by his intense desire to see Lhamo and get her out. On this trip, however, they were laying down a swath of new clients who would need regular repeat trips to supply them with bugs. Essentially, they were now establishing a new trade route around the world, much like what Spanish, Portuguese, Dutch, and English sailors had done in wooden ships five centuries before them.

Brian, Mike, Lhamo, and Stephanie had spent hours debating the risks of doing this, and whether they were really justified by the benefits. After all, it was still less than a year since the tsunami. Maybe the world would snap back from the spasms of chaos that had followed. Maybe ships and planes would again routinely cross the oceans between the continents. They'd asked themselves, "why do this now if, come a year from now, everything is pretty much back to normal?"

Stephanie in particular was anxious about Mike making another trip to Lhasa. Yes, she'd supported his decision to go the first time, but now they had Lhamo back, and the School Milk Project was getting back on track. Why did Mike need to go again? She had wanted to tell him: "First I lost my husband, and now I've lost my brother, Mikie. I can't bear the thought of losing you, too!"

Two weeks after their return from Lhasa, they'd all gotten together for a three day meeting at the Newdle lodge in Idaho. Along with Barry, Ivan, and Dave, they'd discussed the full implications of the world situation and how their airships could contribute to bringing some order back to the chaos, at least in selected locations that were receptive. A few things were apparent. In most places where a Rum Works operation had been set up, it improved the lives and social order of the people it served. Additionally, where Newdle was able to maintain its communications nodes, the flow of information in and out of that locality facilitated the rebuilding process.

By the third day of this meeting, however, if they were not convinced before, they had all come to the conclusion that the world was not going to return to its pre-tsunami 'normal state'. The petroleum industry had been hyper-extended before the tsunami hit. Almost all of the 'cheap oil' in shallow waters and on-shore locations had been extracted. When the tsunami hit, the remaining oil was mostly offshore and very deep. Now much of that infrastructure was destroyed beyond repair. As a major source of fossil carbon accumulating in the atmosphere, the oil economy had been a significant contributor to the global warming that caused of the tsunami. No reasonable person wanted to go back to that paradigm.

As an alternative, regions with coal had turned back to this fuel, but the lack of oil made coal mining difficult, inefficient, and dangerous. Coal too contributed to the atmospheric carbon burden. People with a regional perspective dug coal. People with a global perspective wondered why.

Most importantly, however, the breakdown in social order, especially in the big cities that were not close to agricultural production,
had been devastating. Every city with more than five million inhabitants had destroyed itself, and many cities with more than a million
had suffered a similar fate. Those in desert regions were particularly
hard hit. The lack of food and water had either driven people out
of the major population centers, or driven them to fight over what
little was left. These cities were not just centers of business – they
were also the hubs for roads, rail, and shipping. Clearly these cored
out metropolitan centers could not be counted on to return to full
function any time soon. Until then, they'd need to bypass the cities
and find alternatives for communications and commerce.

These were the issues that led to making this trip, hoping to create
small centers of stability along their path by enabling wood ethanol production, providing sun-powered milk machines, and Newdle
communications nodes. It was a bit like seeding green islands of
self-sufficiency in a desert of chaos. The boys from Newdle had not
pressured them to do this, but they had provided invaluable information that helped them come to grips with the terribly damaged
world passing underneath their diamond-fabric airship.

This reality was now very present in their thoughts as they approached
the Baltic coast. This little group of countries down there had survived more or less intact, but in part this was due to their relative ho-
mogeneity in language and culture. Newdle's analysis indicated that
if you spoke the local language without an accent, you tended to stay.
Non-native speakers tended to leave. No one there had passed a law
that mandated ethnic cleansing. It came down to simple things like
food and water. It did not matter if you were from Byelorussia or Bir-
mingham, or if you had money or not. At life's most basic level, you
can't eat or drink money. If you survived in the post-tsunami world,
in many places, it was because basic tribal instincts prevailed.

The Baltic States had some of the less deadly instances of ethnic
cleansing that had convulsed populations deprived of power, food,
and commerce. In Russia, only the smallest cities and towns had
survived unscathed; the exceptions being where the army pulled
back to defend themselves within national and regional capitols. B[3]

had to stay well clear of such areas under totalitarian military rule, like Minsk and Moscow, just in case someone down there had an old missile or laser and an itchy trigger finger. In the smaller towns and cities, all they had were small caliber stuff that could not get above a few thousand meters, and the diamond fabric outer skin of B^3 was impervious to anything up to .50 caliber, even up close. Bottom line: they were probably pretty safe crossing this region as long as they didn't try something really stupid, like landing in downtown Moscow for a meal of borsht and vodka.

So far on this trip, things seemed to be going their way, literally. The winds were generally good, and the NAF navigator was consistently getting them into the areas of best flow. That was, in part, due to the density of Newdle's monitoring stations across the Atlantic and in Scandinavia, providing detailed three-dimensional maps of airflow. To their delight, they'd only run B^3's turbines for just a few hours, so they still had most of their initial load of fuel aboard.

But as they proceeded inland from here, they'd be more on their own with much less guidance from the NAF navigator. There were some high altitude drifters out ahead of them with look-down Doppler, and they had their own on-board Doppler system that could reach out to examine the winds up to 100 km ahead. However, using their on-board Doppler system told anyone with a radiation monitor precisely where they were, so they could only use it when the potential threat from the ground was low. For now, they were drifting high and silent with their transponder off, emitting no radiation. They planned to stay this way until they had passed well to the east of Moscow.

One limitation of their passive drifting rather than powered flight was that they could only make delivery drops to sites within a swath 30 km wide along their path. This was mandated by the maximum range of their best tethered glider, which was 15 km. As they flew inland from the Baltic coast, however, Brian shared an idea with Mike that was truly exciting. It was like an untethered glider going down, but one that was modified with a novel propulsion system that would allow it to fly back up under its own power.

Brian had taken the diamond fabric doped with aluminum, the stuff that contracted like muscle when subjected to an electric current, and used it to form a pouch under the belly of the glider. Using a small hydrogen fuel cell for power, the pouch was periodically contracted, expelling air out a pair of nozzles in the back to propel the 'glider' forward. Without the restraint of a tether, with a glide ratio of 30:1 fully loaded, it had the potential to deliver its payload up to 300 km off of B³'s path when dropped from an altitude of ten km. With little or no payload aboard on the return flight, however, it became a lighter-than-air vehicle able to fly back up to B³ under its own power.

Brian's team in Alberta had constructed their first working prototype two weeks ago, but the idea had seemed so far-fetched that Brian kept it to himself until they had some performance data. Now that they had modified the pouch's forward air inlets and exit nozzles to give more efficient propulsion and better directional steering, their prototype could sustain a flight speed of 30 kph and fly for eight hours using just 30 grams of hydrogen to power its fuel cell.

Brian showed Mike the latest test video. "It looks like a jelly fish with wings," Mike exclaimed. "It has a jellyfish belly!"

Thus was born the famous Diamond Fabrics' Jellybelly. It would enable them to dependably deliver a ten kg load up to 250 km to either side of their path and then fly back up with a return payload of 1 kg or less and catch up with B³ as long as she was in drifting mode.

As Mike watched the latest test-flight video that Brian had just received, he thought about the practical implications of adding the Jellybelly's capabilities to the Rum Works ethanol and milk business. He immediately knew that this was another important step forward. To get a delivery of bugs to an ethanol or milk machine site, they no longer had to fly over it. Rather than service a swath 30 km wide, now they could cover 15 times the area on an Alberta-burg or B³ flight without altering course. They just needed to get within a 250 km radius, drop a Jellybelly, track it out and back, and recover it within its active flight range.

Then Brian added something else.   They were working on adding a solar fabric array across the top of the Jellybelly's wings. Given its light-as-air efficiency, this would give it an in-sunlight flight speed of 30 kph, drawing its power directly off the solar array. This way, the need for hydrogen-fueled flight was reserved for darkness and clouds. To be sure, the Jellybelly's powered flight speed of 30 kph limited its ability to work against even a modest wind, but that was unimportant as long as it was working from an airship that remained in drifting mode.

Mike's mind wandered to other uses for the Jellybelly. It could function like B^3's bird dog, going out ahead of them when they were in drifting mode, monitoring airflow patterns up ahead, staying alert for possible threats in the air or on the ground, and checking out landing sites.

Brian was watching Mike and read his thoughts. "Now that we've got these catheters in, Amigo, it would not be a good idea to send that little pooch down to fetch a burger with fries," Brian said, chuckling.

Mike smiled. They both knew that the colonic catheters would completely plug up if they ate solid food. They'd had the catheters in for a week to test them out before leaving on this flight. It had taken a few days of trial and error to get the port pressures right for the catheter's rinse and high pressure return functions to operate properly, and neither of them wanted to mess with them now that they were working.

About half way through that test week on the ground, Mike had been pleasantly surprised when all sensations from his lower intestine seemed to disappear. It was like his colon had been put to sleep under general anesthesia. He had no urge to take a crap, no gas, no pressure, or any sense of anything moving. Nothing. It was almost surreal, making a previously regular bodily function completely disappear; and he didn't miss it at all. Now that it no longer happened, he realized that the only feedback he had previously gotten from taking a crap was relief. So not having to find a bathroom and waste some toilet paper was even more of a relief, especially aboard B^3 where their 'head' was a collection chute behind a curtain.

The smooth transition to the colon catheter had come as a pleasant surprise to both Brian and Mike because they'd had trouble with the early Mars project catheters back in St. Louis before the tsunami. Their first research subjects there had experienced intestinal cramping and inflammation of the cells lining the colon during those early tests. They thought that might be due to the lack of fiber in their liquid diet. Normally, intestinal bacteria turn fiber into short chain fats that provide fuel to the cells lining the colon. But on their liquid diet there was no fiber, and with the catheter in the colon there were very few bacteria. This combination resulted in the colon cells being essentially starved, even when the rest of the body was being well fed.

Back then, someone had suggested they inject some of those short chain fatty acids through the tip of catheter to 'feed' the colon lining, but they'd never actually tested that until a couple of months before this flight. It had taken a few weeks to get the dose right, and as a result, Mike had to add something called 'butyrate' to the list of things made by his bugs and extracted by Lhamo's machine. This was infused out of the tip of the catheter along with a basic electrolyte rinse solution, providing the cells lining the colon with their preferred source of energy. The leftovers that didn't get used were sucked out further down and recycled back into the bacterial soup. So far, it seemed to be working just fine. Mike's colon seemed to be happy as a clam doing nothing at all, so long as it was supplied with a continuous dose of butyrate.

Mike chuckled to himself and thought: my great grandparents made the transition from outhouse to indoor plumbing. My hippie grandparents gave up indoor plumbing for an outhouse, and now 60 years later, I have internal plumbing. No muss, no fuss...

Again reading Mike's thoughts, Brian said: "It kind of makes you not want to go back to ground mode, eh?" Although Brian had grown up in Texas, just 6 months in Alberta and he'd already adopted the classic Canadian verbal question mark 'eh'. "Up here we've got no worries about food, water, power failures, clean air, social strife, or cold toilet seats. The view is great and changes every day, and now with the Jellybelly, we've even got us a dog that can hunt and fetch."

"Indeed! But if we stay up here much longer, we'll fry our DNA," Mike replied. "From what you told me before, I'm guessing this will have to be our last flight for quite a while unless we want to get overdosed with gamma radiation."

That's something else I've been working on, Amigo," Brian replied. "When we were in Idaho last month, I had some face time with Newdle's technical guy charged with coordinating our drifting balloon project. He'd been trying to figure out how to have their people do the balloon flights in tag-team mode, so no one individual accumulates too much radiation exposure. But that gets messy when you don't have precise control of where you come down after a month of drifting. To make that work, they would have to transport new drifters to each landing site and bring the previous pilot back. They ran a simulation of doing this by tasking crew transport to the two 'Burgs' that Newdle is buying, but that didn't work either.

"So what's going to happen to that project?" Mike asked.

"Well, this is where it gets interesting," Brian replied. "After we left, the Newdle guy had some of his kids do a problem solving session on the radiation issue. They put 21 of them in a virtual room and told them to keep at it until they had a solution. I got to sit in as a fly on the wall, and it was fun to watch. Imagine 21 kids like you when you were at MIT. They were divided into seven teams of three each, with the team that came up with a viable answer sharing a $150,000 bonus. I thought they'd be at it for days, but it took them less than 2 hours. What they came up with was totally outside the box, but it's intriguing. Get this: they think that if we change the composition of our diet, we can reduce radiation damage enough that we can stay up here indefinitely."

"That's crazy," Mike interjected. "There's nothing in food that can stop an x-ray. And even my best bugs can't make a lead shield out of shit, water, and sunlight!"

"Yeah, that was my initial reaction, too, Amigo. But I watched as this idea unfolded, and while it's pretty far-fetched, it isn't crazy. They started from the fact that our DNA is constantly under attack by many factors besides radiation, so our cells are actually in a constant state of DNA repair. The fact that the radiation up here is about three times greater than down at sea level just adds more to the ongoing repair burden. As a result, too much time up here at altitude eventually overloads the repair system. Their novel idea is that rather than spend 70% of our time on the ground to let the DNA repair process catch up, we could extend our time up if we found ways to reduce other causes of ongoing DNA damage. Take away other causes of damage, and our normal repair capability might be able to keep up with the increased rate of gamma ray damage up here."

"Okay," Mike said. "So what drug do we add to the diet to do that?"

"We don't know of any drug that will do that," Brian continued. "What they came up with is actually simpler and safer than taking some drug. They want us to try taking all of the starch and sugar out of our diet, so that most of our energy will come from fat and some from protein. Its composition would be something like a traditional Inuit diet. What led them to this was that 25 years ago, some diet doctors showed that a low carbohydrate diet reduced the body's level of inflammation and its production of free radicals [15]. Those free radicals are mostly made up of reactive forms of oxygen that can attack DNA and cause damage similar to ionizing radiation. Back then these guys were actually on track to determine if this type of diet could slow aging, but their funding got cut."

"Let me guess," Mike said sarcastically. "Their grants got rejected because if they'd proven that a low carbohydrate diet slowed aging, it would have messed up some food company's market share? Or maybe their research threatened a cosmetic company's new anti-aging product line?"

"Your milk machines weren't the first disruptive innovation to run afoul of an entitled industry, Mike."

"Tell that to my dead uncle!" Mike said bitterly, but then remembered kicking the door in St. Louis and softened his tone. "So what you're telling me, bottom line, is that it's an interesting theory, but we don't know for sure that cutting out carbs in the smoothies will reduce our overall DNA damage up here," Mike concluded.

"Correct. Right now we don't know if this would help, and if so, by how much," Brian replied seriously, but then he raised his right index finger and grinned mischievously. "However, in three more weeks we will. We've got a group of scientists at the University of Alberta all over this question like a cold sweat. They've already sent a bunch of radiation-sensitive mice up in our prototype gondola on a tether 15 km above Edmonton. Our life-support system is keeping them warm and supplying them with oxygen. Meanwhile, half of those mice are being fed regular mouse chow rich in carbohydrates, and the other half are on the low carb mouse diet invented by those docs 25 years ago. We'll know if it works soon after we get back."

Mike sat back on his bench with a sigh. Ever since the tsunami, his life seemed to be running in fast forward, and sometimes processing all of its implications was daunting. Less than a year ago, the world had devolved from a community of nations into a patchwork of communities studded by a few nations. Most of these few "nations" were now functionally totalitarian states that had taken draconian measures to reduce the number of mouths to feed to match the amount of food they could produce. The best estimates were that in a year the Earth's population had dropped from 9 to 7 billion; and among those, half of the remaining seven billion lived in semi-starvation or just barely hand to mouth.

Here above it all, he was drifting in complete comfort, free of worry about his next meal – albeit with a tube up his ass and another in his penis. However, even these tubes, as bad as they sounded, contributed to his sense of complete freedom. No one had planned this path they were following, but it was offering Mike a dream reality – a life above evil. This would not be the life of an isolated hermit hunkering in a cave. Rather, what beckoned was a life without concern for the daily necessities while providing awesome bandwidth and instantaneous access to all of the world's accumulated knowledge.

Instinctively, Mike realized that to earn the privilege of being up here, he'd have to remain fully aware of how bad things were on the ground, and just maybe, bit by bit, make it better. It was his first glimpse into his future life as a high-tech nomad, producing more energy than he consumed, living well and being useful with a negative energy footprint. The possibility was strangely enticing...and it was almost within their grasp.

Then reality called. He still needed to take this one step at a time. For now he grappled with the possibility – no, the likelihood – that he had to reprogram his bugs to make new smoothies fit for folks living in igloos.

"Hey, Brian" Mike said after a minute of contemplation. "Can you take B^3 for the next 8 hours or so? I think I'd better get to work on some new bugs."

CHAPTER 20

THE MAUI CONNECTION
Late November 2030

Over the mid-Pacific, Mike and Brian were looking forward to ground time on Maui. Lhamo's brother Dorje, on the other hand, was looking forward to ground time anywhere. They'd made a textbook nighttime drop into Lhasa, off-loaded their bugs and equipment, taken on a cargo of discs for the milk machines, and lifted off in less than half an hour. It was a classic touch-and-go stop. Their upgraded NAF navigation software was performing beautifully, so they still had 80% of their initial fuel load. There was no need to take on any of the precious fossil fuel that the Tibetans had stockpiled for them.

In the days before Mike and Brian arrived, Dorje had struggled with whether it was better for him to move to Edmonton or stay in Lhasa. In the end, Lhamo convinced her brother that they needed to move their primary disc production to Edmonton. There they'd have better access to power and raw materials; and to do this, she needed Dorje in Edmonton to set up the equipment and train the staff. Their cousin could run the lab in the Potala to make discs for use in Tibet.

And so they had Dorje aboard, but his colon wished it was still back in Lhasa. There had been no time to adapt him to a catheter, or to the smoothie diet. That meant that he'd spent a lot of his flight time behind the curtain using the waste chute. They had plenty of smoothies, but no yak butter or oat porridge. Dorje was taking it well, but he was definitely looking forward to getting back on the ground.

Luckily, that looked like it might be happening surprisingly soon. North of the Philippines they'd hooked the rapidly moving edge of a winter cold front that took them straight east across the Pacific along the 20 degrees north parallel at over 200 kph in drifting mode, hour after hour. In 20 hrs they logged a bit over 4000 km, more than half the remaining distance to Maui. And it wasn't letting up. It felt like they'd jumped on a freight train.

Now that they knew that they could hit Hawaii, rather than being swept farther north like on their last trip, they began serious planning. During their Idaho strategy session, Dave had asked that they try for a stop somewhere in Hawaii this time around. Before starting out from Vermont, they'd picked Kauai and Maui as the best contingencies. Both seemed to have sizeable functioning communities with radio communication to the mainland, and neither had a large military population, which tended to promote authoritarian rule. Once past the Philippines, they came out of transmission silence and began active planning with Dave at Newdle. They had four complete milk machines on board, which was enough to make a difference for a couple of thousand people, so that was the community size they were looking for.

After discussing the various options, they settled on the coastal village of Hana on the east side of Maui. Separated from the rest of the island by the massive Haleakala volcano, they were relatively isolated. Another factor was that the area around Hana was pretty rugged, which limited their agricultural production. Dave was in contact with a Coast Guard unit in the village. This was curious because Hana had not had a Coast Guard Station before the tsunami. The story he got was that a cutter that had been underway north of the island survived intact but had no home port to return to after the tsunami swept across the middle of the island and wiped out Kahului. So they'd pulled in to Hana and stayed. All of this sounded good, but there was still some uncertainty as to how they'd actually be received when they landed.

•   •   •

"This is Hana Coast Guard. Go ahead."

"Hana, this is Airship B3. Request permission to land at your facility. Over"

Calling their airship 'B-three' was a nod to social pressure. Only the most dedicated geek 'got it' if they identified themselves as 'B-cubed'.

"Airship whatever. We've got a dock, a boat with no fuel, and a bunch of hungry people here. Unless you are a helicopter, I suggest you land at the airstrip 10 km north of us. Over."

"Hana. We understand you have a prior communication from Newdle concerning delivery of some milk machines for your community. That would be us. All we need is 100 meters of downwind clearance and four or five people to assist with our mooring lines. Over."

"Airship Bee-Three, huh. Are you a blimp? We assumed the Newdle delivery would come via an ocean-going ship out of San Fran. But we're not picky. How about you use the ballpark on the south side of the village? You should be able to pick it out easy from the air. It's about 300 meters west of the dock in the bay. If the light towers there are a problem, you could also use the pasture just north of the main road. Over."

"Thank you, Hana. The ballpark looks like it should work. Can you run a wind-sock up your flagpole for us? And Hana, uh, how's civil order in the village? Anybody there unhappy enough to take a shot at us? Over."

"You'll be safe landing here, Bee-Three. We've had more than enough unhappiness to last us a lifetime, but so far things here have remained pretty calm. And we'll be truly grateful for any help you can bring us. Over."

Brian, Mike, and Dorje all had visual images of Hana on their displays. Within a few minutes, seven people in uniform collected on the ball field and started scanning the sky. None seemed to be carrying weapons. A few other people started moving down the streets towards the ball field, and they too looked more curious than threatening.

Brian increased power on the turbines and pushed B³ around the shoulder of Haleakala where they'd been holding position in one of the deep canyons high up on the mountain and began his descent to the village. Pretty soon folks on the ground were pointing at them, but overall things seemed to remain calm down there. As Brian brought the ship in over the field, Mike scanned the surrounding area. Lots of garden plots were visible around the village, and there were sailing outriggers off the coast, apparently fishing.

"Hana. Please make the bow line fast. Over."

"Roger that, Bee-Three. We have you secured. Interesting 'ship'! I don't see any doors or windows. You guys in there somewhere?"

Brian initiated the pump-down, then released the electrostatic flap, and the three drifters (a term they'd begun to use to describe themselves) exited the airship onto the green ball field.

They were confronted by a gaunt man in a frayed uniform that seemed cut for someone twice his size.

"Who the hell are you guys?"

"We're from Newdle" was the best reply Mike could think of. "Could you and your people help us with the cargo?"

"Yes sir. My name's Clark – Master Chief Horatio H. Clark, US Coast Guard."

"Pleased to meet you, Master Chief. I'm Mike, this is Brian, and this is Dorje. Let's get these bundles out of here," Mike said as he released the opening to the cargo bay. "It's easier to do this now before the ship is fully deflated."

"I've never seen anything like her before. What's she filled with? Helium?" The Master Chief asked, feeling a fold of the diamond fabric between his fingers.

"Hydrogen," Mike replied casually as he watched a look of concern cross the Master Chief's face. "But don't worry. She won't burn."

"I'll hold you to that, mister," the sailor replied. "Did you fly this slick lady out from California?"

"Nope. We left Vermont seven days ago, overflew Scotland, Sweden, the Baltic, and Russia, made a touch-and-go stop in Tibet, and then sailed across the Pacific riding that cold front," Mike replied, pointing to the distant line of clouds just visible on the northern horizon.

"You're joking, right? No way you fly a blimp three-fourths of the way around the world in 7 days."

"She's not a blimp," Brian interjected. "She's a hyperbaric dirigible with a state-of-the-art brain, designed to sail the prevailing winds. And no, Mike's not joking. If we'd kept going on this trip, we could have done a complete circumnavigation in 9 or 10 days."

"Well, look, if you boys need another 'sailor' on your crew, please keep me in mind." The Master Chief said dolefully. "I've got 23 years in the Coast Guard, but Uncle Sam hasn't paid us in almost a year, so I'm open to alternatives."

"Okay, we'll keep that in mind," Mike replied. "But first, can we talk to whoever governs this town? We'd like to get these milk rigs set up and operating."

"Well, we have a town council, and I guess I'm kind of running the police operation. The real police chief and his one remaining officer got killed in a battle with cattle poachers up on the mountain a couple of months ago."

"When can we meet the council?" Brian asked.

"Let's ask them. Most of them are right here watching," Clark replied, pointing to the couple of hundred people who now lined the edge of the field.

•   •   •

Mike scanned the faces around the table – women, men, ethnic Hawaiians, Asians, Blacks, Caucasians – a diverse mix. Everyone looked about as gaunt as the Master Chief. Clearly the privation after the tsunami was being pretty much equally shared. The discussion, while sometimes tense, was polite and purposeful. There were four milk machines, and they finally decided to distribute them one each to the school, the senior center, and the two major churches. Each unit would have an appointed support staff that was tasked to manage the distribution of the milk output. Equally as important, they also had to manage the controlled input of human waste necessary to provide a recurring supply of nitrogen, calcium, potassium, and phosphorus to feed Mike's bugs growing in translucent sunlit tubes up on the roof.

Mike had tried to introduce this as delicately as possible because this was often an emotional hurdle when communities first came to grips with how the milk machines worked. Turning human urine and feces directly into milk was often a problem for people who were many generations detached from the organic realities of farming.

But this group was different. Both the Hawaiians and Asians on the council had cultural ties to the practice of recycling human waste directly into village agriculture. Furthermore, the Caucasians in Hana were often the grandchildren of hippies like Mike's grandparents in Vermont, among whom outhouses and composting were the norm. It seemed that even the most refined among them had only two degrees of separation from the likes of Helen and Scott Nearing[16]. Rather than scowls and cries of consternation, he saw nodding heads and even a few suppressed smiles. For the first time in many months, Mike relaxed. These people got it. Hana kind of felt like Jamaica, Vermont – but with palm trees and bananas.

•   •   •

Three days later, on December 5th, 2030, the village of Hana held a celebration feast. It was too late for Thanksgiving and too soon for Christmas. But that didn't matter. All 4 milk machines were functioning, each one producing 100 glasses of cold creamy milk per hour of daylight. At the senior center, someone actually got out an old crank and bucket and made home-churned ice cream. Kids were smiling; parents had that sense of special satisfaction that comes with seeing their children properly nourished, and the three drifters basked in the knowledge that they had accomplished something inherently good.

Using the Newdle node they'd installed in the village, Mike linked up with Lhamo in Edmonton and shared the real-time video with her as well. It was a feel-good moment. Mike and Brian had already dropped milk machines into quite a few towns, and they'd been there to see them start up in Jamaica and Lhasa. As a result, they'd already had lots of satisfaction doing this work, but this place felt special.

The next afternoon, as the town council met again, they were confronted by a unique characteristic that made Hana particularly special. The meeting was called to focus on one issue – how do we share this wealth with our brothers, sisters, and cousins up the coast and on the other side of the island? Mike's calculation of 4000 glasses of milk per day for 2000 people had run headlong into the Hawaiian cultural icon of 'ohana'. Simply put, ohana means: 'if we have enough and they have none, we need to share so that they get some, even if then we don't have enough'.

The obvious solution was to bring in more milk machines; but then there were distribution and resupply issues, and these in turn depended on transport either by truck or boat. They debated using sailing outriggers or catamarans, but milk is a fragile biological, especially in a tropical climate. It needs to stay cool and be delivered on time. As Mike sat listening to the debate, he kept looking out the windows to the mountainside lush with green plants. The growth up there was not as dense as a Vermont forest in summer, but here they had no winter. That meant there was no 'down time' in the annual growth cycle.

Mike raised his hand. "What if I could set you up with a system to produce half a million liters of bio-fuel ethanol per year. Do you have flex-fueled trucks or boats that can run on it?"

"What are we supposed to make it from?" a chorus of voices asked. "The sugar cane fields across the middle of the island were wiped out by the tsunami."

"Wood," Mike replied, pointing out the window at the mountainside.

"I used your new communications node to go on-line and read about you last night," responded a delicate, elderly Asian woman. "You're the 'Rum Works' guy. They say you've been delivering the homegrown, renewable energy message around the world. What do we need to do to set up your Rum Works thing here?"

"You need a wood chipper and a tank that holds at least 40,000 liters as a fermenter. Most communities just dig up an empty tank from an old gas station. Then you need a few thousand bricks and a hundred meters of copper pipe. You can find these things inside 5 or 10 abandoned homes. We supply the wood-eating bacteria, a couple of pumps, the balloon harvester, and you are in the ethanol business. It's kind of elegant, but actually, it's really low tech."

The diminutive Asian woman made eye contact with Mike. She could have been Lhamo's grandmother. "When could you get these things to us? And how much will it cost?"

The Master Chief held his hand up palm out towards the woman. "Please Noriko. Take it easy on this guy. He's already told us that our first four milk machines are funded by the Newdle Foundation, so let's not worry too much about his price for this additional stuff right now."

Noriko folded her hands on the table in front of her and bowed her head ever so slightly towards the Master Chief, who then turned to Mike across the table and asked. "How can we help you make this happen?"

Mike smiled back across the table at Clark. "How soon can you leave, Master Chief?"

"At your service, Mister," the Master Chief replied with a nod of his head.

Mike turned and looked a Brian. "Have we got a pilot at Newdle or in Alberta who can make the next run right away with the Master Chief?"

"No problem, Mike. If we leave tomorrow, and if these weather patterns hold, B³ could be back here with the Master Chief, 8 more milk machines, and an ethanol rig in 10-15 days."

• • •

Brian was wrong, but not by much. It took all of 16 days before the Master Chief and Dave Erickson released the electrostatic panel and stepped out onto the ball field in Hana. They'd had 2 days delay on the ground in Alberta before Lhamo had 8 milk machines ready to load, but that was okay because it gave them just enough time to get the Master Chief on-catheter. Then they spent a day sitting in dead air over Newfoundland after a touch-and-go in Vermont to pick up a supply of bugs from Tina. In Lhasa they had to wait another 48 hours for winds that would not blow them way off course out over central China. When they passed over the Philippines, there was still a good eastward flow along latitude 20 degrees north, but nothing like the 'freight train' that Mike, Brian, and Dorje had ridden just a couple of weeks earlier.

In spite of these delays, once again, B³ and their NAF navigator had performed remarkably well. Yes, sometimes they had to wait for the right winds to blow, but they were never forced to go someplace they didn't want to, and again, they had used less than 20% of their initial fuel load. With three circumnavigations behind them, they were beginning to realize that most of their travel could be driven by the wind. The idea of an unpowered, human-occupied balloon navigated by NAF was looking more and more credible.

The Master Chief had been a quick study. Or as he put it, "I'm just a natural sailor". He loved the big, white ship he called Bee-Three, and he was reluctant to leave her in Hana. He and Dave had gotten along well. They parted with a warm embrace. Dave had arranged for Newdle to hire the Master Chief as their 'Chief of Equipment' on Maui, taking pains to emphasize that it was strictly temporary until the Coast Guard could again functionally support their unit.

And as a bonus, Dave gave the Master Chief 500 liters of B³'s ethanol – half of his fuel reserve – to jump-start the milk delivery outreach program until the Rum Works ethanol rig could be assembled and brought on line in Hana.

•   •   •

Mike and Lhamo were sitting in her apartment in Edmonton watching the B³'s landing in Hana through a piggy-back feed from Dave's headset. They had been debating the role of choice versus fate in human lives. As the Master Chief walked off of the ball field, he was met by the elderly Asian woman named Noriko, a much younger Asian woman who looked just like her, and two teen-age boys who looked a lot like the Master Chief.

"It was choice that he married her, and choice that she and her kids were visiting her mother in Hana for the New Year when the tsunami hit. I'll concede that it was fate that the Master Chief was north of the island on the boat when the tsunami hit," Lhamo said.

Mike shook his head slightly as he gave up trying to decide if Lhamo was declaring victory or conceding defeat. "All things being equal, he's a good man," Mike replied. "I trust him."

"On that we agree," Lhamo said as she turned, put her hand on Mike's chest, and kissed him gently.

CHAPTER 21

UNO UNO

11 February 2031

On December 25th, as an unintended and rather morbid Christmas present for Brian, the first mouse eating standard mouse chow while suspended 15 kilometers above Edmonton died. Most of its other 24 other mess-mates were looking either a bit weak or outright sick. By contrast, the 25 mice up there being fed the low carbohydrate diet all looked hale and hearty.

They'd known that this was coming. Two weeks before, the team of scientists from the university had briefly reeled in the tethered gondoloon and done tests on all of the animals. Those on the regular food had had very low white blood cell counts and evidence of extensive DNA damage. The opposite was true for the low carb animals, whose DNA still appeared normal.

But now compassion dictated that the rest of the regular chow animals be mercifully dispatched to spare them a long, slow death. The low carb animals, on the other hand, would be maintained under observation back on the ground at the University lab to see if there were any delayed effects of their three months of high radiation exposure. However, based on these preliminary data, it looked like an Inuit diet had unique properties that protected against cumulative radiation injury.

Of course, everything that works on mice doesn't automatically translate to humans. But these mouse results clearly indicated the next step – revise the bugs and extractors, and then closely moni-

tor some humans as they accumulated exposure time at altitude on
the new diet. Brian left little doubt in anyone's mind as to how that
would proceed. He and his team at Diamond Fabrics were hard
at work refining the prototype balloon and gondola combination
designed to carry a single drifter around the globe in unpowered
flight. He gave Mike and Dave an estimate of four to six weeks until
it was ready for sustained flight, and Brian insisted on personally
taking the "Uno" around on its first circumnavigation.

At Newdle, Dave had initiated a separate unit to further refine the
guidance software – the Newdle Air Flow group. Starting with the
weather prediction software they'd adapted for the guidance system used initially for B^3, this group had already pushed the effective course prediction out past their previous three day horizon towards seven days. Their key limitation was volume of input data
which they mostly obtained from Newdle's ground nodes and high
altitude drifters. Their model indicated that if they added the full
complement of 100 drifters that Newdle planned to order, distribut-
ing them around the globe collecting and transmitting local airflow
data, they could achieve a dependable seven day course prediction.
And then someone had a fantasy moment and plugged in 1000
drifters. The model responded with the claim of 80% likelihood of
getting any individual balloon to within ten kilometers of any point
on Earth within 21 days. When 10,000 drifters were plugged in, the
likelihood went up to 90% – 100,000 drifters, and it became 95%.
Clearly, the need for powered flight in the future could be replaced
by a combination of time and data density.

Their other big step forward could be seen around the Diamond
Fabrics factory in Alberta. Inside the factory, and occasionally outside when wind conditions allowed, the graceful winged Jellybelly
prototypes flew about with their characteristic oscillating motion.
The aluminum-doped contractile fabric used to power the belly
pouch had proved to be both efficient and resilient. Brian had, in
essence, created a motor with no moving parts. One of their earliest pouches had been running continuously in stationary testing for
more than 90 days, and there was no sign of wear.

The first operational Jellybelly was used on a B³ delivery run out to Jamaica and back in January, successfully making a total of 9 deliveries up to 100 km out from its mother ship. While on an overnight layover in Jamaica, the B³ pilot was demonstrating the Jellybelly to Stephanie who immediately turned to Mike and said: "Can you make me one with a light under its chin? If I had it with me when I'm out at night, I wouldn't miss the streetlights anymore."

Now why didn't I think of that? Mike thought. But then, he consoled himself, mom is Uncle Mike's sister.

• • •

They had not intentionally planned to depart on the Chinese New Year. This year it came on February 11th, beginning the year of the rat. The world held its breath. This year, however, the combined gravitational pull of the sun and moon directed at the South Pole didn't pull another massive sheet of ice off of the Antarctic plateau like it had the year before. The connected World breathed a sigh of relief.

They were gathered in Alberta. It was dark and cold. Brian had Uno, his gondoloon, inflated and tethered inside the big cutting shed. The New-New-Burg was laid out on the snow outside, fully provisioned and ready for pump up. A group from Newdle, headed by Dave Erickson, had come up from California, and they'd brought in the Master Chief from Hana on the last 'Burg' run down the northern route and across the Pacific.

They'd had extensive debates about the best path for Uno's first flight. The prevailing winds right now were best for the northern route, but it was winter in the northern hemisphere, so that path had far less sunlight than one further south. Another concern was that the weather on the ground would be lousy if anything went wrong with Uno and Brian had to come down. So they'd waited a few days until a high pressure ridge started surging down from the Arctic. NAF predicted that this would carry them far enough south to catch an easy easterly flow over the Atlantic north of the equator.

Brian had wanted to do the trip alone without any support, but every-one else concluded that it would be better to send the NNB along as an escort. Brian felt that his small size would make him essentially in-visible and thus protect him. The compromise they reached was that Mike and the Master Chief would fly the NNB out of sight between 50 and 100 km behind Brian, but from there they could power up and catch up to Uno in less than 30 minutes if need be.

In preparation, all three of them had started the catheter adaptation process two weeks ago, and they had all started on the new low carb smoothies at the same time. The Master Chief, who'd managed to gain back 20 pounds of muscle in the last two months, was concerned that this new low carbohydrate diet would cause him to lose weight again. Indeed, everyone did feel a bit slowed down in the first week of the diet change, but surprisingly, after that nothing seemed to be really different. They'd all promptly regained their normal energy level and function. Mike mentioned to Dave that this might be a novel finding, but Dave held up a finger for Mike to wait a second and then popped a scanned, printed page up on Mike's display. The header said it was from the diary of an Arctic explorer named Fred-rick Schwatka, dated February 1878, published by the Marine Histori-cal Association in Mystic CT in 1965, and scanned by Newdle in 2012.

Mike read; *'When first thrown wholly on a diet of reindeer meat, it seems inadequate to properly nourish the system, and there is an apparent weakness and inability to perform severe, exertive, fatiguing journeys. But this soon passes away in the course of two to three weeks.'*

"Okay," Mike conceded. "Seems like I got scooped on this one."

At five in the afternoon, everything was ready. They pumped up NNB and warmed up the crew gondola. Mike gave Lhamo a hug, Brian shook his dad's hand and kissed his mother, and there were handshakes all around. Brian closed his access flap, dropped Uno's tether, and rose up into the gathering darkness, riding the wind off to the southeast. Master Chief Clark slipped NNB's mooring line and matched Brian's rate of climb. Within a minute, the February twilight swallowed them both.

•   •   •

On the third day, they broke transmission silence over the Atlantic when they were about 800 km west of the African coast. Mike downloaded some new bug designs to Tina at the Rum Works lab. For some reason he'd become enticed by cheese and onion flavors. The Master Chief had asked about adapting the smoothie machine to make an occasional beer, but Mike had convinced him that even the best low carbohydrate beer wasn't worth drinking.

As on all prior circumnavigations, they'd kept their departure date and planned route completely secret. Since no one had the authority to grant them permission for the trip, they felt no need to tell anyone about it. On this third day out they updated Dave about their route and talked through the pros and cons of a potential stop. At this point, it looked like they would cross Africa north of the Equator, and overfly the southern tip of India. From there, they might be able to swing south of the Philippines and then chart a course for Guam.

Given the extent of the social unrest on the US mainland in the last year, it was surprising how much public concern there was for the fate of the people on Guam. A rugged island in deep water, and one accustomed to the massive typhoons characteristic of the western Pacific, Guam had been pretty much spared by the initial tsunami. However, it could not escape the ravages of the tsunami's after-effects on Pacific basin commerce. With the massive loss of shipping, and especially the loss of oil production and transport, Guam was particularly vulnerable.

With the rise of China as a superpower in the two decades before the tsunami, the US had long ago conceded military control of most of the western Pacific, pulling its remaining military forces out of Korea, Japan, the Philippines, and Taiwan. As a result, Guam had become the westernmost outpost for the US military in the Pacific. After the tsunami and the collapse of international trade in petroleum products, there were calls for the prompt evacuation of the US military from Guam, but the dominant view in Washington was that the US should keep its forward units strong and ready until they could determine the course of events in China.

Once it became clear that China was taking an involutional path towards self-isolation, however, there was no longer enough available fuel for ships and planes to evacuate all of the more than 80,000 military personnel, dependents, and contractors stationed on Guam. The only operational ships on the west coast of the US Mainland with the range to get there and back were the Pacific Fleet's four remaining aged nuclear-powered aircraft carriers; and they were considered far too important to risk in an evacuation effort. Besides, the realists asked, once they got the evacuees back to the mainland, where was there enough food and housing to provide for all 80,000 of them? Some boats and planes did make it out, going primarily to the Philippines, Australia, and Japan. But three months after the tsunami, it was estimated that close to half of the island's military garrison remained there.

For those who remained, simply put, Guam was left to its own devices. Lacking most satellite and all cable communications, their primary means of contact with the outside world was by shortwave radio, and while most of that came through military channels, some private 'ham radio' operators from Guam remained on the air as well. By late May, the military was reporting severe shortages of fuel and fresh food, and also problems with the civilian population. The private non-military radio contacts provided two very different views. Civilian US citizens reported that the indigenous Chamoru people had become hostile, whereas Chamorro contacts indicated that bands of armed contractors were foraging the island for food and fuel, taking what they wanted at gunpoint. There were similar reports of an ethnic divide on the island of Saipan, 100 km to the north.

The last straw came in July, when a force-five typhoon swept over both islands with high winds and heavy rain, after which there were no further radio contacts, either military or civilian. And curiously, while there were some sailing ships beginning to serve as links between islands in the Philippines and Indonesia, there were no reports of sailing vessels bringing information out of the Marshall Islands – Guam, Tinian, and Saipan simply disappeared.

Dave's interest in Guam was both practical and humanitarian. "At a minimum, if you can fly over and get some close-up imagery, we can figure out how many folks are still alive and begin to mount an assistance effort. Better yet would be placement of one of our flower pot nodes to open up communication with the remaining population. Best of all would be making contact with a group that could benefit from your milk machines and ethanol production equipment. We'd love to develop another Hana in the western Pacific," he said, referring to the Master Chief's adopted home on Maui.

"Roger that, Dave," Clark replied. "We should be able to take the NNB in for a close-up recon. But like I told you back in Alberta, I have a bad feeling about that place. I did five years there from '15 through '19. That's where I met my wife. Even back then, the Chamorros resented the military buildup, and they particularly hated the Japanese who bought property there as a hedge against problems on the home islands. You know, they never got over how the Japanese treated them during WWII. My wife is ethnic Japanese. She and her family were delighted to leave when I rotated out of there in '19."

"So you believe that things got ugly there, Master Chief".

"Yes, sir. You had roughly 20,000 military personnel, 10,000 contractors, and 50,000 dependents on an isolated island with 40,000 Chamorros, 15,000 Philippinos and 5000 Japanese. Then you cut off fuel and food imports. The locals are excellent fisherman, but they could feed at most a few thousand, and agriculture on that island is strictly piss-ante. Frankly sir, I would not want to be there when the MREs ran out. No way that mix of folks is going to get along in a pinch."

"What about Saipan and Tinian?" Dave asked. "They have more agriculture, don't they?"

"Did." The master chief replied, flatly. "There used to be sugar plantations on both of the northern islands, but that ended more than 20 years ago. The Chinese and Japanese maintained some offshore industries on Saipan, but that translates to more mouths to feed than local agriculture and seafood production could support. And again, you had major Chamoru resentment up there, and on Saipan there was no large military presence as a stabilizing force."

"So you think that the military on Guam might have helped hold things together?" Dave asked.

"Yes Sir, but only for a time. Military discipline will last only so long when you see your dependents starving. To be blunt, I do not know how I would be behaving right now in Hana if you guys hadn't turned up three months ago. We were close to the edge even then."

"So how do you guys want to handle this?" Dave asked the drifters, making eye contact with each one in turn.

"I think we should go in with the NNB and take a look," Mike volunteered. "I think we should park Brian in his gondoloon at sea anchor somewhere off-shore. That way he won't get too far ahead of us. And I vote we give the Master Chief operational command once we are there. If anyone there poses a risk to us, it will most likely be residual military forces or ex-military contractors, and neither Brian nor I have any military experience."

Dave looked at each of the other two, and both nodded agreement. "Okay, gentleman. The primary goals are to get some clue about who if anyone is left on the island and also to have all of you get back out alive. I don't want anybody pulling a Magellan on us."

"Sir, you might want to Newdle that," Clark deadpanned. "Magellan did just fine when he landed on Guam. It was the Filipinos who cut him up for bait a bit later in his voyage."

"I stand corrected, Master Chief" Dave smiled. "So what's the plan from here?"

"We're planning to stay silent across northern Africa and the Indian Ocean," Brian replied. "We don't know what's down there yet, so for this first transit we're going to be real quiet and just look and listen."

"And our communication nodes?" Dave asked.

"We'll look for evidence of community activity and drop them in by Jellybelly where possible. Barring that, we'll set down at least three across Africa in suitable isolated locations."

"Great." Dave said. "You all be safe, and call home when you can."

"Roger that," the Master Chief replied. "NNB out."

CHAPTER 22

UNO DOS
21 February 2031

They received the Jellybelly into the airlock behind the crew cabin. The Master Chief and Mike accessed its memory and watched the video clip sent to them from Brian up ahead in Uno. All the way across Malaysia, Indonesia, and then out towards the southern Philippines, they'd been observing active surface radars – not just one, but many of them. This was the kind that ships used to avoid hitting land, or to find other ships. Luckily their diamond fabric had zero radar reflectivity, making them totally stealthy. Those surface radars were no threat to them as long as no one could see or hear them, but clearly there were ships down there with enough power to operate radar, and if they were military, that might mean they had missiles. So they'd stayed quiet.

Now they were out over the Pacific east of the Philippine island of Mindanao, and Brian was about 50 km ahead of them. His recorded message was short. "No radar out ahead, nothing on visual. Suggest we power up and call home."

"Hey, Brian," Mike said as Brian's stubble coated face came up on his display. "How've you been?"

"Fine. So what do you think?" Brian asked. "Are those radars down there pirates?"

"Yes, Sir," Master Chief Clark replied. "We got visuals of a medium-sized freighter being pursued by what looked like a patrol boat.

And last night we saw muzzle-flashes down on the surface back behind us. The Straits of Malacca have been home to pirates ever since ships were invented. Anyone trying to get cargo between the Middle East or India to the west and China or Japan to the east has to pass through them. So either we are seeing pirates in action, or the Chinese are trying to deploy enough surface units to protect and control commerce through the Straits."

"If it's Chinese naval activity," Mike said, "that could spell trouble for our 'Burgs' taking the southern route out of Lhasa. If they are operating south into the Straits of Malacca, that means they control the South China Sea, which we need to fly over to get home."

"So let's get on the horn and tell Dave the good news," Brian suggested, sarcastically.

After six days of silence, Dave was happy to hear from them. He didn't seem surprised by their report of apparent pirate activity in the Straits of Malacca. But then, Newdle did have their high altitude drifters that could cobble together enough pixels to create pretty good pictures on the surface if the brown layer wasn't too thick. They agreed that it was important to find out if Chinese naval units were active that far south and discussed equipping a Jellybelly with a camera and using it to do stealth low altitude flyovers of surface ships on their next run out of Lhasa. That resolved, since there was nothing else urgent to discuss and it was 2 o'clock am in California, they let Dave go back to sleep.

There in the western Pacific, however, it was still early evening. They were drifting east-northeast at 40 kph on a course that would take them a bit north of Palau and then somewhere north of Guam near Tinian. Their NAF software told them that the earliest they'd reach the Guam area was tomorrow evening. They discussed the various scenarios for managing their 'visit'. The key question was what to do with Brian and his gondoloon while Mike and the Master Chief nosed around the area in the NNB.

One option was to take the gondoloon up to its maximum altitude of 15 km where the winds were much reduced, essentially 'parking' up there until the NNB was done with its reconnaissance and ready to rejoin them. The downsides of that were that it was too cold up there to process water to make oxygen or grow bugs to make food, so he'd have to use his reserves. In addition, the radiation intensity up at 15 km was greatly increased, and they were still in the beta-testing phase of their low carbohydrate diet. Until they knew for certain precisely how effective it was in protecting human cells against high altitude radiation, they didn't want to press their luck.

They opted for plan B, which was to have Brian drop down to sea level, hopefully well away from inhabited land but in protected water without large waves. He would then deploy his sea anchor. This involved dropping an empty 1000 liter diamond fabric sack on a tether into the water and activating a mini-pump to fill the sack with a ton of seawater. With positive buoyancy in the balloon, the tether would pull the sack of water up to the surface, where it would then hold the balloon steady. Given the large amount of water involved, the balloon would simply go where the water went, independent of the wind.

The one potential comfort issue with the sea anchor is that big waves would cause the gondola to bob up and down in harmony with the sea surface, which most people found unpleasant when confined inside the gondola. In addition, the one real risk for Brian when riding at sea anchor would be that the tethered gondoloon might be approached by a boat. However this could be easily observed by Brian's surveillance system, and in a worst case scenario, the sea anchor could be cast loose to allow the gondoloon to climb rapidly away from danger.

•   •   •

They had almost pulled it off, making a picture-perfect arrival at sunset over the tiny island of Rota just north of Guam. But sunset meant there was reduced warmth of the sun on the land, and that in turn caused a prompt reversal of the low altitude onshore breeze. As a result, Uno and Brian did an unintended U-turn and began drifting out to sea, away from the sheltered water in a bay at the south end of the island where he wanted to drop his sea anchor.

The Master Chief didn't miss a beat. "We need a tow line, Brian," he commanded. "Attach your tether to your Jellybelly and send it over... NOW Mister!... I mean, Sir."

It took the Jellybelly two minutes to cover the distance to the NNB, which the Master Chief had lovingly renamed the 'Enenburg'. "She's a big, white, beautiful ship!" He'd protested. "She needs a real name – not a bunch of letters like an ugly LST!"

Once inside the airlock, the access door was closed tight, and then Clark raised his finger tips into the control plane and gently eased the throttles forward. Like a reluctant dog on a leash, Brian and his gondoloon swung into line about 70 meters behind the Enenburg's tail. Positioned as he was, he was towed half a mile upwind to the middle of the bay off a nonexistent town – a victim of the tsunami – that the map ironically identified as 'Songsong'. There, his fingertips dancing over the virtual controls on his display, the Master Chief held Brian perfectly still 50 meters above the water until he had deployed and filled his sea anchor.

"Ready to cast off?" Clark asked.

"Roger that, Master Chief. Thanks for the tow. Good hunting."

"You're welcome, Uno. Try to stay put until we get back. Enenburg out."

•   •   •

Mike and Master Chief Clark had spent from nine PM to two AM in the Enenburg, nosing around Guam. Using starlight and infrared sensors, they saw nothing characteristic of human life – no movement, no fire, no radio or radar-frequency emissions. "It looks like they are all either dead or gone, Sir," the Master Chief finally admitted. "I was really hoping I wasn't right".

They took the Enenburg up to 2800 meters where the west-wind was gentle and steady, pointed her nose into it, set the turbines to seven per cent power to hold her stationary, and both sacked out until dawn.

• • •

Mike awoke with a start. A soft beep in his headset was accompanied by a flashing visual pip. It was 5:52 AM. The Enenburg had strayed to the east end of the island over the military complex surrounding Anderson Air Force Base. In the predawn gloom, three infrared images were moving. Two stood vertical, and the third was horizontal – perhaps a dog. Against the surface temperature of 21°C, the three moving figures registered at 33-35 °C. They stopped and held position for a few minutes. As the Master Chief stirred, sat up, and rubbed his face, a fourth warm figure emerged into the VR scene. Mike's map overlay indicated that it came from what was labeled as a 'munitions bunker'. Instantaneously there was a brilliant infrared bloom from one of the first two vertical figures – a muzzle flash. The fourth figure fell and the third horizontal figure lunged forward, merging with the fourth. Mike tore off his headset and shook his head, trying to clear the image from his visual memory.

"Hunters one, prey zero," the Master Chief said softly.

• • •

Two hours later, they thought they had a pretty good sense of the situation on Guam. A few hundred humans and maybe 20 dogs were out and about on the west end of Guam, and an unknown number of humans lived within a five kilometer perimeter on the east end of the island. At night, it appeared that everyone resided underground; but at dawn, those on the west end came out and hunted the east end.

They were about to share this with Dave when their preconceptions were shattered. At 8:33 AM, a vehicle emerged from one of the east end bunkers and proceeded rapidly into the west end of the island. Its path took it into a group of what the visual image showed to be humans and dogs. The group scattered, except for two of the dogs, which fell in a hail of gunfire and were scooped up by the vehicle's occupants, who then rapidly returned to their bunker within the east end perimeter.

"This is going to be really messy," predicted the Master Chief. "Before the tsunami there were four major ethnic groups on the island, now there seem to be just two enclaves. And the $64 questions are: how many are left? And who's eating whom?"

•   •   •

"Enenburg, this is Brian. Do you read me? Over." Brian sounded excited.

Like I need this right now, Mike thought. "Go ahead, Brian. What's up?"

"Hey Mike. Look, I was approached by an outrigger canoe paddled by girls in rags asking for food. While I was talking with them, a high speed Zodiac came around the point with guys firing AK 47's and an RPG. Felt like I was back in St. Louis again. I've cast off and am drifting southeast, over."

"You okay, Brother?"

"Hale and hearty, Amigo. God love this diamond fabric! Like nothing goes through it!"

"Good. Look, the Master Chief and I are trying to figure out who's eating who down here. Literally! Can you try to slow your movement as much as possible for a few hours?"

"I hear you. Will do. I'll be parking up at 15K until further notice. Uno out."

•   •   •

"White blimp. This is Major Gonzalez, USMC. Do you read? Over"

"We read you five-by-five, Major. This is Airship Enenburg, and we are not a blimp. Please describe your tactical situation. Over." The Master Chief looked like he was functioning above his pay grade.

"Nen Nen Burg. We are under attack by hostile forces. Need assistance. Can you help us? Over."

"Major Gonzalez, this is Doctor Anderson. Report your tactical situation." Mike cast an apologetic look at Clark and continued. "We cannot assist unless we have a full situation report. Over."

"Look, Anderson. We are in a classic standoff. They eat our pogues, and we eat their dogs. Over."

"Major Gonzalez. Please state your force strength and the number of your 'pogues'... Over." Mike cast another apologetic look at Clark who responded by sternly holding his index finger to his lips.

"Look, Anderson. I don't know your rank, and I don't care. We are down to 600 combatants plus 800 dependents. We only have another 150 Nips and Pinays to give them, so we are running short of ammo, so to speak.

Mike suddenly felt like retching. He held his tongue.

"This is Master Chief Clark, US Coast Guard. My wife is a 'Nip' from Guam, soldier! If we see another body pushed out of your bunker, it's sayonara, baby! You with me, Gonzalez?"

There was a long pause. Clark again held his index finger to his lips and looked sternly at Mike.

"Do I know you, Clark?"

"Not in this life, Gonzalez... Sir! But in the next one, I'll cut off your balls and feed them to my chickens. Are you with me, *MAJOR Gonzalez, SIR?*

"That's no way for a non-com to address an officer, Clark!"

"Officer? Bullshit! No way I acknowledge a murderer as my superior." Clark spat out his response.

"That's easy for you to say, Coastie! Why don't you come down here and let me show you what's going on here. Most of my people are dead from starvation. My strongest men can barely lift a gun. When I send soldiers into battle, people die. How is any of this that much different?

"Like I asked you before, Gonzalez. You with me?"

Another long pause.

"What do I get in return?"

"You are not listening, Sir! In the next life, I might or might not feed your balls to my chickens. That's an unknown. But in this one, it looks a lot like the Chamorros and their dogs are going to eat you, Sir, balls and all!"

They sat there in silence for seven minutes. Brian was working his way up to 15K, the Chamorros' dogs were digesting their morning's catch, and Gonzalez' friends were trying to digest their two dogs – a classic standoff.

"Master Chief Clark. This is Gonzalez. Do you read me? Over."

"Still five by five, Gonzalez. Over."

"How do we make this work, Master Chief?"

"First, Major, who's the senior officer on the island?"

"I am, Clark. All the old bastards with stars and birds found an excuse to leave," Gonzalez spat out.

"Can you maintain your perimeter, Major? Over."

"Yes, but we'll just starve faster doing it. Over."

"If we feed you, can you maintain your perimeter? Over."

"Roger, Master Chief."

"Okay, Major. We are making progress. Now how do I talk to your OpFor command? Over"

"You mean the Locals? Why talk to them? Over."

"Yes sir, Major. I mean the 'Locals'. Because if I can talk with them, perhaps I can buy some lives. Both yours and theirs. Over"

"We don't have a clue how to talk to them, Master Chief. They live underground and come out of hundreds of openings. We think they've reopened World War Two tunnels dug by the Japs. Over."

"Yo, Brian. From your vantage point up there, can you see any fishing boats close to Guam? " Mike asked.

"Funny you should ask, Amigo. There's a cluster of nine sailboats about five kilometers north of the island."

"You see anything else moving on the surface?"

"There are three clusters of sails way further to the north off Tinian that I can see, but I don't see any other sails or wakes near Guam," Brian replied.

"How about we go talk to the 'Locals', Master Chief?" Mike suggested.

They sealed a headset in a waterproof container and loaded it aboard a Jellybelly. This was then dropped onto the deck of the largest boat in the offshore group as the Enenburg kept a respectful 1500 meter distance overhead.

After ten minutes, they got an audio response to Mike's repeated message, "This is airship Enenburg. We are not armed. Can we talk?"

"Who are you?"

"We are unarmed, and we do not threaten you. We would like to help."

"Can you get those military pigs off our island?"

"Not immediately, no."

"Can you protect us from the pirates in the Zodiacs?"

"No."

"Then go away and leave us alone."

"We can help feed you. We can help feed your children," Mike tried.

"Most of our children have died. Killed or starved. You are too late. Go away." As if to emphasize this message, someone below opened fire at the belly of the Enenburg with an assault rifle. Even at close range, the diamond fabric skin was impervious to small arms fire, and at 1500 meters straight up, the few rounds that reached them had no effect.

Mike looked over at Clark and raised his eyebrows in question.

"I'm sorry, sir. I'm afraid this situation has spiraled way beyond any help we can provide."

"If we drop our milk machines to Gonzalez, do you think they would use them?"

"I don't know. I really don't know. But for sure you don't go down there and try to reason with Gonzalez and his people. If we land, I give you hundred-to-one odds we never take off. It's gotta be like World War Two Bataan down there. Back then, the few who survived to fight on broke ranks and hid in the forest. Forget about military discipline down there." Clark rubbed his eyes for a minute. "We can give them a Newdle node plus the four milk machines and maybe someone back in Alberta can talk them through the setup. I think I've lost my 'cred' with this guy. We've got enough bugs to run them for three months. If that works, it might be enough to keep them going – that is, if they can hold their perimeter, defend the milk machines, and not kill each other over who gets the product."

"A least that gives them a chance. Let's get over there and make the drop," Mike said.

• • •

Gonzalez response was not unexpected. "Fuck you, Coastie. We don't need milk, we need meat and potatoes, and then we need a ship. When are you bastards going to come and get us off of this piece of shit rock?"

"We're sorry, Major Gonzalez, this is the best we can do for now," Clark replied. "We were sent here to do recon, not rescue. We've given you a communications node that you can use to talk to San Diego and Pendleton."

"Well, tell the REMFs that sent you to send us a cutter from Pearl, Coastie."

"Pearl took a direct hit from the tsunami, Major, and they haven't resumed operations. Frankly sir, the situation on Oahu isn't that much better than yours. The biggest thing CG has in the islands is a 50-footer, and it's got neither the fuel nor the range to get here and back. Your best bet is San Diego. And just so you know, this ship we are in is private, not military."

"So what's your chain of command, Coastie. Who's that doctor with you, and who does he answer to?"

"The doctor is a civvie, Major. He owns this rig. We work with Newdle, and we're trying to figure out how to glue a few pieces of this FUBAR world back together. Trust me, we will do our best to get some help out to you."

"You do that, Coastie. Clark, right?"

"Right. You use the stuff we gave you, you get all of your people out of there – combatants, dependents, AND pogues – and damn it Gonzalez, I'll personally buy every one of you a beer in 'Diego'."

"I'll hold you to that, Clark."

CHAPTER 23

UNO TRES

22 February 2031

Almost as an afterthought, they decided to use a Jellybelly to drop one more communications node on the island in case the Marines inactivated theirs. They looked for a remote and protected high point on the island where it would not be tampered with. The problem was that the promising locations were all in Chamoru territory, and the best spots were probably used as lookouts for pirates. Then they noticed a stone church standing alone near the center of the island, the group of surrounding homes having all been burned. The bell tower was made of stone, and the top of the tower was open like a castle watchtower. That would probably be the last place anyone would climb up to any time soon, so they hovered at 2000 meters and sent the Jellybelly down with the Newdle node slung beneath it on a tether.

To their surprise, as the Jellybelly was flaring out to do a soft drop, a man emerged from a trap door and was almost knocked over by the node as it dropped from the Jellybelly. Recovering, he crouched to shout down the trap door, and then stood to wave frantically at the big white object above him. In a moment he was joined by a woman and a girl. Mike and Clark scanned the surrounding area and saw no one else, and no more people came up onto the tower.

"What do you think, Master Chief?" Mike asked.

"They are outside the military perimeter, and the kid is blonde, so they don't look like Chamorros. Can we take three people out with us?"

"I'm with you, Master Chief. Can you get us down there and pluck them off that tower."

"Piece of cake, Mister," Clark replied as he swung the Enenburg into the wind, pumped buoyancy out of the nose, and carved a rapid descent towards the tower.

At that instant, Mike was alerted to movement by his headset. The image quickly resolved into three armed men running towards them from the east about 400 yards distant.

"We've got hostile company," Mike shouted.

"This thing is bullet proof, right?" The Master Chief asked calmly.

"Absolutely."

"Then no worries, Mister," the Master Chief replied. He was a master sailor in his element. Clark loved navigating this big white ship in three dimensions. His fingers danced on the virtual controls, his eyes fixed on the trio of figures standing on top of the tower. Surprisingly they stood their ground as the large white object dropped rapidly towards them out of the azure sky and the armed contractors came in shooting from the east. At 200 meters Clark quickly reinflated the nose trim bag, bringing the Enenburg back to level and killing their rate of descent. They came to a standstill one meter above and one meter to the left of the trio standing on the tower, effectively putting the Enenburg between the trio on the tower and the attacking men. There the Master Chief held them against the breeze by gently plying the two turbines to hold them between the tower and the advancing assailants.

Watching the Master Chief in his element, Mike had the sudden thought that giving him the helm of the Enenburg was like handing Rembrandt a paintbrush. His uncle would have loved to see the Master Chief do this. Tearing his thoughts back to the present, Mike released the entry flap of the crew cabin and knelt in the opening. They looked up at him with tears in their eyes, and the woman said softly, "Thank God you've come."

As Clark eased the ship down a bit closer to the tower, the man handed up the blonde girl, who clutched her arms around Mike with surprising strength. The Master Chief was busy with the controls, so Mike held her with his left arm as he used his right to pull the woman up into the cabin. Gently peeling the sobbing girl off his shoulder, he wiped away her tears and handed her to the woman. Then Mike assisted the man up into the crew cabin. Besides their tattered clothes, their only possession was a book, which the man handed to Mike before he reached up and struggled to pull himself aboard. Mike looked at the worn cover and read silently: The Book of Mormon.

As Mike got the man in and rapidly zipped the hatch closed, Clark pulled up the nose by rapidly adding lift forward and pumping water aft. Then the Master Chief used the turbines at full power to quickly drive them back up to the relative safety above 2000 meters. The trio, arms around each other and kneeling in prayer, struggled to maintain balance in the tilting cabin. All three were barely skin and bones. Mike judged the girl to be about twelve. The other two could be her parents.

Eventually the man looked up at Clark and Mike and said, "He answered our prayers and sent you to save us. You must be from Heaven?"

"No." Mike started to shake his head, and then thought of Lhasa, Jamaica, and Hana. "Well, compared to this place, perhaps we are".

As they climbed up to meet Brian, they got the essence of the Bradleys' story. They were missionaries who had been here for six years working among the Chamoru. As the island sank deeper into ethnic strife, more and more of their flock were drawn into the conflict. The worst problem had been the roving bands of civilian contractors, particularly once they discovered that Mormon families kept substantial food reserves. In the end, only the church had been spared. The Bradley's had shared what they had with the few of their flock who remained, but now that was gone. For the last month, all they'd had to eat was a tin of peanut butter, some powdered milk, and rainwater.

Mike asked if it was just the three of them together on the island. He was answered by sobs from the woman and a devastated look on the girl's face. The Reverend Bradley told him of their older two sons who were left in Utah, and of the two younger sons who had died here trying to defend his flock.

•   •   •

"What do you suggest, Brian?" Mike asked.

"I think you need to drop them in Hana. There's no high speed front right now, but the eastward flow along 20-north is still pretty good. You can be there in three days. They've got no clean clothes, and hygiene might be a problem if you try to keep them with you too long. We've not run this model digester and extractor system with five people in a real life test."

"I agree with you that we should take them to Hana. How about you?"

In response, Brian asked "Have you checked your white cell count and DNA recently?"

"Yeah. As of last night, mine hasn't budged since we started. Both are solid in the green," Mike replied.

"Mine too," Brian said. "This diet seems to be working. I want to go around again, and if I avoid dropping into any more war zones, I don't think I need you riding shotgun for me. You okay with that, Amigo?"

"Yeah, I guess so, Brian. Is there anything we can give you to top off your supplies?"

"Actually, what I'd like to do is give you the 60 kg of hydrogen I've made so far this trip. Can you maneuver down under me so I can drop it down to you with the Jellybelly, ten keys at a time?"

"Can do," Clark replied. "And when you're done with that, you should take an extra one of our Jellybellys with you. Never know when you might need a spare. Oh yeah, and we'll send up our sea anchor and tether. Try not to lose this one while messing with mermaids, Mister."

•   •   •

During the transfers to and from Brian up above in Uno, the Bradley family sat on one crew bench, the daughter asleep on her mother's lap, the mother leaning against her husband, her eyes open and staring blankly. The Reverend sat perfectly still, but his eyes watched Mike and Clark.

On the first transfer of his hydrogen down to the Ellenburg, Brian also sent a smoothie, which Mike gave to the husband, who shared it with his wife. Mike cautioned them to drink it slowly because they were not used to a beverage this rich. An hour later, Brian sent down a second smoothie. He was obviously giving up his lunch and dinner to give the Bradleys a start on their recovery. The couple woke the daughter and fed her most of the second smoothie, sharing the rest. Within a few minutes, the child seemed to perk up a bit.

"What's your name, young lady?" Mike asked.

"Hannah," she replied. "What's yours?"

"I'm Mike Anderson, and this is Master Chief Clark. He's from the Coast Guard, and as you saw, he's a master at rescuing people," Mike said with a smile.

"Where are you taking us, and are we in a blimp?" she asked earnestly. "Daddy said this was a giant, white angel coming to take us to heaven, but it kind of looked like a blimp to me."

"Well, Hannah, we're taking you and your folks to a place we think you will like. It's called Hana, almost like your name, and it's on the island of Maui, in Hawaii," Mike told her, gently.

"Hawaii?" Bradley asked with a frown. "We heard they were hit hard. Are they any better off than Guam?"

"You're right, Mister," Clark said softly. "The tsunami hit us really hard – lost a lot of good people. Conditions on Oahu are still pretty grim. We were getting close to the edge on Maui as well, until Dr. Anderson here dropped out of the sky and helped us."

"Are you really a doctor?" Hannah asked. "That's what I want to be someday."

"I'm not that kind of 'doctor', honey," Mike said, directing a quizzical grin at the child's searching blue eyes. "I have a doctorate, a PhD, in molecular genetics. I convince bacteria do special things, like make the stuff in that smoothie you just drank."

"He also makes bacteria that make milk from water and sunlight" said Clark, leaving out a few delicate details. "We were on the verge of starvation in Hana when Dr. Anderson brought us his sun powered milk machines, and now everyone in town has fresh milk to drink every day."

"It's not just me. My team makes the bacteria; my friend's team makes the machine that collects the good stuff together, and the guy who sent you the smoothies directs a team that built this ship that's taking us to Maui."

"Did you bring any of your milk machines to Guam?" Bradley asked.

"Yes, we dropped four of them into the Marine's perimeter," Mike said. "Enough to make a difference for 2000 people."

"What about the Chamorros?" Bradley asked.

"We tried to talk to them. We established a communication link with a group of fishing boats, but all we got for our trouble was a full clip from an assault rifle."

"You can't imagine what it's been like for them these last months. After all, it is their island. I wish I'd been there when you talked with them. I could have helped," Bradley said sadly. "After we drop my wife and daughter in Hawaii, can we turn around and go back?"

Mike looked at Clark who shook his head and said: "I'm sorry, Reverend. It's 3800 miles, a bit over 6000 km, from Maui to Guam, and going the other direction, it's mostly upwind. That puts it outside of our operational range."

"I don't understand. We're going to Maui in this thing now, but we can't go back? Why not?"

Mike looked at Clark and shrugged. "This ship, the Enenburg, is a hyperbaric dirigible, designed to sail mostly with the prevailing winds. We use the turbines as auxiliary power only when necessary, kind of like an auxiliary motor on a sailboat. Right now the motors are shut off, and we are sailing towards Hawaii at ..." Mike consulted his headset "...71 kilometers per hour. To get to Guam, we left our base in Canada almost 11 days ago, crossing the Atlantic, Africa, and the Indian Ocean to get here."

"So when can you go back?" Bradley asked. "To Guam, I mean."

Mike nodded. "We can have an airship like this one pass through that area in four or five days." He looked at Clark with eyebrows raised. Clark in turn nodded. "The thing that almost knocked you off your bell tower, the thing that looks like a flowerpot, is a communications node." Mike continued. "Newdle makes them. They work as a universal uplink for almost any form of communication equipment, from antique radios with tubes to cell phones to state of the art headsets. Do any of the Chamorros have radios of any kind?"

"Yes. They used cell phones until the towers went dead, and now they use walky-talkies that they charge from solar panels."

"If we linked you into the node in your bell-tower, would you try talking to them?"

"Absolutely." With his wife squeezing his hand, the look on Bradley's face told them there was hope.

CHAPTER 24

JAMAICA

21 December 2034

Mike pulled the straps tight and waited. First there was the lurch of the drop, a few gut-wrenching seconds of falling nose down to pick up speed, and then he felt the thump of engine ignition. He kept his head back. He knew what was coming. Once they had power, the Virgin Galactic[17] shuttle swung its nose skyward and in a matter of seconds the ram-jets turned a thousand kilos of hydrogen back into water. The g's they pulled were awesome. Starting from their drop from the balloon at an altitude of 15 km, the 52 passengers were propelled to an altitude of 200 km in the first few minutes of the ride. Now they were in ballistic mode, guided by chemical thrusters, and into the weightless phase.

Twenty years ago, in the same year that Mike had first used wood eating bacteria to make ethanol, a music guy named Branson and the Rutan brothers had charged rich folks $200,000 for a ten minute ride about half this high into space[18]. Back then, they'd used a mixture of laughing gas and rubber to power the ride, leaving a thick black trail of smoke behind them. Now they were burning Mike's hydrogen – plus that from a few other drifters – and behind them there was a column of pure, white steam. Mike was happy. He was headed home for Christmas.

• • •

A little over an hour later, Mike felt the straps begin to dig into his shoulders. They were starting re-entry. He'd been reviewing the Con-

sortium's petition to Congress. They needed the recovering US Government to stand behind their 'Freedom of the Skies' manifesto. This
was critical to the continued growth and function of the NC. They had
to have free access to the airspace over every political entity around the
globe. Yes, they had over 10,000 drifters 'up', and data from that many
atmospheric sensors allowed the NAF software to help them avoid flying over the 'bad guys' with over 99% certainty. But if the other one per
cent of those 10,000 went off course and got into trouble, that made
100 'lost sheep' whose release the NC had to negotiate every year, and
NC membership was growing at close to 20% per year, so every year,
more drifters were likely to get into trouble.

They were easing down into Boston, and Mike felt the faint shud-
der of turbulence as the high lift wing extensions deployed. They
lined up on the Logan landing zone east of the city as the autopilot brought them in with one centimeter precision. The ultra-light
shuttle, free of its fuel load and gliding without power, bled off
speed. Over their designated touchdown point the nose pitched
up, the tricycle gear popped down, and they set down like a bird on
its perch. Mike could barely feel when the gear touched down. A
robot tow engine latched onto the front gear, and in moments they
were at the gate.

Mike got out of his seat in the 13th row, followed the other 51 passengers off, took the escalator down to the metro, and then stepped
aboard a Blue Line car going west. Three minutes later his headset
told him to exit and take the Green Line north. At the I-93 station
he found his group capsule to White River Junction. Slipping into
the seat, his display told him that it would drop him in WRJ in 58
minutes, where he'd change for Brattleboro.

In White River, he followed the arrows on his headset. Two minutes
later his solo capsule was launched out onto the hyperbaric, diamond fabric, mag-lev rail, driving him south at a relatively slow 185
km per hour towards Brattleboro, VT. There, in a total elapsed time
of a little over 3 hours since the balloon carrying the shuttle lifted
off from Maui, Mike stepped out of his capsule.

Not counting his many trips directly into Jamaica and Townshend in the 'Burgs' and a few 'drop-ins' with his gondoloon, this was his first trip home via ground transportation since the carbon revolution had spread this far north. He'd heard that for every mile of black-top road they had torn up, the tar that they recovered provided enough helical carbon to build five miles of hyperbaric rail service. The result was that for travel between most New England towns and cities, roads and automobiles had all but disappeared, replaced by multiple and single rider capsules in automated "flight" over hyper-baric mag-lev rails at speeds up to 300 kph.

Not so in Brattleboro, because west of this small Vermont city, ethanol was plentiful. When Mike got out of his capsule, there was Stephanie, standing next to Uncle Mike's goatmobile. She wrapped her arms around him for a few seconds and then let him go. "You look good, Mikie, but you're way too thin."

"This is my drifting weight, Mom. If I stayed down, ate your cooking for a month, and worked in the receiving yard at the Rum Works, I'd bulk right back up."

"So are you on-catheter this visit, or can you eat my food?" she asked with a tilt of her head.

"I went off-catheter in Maui a week ago, and I got a start on my tan from surfing," Mike replied, pulling back his sleeve to reveal a light brown arm. "I'm really looking forward to eating your food. It's been a long time".

They climbed into the truck. "Good." Stephanie said. "We'll make a stop here in town to see what's available in the store. They've been getting some fruit in these days, and we have a good supply of vegetables from the community greenhouses attached to the Rum Works. Am I cooking for Lhamo, too? When's she arriving?"

"Yes, if you don't mind. We spent last week together on Maui, and we both went off-catheter and readapted to solids at the same time. She took the shuttle into Vancouver yesterday and then the Trans-Canada mag-lev up to Edmonton to spend a few days with her brother. She's planning to come down with the next 'Burg' run, probably in 3 or 4 days." Mike paused and gave Stephanie an apologetic look. "And Mom, you know that it's easier to go back to our drifting diet if we don't eat much carbs, so I can't have your apple pie. Sorry."

"I know, Mikie. The anti-aging movement has been writing a lot about your drifting diet. It's still a struggle for many people to understand how a diet that high in fat can actually be better for you, but there are some experts out there that are becoming convinced. I've been reading up on it. I've cut back a lot on carbs myself, and I feel great. So we'll focus on meat, cheese, vegetables and salads; and go light on the carbs and sweet stuff."

The truck wound its way off the main road and came to a stop in front of a store. Before opening the door, Stephanie turned to Mike and said, "Oh, by the way, I had a surprise visit yesterday from Senator Nyce. He and your father were good friends a long time ago, before he got elected to the Senate, but I haven't seen or spoken to him since your dad died. He stopped in at the Rum Works up in Jamaica and asked for you and then came down to the Townshend house."

"You're kidding me!" Mike interjected.

"No kidding, Mikie". Stephanie said with a vexed look. "Do you know what he wants? He was very pleasant, but he wouldn't tell me anything. He didn't act like he was looking for money."

"I've been trying to talk with him for more than a month, and all I got was the run around from his staff. I wasn't even trying to get face time in person – all I wanted was a 15 minute video hookup."

"Well, he said to tell you he'd be at home in Waitsfield for the next week, and he'd be happy to see you anytime except Christmas morning."

"Why the hell does he need me to come there?" Mike countered. "All I want is 15 minutes to pitch our 'Freedom of the Skies' initiative."

What's this all about, Mikie?"

"Our group of drifters, we call it the Newdle Consortium, or NC for short…"

"I know about the NC, Mikie", Stephanie said with a patient smile. "Some folks love you, and some hate you. Your use of the 'hydrogen spigot' – turning it on and off whenever and where ever you want – has accomplished some great things, but it's made you some important enemies, too."

"Mom, we're a true democracy – maybe the only one functioning in the world right now," Mike said, pointedly. "We are ethnically, culturally, and educationally diverse; but we are bonded by a common set of needs and goals. Every member gets a vote, we actively debate every issue before we vote, and we never withhold hydrogen for frivolous reasons or personal gain. We work to reduce conflict and repression, and to promote the free flow of information and equality of all people. The people who hate us are usually on the wrong sides of these issues."

"Your critics say you are a bunch of spoiled rich kids floating around in the sky, messing with international politics"

"They are right on that last part," Mike said firmly, "because no one else has had the will or ability to take on any of the important global issues these last four years. As a result of direct or implied pressure from the NC, to name a few things, China has not moved back into Tibet, and they've agreed to keep the South China Sea free of pirates and open to international shipping. Most countries now allow unrestricted over-flight by NC drifters, and they also allow their people unrestricted access to the information we carry. So yes, on the charge of messing in international politics, I plead 'guilty'"

"But," Mike continued, "I don't see how anyone can claim we're 'spoiled'. Every drifter who attains NC membership commits to living a lifestyle with a negative carbon footprint. All of us produce more clean energy than we use, and each of us donates a minimum of ten per cent of our profit as hydrogen to promote education around the world, like to power schools, virtual libraries, and to pay teachers. Those drifters who get wealthy do so by living a frugal life while producing useful products like software, intellectual property, and entertainment. Are we unconventional free spirits? Maybe. Intellectual nomads? To quote your favorite cartoon cat: 'I resemble that!' But spoiled? Hardly!"

"I love what you do, Mikie. It started when you and my brother figured out how to use your bacteria to bring energy independence to this neck of the woods, then the milk project, and now your collaboration with Newdle to build a stable hydrogen economy. But it makes some people jealous, and there are many vested interests out there who can't deal with the competition – the oil industry for example. They say that you have used unfair tactics to prevent their recovery after the tsunami."

"Come on, Mom! The oil industry was on life support even before the tsunami. That wave just pulled their plug. And frankly, they were an industry that truly deserved to die. Burning fossil carbon was a major factor leading up to the tsunami. That caused the immediate deaths of more than 80 million innocent humans, plus another 2 billion who died in the post-tsunami unrest!"

"What did my brother use to say at times like this: 'Calm down, Wonderboy!'?" Stephanie said with a quizzical smile. "Look, we need to get some groceries and go home. And on the way, you can tell me what you want to do with Senator Nyce."

"I miss Uncle Mike," Mike said.

"I miss him, too. Stephanie said quietly, placing her hand on Mike's arm. "I miss him, too.'

•   •   •

On the way home, they talked about other things, like people in town and local politics. During dinner, they discussed the Rum Works business, how best to manage its network of far-flung franchises, and their business relationship with Diamond Fabrics. The two businesses had continued to grow in parallel, since the Rum Works franchises used DF balloons, and their bugs were delivered monthly by drops either from gondoloons or from one of the 'Burgs'. And then the gondoloons, all of which were built by Diamond Fabrics, needed Mike's bugs for their smoothie machines to function, and his bugs still came from a business within the Rum Works.

There were many reasons why the two companies might have been merged into one business, not the least being that Mike and Stephanie functionally owned most of the Rum Works and close to a majority interest in Diamond Fabrics. However any merger would have required a prior resolution to the problem posed by Uncle Mike's untimely and unofficial death – something they hadn't effectively resolved until 6 months ago.

In the end, it had turned out to be pretty simple. For the three years after the tsunami, they and a core group of Rum Works employees in Jamaica and Townshend had kept Uncle Mike "alive" as a business entity, telling any curious person that he had become a recluse. They had faithfully paid his taxes even when the state and federal governments were providing no services in return. They made sure that they plowed his driveway in the winter and mowed his lawn and the farm's meadows in the summer. The only thing they didn't do was vote for him.

Over those three years, 'Uncle Mike' had made the two of them regular gifts of discounted Rum Works and Diamond Fabrics stock, plus small contributions to a trust for Angela. Mike had also used his royalty income to buy a lot more of Uncle Mike's stock in both companies at market price, so by the Spring of '34, Uncle Mike owned less than five per cent of both businesses. At that time, Stephanie declared her brother 'missing', stating that she believed he had gone out and not come home. This of course was technically true because she declared that she did not know exactly when he had done so. No one bothered to ask if her window of uncertainty on his time of departure was three days or three years.

A search, mounted mostly by Rum Works employees, found no trace of the old geezer with a red beard. Luckily, Uncle Mike had filed an official will many years before, leaving 40% of his estate to Stephanie, 40% to Mike, and 20% to the Nature Conservancy. Six months after he was claimed to be missing, a probate court judge in Brattleboro signed a piece of paper declaring Michael Barber officially deceased.

The Nature Conservancy made out very well in the transaction, receiving a check for $85.8 million…but not as well as Stephanie and Mike. When the dust finally settled a few weeks before Mike came home for Christmas, their accountant informed Stephanie that she was hands down the richest woman in Vermont. Tammy was about to find out that 14-year old Angela now had a trust valued at $4.2 million, and Mike was among the Forbes's list of the top 25 richest men in the world. In a word, they were financially comfortable.

•   •   •

They'd finished a dinner of Waldorf salad and rosemary chicken roasted over Vermont maple charcoal. The dishes were done. The ethanol burner faithfully simulated a wood fire.

"So Mikie, what do you want from Donald Nyce, and what does he want from you?"

On its surface, that's pretty simple," Mike replied. "I want an open skies agreement that is fully backed by the economic and military might of the United States; and he wants to buy me off – to give Congress *de facto* control over the NC. But since I'm not for sale, I win."

"I'm sorry, but it's not that simple, Mikie," Stephanie responded somberly.

After a pause, Mike asked: "Why not?"

They locked eyes. Mike thought, I learned to do this from Lhamo.

Stephanie looked away. "Many years ago, long before you were born, I had an affair with Don Nyce. It happened back when your father was spending most of his time down in New York. My brother found out, and he and Nyce came to blows over it."

"How long before I was born?" Mike asked.

"Three years" his mother responded.

"You're sure?"

"Yes," she said, and met his gaze.

"Good." Mike said, smiling at his mother. "Then nothing has changed. I'm not for sale, and I'm not his 'boy'. I win."

CHAPTER 25

WAITSFIELD

26 December 2034

Suzy Adams stood, arms crossed, looking out the window and down the long driveway that snaked its way up the hillside from Route 100 below. She thought about the last five years working for Nyce. Other than being obstinate at times and always an insufferable lecher, he was otherwise a pretty good a man. That, and the fact that she loved watching him work his political guile, made her sad about what she would do today.

Suzy had led a complex life, making her prone to the occasional moment of introspection. Am I making him pay for other men's sins, she wondered? As a high school valedictorian, she'd been aggressively groped by a teacher supposedly helping her write her speech. In college and graduate school, she'd learned that 'equal access' equated academic opportunity to sex with her mentors. She could have said 'no', but then she might have failed to achieve her potential.

Despite all of that, fate had favored her. Following her graduation from Georgetown with a Masters in Poly-Sci, she'd landed an internship with Santo Dominus' DC lobbyist. After a 'meet and greet' in their Washington office that year, Bob Tharp had taken her home (well, actually to his hotel suite). Seven years later, Bob had long since become more interested in less fit and softer women, but she in turn had risen to be the head K-Street lobbyist for Santo Dominus.

And then, five years ago, Bob had called to request that she go to work for Don Nyce. How he'd maneuvered her selection for the job had never been discussed. His expectations, however, were crystal clear. "I want to know what that bastard is thinking before he knows he's thinking it." Two days ago, his message was equally clear. "Get your skinny ass out of there the minute that hippy kid finally arrives."

Suzy wondered what it was about this kid that made Bob so toxic. Yes, he'd rejected an offer he shouldn't have refused and launched his school milk project anyway. But then came the tsunami, and Santo Dominus had been forever changed. Before it, they were all about chemicals and hormones; now they were more focused on seeds and food. Other than leading a few thousand monk-like geeks in balloons who didn't need their seeds, what was Bob's problem with this guy? Not knowing why today's event was coming down made her uneasy.

At that moment, she caught sight of an unusual vehicle slowing down on Route 100 to make the left turn into the driveway. It looked like one of those new super-efficient trucks being mass-produced at the old Navy yard in Portsmouth, New Hampshire. She turned to face Nyce, who was pouring over a sheaf of documents spread across his desk. "I think that's him coming up the driveway now," she announced.

Nyce looked up at her and smiled. "This looks like we have enough on him and his dealings to get him into line." He swept the documents into a pile and dumped it into a drawer. "Thanks for summarizing all this material on him. It was a lot of work for you, but I'll give you three-to-one odds that within an hour he'll be working with us."

"That's great, Don. I know you can pull this off. Look, I want to run up to Waterbury to meet someone for lunch." She could see his face begin to tighten. "It's a woman, Don – a friend of my sister who came up to Stowe for the holidays."

Nyce relaxed. "Okay, Suzy. Take the four-wheel drive. I wouldn't want you caught out on a scooter if it starts to snow."

"Thanks, darling." She gave him her warmest smile. "See you later."

•   •   •

At the Senator's front door, Mike passed a woman coming out who gave him a brief smile and a nod. He was struck by her looks. If her hair had been worn up rather than down, she could have been his mother 20 years ago. Having learned just days ago of his mom's infidelity, he toyed with the idea that he might have a long-lost half-sister but promptly dismissed the thought. He had more important issues at hand.

•   •   •

"Thanks for coming, Mike." Senator Nyce extended his hand. Mike gave him a firm grasp.

"I appreciate your time, Senator," Mike replied.

"So," the Senator said, "first things first. Can we have this conversation off-line?"

"That's fine with me," Mike replied. "How do we do this?"

"Simple. We both turn everything off." The senator replied.

Mike removed his headset, turned it around so the senator could see that it was turned off, and set it on the senator's desk. Nyce spread his arms wide, indicating that the room was not bugged.

After a pause, Nyce said: "I read your 'Freedom of the Skies' proposal. It's very well written."

"Thank you," Mike responded. "We have some very good people in our group."

"Tell me about your group, the Consortium."

"Well, it's kind of complex," Mike replied. "The NC is a consortium of individuals working in common purpose, using Newdle software, facilitated by technologies developed at the Rum Works down in Jamaica and at Diamond Fabrics in Alberta."

"What you are saying is that it's a cabal," the senator replied.

"No," Mike said, "I don't think so. A cabal involves a conspiracy to carry out some harmful or illegal act. The NC is an open consortium that promotes the free flow of information and the production of clean energy. We were born of necessity in a period of lawlessness, and we are now promoting an international agreement to make the skies safe for any and all who wish to use them. And that's precisely why I'm here, Senator."

"I'm told that you rent your balloons to bright, young people and then extort a tithe from them, in essence making them your indentured servants," the senator countered.

"I appreciate this opportunity to clear things up," Mike said with a patient smile. "I'm afraid you might be hearing a distorted view of the NC. Because of the high cost of purchasing a gondoloon rig, I work with the management of Diamond Fabrics to allow people without a lot of equity up front to try drifting to see how it works for them. It's kind of like a rent-to-own agreement. If it works out, they use their income to buy the rig. And if it doesn't, nobody loses. For those that do complete the purchase, most agree to pay ten per cent of their net profit into a fund to promote education around the world. It's all voluntary, and there is no extortion in the process."

"But you need to see it from our perspective in Washington, Mike. You are running an international business without any control or oversight. You fly around the world, dropping who knows what from the sky, initiating energy boycotts, and sticking your nose into places where you don't belong. You're acting like a bunch of hippies who want everything for free."

"Kind of like Helen and Scott Nearing?" Mike asked pointedly.

"They died long before you were born. Who told you about them, your crazy Uncle?"

"Uncle Mike and I hunted over in East Stratton when I was a kid, and he showed me the elegantly simple stone farmhouse they built. Our gondoloons are kind of a high-tech version of the self-sufficient mountain farm the Nearings built there a century ago. If you are willing to look at it that way, Senator, the NC is just the continuation of our Vermont heritage."

"Listen to me, Mike, your balloon existence is based upon a false premise; that you can float around up there for free, snatching up the sunshine and the forcing us down here to pay for it in the form of hydrogen. And I'd caution you to take what your uncle tells you with a grain of salt. Unfortunately he doesn't like me – never has."

"First, Senator, I know precisely why my uncle didn't like you," Mike said softly, finding the Senator's eyes and holding them with the Lhamo stare until the senator looked away.

"Second, Michael Barber is dead. He became a recluse after the tsunami, and then he went missing. We just recently closed his estate through probate."

"I guess, um, well, I'd heard rumors, you know..." Nyce stammered, but then was interrupted by a rapid crescendo of six explosions, the last of which blew out the window and shook the building.

Mike and the Senator found themselves together on the floor behind the desk, covered with dust and bits of glass.

In addition to fear, there was also a dark look on Nyce's face. "What the hell's going on here?" He shouted above the ringing in his ears.

Mike shook his head to clear it. "The last time something like this happened to me, it was a kinetic weapon attack by someone who couldn't buy me off," he replied. "Those weapons are deadly accurate, but that time my ass was saved by my friends at Newdle."
Mike looked the senator squarely in the eyes. "And once again, the bad guys seem to have missed."

"But…but they said that they just wanted me to talk some sense into you. They'd never try anything like this against me?" the Senator blurted out.

"Who?" Mike queried.

"Santo Dominus, who else?" The senator spat out angrily.

Mike picked up his headset from the desk, blew off the dust, and put it on. At that moment, two men burst into the room, one with a drawn pistol. The senator made a downward motion with his palms, directing the gunman to lower his weapon.

Keeping his eyes on the two men – obviously employees of Nyce, Mike asked. "May I use my headset to try and figure out what's going on, Senator?"

"Sure, go ahead." Nyce replied as he walked gingerly through the broken glass to converse with his staff.

Mike turned his back to the other three and tipped the flashing red emergency communication icon at the upper right of his screen. Immediately Dave Erickson's live image appeared. His attention was obviously riveted on something else, but then he briefly glanced towards Mike and said, "Lhamo, he looks okay, can you talk to him?"

Lhamo's image appeared in Dave's place, her normally placid face showing obvious concern. "Are you injured, Mike?"

"No, Lhamo, I'm fine. By the time the last one blew out the window, we were already on the floor under the desk. The senator has one staffer and a bodyguard here, and they both look okay as well. How many rigs are involved this time?"

"Just one, Mike. I'm sorry they came so close. He was using an unusual laser protocol to target you, and it took us a few extra seconds to over-ride it and draw them off target."

"Where's that rig now? Was it occupied or on autopilot?"

"It's occupied, and the pilot obviously doesn't want to die trying to escape," Lhamo replied as she glanced away from Mike to observe something else on her display for a moment. "We are right on top of his disk, and Dave is forcing him down with the Enenberg. We should have him on the ground just east of the senator's house within a few minutes. Can you ask the bodyguard to come out and take control of him for us? We're not armed."

At that moment, the bodyguard tapped Mike on the shoulder and pointed towards the door. Mike turned, and the senator said, "Mike, my guys think we should get out of here now!"

Mike held up his index finger and asked Lhamo "Any other potential threats up there?"

"No Mike. Immediately upon weapons release, Julian and Brian instructed all Consortium members within 40 km upwind to divert outside that radius or go to ground. There are no potential threats to you from above at this time."

Mike put his hand on the bodyguard's arm, pointed to his headset and then his own to indicate that they do a linkup. The green icon appeared and Mike said, "Lhamo, this is the senator's bodyguard. Please tell him what you just told me."

"While I do that, Mike, you need to talk to Anton Brinkmann. We've got much more than just one drifter this time." Lhamo shifted her gaze and smiled at the bodyguard.

Mike turned to the senator who stood at the door with a quizzical expression, obviously wishing he had a headset. "We are safer in here than outside, Senator. My Consortium friends have the situation overhead under control. But please give me a moment. There's something else I've got to check on."

Nyce nodded. Mike typed in 'AB' on his query bar and within a second Anton appeared. "Hi Mike. You know I was against sending you in there as bait. They came uncomfortably close to threading one of those uranium needles into the Senator's house. But the good news is that your gamble has paid off. When his six weapons all missed, your attacker sent a flash message to an address that let us backtrack through his communications for the last 9 months. We've got those bastards cold. It goes right to Bob Tharp at the top at Santo Dominus."

"That's great, Anton, because I'm starting to get tired of ducking those suckers," Mike said with a grim smile. "And I think the Senator's now convinced that it's better to play ball on our team."

"Good. Maybe this will work out okay after all. But there is one thing I'm sad to report," Anton continued with a shake of his head. "We haven't been able to tie this to that snake Klink. Maybe we'll get lucky when we sweat some more details out of the bastard that Dave and Lhamo just forced down into the Senator's meadow."

Mike looked out through the shattered window and saw the massive Enenburg pinning a disk and gondola horizontal against the grass as the senator's bodyguard warily approached it with his weapon drawn. "Maybe we will, Anton. But without Santo Dominus backing him, I'm guessing that Klink has lost his fangs," he replied.

In response, Anton just shook his head skeptically.

Two minutes later, the senator's staffer escorted Dave and Lhamo into the room. "Senator, this is Lhamo Rinpoche, CEO of Djore Enterprises in Lhasa and Edmonton; and David Erickson, Senior Vice President of Newdle," Mike said.

"Let me guess," Nyce said with a combination of sarcasm and a sly smile. "You just happened to be passing by."

"In fact, Senator," Dave responded evenly, "you have us to thank for diverting all six of those depleted uranium weapons into your meadow rather than here on your house. Luckily, we were on our way from Alberta to Townshend and decided to provide some top cover for your meeting with Dr. Anderson. You thought you could work with these murderers, but you were double-crossed. These people attacked you because they decided they can't trust you. But

now we have the evidence to connect your attackers directly to Santo Dominus. With our help, you can use it to put them away for life,
along with your traitor of an assistant, Suzy Adams. She set you up
for this attempt on your life."

Senator Nyce looked thunderstruck. "That's outrageous," the senator blurted, struggling to come to grips with her betrayal. "She'd
never do anything to hurt me. This just doesn't make sense."

"Yes, it does, Senator," Mike said earnestly. "Some very powerful
people can't accept the fact that the world has irreversibly changed.
But we both know that it has. Now that they have turned on you,
this would be a good time for us to build a relationship based on
trust and understanding. If we can accomplish that, Senator Nyce,
I think we can find common ground from which both the needs of
the US Government and those of the NC are effectively served."

Lhamo smiled to herself, the kind of smile that Mike had learned to
see only in the corners of her eyes.

Later that evening she would tell him: "You are not a foolish boy
anymore, Dr. Anderson."

CHAPTER 26

ANGEL
January 2036

"Hi Mike".

"Hi Angel".

Most incoming calls got shunted into the protective cocoon that terabytes of avatar-hosted message management afforded. Almost everyone attempting a real-time connection with Mike got to talk with his polite 'alter-Mike', explaining how busy Mike was and that he'd pass the message along as soon as Mike had a free moment. Angela was in a different class. If she wanted real-time, she got it.

"Where are you? And is that really you, or another one of your avatar images? You still look pretty okay."

"Whoa, easy girl. One question at a time. Why shouldn't I look okay?"

"Mom says that everybody who goes up drifting gets really skinny and then gets sick. Too much radiation or something."

"Well, Tammy's right...or was right as of a few years ago. But we've fixed that, so you don't need to worry about me".

"How'd you fix it? We learned about radiation in advanced biology class. It damages the DNA in your genes, and it goes through almost everything but lead. And don't tell me you've got a lead shield up there."

"Nope. I'm not hanging underneath a lead balloon, Angel." Mike smiled and gestured up above his head. "Actually, the way we solved it was pretty cool...if you want to hear about it."

"Sure," Angela nodded, cocking her head to the side until her blonde hair partly covered one eye.

"Well, you know about the Consortium, right?" Angela nodded. Mike continued: "We're up close to 15,000 members now, but five years ago there were just a few of us. Back in the early days of drifting, we could only spend at most a third of our time up, and the rest of the time we were on the ground recovering from the side effects. And as Tammy told you, a big problem was the cosmic radiation up here. That's because in prime drifting space six miles up, more than two-thirds of the atmosphere is below us."

Angela nodded again, and Mike continued. "So the Consortium assigned the problem of how to deal with this to Brian, my former boss from the Mars project. He was the first modern solo drifter to come up, even before me, and he had already been grappling with the radiation issue for the Mars Mission. He worked with a team at Newdle, and their solution to this problem was not to reduce the radiation level up here. Instead, they figured out how to increase the body's tolerance of radiation and its ability to repair radiation damage."

"Wait a minute," Angela objected with a frown. "We were taught that radiation damage to DNA is permanent."

"I know that's what the text books say," Mike agreed, "but it turns out that most DNA damage can be repaired by special enzymes before the cell suffers any permanent effects. It's kind of like workers on a suspension bridge continually repairing the cables strand-by-strand so they don't rust through and let the bridge fall down. So Brian looked for ways to make the repair process work better. None of our modern gene-splicing tricks worked well enough or were safe enough. In the end, his answer came from the distant past."

"So, what happened?" Angela interjected. "Did space aliens bring the answer to Earth and carve it on a Mayan stone tablet?"

"Right continent, wrong tribe, Honey," Mike replied with a chuckle. "Actually, it came from a bunch of aboriginal groups like the Lakota, Kiowa, Athabasca, Assiniboine, and Inuit who developed essentially pure hunting cultures. They figured out how to live without a lot of sugars and carbohydrate in their diet. Brian worked with a group of whiz kids from Newdle. They scanned the literature for things that tipped the balance in favor of DNA repair and up popped this aboriginal diet stuff. Their conclusion was that cutting out most dietary carbohydrates seemed to be our best bet. So we revised the mix of things my bugs make; Lhamo changed the extractor surfaces, and now we feast up here on buffalo steak and seal blubber!"

Angela made a face. "Yuk!"

"Just joking, Angel. No, it's still pretty much like my original milk – the stuff you drink at school. It comes out of the machine as a beverage, so I can choose a fruit smoothie, a mocha, cream of broccoli soup, chicken soup, or any of a number of other flavors. But like the diets of the pre-contact Lakota Nation or the Inuit, there's very little carbohydrate in the food. We provide just enough protein to meet the body's needs, but most of the energy in the diet comes from fat. It sounds weird, but it worked in mice on the ground, then in mice under a balloon high above Alberta, and when we tried it on ourselves up here, the level of DNA damage went way down."

"How do you know that?" Angela asked, wrinkling her forehead.

"Because we have a system that continuously monitors how many white blood cells we have, and how much damage is being done to the DNA in those cells. White blood cells are like the body's canary in the mine shaft – if anything is going wrong, these cells show it first. If there is even a slight trend in the wrong direction, a warning icon pops up on my display. Want to see my levels for the last six months?" Mike tipped the icon on his display to open it, dragged its graphic over to the 'share space', and activated it. He watched Angela's eyes scan over the graphic in front of her, undisguised curiosity showing on her face. He remembered looking through Uncle Mike's microscope when he was her age. Was Angela developing his thirst for finding the new and different?

Her eyes shifted back to Mike's. "So what happened back in November? There was a dip down into the yellow warning zone for a week. Did you eat a bunch of junk food up there?"

"Good for you! I wondered if you'd catch that. No junk food, Angel. I was trying to get into Lhasa, I was over Kashmir, and the winds totally sucked! – they seemed determined to push me hundreds of miles too far to the north. I could have come down in Kashmir and waited, but that's not real safe ground, so I dumped most of my water and went up to my rig's absolute maximum altitude of 55,000 feet. That's almost 17 kilometers high, which put 90% of the atmosphere and its protective shielding below me. I parked up there above the winds for 8 days waiting for the weather pattern to change. The mountain scenery was great, but I was up too high for too long. But scouts' honor," Mike said with a guilty smile, holding up three fingers of his right hand, "I won't do that again".

Angela knew about Lhamo – that her home was in Lhasa – but didn't take the bait. Instead she asked: "So how do you get white blood cells to test? Do you have an implant in a vein, or stick yourself with a needle?"

"Neither. We're a lot more advanced than that. But it's kind of delicate, Honey. Are you sure you want to know?"

"Try me," Angela said firmly.

"Okay," Mike said. "You know that we don't have toilets up here, right?"

"Yes, Mike, I KNOW. You've got a pair of catheters – one for pee and one for poop".

"How'd you find that out?" he asked, surprised.

"How do you think? I Newdled it. And then I found the catheter patents that the Consortium owns and read those, just like I read your patents. I'm not a dummy, Mike."

Mike took a second to process all this. Over the years, most of his conversations with Angela had been about her friends, her tennis game, school, and the dog Tammy wouldn't let her have. But this interest in the details of life in a gondoloon was something new. He wondered where it was going.

"I know you're smart, Angel. Okay, so the lining of the colon is thin, much thinner and more transparent than our skin, so there's a sensor in the catheter that can see through into small blood vessels and count the number of white blood cells that go by. Also, because the catheter tip has gentle little fingers that are constantly moving to hold it in place, it sort of tickles the colon surface enough that a few cells are released, and these are analyzed for DNA damage by another sensor embedded in the tip. But since all of this happens automatically, Hal only bothers me about it if something is going in the wrong direction, like last November."

"Mike, naming your computer 'Hal' is so retro.   Between your thing with the Grateful Dead and Kubrick, aren't you kind of stuck on the past?"

"Look at where I live, Angel. Perhaps it's a fantasy world, but it's definitely not the past. And besides, the past is how I got to where I am now. Just like our low carb diet up here, some things from the past turn out to be pretty useful. And as for the Grateful Dead, Uncle Mike was a dedicated Deadhead, and he was always on the cutting edge."

"So what happened to your uncle, anyway? For years he'd send me those little video post-its on my birthday. I'd get to talk to Grandma Anderson but never him. And then last year he just disappeared, and now mom tells me that he left me a big trust fund."

"He was kind of a 'mad scientist', Honey. He invented lots of really useful things, but he was way ahead of his time. Most people didn't understand him. And then came the tsunami that he thought could have been prevented. That really upset him – so many people dying and the misery that followed. He was never at ease around people, but he felt very bad about all the suffering. It really affected him."

"Yeah, mom says he was pretty strange. But you liked him a lot, didn't you, Mike?"

"Yes, Angel, I did. You know, Grandpa Anderson crashed his plane and died when I was only four, so Uncle Mike was kind of like my father when I was growing up in Vermont. He'd take me hunting and fishing, and he taught me a lot about science."

"Is it really as pretty there as in the pictures. We see lots of pictures of Vermont now that the new president is from there. Have you ever met him?"

"President Nyce? Yeah, I have. He's an old friend of Grandma Anderson."

"Mom says that he's too liberal, and that he's giving up too much of our country's power. Do you think he's good for our country, Mike?"

"I think we can trust him, Angel. The world is a very different place now, and a lot of the old rules don't work, like single super power countries telling the rest of the world what to do. President Nyce has agreed to support an international treaty to protect all drifters, no matter what country they are from. That will help make drifting a lot safer."

"That's good, Mike, because I just want to ask this and hear what you say." Angela gave him that look with the tilted head and loose blonde lock. "Can I come up in a gondoloon with you this summer? Just for a few months – you know, like see the world?"

"Wow, Honey! You're only 15. And I'm sure that your Newdle search told you that two person gondoloons don't work out too well. I don't even own any. So you'd be up all by yourself. What does Tammy say about this?"

"I'll be 16 in April. And I haven't talked to mom about it, 'cause I know what she'll say. I wanted to talk with you first."

"So you think I'm an easier mark than Tammy?" Mike asked with a wry smile.

"Absolutely!" his daughter deadpanned.

"But if you went up you'd have to use catheters, and you're a bit young for that, aren't you?"

It's not a big deal, Mike. I already use a catheter with a portable mini-pump when I'm on my period. A lot of my friends do, too. You've seen the advertisements, haven't you? 'No mess. No moods!' You need to come down to Earth occasionally, Daddy Dearest! The catheters won't be an issue."

"So what would you do if you had to go to ground in Kashmir?" Mike asked. "Even if most countries sign the new treaty, there will be some holdouts that don't."

"What would Lhamo do if she landed there?" Angela shot back, a bit too quickly. But before Mike could respond, she tried a different tack: "If they took me hostage, your Consortium could cut off their hydrogen and information access until they let me go. I read about how you do that in the Wall Street Journal. They said you guys act like a bunch of spoiled kids, but I think it's cool."

"We only do that when we've tried everything else, and we don't apprentice anyone into the Consortium who we think might act like a cowboy – or a cowgirl. Frankly, Angel, I'm not real happy with the idea of you coming up just yet. You should keep working on your tennis and enjoy being a kid. How's your game compared to Tammy's. Is she still beating you two sets out of three?"

"No, it's been months since she won a match against me. I'm good at tennis, Mike, but I'm not going to do it in college, and it's not like I'm going to turn pro. That's all about short skirts, boobs, and attitude. That's just not me."

Mike paused and took a breath. This process of a woman emerging from his blonde kid was amazing but also kind of scary. "I like it a lot when you are strong, Angel," Mike said. "But this is serious stuff, drifting. Each of my rigs is flown by someone who works for me, solving problems for the Consortium or for people on the ground, writing patents, and generating income. Why should I drop one of them, so you can play tourist for the summer?"

Angela smiled at Mike. As long as he could remember, she would use it as her trump card. "Mom says that you're rich, so I thought you could afford it. And while I'm up, I plan to take AP Biochem and first year college Biology. That way, I can jump start my premed courses at the University of Chicago. They have a six year MD program, and I've just been accepted into next year's class."

"Congratulations, Angel. That's awesome! Sounds like you've got all of this planned. But please think this through, Honey. Yes, I went to MIT when I was 16, but it wasn't all that easy for me to adjust. In the classroom, I got all "A's, but after the bell rang, except for tennis with your mother and hunting with Uncle Mike, the rest of my life sucked. Why not take some time and enjoy being a kid?"

"When you were 16, Mike, did you feel like an ordinary kid? I don't feel like most of the other kids in my class, and I don't want to play at being something I'm not."

"So, at 15, you're not a kid?"

"Well, maybe a bit, but not for much longer." She paused. "And... Mike?"

"Yes?"

"There's another reason I want to come up this summer." Mike nodded, and Angela continued. "I really want to drop into Maui and spend some time with Hannah, Herman, and Henry."

Mike's look of total surprise was obviously apparent to his daughter. "You can't seriously believe that I wouldn't know about your friends there, Mike. I know that you call them your second family. I hooked up with Hannah on the web two weeks after you rescued her from Guam five years ago, and she introduced me to the Master Chief's two boys. They love you, Mike – maybe the same way you loved your uncle. Mom and I have kind of taken Hannah under our wing. She and her mother are coming here to look at the University of Chicago this summer because Hannah and I want to do med school together."

"All these times we've talked, Angel, you never mentioned you knew about Hannah..." Mike's question trailed off as he struggled to process this unexpected gemisch of two previously separate parts of his life.

"You never told me about your trips to Guam, Mike. The whole connected world sat on the edge of their seats as the Marines were rescued and the Chamorros got their island back. You did something really good, but you hid your part in it from the world, and you never told me about it."

"And frankly, Mike," Angela continued with an injured tone, "I didn't tell you about hooking up with Hannah because at first I was kind of jealous of her. She got to hug you when you lifted her aboard your big white blimp, and you taught her to surf. But I've never had the chance to hug you or go surfing with you."

The eyes of daughter and father embraced for a second. Something good happened between them.

But in almost the same instant, Mike had a terrible thought. They knew when he'd be in Hawaii a year ago December because he'd told Angela, and she'd probably told Hannah he was coming. That's how they'd timed their attack on him. One or both of the girls were being stalked. He struggled to keep his face from revealing his thoughts.

But then Angela shook her head as if she was being bothered by a mosquito.

"So, Mike. How many rigs do you own?"

"Rigs? You mean gondoloons?"

"Yes! Gondoloons."

"Quite a few."

"How many?"

"Maybe a couple of hundred?"

"How many?"

"386"

"I saw an older model sell on eBay recently for a bit over a million dollars. So you are rich."

"Yeah, I guess."

"Mike. You can afford it, and this is important to me. Let me come up this June – please?"

Before Mike could think of a response, she tilted her head, the lock of blonde hair passed between them, and Angela cut the connection.

Mike sat back and exhaled. "Yes, Angel," he said to himself. "Both you and Hannah will need to come up this summer; because, for the time being, drifting may be the only place the two of you can be safe."

(ENDNOTES)

1   Heads Up Display. Mike has a wrap-around visor in front of his eyes on which is projected one of many three-dimensional images of his choosing. For instance, the control panel for his gondoloon appears to be 15 inches in front of him, and he operates it by raising his fingertips up to the virtual controls, and it functions like a virtual touch-screen.

2   JellyBelly glider. An ultra-light aircraft constructed of diamond fabric and filled with one cubic meter of hydrogen designed to descend with a 10 kg payload at a glide-ratio of 30:1. It can perform this function attached to a tether that allows it to be reeled back up with a similar payload. Untethered, it can fly back up to its base vehicle (either a gondoloon or a 'Burg') under its own power with a payload up to 1 kg.

3   Steve Fossett was a sports balloonist and the first human to circumnavigate the globe in unpowered flight.

4   'Burgs' (as in 'Hindenburg') refers to ultra-light dirigibles designed to navigate by either passive drifting or powered flight. They are equipped with life-support systems similar to Mike's gondoloon, allowing very high altitude operation and prolonged periods of flight.

5   Rum Works. A biofuel ethanol business started by Mike Anderson and his uncle Mike Barber in 2014. This technology was enabled by the younger Mike's discovery of a unique bacteria capable of efficiently reducing the cellulose and lignin in wood to ethanol. Because the uncle lived in Jamaica, Vermont and they were producing ethanol, they named their business 'The Jamaica Rum Works'.

6   'Hayflick gene'. In 1962, Dr. Leonard Hayflick at the University of Pennsylvania made a key discovery in the mechanism which causes some types of cells to become senescent and die, whereas others were able to reproduce and essentially live forever. The 'Hayflick gene' referred to here is a hypothetical gene inserted in the DNA of bacteria that prevents them from reproducing forever.

7   Buckyball refers to a member of the fullerene class of molecules, composed entirely of carbon, in the form of a hollow sphere. Named after Buckminster Fuller, this 60-carbon structure resembles the geodesic dome designed by Fuller. Subsequent fullerene structures also include cylindrical nanotubes, but the helical structure proposed herein remains undiscovered.

8   E. F. Schumaker. A German-born economist who emigrated to Great Britain before WWII and helped reconstruct both the post-war British and German economies. He became a vocal advocate of small regional industry over large centrally-controlled industry. His 1973 treatise, 'Small is Beautiful' became one of the most influential books of the 20th Century.

9   Clayton Christensen. (1997), The innovator's dilemma: when new technologies cause great firms to fail, Boston, Massachusetts, USA: Harvard Business School Press, ISBN 978-0-87584-585-2.

10   Brass Rat. The MIT mascot is the beaver, which is the motif of the MIT class ring. With typical Cambridge cynicism, the locals refer to it as a rat rather than a beaver. Thus someone who has graduated from MIT is referred to colloquially as a brass rat. Someone like Mike Anderson with both his undergraduate and graduate degrees from The Institute is therefore a 'double brass rat'.

11   Think of a block of ice 240 miles by 100 miles and a mile thick perched 2 miles up on a sloping plateau. Once its margins have ruptured, the only thing slowing its acceleration is friction at its base. Assuming that this ice sheet has been glaciating its way slowly downhill for the last 100,000 years, that path will be pretty polished. One can thus assume that both the friction at its base and wind resistance over its surface will be negligible relative to its total mass, and that it will behave almost as if it is falling straight down. Even small avalanches less than 50 feet thick descending a few thousand feet have been clocked at speeds in excess of 200 miles per hour.

12   Rutan brothers. Burt Rutan revolutionized aviation with his light and efficient aircraft designs, many of which were piloted in record setting flights by his brother Dick. They became well known when their Voyager aircraft flew around the world nonstop and without refueling (i.e., 'on one tank of gas') in 1986. They then designed and built the first civilian space plane (Starship One), winning the Ansari X-Prize in 2004.

13   Paul MacCready, Jr. at AeroVironment designed and built ultra-light aircraft, both human powered and solar powered. His solar powered Helios aircraft was able to fly at altitudes of 60,000 to 95,000 feet; paradoxically remaining in that altitude range overnight by employing solar-charged batteries and a very high glide ratio, climbing back to the apex of its flight cycle after dawn the next day. Because their operational altitudes were well above both the weather and jet-streams, they were able to remain in one location indefinitely despite their low flight speeds, thus earning them the nickname of 'atmospheric satellites'.

14   The Tantric form of Buddhism typical of Himalayan cultures, called the Diamond Path.

15   Dr. Cassandra Forsythe, et al. Comparison of low fat and low carbohydrate diets on circulating fatty acid composition and markers of inflammation. Lipids. 2008: 43:65-77.

16   Helen and Scott Nearing. US educators and socialists who adopted a self-sufficient agrarian lifestyle in southern Vermont beginning in 1932. Their 1954 how-to testimonial 'Living the Good Life' became a beacon for the back-to-the-land (hippie) movement in the 1960's.

17   www.virgingalactic.com. Imagine what this technology will lead to in the next 20 years.

18   Sir Richard Branson's Virgin Group and Rutan's Scaled Composites have a joint venture to build commercial spaceships to take paying customers on sub-orbital spaceflights.

Made in the USA
Lexington, KY
18 March 2012